Eviskar Island

By Warren Dalzell

"Eviskar Island" is dedicated to its readers, especially to those who possess a keen sense of adventure and who can appreciate the occasional curveball Mother Nature throws our way.

WD July 2015

"Fiction is obliged to stick to possibilities. Truth isn't."
Mark Twain

I

S hock and surprise registered with the man as he fell. Tumbling through space, he flailed his arms and legs trying to find purchase on solid ground his subconscious knew wasn't there. But the ground would be there soon. In the horrifying seconds before impact he imagined what it was going to be like, what the exact consequences would be: the pain, the severity of his injuries.

The rock-strewn slope came up to meet him with crushing violence. Stabbing sensations shot through his body as he felt and heard his bones break: ankle, arm, ribs. In an instant he stopped moving. There was a brief moment when, knowing he'd been badly hurt, he maintained a certain clarity of mind, waiting for the overwhelming pain that would consume his senses. He moved his head slightly to one side, facing back in the direction from which he'd fallen. Tall, jagged, snow-capped peaks ascended into a dense, impenetrable fog layer just below their summits. The cold, inhospitable appearance of the mountains provided mocking contrast to the warmer, almost jungle-like conditions in which he lay. What he'd seen and experienced in the last few hours had yet to register firmly in his psyche, but, even in his present condition, a fleeting thought flew by: "What kind of world have I entered?"

Was that one of his colleagues standing on the cliff above him? A second glance showed no one there. The pain was now excruciating; the mere act of breathing felt like someone was jabbing a dagger into his chest from within. But the physical discomfort was nothing compared to the psychological. There would be no rescue from this place. It was far, far too remote. Dr. Aage Randrup knew that if he were to survive it would be up to him and him alone, one man against this new, unpredictable and isolated valley. Summoning his courage he attempted to move, to roll onto his side. After a heroic effort he succeeded, but that simple act sent waves of pain through his body, reinforcing his awareness of the horrendous damage inflicted upon him. Contemplating death, he closed his eyes and welcomed the quiet, pain-free oblivion of unconsciousness.

II

Hallelujah!" Dr. Morgan Holloway exclaimed. He pumped his fist and did a quick 'moon walk' before continuing to peruse the rest of the document, the one that had arrived in the morning mail. It wasn't quite what he'd hoped for, but he was still enormously relieved. Morgan made his way through the kitchen to the back door where his wife, Debbie, was dressing for an afternoon ski workout.

On a day like today, most of the residents of their small town in northern Minnesota were contentedly ensconced in their homes, reading by the fire or otherwise engaged in indoor projects. Only the hardiest of souls, like Debbie, dared to brave the single-digit cold that had descended from Canada following last night's snowfall. The additional eight inches of fresh powder beckoned as Debbie laced the insulated gaiters fitted around her cross-country boots. Today's route would take her on a beautiful six-mile loop out past Granite Lake. An hour or so earlier she'd spied a group of skiers, probably students given their high fitness level, shushing behind their house, moving along the path she would take. It was then she'd made the decision to follow in their tracks. Not having to break trail would permit her to glide along at a comfortable pace and enjoy the sharp air and clear blue sky delivered by the cold front.

"Would you like to know where we'll be spending our summer?" Morgan asked as he approached. The grin on his face spoke volumes.

"I'd love to go back to Eviskar Island!" she replied with enthusiasm, "Did your Ash-Driscoll grant get approved?"

"No, I haven't heard back from them yet. I don't expect to either. Marcus Friedman at Cal Fullerton told me that if they haven't responded by now we haven't got a prayer. Today's letter, surprisingly, came from our new best friends in the Federal Education Department."

"I don't get it. How can the country's most prestigious organization for the support of archeological research ignore a small proposal to share in one of the most important digs in recent memory, while an education grant gets approved to send a bunch of high school kids to the middle of nowhere?" She pulled a brightly colored woolen cap over her head and began to wrap a scarf around her neck. "Heck, all that matters is that your research continues. Congratulations, you archeological stud." She stood and kissed him, "So, how many kids are we going to chaperone?"

Morgan flipped through the document. "Let's see. They were kind enough to give me pretty much what I asked for. The main cost the students add to the expedition is for transportation to and from the island. I looked at air fares from New York to Reykjavik a while back and they've gone up since last year." He frowned, "They've set aside a specific amount for travel." After a quick mental calculation he remarked, "We can't take more than half a dozen people besides ourselves. It also stipulates on the very first page that we need a mix of ages—fourteen through eighteen years old. Hah! That was something I injected into the proposal thinking that it sounded really pedagogical, something that might appeal to an educational bureaucrat. Looks like it worked. Well, if the downside of obtaining an education grant instead of a research grant is that we'll have to babysit a bunch of snot-nosed kids, I can live with it."

Debbie smiled, "I think it will be wonderful having them along. And your use of the moniker 'snot-nosed' is a bit condescending, don't you think? My hunch is that they'll be extremely useful. You'll be eating your words come next fall. Besides," she purred, pressing her lithe spandex-clad form against him and putting her arms around his neck, "chaperoning these kids will be great practice for when we start our own family."

He hugged her. "I suppose you're right. Now, you're going to have to remind me again how this works. What is it we have to do to make a baby?"

"I tell you what. When I get back from my ski, I'll give you an extended lesson in baby making. In fact it may take up the rest of the afternoon."

Before things got too steamy, Debbie hurried out the door to grab her skis and poles. Morgan padded back to his study and examined, in more detail, the grant he'd just been awarded.

Although it was late December and the archeological site wouldn't be accessible until June, there wasn't much time to plan. How was he going to choose his students? The grant offered no guidance on that issue. He couldn't just pay a visit to the local high school and middle school and post notice of the endeavor on their activities boards. Of that he was certain. The selection process had to be geographically far-reaching. Also, if he didn't end up with a "proper" demographic mix, some politically correct knucklehead from the ACLU or some other watchdog organization would make his life miserable. Morgan sat back in his desk chair and absentmindedly chewed the end of his pipe stem, a typical action whenever he was deep in thought.

A smile crossed his lips as the idea came to him: an essay contest. It made perfect sense. A final group of perhaps fifty applicants would be selected solely on the basis of essay content. That part would be based purely on merit. Further culling could then be done through careful re-reading of the submissions in concert with consideration of the obligatory gender, race and ethnicity factors. He had colleagues for whom a decision based upon anything other than merit would be morally reprehensible. Morgan didn't harbor such sentiments. He was a pragmatist who accepted political correctness as a job requirement. One's morals sometimes had to be set aside when made necessary by life's inescapable realities.

Morgan was delighted with his selection process. "So far, so good," he thought with a sense of self-congratulation. He jotted down the topic to be addressed by the applicants in their essays: "Why I would like to spend my summer in one of the world's most remote locales unearthing evidence of an Old Norse settlement." Now all that remained was to spread the word about the contest, set an application deadline and take another look at the expenses for the expedition.

After an hours' worth of number crunching and web research, he arrived at a sobering conclusion. He was going to have to limit the number of students to just four. The Danish and Greenlandic archeologists who collaborated in the endeavor looked to him to provide substantial support for the project. The unstated understanding on this dig was that he was an outsider who was graciously being allowed to participate in their undertaking. Only shoestring support was being provided by the Danish government, and he was expected to carry more than his share of the expedition's financial burden. Last year the dig had been extended through mid-September thanks to Morgan's heroic efforts to secure additional NSF funds. Part of the generous travel allowance in this new grant could be used to help offset the travel expenses of some of the other researchers—if he dropped the number of tag-along kids to four. For political reasons it had to be done. He hoped the Department of Education overseers would either not notice what he was doing or would let it slide, allowing him some discretion with trip logistics.   In any case, Morgan felt confident he could argue his way out of any resulting difficulty.

With all the belt tightening going on at colleges throughout the country, money for research was taking a big hit, especially in areas such as archeology and anthropology. It was so much easier, Morgan thought, if your research affected society in some dramatic way: finding a promising new treatment for a lethal cancer, cracking the genetic code for an inherited disease, or, he thought with amusement, making motor fuel from one's own urine. The latter idea had sprung from the mind of a colleague in the Chemistry Department at his school. Of course the fellow hadn't actually said he was turning piss into gasoline. His research involved a compound normally found at trace levels in urine that could be incorporated into a catalyst for refining oil. There were better and cheaper sources for the material, but the way in which the Chemistry professor, Dr. Loyd, had put the urine spin into his proposal was, in Morgan's mind, a stroke of genius. Attention from the press, not to mention the large award itself, had almost assuredly sprung from this clever association.

Dr. Morgan Holloway loved his job. Unlike many of his peers, it wasn't so much the subject of his work that beckoned him, it was the aura of being a full professor, a distinguished member of academia, that provided his motivation. He didn't mind doing field work or helping to prepare manuscripts as long as generous recognition and accolades resulted. These were like an aphrodisiac for him. No one loved seeing his name in print as much as Morgan Holloway, PhD.

In his earliest years at the college, Morgan's wardrobe portrayed him as a rough-and-tumble man of action, someone accustomed to sleeping with scorpions in the desert, piloting a canoe through dangerous rapids, or evading marauding cannibals. Of course, his look also had to suggest that while he was flirting with danger, he'd also be unearthing the precious secrets of antiquity. In short, he wanted to be viewed as a real life "Indiana Jones." Most days back then he'd sported an expensive custom-fit bomber jacket, safari pants held up by suspenders, and a wide-brimmed, faux-leather Australian bush hat. The latter accoutrement not only served to enhance his swashbuckling appearance, it also provided him with a means to cover his fast-receding hairline, a gift of his father's lineage.

Over time, his image softened and his dress became decidedly less ostentatious, but he did retain what had become his signature feature, one that now defined him and, in his mind, made him stand out among his peers—his pipe. In fact, Morgan had quite a collection of pipes. Antismoking rules didn't faze him much. Sure, he enjoyed lighting up while at home in his study, but the majority of the time the pipe was just a prop, a device to enhance the distinguished aura he hoped to project. For someone so blessed with a youthful appearance, he desperately wanted to appear older and refined, and the pipe was the key tool he used to achieve that goal.

Morgan bore the title of 'professor' as though he'd been bred for the job. While many faculty members were bothered by the political side of the academic world, Morgan reveled in it. He craved fundraisers and mixers. He was adept at schmoozing with deans, administrators, benefactors—anyone of influence who could help to advance his career. Disingenuous smiles and feigned interest in the work of others came naturally to him as he constantly worked to climb the University's social ladder, seeking committee and departmental chairmanships and other, high- visibility positions. But despite his prodigious interpersonal skills, he knew that the most important attribute leading to success in academia was, as the saying goes, "bringing home the bacon." Money was power. Everything else took a back seat to the acquisition of enough funding to pay his own salary and to swell the coffers of the institutional bureaucracy. This was the reason behind the overwhelming relief Morgan felt when his backup request came through, the one submitted on a whim through the educational sector. Simply by mentoring a bunch of high school kids, he had solidified his standing at the university and guaranteed the production of more research papers bearing his name.

At the back of the house a door slammed. He could hear Debbie stomping the snow off her ski boots. Putting aside his mail, Morgan sighed contentedly and went to welcome his wife's return.

Spencer Bowen

Spencer Bowen rounded the corner to the street where he lived. It was mid-March in Brooklyn, NY. Patches of dirty snow remained along the street corners, remnants of piles left by plows throughout what had been a harsh winter. He limped along, dodging potholes full of water from the aggressive melting currently in progress. Although the sky was largely overcast, it was warm, mid-fifties, and Spencer's foot hurt, a sure sign that the warming trend was about over. More cold and snow were on the way. Winter wasn't yet through with the city.

"Yo, Spence, they teach you anything in that 'ol brick prison today?" The owner/operator of "Charlie's Dog Stand" always greeted the young man on his walk home from school.

"Nah, that school's a friggin' waste of time, ya ask me," Spencer replied, shifting his backpack to his right shoulder. He reached into his pocket and pulled out a handful of bills, quickly figuring out what he could afford for dinner. "Gimme a Coney doag wit' extra onions," he said, his speech laced with its heavy New York accent. "'An hold the relish."

"You got it. Anything else?"

"Yeah, gimme extra mustud. 'An don't get stingy wit' it."

"How's about you put it on yourself, hotshot? That way I don't get accused of bein' a cheapskate." Charlie flashed Spencer a half grin and handed him his hot dog. "Mom's workin' late again?"

Spencer nodded, "She hadda work the afternoon shift on accounta' Mrs. Romanov called in sick." He took a large bite of his condiment-laden hot dog, chewed and swallowed. "Got any root beah that's cold?" Charlie fished out a cold can of A&W and handed it to his charge. Spencer nodded in thanks and then flashed a rare smile. "When they both get home, I got big news for my mom and dad." Charlie raised a questioning eyebrow. "Yeah, I'm not gonna be heah this summah. I gotta job diggin' up bones an' stuff."

"Don't say. Where at?"

"On an island off the coast of Greenland."

Charlie frowned and waited for Spencer to wolf down the rest of his meal. "Greenland? That's pretty far away in't it? You sure your folks'll let you go?"

"'Course they will. They encouraged me to apply for the job. Only, I figure what they really want is to get ridda me for a while so's they don't hafta pay old lady Bartoli to look afta me during the daytime. Ya ask me, that's all school's good for anyway—to baby sit kids while their folks're at work."

Hey, you shouldn't talk smack like that about your folks, Spence. They're good people, know what I mean? They're gonna miss ya. I know your grades are top notch an' I think they realize this is a great opportunity for ya."

"Yeah, whateveh."

"'An thanks for lettin' me know. What I mean is I gotta plan my inventory for the summer, and seein's how my best customer is goin' away…" Charlie paused, his gaze was now fixed up the street, behind Spencer. "Speakin' of customers, here comes another one." Spencer turned to look and blushed as Carmen de Jesus, one of his classmates, approached.

"Hi, Charlie. Bonjour, Spencer," Carmen said brightly as she passed by.

"Yo, how's it goin'," Spencer muttered, barely making eye contact.

Charlie and Carmen spoke briefly while Spencer sullenly sipped his soda and tried to act casual. When the girl was gone, Charlie did his best Spencer imitation: "'Yo, how's it goin'?' Want my advice? That attitude ain't gonna get you very far with her."

"So? You think I care about Carmen de Jesus? 'Sides, why should I? 'An what's it to you?"

Charlie held up his hands defensively. "I'm just sayin' you could be a bit friendlier is all. I can tell she likes you. Beats me why, though. I guess it could be those condescending looks you're always giving people, or maybe it's those sarcastic comments you're so good at. Wait…I know, it's your sexy, elitist attitude."

"Whateveh"

"She's real cute, Spence. You guys have any classes together?"

"She's in my French class. What about it?" Charlie just smiled. "Well, I gotta go. Thanks for the doag, Chahley," Spencer hoisted his backpack. His eyes were fixed on Carmen as he trudged home.

Charlie was a neighborhood fixture in the part of East Williamsburg where Spencer lived. It was one of the many working class neighborhoods in the great melting pot of Brooklyn, NY. During the winter he worked part time for the city, shoveling people's steps clear of snow and driving a small snow blower around sidewalks. When the weather was warm enough, and for

Charlie that meant anything above freezing, he operated a small, but quite lucrative, hot dog stand that he would set up on any of several street corners. His friendly, loquacious personality lent itself perfectly to such a job, and Charlie, having no kids of his own, took it upon himself to look after the children in the area. The avuncular septuagenarian was appreciated by all of the parents in the close-knit neighborhood, and his constant presence helped to keep the crime rate well below what would be considered normal in other parts of New York.

Having known Spencer for most of his fifteen years, the two had become quite close. From what other kids said about him, Charlie learned that Spencer was intellectually gifted, a curious boy who always helped his fellow students while struggling with boredom for his own part.

Spencer was lanky and handsome, sporting the aquiline nose and high cheekbones of his Mohawk Indian father, and the dark skin, curly black hair and expressive brown eyes of a mother who was born in Haiti and who emigrated to New York by way of Puerto Rico. Such an ethnic mix would have made him stand out anywhere else in the country, but he blended perfectly with all of his neighbors in East Williamsburg. Most of the residents on his block were East Indian, the majority of them Haitian, like his mother. He could carry on a passable conversation in the Patois French heard up and down his street and, in the Dominican enclave two blocks away, he picked up enough Spanish to speak and play comfortably with the friends he had over there. Spencer's grandfather had been a high-rise iron worker, one of the fabled Mohawks who had performed much of the dangerous work dozens of stories above the metropolis. As a very young child Spencer had absorbed enough of the complex Iroquoian language spoken by his grandparents to carry on intelligible dialog with them. In short, Spencer Bowen was borderline genius, a gifted offspring whom his parents had yet to fully appreciate.

Despite his prodigious intellect, however, Spencer was a troubled youth. He'd been born with a slightly clubbed right foot. Charlie knew of the problem but wisely never discussed it unless Spencer brought it up. And the emotional pain Spencer felt was particularly acute at this time of year: basketball season.

Spencer loved the game. Back in November he'd been crushed when, for the second year in a row, he didn't make the final cut to be part of his school team. No one could hit threes like Spencer Bowen, and none of his peers, even the standouts in the fast-paced offense the coach liked to run, could match him in free throw percentage. But Spence just couldn't keep up. He lacked the necessary agility to play at a high enough level.

Spencer never blamed his folks for not seeking treatment for his foot. The condition wasn't even diagnosed until he was almost a year old. When he began to walk, his mother noticed his decided limp and brought it to the attention of her "doctor." Unfortunately Mrs. Bowen possessed a strong mistrust of M.D.s, preferring instead the advice and care rendered by a local medicine woman, an elderly Haitian crone with legendary healing powers. After the sacrifice of innumerable chickens and goats, Spencer's foot hadn't gotten any better. His mother had then gone into a funk, entertaining the notion that it must have been something she'd done to condemn her young son to a crippled existence. Despite her anguish at having wronged her child, she still felt compelled to eschew modern medicine as an alternative for his care.

Spencer's father, Markus, was swing shift manager at a shipping warehouse on the East River. A confirmed acrophobe, he'd broken from his family's tradition of lucrative employment in high-altitude construction work, vowing to keep his feet as close as possible to terra firma. He and Spencer were close, and they enjoyed going to ball games and movies whenever his working hours and his son's time in school allowed. Markus was not an educated man and he also lacked the common sense and backbone to combat his wife's forceful enthusiasm for what he called "voodoo treatment." As long as the boy's health was never at risk, he reasoned, Caribbean faith healing was probably good for his wife's psyche and had the added benefit of broadening Spencer's awareness of the human experience. Thus, Spencer's club foot went untreated. Aside from routine visits to a local clinic for school-mandated vaccinations and checkups, he received no real medical care.

Spencer stoically accepted his fate and made the best of things. Frustrated in athletics, but driven to excel in other areas, he'd become an academic standout. Archeology and paleontology were among his personal interests, so when he'd heard of the opportunity to participate in a serious archeological project, he'd dashed off his application immediately. Although he didn't know it, his essay had placed him at the very top of Morgan Holloway's short list. Morgan had immediately sent him an invitation to join "the dig."

Jacek Malinowski

"Gdzie to jest?" ("Where is this place?") Despite having lived in the United States for fifteen years, Jacek Malinowski's mother didn't like to speak English. She was self-conscious about her accent and insisted upon conversing in her native Polish while at home.

"It's well north of the Arctic Circle, momma, off the northeast coast of Greenland."

"Why would anyone, especially my son, want to go way up there?"

"I think it is great opportunity," interjected Jacek's father, Stanislaw. He turned to his son. "We will miss you in garage this summer, but you must go on this trip. It is best for you, Jack."

"His name is *Jacek*," Mrs. Malinowski said disapprovingly, "it is Polish name, not American."

"Yes, yes," her husband replied." He laughed and got up to hug his wife. "I too have read his birth certificate. You are indeed correct. But his friends call him Jack. It is the way with Americans, my dear; they have diminutive names for one another. It is quaint custom."

"I wanted your blessing before writing to Dr. Holloway and accepting his offer," Jack said. "I know I told you about it when I wrote the essay, but..." he shrugged. "I guess I never expected to be selected."

"Nonsense," his father gave him a hearty slap on the back. "They will soon learn how fortunate they are to have Jack Malinowski on their team. He will ensure the success of their project. In fact, I suspect he will make great discoveries for them."

Jack smiled wanly, "You sure you don't need me in the shop, dad?"

His father gave a dismissive wave, "You are great mechanic, Jack, but we have others. You go. Make us proud. You deserve opportunity."

Jack nodded and took his dinner dishes to the kitchen. He returned momentarily. "Well, I guess I'd better send in my reply; wouldn't want someone else to get my spot." He turned and headed up the narrow staircase to his room.

The Malinowskis lived in Parma, Ohio, a suburb of Cleveland with a substantial Polish-American population. The family's journey to get there was one of perseverance, sacrifice and hard work, a story typical of many immigrants who seek economic prosperity and a better life in America.

Stanislaw ('Stas') and Dagmara Malinowski grew up in an exciting but difficult time in their native land. The eighties were a decade of tumultuous unrest and change, an era when their native Poland led the fight in Eastern Europe to break from the stranglehold of communism. Perhaps, as Stas felt, it was the rise of the Bishop from his hometown of Krakow, Karol Wojtyla, to become Pope John Paul II, that kindled the great popular uprising that brought forth political change. Maybe it was simply the death of the faulty social economic system. Whatever the root cause, labor strikes and the formation of the Solidarity union exerted tremendous pressure on the authoritarian, atheistic regime to force it to negotiate with the reformist leaders.

Times were hard back then. Strikes, martial law, international sanctions and triple digit inflation threatened to undermine the labor revolt, but Poland and her people persevered. In 1990, decades of communist rule finally came to an end.

The couple celebrated by getting married, and as the economy slowly improved, they worked to build a future together. Dagmara finished her degree and found a job in the clinical laboratory at a local hospital. Stas, who was an acknowledged genius with machinery, rose to be a foreman on a large farm. He assumed responsibility for maintaining all of the antiquated equipment so essential during the periods of planting and harvest.

Despite Poland's transition to a free-market state, and the gradual improvement in their financial situation, the Malinowskis grew restless. When one of Dagmara's cousins suggested she apply for a temporary position at the Cleveland Clinic, she tentatively asked her husband if he would consider taking a leave of absence from his job. She needn't have been apprehensive. Stas didn't need any encouragement when presented with an opportunity to chase the American Dream. In 1999, the young couple packed their belongings into two large trunks, sold their house, and they and their toddler son, Jacek, headed overseas toward a new life.

Parma was the perfect place for them to settle. Dagmara loved her job at the Clinic, working at the forefront of medical science. Stas, a determined entrepreneur, started his own business as a specialty auto mechanic. The business thrived, and it wasn't long before most of the power brokers in the city became regular customers, unwilling to entrust their precious Bentleys, Mercedes and Beemers to any other shop.

Young Jacek grew up in the garage. While other boys in his neighborhood occupied their nonschool hours playing sports and video games, 'Jack' helped in the family business, gradually learning the design subtleties of various high-performance internal combustion engines. Like his father, he had a flair for all things mechanical, and his capable, easygoing manner endeared him to their customers. Everyone who knew him assumed he would take over the workshop when his dad retired.

However, in his teens, Jack's interests expanded beyond those of school and helping his father. As a boy he'd been fascinated by the mechanics of cars, but in recent years he'd gradually become bored hanging around the garage. A few days after his sixteenth birthday he'd gone with a friend to a local gym to work out, and on that fateful day he'd become captivated by the demanding sport of rock climbing. He soon became a regular member of a climbing club, and Monday, Wednesday and Friday afternoons were now spent at the climbing wall, setting routes and developing the strength and balance he needed to become an elite climber.

Integrating work, school and his new time-consuming hobby required real discipline on Jack's part. During the week his schedule was exhausting. He labored hard to satisfy all of his obligations, but most evenings, after finishing his homework, he increasingly made time to pursue yet another newfound passion.   It was a subject quite apart from those he studied in school, and it fascinated him to the point where he began to think about maybe going to college, to learn more about it from experts in the field. Jack had fallen in love with astronomy.

Books on the subject now lined the shelves in his room. He subscribed to 'Astronomy' magazine and 'Sky and Telescope,' and on weekends he would often journey to the local planetarium, or drive to Cuyahoga Park on moonless nights where he could look up at the stars without interference from city lights. Navigating through the heavens became as easy for Jack as driving through his neighborhood. In the back of his mind, though, he was tormented by a looming problem: should he be accepted at a university, would his father approve of his plans to leave the family business?

Tonight, on this quiet evening in late March, Jack Malinowski had something else on his mind. He sat and stared at Morgan Holloway's offer to participate in that archeology dig up in Greenland. Was this trip really such a good idea? He was beginning to have second thoughts. There wouldn't be much to see in the night sky way up at that latitude, not in the summertime anyway. And he wouldn't be doing any climbing for a while.

"Bah," he muttered.

Before he could talk himself out of it, Jack sealed the envelope containing his acceptance and slapped a stamp onto it. He'd miss his folks and the hobbies he enjoyed, during the months he'd be gone, but he needed to get away for a while. He needed to go somewhere without distractions, to a place where he could contemplate his future and the direction his life was taking. Eviskar Island, he decided, would be the perfect locale.

Marcia Van Wormer

Marcia (Marcie) Van Wormer slammed the door behind her and didn't bother to wipe her feet before stomping across the kitchen in her muddy Nikes. In the breakfast nook, with its ornate bay window, her stepmother murmured a quick sign off into her cell phone and then calmly folded her arms across her chest.

"Please don't start with me, Marcie. You know it's not my decision." She made a show of regarding the footprints on what had previously been a clean floor, now corrupted by herringbone tread marks composed of dirt, sand, road salt and melting snow. Gail Van Wormer was fussy about the cleanliness of her home, and the cleaning woman, who'd left only hours earlier, wouldn't wash the floors again for another two weeks. She glared at Marcie but refrained from raising her voice when she saw the hurt and anger in the girl's eyes. Instead she said calmly, "I wish you'd settle down. You're making too big a deal about this."

Marcie fought back the urge to yell. "Oh great, now Ms. Perfect sees fit to weigh in with the other team. It's so easy to just go along with dad. I've got to hand it to you, Gail; you'll score a lot of points with him this time. Smart move on your part. The only downside, of course, is that the opportunity of a lifetime will pass me by. But, hey," she smiled sardonically, "that's a small price to pay for an approving nod from your hubby, right? Know what? You're right. It's not your decision, so just butt out!"

"Marcie, be reasonable about this..." her words addressed empty space as her stepdaughter stormed down the hallway and up the stairs, leaving small patches of mud on the carpeting.

Gail buried her face in her hands. It had been a miserable day, both at work and now at home. Although she'd grown up here in Albany, New York, and had lived here most of her life, the winters had always been difficult for her. The only time she'd left New York's capital city for any extended period had been during her college years at the University of Georgia. March was always so full of promise down in Athens. By this time the dogwoods, azaleas and rhododendrons would all have buds on them, and the longer days and brisk but mild temperatures carried with them the promise of a colorful spring. It would be another six weeks of cold, wet, overcast weather here in Albany before the tulips in Washington Park would bloom to announce the arrival of spring this far north, a seeming eternity after more than four months of chill and snow.

Gail and Steven Van Wormer had been married now for almost two years. They'd met at the Albany Institute where she worked as deputy curator and he starred as one of its principal members and benefactors.

The Albany Institute of History and Art, AIHA, is one of the oldest museums in the country, housing extensive collections and exhibits which document the history and culture of the upper Hudson Valley and New York State's Capital District. Prominent among its fine art collections is an assemblage of Hudson River School paintings. Works by such luminaries as Thomas Cole and Frederic Church are on permanent display there, along with examples of cast iron pieces from the once great foundries in Troy, and textile goods produced in the late 19th and early 20th centuries in cities along the Mohawk River.

Every schoolchild in Albany remembers when he/she first laid eyes on the two Egyptian mummies, complete with their ornate sarcophagi, that the Institute acquired in 1909. In fact, it was a visit to the Institute fifteen years earlier that had sparked Gail's interest in history, had led her onto her career path to preserve the past. When she was a freshman in high school, on a cold, mid-winter field trip, she'd walked up the snow-covered steps of the building and into a world of 19th century opulence.

Gail smiled briefly as she recalled the events of that day. She and her two best friends, Allison and Francis, had conspired to hold back during the tour and distance themselves from the other students and teachers. They would make it a social outing, a break from all issues academic, a half-day respite from four dull hours of boring lectures, quizzes and assigned homework.

Gail's plans changed abruptly moments after she stomped snow off her shoes and doffed her coat in the large foyer in the front hall. Greeted by docents and staff dressed in clothing period to the mid-1800s, she and her classmates began their trek through the museum. As they wound their way across creaky, polished hardwood floors, gliding through rooms filled with beautiful inlaid furniture and masterfully engraved silver pieces that had once belonged to families named Van Rensselaer, Schuyler, and Corning, Gail felt the past come alive. Transported back in time, she sensed that in some way she belonged to that earlier period; it was as though she'd been born 150 years too late. History and genealogy, she realized on that fateful day, were subjects that captivated her.

After high school, Gail had poured her soul into her history/fine art studies at UGA with the goal of gaining employment at either the Albany Institute or at the New York State Museum located only a few blocks away. Last September she'd celebrated her fifth anniversary at the Institute, and despite the occasional rough day, like today, her job had turned out to be everything she'd hoped it would be. She loved giving tours to groups of all ages, often awakening in her charges new awareness and appreciation of the region's cultured past.

Life was grand for the not yet twenty-nine-year-old Gail when, suddenly and unexpectedly, Steven Van Wormer entered her life. A scion of Albany society, Steven was one of the Institute's biggest benefactors. He was a good-looking, articulate, successful orthopedic surgeon who also happened to be recently divorced. The two of them met at a fundraiser and, after a whirlwind courtship of six months, were married. That was two years ago.

Angela, Steven's ex-wife, had run off to Buffalo with a roguish young man whom she had hired to paint the inside of the house. Apparently much more than painting had gone on in the upstairs bedrooms, not to mention the den, the living room and even on the basement workbench. One day Marcie had come home from school to an empty house save for a folder addressed to her dad. It had contained papers from the office of a local lawyer, announcing Angela's desire for a divorce. Marcie was understandably hurt. The strong feeling of abandonment resulting from her mother's deplorable departure had brought her much closer, emotionally, to her father. Gail was aware of the situation and had worked hard to fit in without threatening the close ties between father and daughter. For the most part her efforts had been successful. Gail's love for Steven was apparent to Marcie, and the girl appreciated how happy her father was in his new marriage.

Marcie was an extremely bright, studious tomboy of a girl who was currently experiencing the throes of adolescence. In general she and Gail got along well. They admired one another, accepting the roles they had been forced to assume. In the last few months Marcie had guardedly begun to open up to Gail about some of the social problems she was experiencing in school. The soccer coach had placed her on the "C" team rather than the Junior varsity where Marcie felt she belonged, and one of her better friends was giving her the cold shoulder for some unknown reason. But there were other issues, those relating to the physical changes associated with puberty, which Marcie refused to discuss with anyone, not even with her father, a physician. Gail wanted desperately to play a greater role as confidant and parent to the young woman, but that wouldn't happen unless Marcie wanted it.

Gail wiped a tear from her eye. Over the last two days, Marcie had plummeted into a deep funk over her dad's unwillingness to allow her to go on that summer archeological trip to Greenland. "You're just too young to be that far from home and for such a long period of time," Steven had blurted out the night before. "I don't want to hear another word about this, young lady. The issue is closed. Do you hear me? Closed!" Never before had Gail heard Steven get cross like that, especially with his daughter. She knew he was stressed at work and Marcie had been nagging him incessantly about the trip, but that conversation had resulted in hard feelings between father and daughter. On previous occasions when Steven had declined to grant permission to Marcie for something—usually with regard to attending unsupervised parties—Marcie had reluctantly accepted her dad's denials. But this time things were different. Both Marcie and Steven were firmly anchored to their respective positions. Marcie insisted upon joining the expedition and Steven was just as steadfast about his veto. The household was laden with tension and Gail felt caught in the middle.

Abruptly Gail stood up. Her love for both Steven and Marcie demanded she become involved. "Damn it," she thought, "Maybe I shouldn't do this, but..." She strode through the house and bounded up the stairs, taking them two at a time. Outside the door to Marcie's room she stopped. Taking a moment to compose herself, and to gather her courage and her thoughts, she took a deep breath and knocked.

"Marcie, it's me, Gail. We have to talk." (no answer) "Marcie Van Wormer, open this door!"

A feeble voice, attributable to someone who'd been crying, answered, "Go away!" Gail opened the door and stepped into the room. Marcie was lying on the bed facing away from her. She was staring blankly out the room's solitary window that overlooked the street.

"This can't go on, Marcie. It kills me to see both you and your father so unhappy."

"So, you want *me* to pity *you* because, as an 'impartial' observer you feel uncomfortable? Get real, Gail. I know why you're here. Mission accomplished. When dad gets home you can now honestly tell him that you and I had a talk, and that 'little Marcie' his 'child' is still upset. You did your duty, Gail," she said despondently, "now please leave me alone."

"You mean you're going to accept your dad's decision?"

"What choice do I have, Gail? I'm a minor. If he doesn't sign the consent form, I don't go on this trip. Period. I'm fucked!"

Gail bristled at her stepdaughter's language, but didn't admonish her. The girl was understandably upset. "For what it's worth, Marcie, I came here to support you. I think you're right."

Marcie sat up and turned to face her. "What?"

"Hey, I'm entitled to an opinion on this matter even though I have no authority. And make no mistake, Marcie, I'm not here to win brownie points with anyone, neither you nor your father." She sat on the bed and looked into the girl's eyes. Marcie returned her gaze, noting the anguish in Gail's countenance.

"You're going to be fifteen in less than two months," Gail continued quietly. "You're also exceptionally mature for your age and your grades are top notch. There will be other kids, I mean, other young adults, on this trip as well. It is a true scientific expedition and possibly a once-in-a-lifetime opportunity." She smiled. "Also, believe it or not, I was fifteen once. I know how important an experience like this can be."

"Thanks, Gail," Marcie said with true sincerity. She slid across the bed and gave her stepmom a hug. "Thanks for believing in me."

"All I can promise is that I'll talk to your dad. I'll tell him how I feel and throw in a little guilt trip about the encouragement he gave you when you submitted your essay. I'll remind him of the hypocrisy of denying your participation after having supported your application."

Marcie laughed. "Yeah, that's good. I hadn't thought about that."

"But I also want you to consider why your dad feels the way he does. I don't mean to sound overly patronizing, Marcie," she smiled sheepishly. The young woman seated next to her was extraordinarily astute. "He's scared. If you go, it will be the first time he's been separated from his little girl, both in duration and geographically, since you were born. It's weighing on him."

"I guess you're right," Marcie admitted.

"His angst isn't a very good reason for denying you this opportunity, and I'll try my best to make him realize that. But," Gail continued soberly, "just because I don't agree with his position doesn't mean he'll change his mind. As you said earlier, the final decision to give parental consent is his alone. Even if your mother were to disagree, your parents' custody agreement effectively gives him complete control."

"My mom doesn't care one way or the other," Marcie muttered.

"It's settled then," Gail said in a conspiratorial but upbeat tone. She walked to the door and turned to face Marcie. "I'll put as much pressure on your dad as I can, but in return you'll have to accept his final word with dignity."

"Deal," said Marcie.

Jocelyn Delaney

The bell outside room 210 announced the beginning of another class at

Hamilton High School in Corpus Christi, Texas. It was Friday, mid-March. Herb Powell stood leaning against the bench at the front of the room, surveying the mix of juniors and seniors in his eighth period biology class. Off to his right, at the back of the room, sat his "problem children." They were an incorrigible bunch, rude, disruptive and unpredictable. Today, Jocelyn Delaney sat in the middle of the group flanked by Freddy Ramos and Ann Marie Severko. Directly behind her sat Toby Johnson. Powell made note of the seating arrangement chosen by the students and smiled inwardly. All was as he expected.

"Class, before we begin I'd like to introduce you to Miss Diane Thompson." He nodded towards a woman in her late twenties seated near the blackboard. She was pretty, with red hair and freckles. She gave the class an embarrassed wave and flashed a winning smile. "Miss Thompson is a student teacher and has come to observe our class today." Snickers and muted laughter came from the back corner of the room but Powell ignored the noise and continued, raising his voice several decibels. "As you know, today you'll take your midterm exam. Please clear your desks of everything but a number two pencil so that we may begin."

While the students stuffed notebooks into backpacks and backpacks under and behind seats, Powell picked up a neatly stacked pile of test papers and began walking up and down the rows of desks, passing them out. As he walked among those seated in the back, he said, "If you have any questions, please raise your hand and either Miss Thompson or I will come to you. When you're done, bring your test to the front of the room and then work quietly at your seat until everyone has finished. You have forty-five minutes in which to complete the exam."

Powell didn't anticipate any questions from the students. He'd made the test multiple choice. All of the problems were clearly stated and the answer choices were direct and unambiguous. Those who knew the material should finish in thirty minutes or less. He sauntered back to the front of the classroom, donned a pair of dark glasses and pretended to write something in a notebook. Knowing that others would be unable to follow his gaze, he kept a surreptitious eye on the troublemakers seated in the back. Soon, when they thought his attention was directed elsewhere, Ramos and Severko, the students sitting adjacent to Jocelyn Delaney, would blatantly lean over to look at her answers. Powell glanced at Diane Thompson who nodded almost imperceptibly.

Powell then relocated to a chair next to Diane and the two of them engaged in muted conversation. Although his back was now to the room, Thompson had a clear view of what was happening among the cheating students. She gave Powell a blow-by-blow account of events.   At one point, Jocelyn nonchalantly leaned down to scratch her ankle with one hand while simultaneously holding up her test in the other so that the boy sitting in back of her could clearly see her answers. Powell snuck a glance over his shoulder to verify Diane's assessment.

When the bell rang to end the period, the students clambered out of the room conversing excitedly in their collective euphoria over the commencement of the weekend. Mr. Powell tried to ignore the smug looks on the faces of the four dishonest students as they made their way past him. He sincerely hoped they'd be embarrassed and chagrined once he revealed what he'd done.

Years earlier Powell had pulled the same stunt and felt it had made a difference to several of those involved. Three of today's participants would undoubtedly laugh this off as a silly game. But the fourth? Herb shook his head. It would be easy to grade her paper normally. After all, there was little doubt she had done her own work, but there was also no doubt that she was complicit in the schemes of the others. The consequences for her would be heartwrenching, but he, along with several of her other teachers and the principal, had agreed that all should be punished. Cheating was unacceptable.

"Thanks for helping out today, Diane. I wish we could have worked together under happier circumstances."

"No sweat, Herb. Don't let this trouble you. You did the right thing."

The following Friday was overcast and dreary. Cold air spilling in from the north was slamming into warm, moist air roiling up from the Gulf. Winds were high. Heavy rains periodically lashed the windows of the biology lab as squalls made their way across the city. Herb Powell's mood mirrored the weather as he delivered an uninspired lecture to his last class. Halfway through the period, Diane Thompson entered the room and sat demurely by the door. Five minutes before the final bell, Powell handed back the previous week's exam papers, graded and marked with corrections. Scrawled across the tests of the students who'd cheated were the words: 'See Me After Class.'

"There's gotta be some mistake here," complained Toby Johnson as he approached Powell's desk. "I studied hard for this test. I don't see how I could'a got an 'F'."

"Cut the crap, Toby," Powell replied. He arose and closed the door to the hallway, then motioned for the four students to sit down. "I misled the class on Friday when I introduced Miss Thompson as a student teacher. For that I apologize. She is actually dean of students at George Washington High, on the other side of town. She works principally with students who have disciplinary issues."

"I try to get problem students to see the errors of their ways," Diane interjected. "What I saw on Friday made me sick." She gave a hard stare to each student in turn. Jocelyn Delaney went pale when she realized what was happening.

"I handed out two different tests," Powell said. "Superficially the two looked the same. In fact many of the same problems appeared on both, but with the possible answers in different order. I made certain that Miss Delaney took one test and that the rest of you took the other. Mr. Johnson and Mr. Ramos, ALL of your answers were the same as Miss Delaney's. You each received a score of 8% on the exam." At this point Powell allowed himself a hint of a congratulatory smile. "You'd have scored better if you had guessed at every question. The only reason your scores weren't zero is because, coincidentally, the correct choices for four of the fifty questions were tied to the same letter—an oversight on my part."

Freddy snickered, "That's really clever, Mr. Powell. You pulled a fast one on us—must be really proud." He looked at his peers soliciting approval for his macho attitude towards their recent academic disaster. Toby and Anne Marie laughed, but Jocelyn remained stoic.

"I'm really sorry you don't get what's going on here, Fred," Powell replied sadly." It's been years since I've had to do something like this. Cheating is just plain wrong, guys, and I won't tolerate it. What really saddens me, though, is that you're all so bright. Instead of playing childish games trying to scam the system, you could be broadening your knowledge, showing a little discipline and self-respect."

Powell arose, indicating that the lecture was over. None of those in attendance, including him, wanted to waste another minute talking about this. "Diane and I have discussed your punishment and decided that each of you will get a grade of zero on this test. Mathematically, that will drop you at least one letter grade for the course."

"All of your other teachers have been informed of this," Diane added, an ominous tone to her voice. "Another cheating episode will result in expulsion."

Jocelyn was the last student to leave the room. As she walked dejectedly past her teacher he said in a low enough voice so that the others wouldn't hear, "Why did you do it? You won't be valedictorian now, not with a low grade in this class." She just pushed by him, flashing a venomous glare, but saying nothing. "I hope it was worth it, Jocelyn. I really do."

The door slammed behind her.

A salt breeze assaulted Jocelyn as she made her way out to the street. Ann Marie vaulted a large puddle in the parking lot in order to catch up with her. "Hey, Jossy, can you believe what Powell did? What a douche bag." She laughed. "He acted so sad, like giving us a bad grade was going to devastate us. Oh yeah, like going from an 'F' to an 'F minus' is a big freakin' deal for me."

Jocelyn forced a smile, "He's a real turd all right."

"C'mon, let's go to the beach. Toby and Javier are all jazzed to get out on the bay. Hobie Cats are gonna fly in this wind. It'll be awesome. Afterwards we can grab something to eat, maybe get high. Wadda ya say?"

"Nah, maybe tomorrow," Jocelyn replied, "looks like it might rain some more."

"Suit yourself. See you tomorrow, Jossy."

Left alone with her thoughts, Jocelyn walked the nearly two miles to her house instead of taking the bus. She was close to tears. "God," she thought, "What a shitty thing for Powell to do." When she got home she took a minute to compose herself before slipping into the kitchen via the garage.

"Is that you, Jossy?" Her mother hurried past fumbling for her keys in her purse. "I have to show a house in five minutes. I'm late. Hey, you okay? You look sad."

"It's nothing. I just, uh, I'm not feeling well. I think maybe I'm getting a cold."

"Oh, honey, I'm sorry. Look, I won't be home for about an hour. Your dad is going to stop on his way home and get take-out Chinese. You get some rest, okay? See you soon."

Seconds later Jocelyn stood alone in the kitchen, the ticking of the cuckoo clock above the telephone breaking the sudden silence in the room. She plodded silently down the carpeted hallway to her room and dumped her books onto her desk. Fighting the urge to cry, forcing reason to overcome emotion, she sat and stared at the mementos, photos, trophies, and knick-knacks that littered the room, the icons that chronicled her life.

The preponderance of awards indicated that the bearer was a bright, talented and ambitious young woman. Many of the framed certificates staring down at her from the walls were from science fair competitions, something she'd been into in a big way in her youth. The more prominently displayed pieces—those she was most proud of—pertained to her language skills. Jocelyn was a true polyglot. She seemed to absorb foreign languages like a sponge. Several of her native Spanish-speaking friends were hesitant to converse with her; they were intimidated because her vocabulary, diction and grammar were superior to theirs. One of the certificates had been awarded to her by the local Societé de la Culture Française. She'd won a standing ovation for an entertaining speech given entirely in French.

The shelf above her desk was adorned with brass frames containing photos from family vacations: her folks skiing in Taos, NM; Jocelyn, Ricky and their mother hiking in the Okefenokee wilderness; mom and dad laughing in a café in old Quebec City. She stared at her favorite, a blowup of her sitting on the beach on South Padre Island. She'd been to South Padre many times, of course, but on that particular trip she'd met a boy with whom she'd shared her first kiss. That's something a girl never forgets.

Jocelyn's reverie ended with the slamming of the front door. A child's voice yelled, "Mom, Angelo asked if I can sleep over. Can I? Hey, mom?" When he got no answer, Ricky Delaney bounded down the hallway and skidded to a stop outside Jocelyn's room. The door was open so he barged in. At eight years old he had little respect for his sister's privacy. Breathing hard he asked, "Where's mom?"

Jocelyn looked at her sibling with a mixture of annoyance and resignation. Diminutive in stature and with a freckled face and ears that stood out like those of a mouse, most adults considered young Ricky to be adorable. Even Jocelyn had been of that mindset until a few years ago. Her kid brother had since passed through the adorable phase. In fact, he'd rapidly progressed through "cute," "bothersome," and "aggravating," and had now become "insufferable," a royal pain in the derriere. His main goal in life now seemed to be the torment of his older sister.

"She had to show a house, 'Squirt.' Dad's bringing dinner home with him, probably Chinese."

"Oh man, I hate Chink food. It's slimy—and it gives me stinky farts."

"Watch your mouth, young man. Just because mom and dad aren't here doesn't give you permission to make crude statements and disparaging racist remarks."

"Yeah right, and you're perfect. Anyway, Angelo's folks are probably having something good tonight, like tacos or burritos. They asked me to spend the night."

"Did his folks invite you or was it just Angelo?"

"Angelo invited me, but I'm sure it's okay with his mom."

Jocelyn would have liked nothing more than to say, "Sounds great...goodbye!" to her kid brother. It would ensure her a peaceful Friday evening, but it wasn't her place to grant him permission to bother the Cespedes family down the street. Also, for all she knew, Angelo was probably pleading with his folks to spend the night here.

"You know what Angelo calls you? 'Juicy Jossy.' He thinks you're 'Juicy.'" For some reason Ricky considered this to be extremely funny. He laughed heartily and repeated the word "Joo-say" while making some sort of hand gesture combined with a cool dance step.

Jocelyn rolled her eyes. "What a little pervert. Someone should slap some manners into him."

"Hah! Angelo's awesome. Know what he can do? Today at recess he hawked a looie straight up into the air and caught it in his mouth on the way down."

"Gross!"

"And at lunch he taught me how to drink milk through a straw and make it come out my nose."

"Now *that* is a talent I can relate to," said Jocelyn sarcastically. "Maybe you can show that trick to mom and dad some night at dinner. I bet they'd be really impressed."

A car pulled into the driveway. Like radar, Ricky's satellite-dish ears picked up the sound and he ran off to assail his father with the sleepover request.

"I'm NEVER going to have kids," Jocelyn thought with firm resolve. Her attention turned once again to her cluttered desk, and to her earlier despondent mood. She needed radical change in her life, a reprieve from annoying kid brothers, manipulative friends and sanctimonious teachers. She grabbed her school books and dropped them unceremoniously onto the floor. That action uncovered the letter she'd received the week before.

Out of the blue Jocelyn had received an invitation, written on fancy, engraved stationary, to participate in an archeological dig on an island in the far North Atlantic. Having dismissively set the letter aside because of her upcoming biology midterm, she'd forgotten about it. The fog was now lifting from her memory. Months earlier she and several fellow students in her geology class had learned of a competition to apply for work at a real archeological dig site. A few of her colleagues had submitted, with great enthusiasm, well-written essays, hoping against great odds that they might be selected to go. Jocelyn hadn't been nearly as excited about the project as her friends. Her own essay had been a real lackluster effort. She certainly hadn't expected to hear anything further about it, and she now felt bad because she knew several individuals who undoubtedly would be ecstatic to have been offered this opportunity. Intending to decline the offer, she had set the letter aside. Given the day's events, however, she now gave the matter a second thought. "What the heck," she muttered. Although not particularly religious, she couldn't help but feel a sense of divine intervention. This was a chance to get away from the shitty circumstances that were bringing her down here in Corpus Christi.

The envelope contained an acknowledgment form to be returned with a postmark dated no later than April 1st. The deadline was still about a week away. "I'm going to do it," she decided. She filled out the form and then got up and followed the savory aroma of egg rolls, fried rice and sweet-and-sour sauce wafting in from the kitchen.

"Eat your dinner, Rick," said her father. He sounded exhausted. "I'll call Mrs. Cespedes once you've cleaned your plate. If it's okay with her we'll get your sleeping bag and I'll take you over there."

Once the three had eaten, Jocelyn saw her opportunity. "Um, dad?" she began, "When mom comes home there's something I'd like to discuss with you. It has to do with my plans for the summer."

III

Just outside the secure portion of New York's La Guardia airport, Debbie Holloway waited for the young woman from Corpus Christi, Texas. Beside her stood a fit, wiry, broad-shouldered young man who had arrived earlier on an American Airlines flight from Cleveland, Ohio. The two had never met until today, although they'd corresponded extensively over the past several months. In the hour or so they'd been talking, Debbie had grown ever more impressed with Jacek Malinowski. He was easygoing and friendly, and, most importantly, he harbored no romantic illusions about the project they were about to undertake. It would involve dirty, backbreaking work at times, but "Jack" seemed accepting of that fact and showed an eagerness to learn about the ancient settlement they were to unearth. While Debbie was sharing an amusing anecdote about the previous year's progress on the dig, Jack nodded at a woman stumbling towards them along the corridor leading from the gates.

Rolling a large carry-on suitcase behind her while struggling to support a large rucksack, Jocelyn Delaney slowly approached. The suitcase had a broken wheel that caused it to flop from side to side, occasionally falling into the paths of other harried travelers. Once she had made it past the TSA guard at the entrance to the secure area, Jack rushed to her aid.

"You must be Jocelyn. Let me take your rucksack. "Thanks. Yes, I'm Jocelyn Delaney. Who are you?"

"Jack Malinowski, I'm one of the other students. This is Debbie Holloway."

Jocelyn shook hands with her new colleagues and breathed a heavy sigh of relief. "I almost missed my connection in Dallas. The connecting flight was, like, twenty gates away and I had all this stuff. But, hey, here I am."

"It looks like you were able to bring all your stuff as carry-on," Debbie remarked. "Jack did the same. We can go right to the curb and catch a cab to the hotel."

"Oh, I have a couple of checked bags," said Jocelyn. "The flight number is 703. They'll be in bag claim 'C'."

The three gradually made their way down to baggage claim. Jack was loaded down with his and Jocelyn's rucksacks as well as his other satchel, a backpack he'd lashed to the top of his rucksack. Joselyn continued to fight with the damaged roller case as they weaved through a large crowd that encircled the revolving baggage conveyor.

Jack stood to one side while Jocelyn reviewed the passing bags and chatted with Debbie. Until now, he hadn't given much thought to what the other people might be like on this archeology project. It was the nature of the work, the science, the thrill of discovery that had prompted his interest, and that had been the gist of his application essay. Sure, he knew there would be other students on the trip, but until now he'd never considered the social situation he would face.

He watched Jocelyn. She was cute, no doubt about that. Long blond hair, expressive eyes, killer-nice curves—all of the signs indicated she had an active social life back home and probably a steady boyfriend. He suddenly became apprehensive. Here was someone who most certainly wasn't like the studious types Jack hung out with. So, why the heck would she be interested in a field trip like this?

Something Debbie said made Jocelyn laugh and she abruptly turned her head in time to see Jack starring at her. He blushed and averted his gaze.

Soon, a large fabric suitcase emerged from the gullet of the baggage train and plopped onto the carousel. Jocelyn lunged for it and, with some difficulty, wrestled it onto the floor beside her. Jack sauntered over to see if he could be of assistance as Jocelyn grabbed a second nearly identical bag and dragged it alongside the other.

Debbie looked worried. "Jocelyn, I hope you don't plan to take all of this on the trip; I don't think there will be room. The information we sent out specified that each individual, Morgan and me included, can only take one rucksack full of clothing along with a backpack or other easily transportable carrier containing additional clothing and/or personal effects. We sent you your rucksack. All of them, by the way, are the same. They have an internal volume of over forty liters, which should be plenty of space for what you'll need. I seriously doubt you'll be able to take all of this."

Jocelyn's smile disappeared. Her reply was defiant. "Mrs. Holloway, we're going to be gone for almost three months. And, your note said that laundry facilities would be 'primitive.' I've packed the absolute minimum amount of clothing that I need."

"Jack has obviously complied with the rules."

"Yeah? Well, guys are gross. He's probably packed only one set of underwear. We won't be able to get near him when he gets really ripe."

"That's part of my master plan," Jack interjected, attempting to lighten the mood, "The smell should keep the polar bears away." He received condescending looks from both women. "Hey, just kidding; I actually packed two pairs of briefs." The deprecating stares continued. "...plus those I have on," he added meekly.

"Okay, perhaps now isn't the time to talk about gear," Debbie said diplomatically. "We'll discuss it with Morgan when we get to the hotel."

Jack loaded up with his own belongings plus the heavier of Jocelyn's bags—one that didn't have wheels. Debbie towed Jocelyn's other suitcase while Joselyn herself continued to deal with her carryon items. Like heavily laden Sherpas headed for base camp, the three of them slowly slogged to the front of the terminal to a line of waiting taxi cabs.

Amtrak's Empire Service train rolled into Penn Station at 2:30 PM. Gail Van Wormer marked her place in the mystery novel that had occupied her attention, off and on, during their three hour trip from the Albany-Rensselaer station. She nudged her sleeping husband and pointed across the aisle at her stepdaughter. Marcie was once again in her seat and flashed a rare smile at her folks. To say that she'd been looking forward to this day was an understatement. Her preparations had begun the moment her father had given his approval for her to go.

After school had let out she'd spent dozens of hours toiling under the hot summer sun: mowing lawns, weeding gardens, and performing miscellaneous chores throughout the neighborhood. In the evenings she took babysitting jobs. Marcie had plied every cent of her earnings into provisions for the trip. She and Gail had made critical trips to Crossgates Mall and Stuyvesant Plaza, hitting clothing and sporting goods stores, buying everything from water purification tablets to mini-binoculars to LED headlamps. Some of her enthusiasm had even rubbed off on her dad. He'd surprised her with a graduation gift of high-tech, Gortex hiking boots and a rugged windbreaker with a detachable Polartech insert. He'd also purchased a quality backpack to accompany the expedition-supplied rucksack, and Marcie had packed and re-packed both bags so many times, she could now locate anything they contained, blindfolded, within fifteen seconds.

Her personal bag held her laptop, camera, writing materials and stamps, extra batteries, wallet, cell phone, GPS, one hundred feet of parachute cord, a poncho, an emergency blanket, and a wellstocked first aid kit that included: antibiotic ointment, various analgesics, water purification tablets and compression bandages. The rucksack contained clothing, miscellaneous non-perishable food supplies, and a small multitool that wouldn't be allowed in her carry-on gear. All items were packed and stowed with military precision. Marcie Van Wormer was ready for a post-apocalyptic world.

"We're pulling into platform eight," she announced in a businesslike tone, "on track five." She was standing in the aisle now, before the train had come to a full stop, pulling her rucksack from the overhead compartment. Neither parent was allowed to touch her bags. Marcie's fiercely independent mindset demanded that she prove her self-reliance to everyone associated with this trip.

It was the first time Marcie had ever been in either Penn Central Station or Madison Square Garden, but she forged ahead through the crowds with singular purpose, heavily laden with gear and forcing her folks into a brisk power walk. From the layout of the station posted on the internet, she navigated according to landmarks committed to memory. "Hurry up, dad, Gail. I only see three cabs out front. They'll be gone soon."

"We were instructed to be at the hotel by 5:00," said her father, "it's not even 3:00 yet."

Marcie rolled her eyes. "I know, dad, but I want to talk to the Holloways beforehand. There may be something we forgot. You never know."

There wasn't much Steven could say. He wasn't in charge.

The Hotel Chelsea wasn't exactly five star, Steven noted with a frown, but at least it didn't look like the kind of place that rented rooms by the hour.

Located on West 29th street, it was conveniently located to many landmarks in Manhattan, including the Empire State Building. The Van Wormers bundled inside and checked in. Marcie was given a key to a room she would share with another student on the trip, a girl named Jocelyn Delaney. Steven and Gail planned to spend the night there as well. They would see their daughter to the airport in the morning, hit a few museums, and then take an afternoon train back to Albany. Unbeknownst to his daughter, Steven had another, more compelling reason to remain in the city for the night: he wanted to speak with Morgan Holloway, the leader of the project, about trip logistics and safety concerns. Although he'd given tentative approval to allow Marcie to participate, he still commanded veto power if things didn't appear to be on the up-and-up. He was proud of his daughter, proud of her drive, work ethic and the professional way she had prepared for this endeavor. But she had yet to turn fifteen. No matter how maturely she behaved, she was still a child—his child—and he was perfectly willing to withdraw his support and permission if he saw any indication that she would be exposed to undue risk.

Marcie led the way across the lobby's parquet floor to a bank of elevators embedded in the far wall. She was anxious to stow her things in the room and then return to meet and mingle with her summer colleagues. The elevators were ornately trimmed with 1920's style brass molding. Mounted above each one was an arrow that swung in a semicircular arc to indicate the current floor location of the lift. One of them was dropping, preparing to disgorge its cargo to the lobby.

The door opened and a young man exited in a rush, but stopped short when he caught sight of Marcie. He had the appearance of a typical young urban professional: casually but neatly dressed in slacks and a short-sleeved, button-down dress shirt. A pair of expensive soft-leather Italian shoes completed the carefully styled attire. Slim and fit, he had an undistinguished, round face and a receding hairline. Pale blue eyes resided behind trendy wire-rimmed spectacles. He stared momentarily at Marcie before breaking into a winning smile.

"I recognize the rucksack. You must be Marcie. Hi, I'm Dr. Morgan Holloway." He then turned his attention to her parents. "Dr. Morgan Holloway," he repeated. "You must be Marcie's folks.

"I'm going to my room," Marcie announced enthusiastically, "I'll be back in five minutes."

Her father grinned. "Steven Van Wormer. This is my wife, Gail. As you can see, Marcie is rather excited to be a part of your archeology project."

"And we're most happy to have her along," Morgan replied. He looked at his watch. "I'm expecting the other students to show up any time now. We may as well make ourselves comfortable while we wait." He beckoned them towards a cozy seating area away from the thoroughfare around the front desk. A large bay window gave a panoramic view of West 29th.

It was a beautiful summer afternoon in New York, and the city bustled. A shoe and leather goods store across the street advertised a 30% off sale to throngs of people who passed by, all of them in a hurry. Cars rolled along the oneway street, at least every other one a yellow cab, outpaced by pedestrians except for the intermittent spells when traffic lights were in their favor. A double-parked delivery van unloaded produce in front of a Korean grocery store, while just down the block the remains of a late lunch crowd conversed on the patio of an Italian eatery, oblivious to the exhaust and noise only yards away. Steven caught a whiff of garlic and pesto sauce every time the door to the hotel opened. His stomach growled. He was hungry; they had missed lunch on the train.

Steven's thoughts were interrupted by Morgan, who swept an arm towards the scene outside. "It's hard for me to believe that in just a few days I'll have traded the chaos of one of the largest cities on earth for one of its most remote locations. It's humbling to see how man has changed the face of the planet when you get to see our world from such vastly different perspectives in such a short time." He paused for dramatic effect and continued, "I hope the young people, like Marcie, who are joining us on this year's dig, will also appreciate the wild and rugged land that greeted the Norsemen who first ventured to Eviskar Island."

"I know Marcie will," Steven remarked, "She loves the outdoors. She'll pull her weight without complaint and enjoy every minute of the trip despite the lack of creature comforts. And, I certainly agree that the island is remote. When I looked it up on Google Earth I immediately became concerned for my daughter's safety."

Morgan responded with a dismissive wave. "I understand completely. You must consider, though, that this is a major international investigation.

Researchers from many parts of Scandinavia; Denmark, Norway, Greenland, Iceland; in addition to our US contingent, are extremely interested in this find. The fact that such a large Norse settlement was located so far north, and so far from coastal Greenland, is what makes it so fascinating. You see..."

"It is fascinating," Steven agreed, "but scientific interest is distinct from safety preparedness. I simply want to know what emergency measures you have in place for dealing with things like broken bones, lacerations, appendicitis, stroke—incidents that can be life-threatening in such a remote locale. I'm not overly paranoid, and I don't presume that an expedition like this doesn't carry with it some additional risk. I just want to know how prepared you are for the unexpected."

"A fair question indeed," Morgan replied. He leaned back and steepled his fingers together, pausing as though deep in thought. "If an accident were to occur—an extremely unlikely event to be sure—we have enormous resources at our disposal. The scientific importance of this project ensures that to be the case." Morgan droned on, attempting to placate Steven rather than specifically addressing his questions and concerns. Steven's anger flared. This was nothing but runaround. He wanted specifics, not some patronizing, hand-waving homily about how safety follows automatically from the fact that the project is so scientifically important—important, at least, in the mind of Dr. Morgan Holloway.

Steven was about to interrupt Morgan's speech in less than congenial fashion when the speaker abruptly glanced over at the hotel's desk. "There they are," he announced with some relief, "my wife and her charges. Please excuse me. I'll be right back."

Debbie Holloway, flanked by the students she'd met at New York's LaGuardia Airport, was busy signing paperwork. Morgan sauntered over to greet them and waited courteously while an officious desk clerk ran through her spiel about checkout times and the hotel's complimentary continental breakfast. She finished with the requisite "have a nice day," and motioned for the next guest to approach. The students departed for their rooms, but before they were out of earshot Debbie reminded them, "We've reserved a private dining room for our group. Dinner is at 5:30." Jack nodded assent as he muscled Jocelyn's bags into the elevator. Morgan then ushered Debbie towards the

Van Wormers. En route she stopped and grasped his arm. She looked haggard, exasperated. "Before Jocelyn comes back we need to discuss the amount of stuff she intends to bring with her. Morgan, she has at least three times the volume that we've allotted per person. In addition to her rucksack she brought two huge suitcases."

Morgan pondered her statement and frowned, "We certainly sent out very clear instructions to the students. The captain of the Danish naval vessel that will take us to the island specifically stressed the critical issue of space in her correspondence. Bunk space in the cabins is extremely limited and the cargo holds will be filled to the gills. She's going to have to comply with our orders."

"That's what I figured you'd say, but I wanted to make sure. She seems like a strong-minded young woman. I suspect there's going to be an argument over this. As much as I dread it I'm willing to deal with her, but I'm going to need backup." She turned to the van Wormers. "Sorry about that. It seems we've run into our first minor crisis. We took two graduate students to the site last summer, but this year, as you probably know, we're taking along four high school students. It should be an interesting experience for all concerned."

Gail nodded and laughed. "I can assure you, as someone who's getting her first dose of what it's like to parent a teenager, there will never be a dull moment for you this summer. Our Marcie won't be a problem for you though. The only thing you may tire of is having to answer all of the questions she'll ask. She's full of the enthusiasm of youth. Other than that I believe she'll be a real asset to you."

"Speaking of youth, she's only just completed the eighth grade," Stephen interjected. He was settling down after his frustrating talk with Morgan, but still wanted his concerns addressed. He needed some sort of assurance, as detailed as possible, that the trip would be safe for his daughter. "I want to know what sort of care Marcie would receive if she, or anyone else for that matter, were to have a medical emergency in that remote place."

Debbie sensed the conviction that underlay Steven's words. "I understand your concern. Here's the deal. This will be our third year of study out there. Needless to say the operation is significantly more efficient than it was in the beginning. We have an onsite medical station that can handle most routine health problems: cuts, broken bones, infections...that sort of thing. One of our anthropologists is a pathologist, Dr. Liva Strøm. She's on the island already; I received an email from her last night. Her husband is a physician as well. Morgan and I, along with most of the other staff, are trained and licensed to administer CPR and first aid."

Stephen nodded, and asked, "But what if hospitalization is required? How soon can transport to a trauma facility be done?"

"There is a ranger station at Daneborg, Greenland. It's the regional headquarters for the personnel who work at the Northeast Greenland National Park. It's about 150 nautical miles, give or take, southwest of Eviskar. During the winter it's only manned by a skeleton staff, but in summertime the Greenlandic coast guard uses it as a helicopter base. Eviskar lies within their flight range. The medical facilities at Daneborg aren't much better than those we've setup on Eviskar, but Daneborg has an airstrip from which jet ambulance service can transport patients the 610 nautical miles to Reykjavik or to the U.S. Air base at Thule over on Greenland's west coast."

Stephen nodded approvingly, "And what about communication with the outside world? Do you use some sort of satellite phone out there? It would be nice if we can stay in touch with Marcie."

"Yes, we have several sat phone units and emergency communicators out there. Because of the high latitude at Eviskar, they are of the type that use private telecommunications satellites that fly in polar orbits. Ours use the Iridium network. Overall we've been pleased with the way the system has been working." She shrugged, "sometimes one has to wait until a satellite is within range. That can be a bit aggravating, but the delay is never more than about 15 minutes. The neat thing about the system is that it ties into all the major cell phone networks. If need be, Marcie can literally type your number into the sat phone handset and call you at home."

Finally, Steven broached THE subject. He could tell Debbie was expecting him to bring it up, and he also suspected she knew that Marcie's participation hinged on her response. It wasn't until long after he'd signed and mailed the acceptance form that he'd learned about a disturbing incident at Eviskar. When he'd found out about the episode he'd become extremely upset, angry enough to spit nails, and it had taken all the persuasive skill Gail could muster to calm him down. Her advice: Find out what happened, Steven, before you jump to conclusions. Talk to the Holloways before you take this opportunity away from Marcie. Once he'd calmed down he'd reluctantly complied with Gail's request, but this was it; now he wanted answers. "Tell me please, Mrs. Holloway, what exactly happened to the researchers who disappeared last year."

Debbie let out a long breath. During the previous summer, three members of the archeological team had disappeared without a trace. The event had been traumatic for everyone associated with the project, and Steven's concern was understandable. "Three of our party took one of the zodiacs on a trip to circumnavigate the island. Their purpose was to look for evidence of additional old settlements. We expected them to be gone for about a week, but after ten days elapsed without any contact from them whatsoever, we sent out search parties." Hurt crept into her voice as she recalled details of the incident. "We launched the two other boats and scrutinized every inch of coastline. The park rangers in Daneborg also conducted searches by helicopter—without success. Believe me, Dr. Van Wormer, if those scientists had been stranded anywhere around that island, we'd have found them."

She looked down and shook her head, "There was a particularly violent storm that came through while they were gone. All of us now believe that the boat must have capsized and the wreckage was blown out to sea; no other explanation makes sense. But," she added emphatically, "I want to stress that we've learned from that experience. We've invested a lot of money into additional communications gear and safety equipment since then, and I can assure you that everyone at the site is now far more safety conscious. Don't worry; we're going to take very good care of Marcie and the other students."

Before Stephen could ask more questions he felt a hand on his shoulder. Standing behind him, beaming from ear to ear, was his daughter, and beside her stood a pretty young woman with long, blond hair tied back in a ponytail. Jocelyn looked as though she'd just come home from the beach. Her slim physique was accentuated by tight-fitting jeans and open sandals with raised heels. A T-shirt advertising 'Sammy's Crab Shack, Corpus Christi, Texas' hung loosely from her tanned shoulders. With her green eyes and winning smile, Jocelyn Delaney was turning heads in the lobby of the Chelsea hotel.

"Jocelyn, these are my folks. The male is my dad and the female is Gail, my stepmom. Dad, we're going to check out the neighborhood. Dinner's at 5:30 so we'll be back a little before then, OK?"

"Sounds great, sweetie, Gail and I will..."

Debbie interrupted. "Marcie, uh... Jocelyn, perhaps it would be best if you waited a bit. After dinner we're going to go over the logistics of tomorrow's flight along with what we're going to do when we get to Reykjavik. Everyone's got to be packed before we go to bed; there won't be time in the morning. What I'm trying to say is that there won't be time for Jocelyn to repack her things after dinner. It really has to be done now. Jocelyn, I sincerely hope this won't be too difficult, but I'm afraid you're going to have to leave some stuff behind."

She glanced at Morgan, who flashed what he hoped was his patented disarming smile, "Yes, you should definitely repack your things, Jocelyn."

"We have a one rucksack rule," Debbie reminded him.

"Yes, of course. That's certainly true, but let's not get excited until we know what we're up against. Why don't you ladies get started packing. Things may not be as bad as you think."

Debbie glared at him before she and the girls headed for the elevators.

At five minutes past 5:00 three people entered the Chelsea hotel. Leading the way was a large black woman who paused in the doorway, framed by sunlight pouring in from the street. Like a queen, she then strode forward slowly. She was a commanding presence, drawing the attention of everyone in the lobby. A colorful skirt hid the motions of her legs, making her appear to float through the room. Her round, cherubic face broke into a wide grin as she twirled, arms raised as if in victory, scanning her surroundings.

"Will you look 'a this Spencer," she said in awe, her voice booming in throaty Creole, "such a fancy hotel. You be blessed, my son, truly blessed. I tole' you dat Mambo use strong med-sin. Maybe you believe me now."

A thin, curly-haired boy emerged from behind her. He was obviously embarrassed by his mother's pronouncement. On his back he bore a large canvas rucksack of a characteristic design. At the sight of it Morgan approached.

"You must be the Bowens. I'm Dr. Holloway."

The woman beamed, took his hand in both of hers, and gave a slight bow.

"Je suis très herreuse de faire votre connaissance, Monsieur professeur. Very 'appy to meet you. I'm Spencer mother and dis his father." Still gripping Morgan's hand with her left she made a sweep with her right arm in the direction of a short, bronzed, somewhat bowlegged man with brooding eyes. Content to stand off to one side while his wife assumed center stage, Markus Bowen simply acknowledged his host with a smile and a nod.

The Van Wormers approached and introduced themselves. Gail took an immediate liking to the gregarious Yolanda Bowen. The two women chatted in French for some time while Spencer answered a host of questions about himself amongst the men. They soon retired to the private dining room that Morgan had reserved. Jack Malinowski joined the group as the dinner hour approached. He singled Spencer out of the mix and the two students conversed over hors d'oeuvres and refreshments.

"May I have your attention please?" Morgan was tapping the side of his wineglass with a serving fork. "If you all wouldn't mind taking your seats, the waiting staff are now ready to serve us. I'm told we have our choice of either baked scrod or rib-eye steak as entrees, with summer peas, buttered carrots and mashed or julienne potatoes as sides. And, for those of you with more pedestrian tastes, the hotel invites you to try its five-star, double-decker 'Metro Burger.'" He looked around the room apprehensively and glanced at his watch. There was still no sign of his wife or either of the female students. "Once we're settled I'd like to give a short presentation about the archaeological dig that has brought all of us together for the summer."

It wasn't long before the food arrived. Morgan was nearly halfway through his talk, over-emphasizing the historic repercussions of the excavation, when Marcie Van Wormer entered the room. She quietly took the seat next to her father and smiled at him as she sat. Instead of listening to what Morgan had to say about the expedition—the trip she'd been anxiously anticipating for months—she whispered something in a low voice to her father. Stephen listened, then nodded, patted her hand and smiled. He made a deferential sign to Morgan, a gesture apologizing for the interruption. Moments later Jocelyn and Debbie made their appearance. Debbie looked haggard, but she forced a smile when her husband welcomed her belated arrival.

Jocelyn sat sullenly and barely responded to a waitress who sidled up to take her dinner order. Her eyes were puffy and red, and there were hints of defeat mixed with smoldering anger in her countenance. Blood had been drawn back in her room. Not two hours into the project, the first fractious encounter with Jocelyn Delaney had occurred. Marcie and Debbie exchanged worried glances before settling into the social setting.

"We got to be leaving now," Spencer's mother announced once the dinner party had disbanded. Daylight was beginning to fade. "Markus has to go to work." She abruptly grabbed her son and held him against her bosom, a hugely embarrassing event for Spencer but something he knew was inevitable. "You know I was in contac' with the Loa last night, Spencer, my son. I prayed for a successful trip. You'll be fine."

Gail held out her hand. "I share your concerns Mrs. Bowen. After all, Marcie is about Spencer's age and that makes me a bit apprehensive, but they are both smart and resourceful kids. I'm sure the Lord will keep them safe. Not to worry."

Arm-in-arm the Bowens walked out of the hotel. Mrs. Bowen waved an enthusiastic goodbye to the Eviskar island entourage. Spencer's father nodded to everyone before being led away—he hadn't spoken more than ten words all evening.

Gail turned to Spencer. "I really like your mom, Spencer. She's great. And I'm impressed with her strong faith. She's absolutely convinced that the Lord will watch over all of you on this trip."

"The 'Loa,'" said Spencer.

"Yes, that's what I said, the Lord."

"No, Mrs. Van Wormah. Last night she got her priestess to do a ceremony to protect us. She prayed to her Loa—that's a kinda vodou spirit."

"Priestess? Vodou?"

"Yeah, the old lady downa street is a Mambo. Hadda use a live chicken foah the ceremony. She held it up, said some kinda chant in old patois French, then slit its 'troat."

"How horrible," Gail gasped.

"It's not so bad if ya think about it," Spencer said matter-of-factly. "It's the way they do 'em in the market she goes to. 'An from what I heah, that's how they kill the chickens you find in the grocery stoah. Anyway, mom doesn't know this but old lady Perrault cooks 'em when she's done. I don't think she's 'sposed to do that. After she sacrifices a chicken I often see her gnawing on a drumstick the next day. That doesn't botha' me, but I think my mom would have a haht attack if she knew."

Gail strained to overhear the conversation between her stepdaughter and the Malinowski boy. Keeping her distance, she prepped her breakfast—juice and a banana—while she listened. No one else was in the hotel's breakfast area yet, and Marcie, summoning her courage, had approached her fellow traveler.

"Hi, Jacek."

"Good morning. It's Marcia, isn't it?"

"Yeah, but my friends call me Marcie. You can call me Marcie."

"Okay, Marcie. Most people call me Jack. Only in my house, around my mom, do I go by Jacek." Jack selected several sugar-laden sticky buns from among the continental breakfast offerings and poured himself a cup of coffee.

Marcie hovered, contemplating what else she might say. Finally, she said, "Um, it's appropriate that we're having Danish pastries for breakfast. I mean, we're on our way to Greenland after all." Jack smiled. Mesmerized by his blue eyes, her knees became weak, and like a deer caught in a spotlight, her mind went blank. She blushed and looked away, embarrassed.

Jack sensed her unease. Her attention made him a bit uncomfortable as well. He said, "Beats me if the folks in Greenland really eat this stuff, despite the name. I suspect we'll know when we get there; if the people we meet are all fat and diabetic, that will tell us."

Marcie laughed. "I suppose. Look, if you want something better than these coronary-blocking calorie bombs, I've packed a bunch of energy bars. They're specially formulated for bodies under stress—vitamin and mineral fortified, high in protein, and with a mix of simple and complex carbs for both quick energy and endurance. You can have some if you'd like."

Jack stifled a grin and politely declined. "You'd better save 'em for the trip, Marcie."

Watching from across the small room, Gail sighed and waited for her husband to finish his shower and come to breakfast. Soon, Jocelyn arrived and she and Jack sat together by the window. A frustrated Marcie sat with her stepmother and watched the interplay between her older colleagues.

As she sipped her orange juice, Gail pondered the snippets of dialog she'd just heard. Her face wrinkled with concern. Marcie was definitely interested in Jack. He, on the other hand, had been spending considerable time with the other girl, Jocelyn. Fear for Marcie's feelings tugged at Gail's heart. Unexpectedly, she also became concerned for Jack and his emotions. He seemed like a nice guy. As a woman, Gail's sixth sense told her that Jocelyn played the key role in the unfolding social dynamic of this expedition. The girl had easily gotten her hooks into Jack. Was she just being friendly? Was she truly attracted to him or was Jocelyn a player, someone who, even at the tender age of what, seventeen? eighteen? had learned how to manipulate men. She was pretty, charming and smart, and she'd already run into trouble by trying to coerce the Holloways into allowing her to bring extra belongings on the trip. Gail smiled at the remembrance of Debbie not backing down. This archeological project was going to be an eye-opening experience for Marcie. She was about to learn harsh lessons about human behavior and the affairs of the heart, in addition to whatever science and history knowledge came her way.

The breakfast area began to fill up. Guests were trickling in, all of them toting travel bags, many of them bleary eyed. Despite the early hour, the city was buzzing. Although known as the city that never sleeps, the traffic patterns in Manhattan's lower west side varied markedly throughout the day. Most commuters had yet to rise, but at this hour the street bustled with delivery vehicles hoping to offload in time to beat the frantic beginnings of the dreaded rush hour.

A line had formed in front of the coffee dispensers. Marcie sat across from her folks, her gaze fixed toward the large south-facing window of the hotel's breakfast nook and the young couple seated there. Orange rays from a rising sun streaked Jocelyn Delaney's long locks a reddish gold. She nibbled at a muffin, smiling at whenever Jack Malinowski was saying.

"Are you going to give us the pleasure of your company on the way to JFK or are you going to ride with the group?" The question startled Marcie. She turned to face her dad. "Sorry to interrupt your musings," her father continued. "It's a shame they make you get to the airport four hours before an international flight. We could spend the time so much more productively."

He paused. "Is something wrong, princess? You're not having second thoughts I hope."

"Oh, no. Of course not." Marcie took hold of Stevens hand, snuck a glance towards the window and then said, "I'd better go with them, dad. You and Gail should spend the morning in the city; you guys need some quality time." She sighed, "You've done so much for me, both of you... bringing me down here, letting me go on this trip. I just want to thank you for everything."

A beaming Morgan Holloway entered the room and clapped his hands. "The van is here, folks, time to move out. Make sure you have passports ready."

Jack shouldered his bags and held out his hand to Jocelyn. Marcie fixated on the interaction between the two, noting with dismay how easily Jocelyn manipulated her new acquaintance, handing him her rucksack—its seams nearly bursting at every point. She felt a hand on her shoulder and turned to find Gail smiling at her with tears in her eyes. Enveloping her stepdaughter in a hug, she said, "Your dad and I won't be going to the airport." She hesitated and giggled, "He's awfully cute, Marcie. Come to think of it, so's the other young man, Spencer. You behave, now. Write to us often and have a great trip."

"Thanks, Gail."

Marcie turned and gave her dad a hug. "Dad, don't forget about Jocelyn's bags, will you? She's really in a bind."

"Relax, princess, the desk clerk said he'd keep her bags in the back until it's time for Gail and me to catch the train." He popped the rest of his breakfast croissant into his mouth and washed it down with the swill he suspected the hotel had fraudulently labelled '100% Colombian' coffee.

More quick hugs for her parents followed before Marcie grabbed her bags and ran off to catch the waiting van.

It took only seconds for the driver of the shuttle to toss the rucksacks to Morgan, who, in turn, tossed them onto the sidewalk. Moments later, the tires of the van squealed as the vehicle charged back into traffic.

Before the group entered the airport, Debbie began grabbing people by the arm. It was time for an obligatory group photo. "Marcie, you stand in front of Jack, and Spencer, you move over to his right. Jocelyn, I want you in the middle...wait...on second thought, go stand next to Morgan."

Another shuttle pulled in behind them and unloaded its passengers. Most of them walked right in front of the camera, oblivious to the photo operation in progress. That vehicle also left as quickly as it had arrived, and Debbie took advantage of the activity lull to reposition her subjects. "Marcie, move closer to Jack, you're drifting out of view." Jack reached down and pulled Marcie towards him. She looked up to see him smiling down at her and turned bright crimson. Of course, that was the instant Debbie snapped the picture. "That's perfect. Good."

When the photo session was over, a collective sensation of destiny came over the students. It was as though they were standing at the threshold of a great edifice or assembling at the starting line of an important race. All felt as though the journey that would become a significant event in their lives began here, in front of the air terminal at JFK International. This was it.

Jack Malinowski was particularly reflective. He realized that, in fact, he was standing amongst a group of strangers. He turned to the young man standing beside him. "Hey, Spencer."

"Wa 'sup?"

"So, what do you think? You ready for this? Ready to have me as a roommate for the next couple months? I'll try not to snore."

"Wouldn't botha me none if ya did. I can sleep tru most anything. At my house someone's always up makin' noise."

Loud talking nearby interrupted their conversation. The source was a heavyset man in a badly wrinkled suit, waving an outstretched middle finger at a cab that was pulling away from the curb. Obscenities filled the air.

To Jack's amazement, no one nearby was paying much attention. "That the way they hail a cab in New York?" he asked.

"You mean you nevah seen that? You're right, it's a New Yoahk thing. It's called a 'half victory sign'—we use it alla' time. It's a sign 'a respect 'an admiration. You should try usin' it."

Jack kept a straight face. He put a hand on Spencer's shoulder. "Thanks for the tip, buddy. It's nice to be around someone who can give me good advice when I need it."

"Hey, no problem, that's what friends are foah."

"Okay, grab your bags," Morgan announced. He needn't have bothered.

All four students were already loaded up and headed into the terminal, making their way towards the Icelandair desk.

IV

What the heck, it was worth trying. It wasn't the most sophisticated of plans, but, if successful, it would make the flight to Iceland a lot more pleasant. They were at the gate, ready to board, and Marcie Van Wormer's mind was working hard, scheming. Marcie casually wandered amongst her colleagues, pretending to be excited...well, actually she was extremely excited—she was just pretending to be even more excited than she really was—asking seemingly superfluous questions in order to garner valuable information. "So, where are you sitting?" she asked of everyone in the group. She even asked Jocelyn the question—not that it mattered.

The students weren't seated together; they had aisle seats scattered throughout the cabin. Jack's response indicated he was three rows in back of her. Bingo. As important as this info was, Marcie still lamented the seating system. Why couldn't Icelandair use the 'cattle car' method, like Southwest did, she fretted. This whole issue would be a no-brainer then.

Marcie scooted into line right behind Jack. They boarded the plane and as she passed her own seat she dropped off her backpack and continued to talk to him, following him to his seat. She moved from the corridor into the next row, politely clearing the way for others to get past and continued to chat until a petite, elderly woman motioned toward the seat adjacent to Jack's. Marcie pounced. "Pardon me, ma'am," she said, "my friend and I would love to sit next to one another. Would you mind switching with me? I'm right over there, on the aisle."

"I am sorry," the woman replied in heavily accented English, "but my husband is coming." She waved to a portly gentleman who was stuffing a garment bag into an overhead bin. "I would prefer to sit with him."

"Hey, no sweat," Marcie tried to sound cheerful, "Enjoy your flight." Chagrined, she immediately marched back to her seat and let out a deep breath, "Drat!"

Her seatmate, a middle-aged woman who was already deeply immersed in her copy of the inflight "Shopping Mall" magazine, looked over with raised eyebrows.

"Minor problem," was all Marcie said by way of explanation. She then tried to appear more social. Smiling at her neighbor she asked, "So, uh, are you going to Reykjavik?" As soon as she said it, she realized the stupidity of the remark. *Good for you, Marcie,* she chastised herself. *What a dumbass. Keep this up, and soon everyone on the plane will know what a fool you are. If I were you—and I am—I would just shut-up and chill out.*

Jack settled into his aisle seat and stuffed his backpack under the one in front. Sitting back, he contemplated what to do first: continue reading the mystery novel he'd just gotten into, or listen to the awesome collection of tunes he'd downloaded for the trip.

Something bumped his shoulder. He turned and discovered his nose was mere inches from the oversized derriere of an elderly woman trying to heft an enormous carryon suitcase into the overhead compartment above him. The woman grunted, her arms shaking with fatigue under the weight of the swaying object balanced precariously above her head. Jack jumped to her aid, partly out of chivalry but mostly for self-preservation. Together he, the woman and her travelling companion, another female septuagenarian, fought with the bag, turning and shoving it until the compartment door latched successfully. Sarcastic applause broke out from several passengers stuck in the long boarding line stalled by their labors.

Following a withering look at the irate travelers, the woman flopped into the seat across the aisle and addressed Jack. "Thank you, young man. I swear they keep decreasing the amount of storage space on these planes. It's all a conspiracy, you know. They're trying to get folks to check bags so they can charge extra." She turned to her partner, "Right Suzanne?"

The woman named Suzanne glowered. "I warned you before; if you think you can borrow anything from me on this trip, you're sorely mistaken, Ms. Cheapskate. Honestly, trying to cram ten days' worth of clothing into a carryon bag simply to avoid paying a twenty-five dollar fee: you deserve to be inconvenienced."

Ms. 'Cheapskate' introduced herself as Constance Tucker. Jack identified himself and then pointed to the ball cap she was wearing. It was white with the word 'Orioles' embroidered in neat, orange script. "So, do you live in Baltimore?"

"That's right. We decided to spend a few of our vacation days in New York when the Orioles were in town." She glared at her companion. "If we'd gone to the Saturday game, we'd have seen them win, too. Instead, *someone* suggested we wait 'til Sunday afternoon."

"Now how was I to know the Yankees would win that one? Don't place all the blame on me. If you had brought your crystal ball, I would have been perfectly amenable to go on Saturday."

Constance turned to Jack, her tone indignant, "We learned the hard way why the Yanks are called the 'Bronx Bombers'—four home runs by the end of the third inning. We suffered through a twelve to two drubbing and a forty-five minute rain delay. It was a miserable way to start our vacation."

The two women, who Jack learned were sisters, continued to bicker as the plane pulled away from the gate and taxied toward takeoff. Jack did his best to tune them out. Crossing his arms and turning away, he pretended to nap.

It didn't work. As soon as the plane went airborne, he felt someone poking his shoulder. His new acquaintance from Baltimore asked, "So, what brings you to Iceland, business or pleasure?"

Jack had little choice but to respond, "A bit of both, I suppose. I'm one of four students who've been selected to participate in an archeological excavation on an island off the coast of Greenland. The site is an old Norse settlement that existed about a thousand years ago. Its extreme northern location is what makes it so important—or so I'm told."

"Archeology, my, that sounds fascinating. What sorts of fossils do you expect to find?"

Jack contemplated his answer. "To tell you the truth...I don't know."

"My sister, Suzanne, and I are going to spend a week in Reykjavik. We've been planning this trip for a year, ever since a good friend went there and recommended it. She said it was like going to Denmark except you only have to go halfway. Did you know that Iceland used to be part of Denmark?"

"You don't say?" Jack forced a smile that was more suggestive of someone suffering from gas pain. This was going to be a long, tortuous flight.

"Yes, they're decidedly European, very progressive." She leaned across the aisle. Putting her hand on Jack's arm, she continued in a hushed voice, "They have public baths there, heated by volcanoes. Some of them are…clothing optional!" She pulled back with a look of satisfaction, as though she'd somehow revealed the secrets of the universe to him.

"Do you…" Jack stifled a laugh, "Do you and your sister have plans to visit those baths?"

"Why of course! We're very cosmopolitan. You know what they say, 'when in Rome…' Most of our friends wouldn't, but we're quite adventurous. Seeing other people in the buff doesn't bother me at all, not one little bit. Mind you, I am a bit concerned about—and I mean no offense, you understand—I worry about the *men* at those places."

"How so?"

"Well, not ALL men are this way, but a certain portion of the male population, when surrounded by women wearing nothing but smiles, can be a bit…'forward' in their ways."

"She's afraid some Icelandic stud will try to ravish her," Suzanne interjected, "right there in the middle of a public pool."

"No, not in the bath, per se," came Connie's annoyed reply, "but some man charged with primal, hormonal lust—you know the way men get—might decide to follow me to our hotel. One never knows."

"That sounds like wishful thinking to me."

"How dare you suggest such a thing, Suzanne?"

As the argument between the women escalated, Jack excused himself. On the way to the rest room, a trip designed not only to void his bladder, but to purge his mind of images conjured by his latest conversation, he passed Marcie's seat. "Hey, Marcie."

"Jack, what's up?" She pulled out her ear buds and smiled up at him.

"Just taking a break. Look, I'm sorry my neighbor didn't want to swap seats with you." He glanced back at the ongoing flutter between the two Orioles fans. "It would have been great to have someone sane to talk to."

He continued his trek to the front of the plane while Marcie contemplated the significance of what he'd said. She pursed her lips in concentration. It wasn't exactly the declaration of affection she'd dreamed of, but at least he didn't think she was crazy. "It's a start," she mused optimistically as she nodded in time to the beat of Taylor Swift's 'Shake it Off,' "and not a bad start at that."

Jack groaned as he approached his seat. Staring at him, leaning into the corridor, was the beaming face of Constance. "You must be one of those folks with an overactive bladder," she commented loudly enough for all those seated around them to hear. "Just try not to think about going and you won't have to get up as often. It won't be long before we're there." She looked at her watch. "What time do we get in anyway? I left my itinerary in my luggage."

"The plane lands at 8:30," Jack sighed.

"Oh, my. That can't be. Why, it's only half past ten right now."

"Reykjavik is just over 2200 nautical miles from New York," Jack replied, his eyes now closed, wishing she would leave him alone. "That's roughly 2600 statute miles. If you assume an average ground speed of 500 miles-per-hour for this aircraft, that yields a flight time of just over five hours. In addition, we're crossing five time zones, travelling east, which means we lose five hours, so, yeah, local time will be ten hours from now when we land."

"Oh, dear God, I never expected this flight to last ten hours. TEN HOURS! I didn't know Iceland was so far away."

"Well, ma'am, you see it's only five..." he caught himself in midsentence. A hint of a smile appeared and he turned to face her. "My secret to enduring super-long flights like this is to sit back and try to sleep. If you can do that, I guarantee the trip will only seem half that long."

"Yes, yes, I suppose you're right. Thank you; that's good advice."

Keflavik International airport lies thirty miles by road southeast of downtown Reykjavik. Clearing customs in mere minutes, the four students and the Holloways made their way to a line of buses waiting to transport passengers and baggage into the city. Diesel fumes laced the salt air wafting in from offshore. Many of the assembled tourists marveled at the view of the Reykjavik skyline across the bay, bathed in the reddish light of the late afternoon sun.

On the curb outside, Morgan was talking excitedly about the hotel where they'd be staying. Jack wasn't listening. His eyes were focused on the crowd, scanning the line ahead of him, searching for an elderly woman wearing an Orioles cap. Constance had insisted they ride into town together, but Jack was just as determined not to let that happen. Marcie was watching Jack.

They spotted each other at the same time. Connie waved and abruptly addressed the task of wrestling her enormous bag up the steps of the idling bus. Jack didn't hesitate. He exited the line and moved to the growing cue at the door of the next bus—one different from the shuttle carrying Constance, Suzanne and his fellow travelers.

"Jack, what are you doing?" asked a perplexed Marcie. "I don't think that bus goes to our hotel."

He waved his map of the city and pointed to the luminous sign above the windshield. "That other bus looks like it's gonna be really crowded. Besides, this one will get us to within a block of our hotel. They're all going downtown. Reykjavik isn't that big."

Without giving a second thought to her actions, Marcie grabbed her bags and crossed to where Jack stood. She squeezed in front of another fellow who'd arrived just ahead of her. "Excuse me, we're together," she said sweetly. The man frowned but didn't complain.

"You don't want to stay with Morgan and Debbie?" Jack asked.

"Naw, I'm with you. That bus looks crowded."

They soon handed their rucksacks to the driver who tossed them into the cargo space. They boarded carrying their backpacks. Jack pointed to a window seat, and Marcie took the hint. Jack scooted in beside her once she was settled. Having been thwarted in her attempt to sit with Jack on the plane, Marcie had cleverly grasped the opportunity to ride with him from the airport. For the next forty-five minutes it would be just her and Jack riding together in a bus full of strangers. She couldn't have asked for more.

The buses, there were four in all, were loaded and ready in minutes. This routine of shuttling back and forth from the airport was carried out several times per day, and it was so often repeated, the personnel involved had worked out the logistics and timing with military precision. In a cloud of blue-white diesel exhaust, the lead bus pulled out of the parking zone, headed for the highway that would take them along the coast and into the city. With a lurch, the bus containing Jack and Marcie took its place in line and the caravan was under way.

"We've got a long ride ahead," Jack offered as the bus picked up speed, "what do you want to talk about?"

"Heck, I don't know, whatever you want, I suppose."

He looked at her, and his blue eyes fixed upon hers. "I just realized, Marcie, we've hardly spoken with one another on this trip. If we're going to spend the next three months working side by side, we ought to get to know one another better."

That's the plan, she thought, her heart racing. All of the effort she'd put into preparing for this trip: the yard work, the babysitting, countless trips to the store, it was all starting to pay off. She was sitting next to a gorgeous hunk, at the start of what was shaping up to be a long, romantic adventure. Life couldn't get much better. "You first," she said. "Tell me all about Jacek Malinowski."

"Where the heck are Marcie and Jack?"

Morgan Holloway was holding court in the hotel lobby. Somehow, even with his unlit pipe clenched firmly in his teeth, his speech was remarkably clear and understandable.

"I saw 'em get on the otha bus," said Spencer.

"Oh, okay; as long as they're not still at the airport they should be here soon." Morgan turned his attention to the extra baggage he'd brought with him—supplies other than personal effects they'd need in camp. The heaviest was a large duffel that contained a sophisticated total station and collapsible tripod, the kind used by land surveyors. The instrument would be used to establish a precise coordinate system at the site so that the exact location at which each artifact was unearthed could be recorded. Another padded suitcase held two satellite communicators and a sat phone. Debbie had insisted they use some of the precious grant money to enhance their ability to communicate with the outside world, especially since they would be responsible for four young students.

"Hey, doc, sorry we're late." Jack and a flushed, beaming Marcie arrived and tossed their rucksacks beside the others. "Want some help carrying that stuff to your room?"

"Why, yes, thank you, Jack." Morgan then addressed the group as a whole, "You should find your room assignments and dinner vouchers at the front desk. I'm afraid Debbie and I will be too busy this evening to provide much in the way of entertainment, so you folks are on your own. Bear in mind we have to get up early tomorrow to catch the 6:00 bus to Olafsvik, so I strongly suggest you take a moment to freshen up before dinner and then think about getting some sleep. It's already..." he glanced at his watch, "...almost 9:30 PM local time, which means we'll be meeting back here in the lobby for breakfast in only eight hours."

Led by Jocelyn, the students made their way across the small lobby to the hotel desk. "I wondah where the phrase 'freshen up' comes from," Spencer speculated. "It's just a euphemism for 'go to the bathroom.' Why don't people just say what they mean?"

"It's all about manners and class," said Jocelyn. "If you'd like I can give you lessons."

"Yo, bite me."

"Lesson number one," she said sweetly, "is that 'bite me' is an unacceptable and derogatory response in civilized parts of the world. You're obviously from a more 'backward' region."

"It's only 16:30 our time," Jack said as he accepted his room key from the concierge. "I think I'll grab a bite after I 'freshen up,'" he winked at Spencer, "then I'm going for a walk. This may be my only chance to see Reykjavik."

"Me too," Marcie said, her tone brimming with enthusiasm. Her sense of adventure was readily apparent. "After sitting on a plane for five hours, I could use some exercise."

Jocelyn rolled her eyes. "So, I take it the plan is to meet for dinner and then do some sightseeing. Fine. But doc Holloway did have a point; we all have to get up early tomorrow." She looked at Marcie, "The younger ones among us, in particular, need their rest." To Jack, she continued, "see you in fifteen?"

Even in the middle of June there was a nip in the air which infused briskness to Jack's pace as he led the way down Laugavegur, the street in front of the hotel. Armed with a map of downtown and his cell phone with its three-megapixel camera, he was in full tourist mode. The party turned north onto Frakkastigur and within a few blocks hit the Saebraut, the main street and walkway that wound along the Atlantic shoreline. The others followed dutifully because it was obvious Jack knew where he was going. He had a destination in mind.

"There it is," he said to no one in particular.

Glare from the setting Sun bounced off the strange-looking structure located between them and the sea. Constructed of stainless steel to protect it from the corrosive salt air, the impressive sculpture stood resplendent against the backdrop of the western horizon. They crossed the street to get a closer look. Marcie, Jack and Spencer maneuvered around to the other side to take photos with the Sun at their backs.

"What is it?" Marcie asked.

"Looks like a Viking ship, sort of," Spencer replied.

Jack explained, paraphrasing from his Reykjavik guidebook, "It's called the 'Solfario' which means 'Sun Voyager.' Says here it's supposed to be a dream boat, an ode to both the Sun and to the explorers who left these shores heading west into the unknown."

"Cool," Marcie remarked. She took several pictures, all of which included Jack well-positioned in the foreground.

"Make sure you get both dreamboats in those photos," Jocelyn offered. She was standing right behind the younger girl. There was a bored, sarcastic hint to what she said.

"Hey, it's none of your concern what I photograph. Give it a rest, Jocelyn, geez."

"Sounds like I struck a nerve. And don't get all huffy; I'm just trying to help. He's a bit old for you, don't you think? I mean, if we're going to be roommates on this trip, the last thing I want to put up with is you moping around hoping Jack will show some interest. Take my word for it; it's not going to happen."

Marcie gave her a look of disgust and walked away. Jocelyn knew she'd hurt the other girl's feelings, but felt entirely justified in her statement. Marcie's interest was understandable; Jack certainly was cute and they were going to be spending a lot of time together this summer—all of them. The interactions among them would be complicated and difficult if romance were to enter into the equation.

The sodium-vapor lights along the Saebraut had begun to glow, their yellow light heralding the arrival of 'evening' in this most northerly capital of Europe. Lights were turning on all over town, transforming the cityscape from that of a quaint coastal community into that of a cosmopolitan metropolis. Jack stood transfixed at the vista of the foreign city he'd been in for less than two hours now, watching lights wink on as though it were a sprawling giant beast awakening from its diurnal slumber. Although it was a rather small city in terms of population, Reykjavik had played an important role in late 20th century world history. In particular, it had served as a gateway to the thawing of tensions between the democracies of the west and the Soviet communist block to the east. In October of 1986, Ronald Reagan and Mikhail Gorbachev held historic meetings there to set treaty limits on nuclear warheads, an event which significantly lowered the levels of animosity and paranoia between the super powers and led to the fall of the Berlin wall and the Iron Curtain less than a decade later.

"We should probably think about heading back soon—gotta get up in about six hours." Marcie was standing beside him. "What are you looking at?"

Jack smiled sheepishly when he realized he'd been daydreaming. "I was just thinking about what's happened here. When my dad found out we'd be passing through Reykjavik, Iceland on our way to Eviskar, he got really excited and started telling me all about the famous chess match that was played here."

Spencer, a chess aficionado, overheard their conversation and wandered over. "I think I heard 'a that. It was between some Russian guy and a crazy American."

"That's right. It all happened back in the 70s, before any of us were born. At the time my dad was about my age, maybe a bit younger; he was a member of a chess club in Krakow during the communist years. According to him, it was a huge deal in his neighborhood, almost like a heavyweight fight—no, more than that, it was like the Olympics, the Super Bowl and the World Cup all rolled into one—the chess match of the century. Every newspaper around the world carried a list of the moves made in each game.

"The reason for all the interest went beyond the fact that it pitted two of the greatest players in history against one another. It had a lot to do with where they were from. Boris Spassky, the champion, was from Russia. His opponent, the challenger, was a brilliant young upstart from the US named

Bobby Fischer. Reykjavik was chosen for the showdown I suppose because it's remote and lies sort of midway between the capitals of Moscow and Washington.

"During the match, my father and his friends would wait impatiently for the daily paper. As soon as it arrived they would set up their boards and replay each game, talking excitedly about the strategies of the opponents. According to experts, who wrote volumes about the match as it progressed, both participants played brilliantly. It truly was an epic struggle between giants of the sport. The tension throughout the match was incredible. Spassky was the more conventional and methodical of the two. Once he'd taken the lead, he worked hard to wear Fischer down, playing superb defense, knowing that if enough of their remaining games ended in draws he would win the match.

"Fischer, on the other hand, was a risk taker. He made moves that astonished the experts. Some were blunders that got him into serious trouble, but he made others that, well, my dad said they were some of the most clever feints, finesses and gambits anyone had ever seen."

"So, who won?" Marcie asked.

"Many experts considered Spassky to be at the top of his game, nearly unbeatable. His technique was too good; he had no discernable weaknesses."

"Okay, okay, but who WON?"

"Fischer. When it was over, my dad and his chess buddies celebrated. Anti-Russian sentiment had reached a seriously high level by then. A decade later the Solidarity movement began, and Poland began its break from the Soviet sphere of influence. In the eyes of many Poles, Bobby Fischer had brought down the Russian bear. Single-handedly he had dealt a devastating blow to Russian prestige in a sport they'd dominated for decades."

Jack paused to reflect on the major world event that had taken place in this small city. "When you think about it, the match really had nothing to do with the native lands of the participants. It was just great competition between two great minds, men who could have come from anywhere. My dad believes it was actually Spassky rather than Fischer who did more to thaw east-west relations. Fischer was as moody and eccentric as he was brilliant. Spassky could have won the match by default when Fischer suddenly insisted they move the match to a private room attended only by chess officials—no spectators. In a gesture of good sportsmanship, Spassky agreed to Fischer's demand and even applauded his opponent after a particularly well-played game. He was very gracious in defeat, and the respect Spassky showed for Fischer's skill as a fellow chess player transcended the petty political differences between the countries from which they came." Jack paused before concluding, "Maybe the world should re-examine what took place here from that standpoint."

It was getting late. Not much was spoken as the four nascent archeologists wound their way back to the hotel. Everyone, even Jocelyn, who'd been standing in the background listening quietly to Jack's story, was now contemplating the famous chess match in Reykjavik that had galvanized the world forty years earlier.

The bus left the hotel at precisely 6:30 AM local time, 1:30 AM eastern daylight time. All of the students were jet lagged, and none had slept more than a few hours, but the resilience of youth coupled with the extra-large coffees provided through the hotel's free continental breakfast, kept them awake and lucid. The Sun had been up for hours, a factor that had contributed to their inability to sleep.

Marcie sipped her coffee and wrinkled her nose. She didn't normally drink the stuff, but she'd accepted the assertion made by Debbie that it would help to reset her biological clock, help her adapt to the time difference. Yuk, even with about ten packs of added sugar she could barely tolerate it. How could her dad consume gallons of this junk? And he liked it black, unsweetened. Go figure.

Between bites of a breakfast pastry, Jocelyn giggled at something Jack said. The two were seated in the row in front of Marcie. Marcie was pissed. Jocelyn's reproving words from the previous evening, insinuating that she was too young to become romantically involved with Jack, had embarrassed and angered her. Now, Jocelyn had the choice seat next to Jack and was chatting him up. Granted, Jocelyn was already seated when Jack boarded the bus, and he had chosen to sit beside her, but Marcie still felt as though she'd been manipulated.

Strangely enough, Marcie also wanted to get close to Jocelyn. After all, they were going to be roommates for the next three months and it would be hell if they didn't get along. Trying to maintain a thick skin and ignore her companion's hurtful remarks was trying her patience, though. She often wished the girl would just hop on her broomstick and fly back to Texas. There was no denying the trip would be a lot more pleasant without her, but Marcie was trying to adapt. She had no choice.

Beside her, in the window seat, Spencer was absorbed in some sort of game on his computer. "Man," she thought angrily, "if he wants to sit by the window, the least he could do is to appreciate the view." She considered asking him to change seats but decided against it. Her view of the countryside was good enough from her current vantage point. Already the scenery along the route had changed dramatically from that of inner city to individual houses surrounded by verdant fields. They were rapidly leaving Reykjavik behind.

Morgan stood up from his seat in the front of the bus and turned to face his entourage. "Welcome, all," he said cheerfully. "Sorry for the early start. I'm afraid we still have a couple of travel days ahead of us until we reach the shores of Eviskar Island. Hopefully, the ordeal of getting there will reinforce in your minds just how remote our dig site is and how intrepid were those souls who settled there 1000 years ago." Morgan's enthusiasm about their endeavor had an uplifting effect. The students paid close attention as he continued his speech as impromptu tour guide. "The good news is that I've been in touch with the *Stjerne*, the ship that will transport us the final 600 or so nautical miles to the island. They are on schedule to dock in Olafsvik early this afternoon. If all goes well, we should arrive at Eviskar the day after tomorrow." He peered out the window and grinned. "In a few moments we'll be in for a real treat. The Hvalfjordur tunnel is coming up. It's one of the longest tunnels in the world. Here are some facts that may impress you." Morgan produced a pamphlet and donned a pair of reading glasses. "It's over three and a half miles long and dives to a depth of 165 meters. That's over 540 feet below sea level."

The tunnel entrance soon came into view. It was a giant hole in the Earth lying directly in front of a majestic expanse of water, a sight that was both incongruous and surreal. Its gaping maw seemed to swallow vehicles as they drove into its dark throat and disappeared from view. As the bus approached, Marcie noticed a change in Spencer's demeanor. He'd stowed his tablet computer and was now sitting straight and rigid, both hands gripping his arm rest tightly. Spencer was scared.

Marcie became concerned. Clearly the young man seated next to her was upset, and as the bus approached the entrance, he seemed to slump in his seat. When their vehicle finally crossed the threshold, everything abruptly plunged into darkness. To make matters worse, the road grade dropped precipitously, propelling them down beneath the waters of Hvalfjordur Bay.

"Note the rate of descent," Morgan announced, "At depth, we'll be about forty meters, 150 feet, below the sea floor..."

"Please, Dr. Holloway, please shut up," Marcie thought as she monitored Spencer's worsening condition out of the corner of her eye.

"...Imagine the tons of water right above our heads..."

Marcie felt she had to do something. "Hey, Spencer," she said, "think about all the cars that pass through here every day—without incident."

"What are you implying, Marcie? You think I'm scared? Goin' into the tunnel just took me by surprise, that's all. I been tru' the Lincoln tunnel plenty 'a times. It's no big deal. Just mind your own business, will 'ya?"

Marcie wanted to protest, but held her tongue. Calling attention to his plight would itself do the job. She figured Spencer would fight to maintain control over his emotions in order to avoid embarrassment. They rode in silence for several minutes. The road was now flat and straight, a featureless void seemingly without end.

"Sure is dark in heah. In New Yoahk the tunnels are well lit. You'd think they'd put a few lights in this place."

"I'm sure the driver can see where he's going," Marcie replied wearily. "Come to think of it, I don't think I've ever driven through a tunnel before. There are none around Albany."

"Humpf, Albany. It's more like 'Small-bany' 'ya ask me. S'not a city, just a town."

Marcie was mildly offended. She was proud of her hometown. "It is the State Capital, Spence."

"I know. What a mistake. They should'a made New Yoahk the capital. I mean, really, that's where all the people are. Governors only go to 'Small-bany' to give a speech once in a while. The rest 'a the time they're in the city. They hardly eveh spend time in the Governor's Mansion."

"Patterson did."

"Yeah, whateveh."

Jocelyn giggled again. She and Jack appeared to be having a good time. The sound grated on Marcie's nerves. This trip was taking a turn for the worse. The thought of spending three months with a snide, claustrophobic city boy; a spiteful, southern dilettante; and a hunk who barely acknowledged her existence, dampened her enthusiasm. I just have to get through this as best I can, she sighed. Maybe the work itself will be really interesting.

The final stretch of tunnel led upwards toward the proverbial light at the end. Growing ever brighter, the exit beckoned them into a world of bright sunlight and turquoise sky. The psychological effect was palpable. Marcie's melancholy and Spencer's fear evaporated as the somber, brooding, tunnel blackness gave way to an incredible landscape. Most conversation in the bus stopped as its inhabitants, visitors and locals alike, gazed appreciatively out the windows.

For the next thirty miles the highway followed the rugged, undulating Icelandic coast. Majestic cobalt-blue fjords lay to the west. Off to the right, lush, sprawling hills stretched far into the distance, yielding to permanently snow-capped mountains along the horizon. Rivers, with the occasional breathtaking waterfall, rushed under the bridges they crossed, thundering and churning on their way to the sea.

The coastal vistas soon gave way to rolling hills as the road cut across the Snaefellsnes Peninsula. When the ocean once again came into view, the bus hung a left at an isolated crossroads and followed another coastal road into the quaint fishing village of Olafsvik.

"This is the end of the line for us," Morgan announced cheerfully.

Perhaps a dozen people, including the Eviskar group, debarked and crowded around the driver and an assistant who unloaded their belongings from the baggage compartment of the bus. Within minutes the bus was gone, heading for other maritime communities along the country's northwest coast.

Across the street from the bus stop was a small hotel/restaurant. They all headed inside to use the facilities and get a bite to eat before the ship arrived.

"Anybody up for a hike?" Debbie was stuffing fresh pastries into her backpack. "There's a long boat ride ahead of us, guys; this will be your last opportunity to stretch your legs before we get to the island." They were relaxing by the fireplace in the restaurant's small dining area. The kitchen featured a marvelous bakery, and the weary travelers were finishing a sumptuous snack of fresh Icelandic cakes and tarts, washing them down with thick, creamy hot chocolate.

"I'm game." Marcie was on her feet. Grinning broadly, she too started zipping up her backpack in preparation for an outing.

"Go ahead and leave your pack here, Marcie. Morgan is going to stay and watch our stuff. I'll carry everything we need for the hike. Just hand me your water bottle. Anybody else?"

"What the heck, count me in," Spencer replied. "I gotta burn off some 'a these calories."

Only when Jack moved to join the expedition did Jocelyn rise from her chair with an audible moan.

"Good, you'll all appreciate the exercise. When you get a look at some of the local scenery, you'll be glad you came." Addressing her husband, Debbie said, "You're in charge here, sweetie. We'll be back soon."

"Keep an eye out for the ship," Morgan warned, "Remember, they're only stopping briefly to pick us up. I don't want to antagonize the captain or wear out our welcome. Transport to Eviskar is difficult to come by."

"Understood. We'll be back to help carry the gear to the dock."

Debbie led the group out through the hotel's main entrance and turned eastward along the main thoroughfare. The route took them past several marinas containing boats of all shapes and sizes. Most were fishing craft, but smaller, pleasure boats sat interspersed among them, their sterns displaying names the Americans couldn't interpret.

Commercial buildings lined jetties all along the harbor. Some had large, open bays that revealed more boats sitting in dry dock. Others were obviously fish processing facilities, their function divulged by the pungent aromas wafting in on the offshore breeze.

Turning inland, Debbie took a side street through a residential area. The road wound uphill through a neighborhood of small woodframe houses painted in a bright rainbow of colors. A quarter mile from the sea, the road, and the town, ended abruptly. A signpost marked the beginning of a trail that wound southward towards a promontory that overlooked the bay.

"I fell in love with Olafsvik when we came through last year," Debbie mentioned. She was slightly out of breath because the slope of the path they were on had increased significantly. "It's not just a scenic fishing village. I wanted to bring you all out here to see the view from the crest of that hill up ahead." After a glance back at the harbor, she continued the climb. "What Morgan said about the boat is important. It's an oceangoing military craft that patrols along the coast of Greenland. They're scheduled to arrive in about four hours, and we have to be at the dock, waiting, when they pull in. Although it flies the Danish flag, many of the crew are Greenlanders, and it's only because the Eviskar dig is important to Greenland's authorities that we're allowed to hitch a ride."

"You mean, the boat has, like, guns 'n stuff? It's part of the Navy?" Spencer had tuned in to what she'd just said. Although he'd seen US naval vessels in the New York harbor, he'd never imagined sailing on one.

"Yes, and the bad news is that means our accommodations will be quite Spartan. This will be no luxury cruise. The good news is that we won't have to worry about being boarded by pirates."

After negotiating several long switchbacks, the party reached the crest of the hill. The view back towards the sea was breathtaking. All had to admit that Debbie's assessment of the town was spot on. It was indeed an idyllic Scandinavian village, remote, lonely, situated along the vastness of the North Atlantic. But the view in the other direction, to the southwest, was even more impressive.

Debbie grinned when she saw the looks of awe on the faces of the students. "That, my dear friends, is mount Snaefell." Before them, rising into a layer of cloud, was a singular mountain that commanded the lowlying terrain around it. "It's the volcano that lies at the heart of the Snaefellsnes National Park. One of these years I'm going to climb it, if I ever get the chance to break away from this archeological project, that is."

"It must be an extinct volcano," Spencer offered. "Look at all that snow on top."

"What you see is actually the Snaefellsjokull Glacier. They say that to climb the mountain safely you need a guide. There are dangerous crevasses along the way. Falling into one could seriously ruin your day."

"So is it extinct, the volcano I mean?"

"I'm no expert, Spence, but from what I've heard, the answer is 'yes'...and 'no.' The last eruption occurred in about 200 AD, so, yeah, it's not currently active, but like most volcanoes in Iceland it will probably erupt again in due time. Four years ago another one erupted that profoundly affected air travel between the US and Europe. The ash it threw into the air posed a threat to the jet engines on aircraft.

She looked at each of the students and smiled, "Now, can any of you name the famous book in which Mount Snaefell plays a central role?" When she received nothing but blank stares and shrugs she continued, "Have any of you read 'Journey to the Center of the Earth' by Jules Verne?"

"Oh yeah, I read that," Spencer exclaimed, "So, this is where they stahted? This is the volcano?"

"Yep, this is the mountain where Professor Lindenbrock, his nephew Axel and their Icelandic guide Hans began their epic journey. Following writings and signs left by the explorer Arne Saknussemm, the trio overcame a multitude of hazards, traversed a huge subterranean sea and dealt with prehistoric beasts."

"I remembeh the dinosaur parts. It was an awesome book."

"I agree. When I was a girl about your age it was my favorite story. I had vivid dreams about going on an adventure like that." She paused for a moment to reminisce. "You know, in a way our Eviskar excavation is a bit like that Verne novel. It takes place on a remote volcano...but we aren't going to run into any prehistoric animals there or anything like that. We'll have to be content with discovering things about the people who lived there a thousand years ago. A millennium is a long time in human history, but it's hardly worthy of note from a geologic perspective."

"I can see why you like this place so much," Jack said. "When I come back here in twelve years, I think I'll spend a week hiking in this park. It's beautiful."

"Did I hear you right?" Jocelyn asked. "You're coming back in twelve years?"

"Yep"

"Not in eleven years or in, say, thirteen years?"

"Nope"

The others all looked at Jack expectantly. He laughed, "Barring unforeseen circumstances, I'll be here on August 12, 2026." He paused, reveling in their curiosity.

"Okay, I'll bite," said Jocelyn, "What happens then?"

"There's going to be a total solar eclipse on that day. The moon's shadow will pass across far western Iceland and then over the coast of northeast Greenland. Olafsvik is one of the few inhabited places on Earth that lies in the zone of totality. This town is going to be packed with astronomers when that happens."

"Including you?" Jocelyn asked. "Do you plan to be one of those astronomers?" Jack seemed a little embarrassed by the question. "Maybe," he admitted.

"That is so cool," Marcie broke in. "Eclipses are really rare. I'm going to be here as well."

"Oh really?" Jocelyn chided, "as an astronomer or as one of Jack's groupies?"

The spiteful comment stung poor Marcie. It also put a damper on the group's conversation.

"All right, that's enough," Debbie sighed, "we'd better get back to the hotel. I want to make sure Morgan doesn't try to take all of our gear to the dock by himself."

V

The HDMS Stjerne flew both the flag of Greenland and the red and white pennant of the 'Kongelige Danske Marine,' the Royal Danish Navy. A "Thetis class" ocean going vessel, her primary mission was to safeguard the navigable waters off the eastern coast of Greenland. Sleek and fast, she measured 370 feet long, 50 feet abeam and displaced approximately 3500 tonnes—comparable in most respects to a large US Coast Guard cutter. The ship slid into port, appearing as if from nowhere, and before she had even come to a full stop, her able-bodied crew began to transfer the six visitors and their gear aboard. The entire pit stop took fewer than five minutes.

Spencer had little time to study the ominous-looking, bow-mounted canon before he and the others were herded to the ship's stern to receive a short safety and welcoming lecture. The briefing was delivered not by one of the crew but by another researcher and colleague of Morgan's, who, like the recent arrivals, was also en route to the excavation at Eviskar.

Dr. Johan Sørensen was a large hulk of a man with a full beard, booming voice and a jovial, avuncular nature. He'd been a passenger on the Stjerne for almost a week, ever since it had last refueled and provisioned in Nuuk. Because his English was superior to that of the captain and crew, he'd been assigned the job of welcoming and briefing the new arrivals.

Sørensen had two children of his own. Both were considerably younger than the Eviskar students, and saying goodbye to them prior to leaving on this trip had been terribly difficult. Perhaps as a result of some latent parenting need, he felt an immediate attachment to the young members of this group. Sensing his affection, the students reciprocated. Even before setting foot on the island, all knew they'd already made a good friend.

The ship shook mightily when her three powerful diesel engines roared to life and she began to pull away from the dock. Bow and azimuth thrusters swung her around effortlessly and before their introductions were complete, the helmsman had opened up the main throttles and nosed the *Stjerne* down the center of the main channel towards open sea.

During the trip out of port, the Eviskar travelers stood along the rail of the vessel's fantail and watched the town of Olafsvik glide slowly by. This would be their last glimpse of a permanent human settlement until September. As land faded into the distance and the white-capped waves of the ocean beckoned, each considered the ramifications of leaving civilization behind. The cold salt breeze reminded them they were on their way to a forbidding, isolated land, a place where they would have to rely strictly upon themselves and their immediate colleagues for sustenance and safety.

At least that's what most were thinking. Spencer had other things on his mind. The young man was leaning out over the waves, craning his neck to gain a better view of the ship's main gun turret located in front of the bridge. His gaze then moved slowly back along the ship's port side, surveying the superstructure for other signs of armament. At length he asked his host, "Dr. Sørensen, do they have bullets for that gun? 'Ya think it's loaded?"

Sørensen was expecting such a question and laughed heartily. It was a booming laugh, easily heard above the engine noise. He slapped Spencer on the back. "Ja, it is definitely loaded. In fact, several days ago they had a live-fire exercise. Perhaps it was for my benefit, but of that I can't be certain. If you are good passengers, then maybe the captain will demonstrate for you too. That, my boy, is a 76 mm canon capable of firing two rounds per second. When I inquired about the types of ammunition they carry, if they use armor piercing or explosive rounds for example, all I got for an answer was a smile." He chuckled, "It seems there are things they do not want us to know—for security purposes I am sure."

"They got any otha' guns on board?"

"Oh yes, they have several heavy machine guns and I believe there are smaller caliber machine guns that can be mounted on the landing craft. There may be more, but, again, the Danske Marine probably doesn't want to reveal all of her capabilities."

Sørensen addressed the Eviskar entourage as a whole: "What young Spencer brought up is very significant. This is a military craft on active patrol. It is crewed by sailors from Denmark and Greenland, and her mission is to defend the Greenlandic coast and the waters adjacent to it. We, all of us, are guests on board and we must not, under any circumstances, interfere with her duties."

The ship was now outside the protection of the harbor and the seas were noticeably rougher. White caps broke all around them once they were out of sheltered water, and the up and down movement of the ship was quite pronounced. Sørensen waved in acknowledgement to one of the crew and then ushered his charges inside. "The deck area is off limits most of the time while we are at sea. Although they treat us sometimes like prisoners," he said jovially, "it is for safety reasons—to guard against someone falling overboard. If the weather holds up, they will probably allow us to get some fresh air tomorrow afternoon for an hour or so. Let me show you to your quarters and to the break room. That is where we will spend the next day and a half on our way to Eviskar."

The central corridor was so narrow that in order for two people to pass one another they had to turn sideways. Because their quarters were near the front, they had a long way to walk. Finally, after traversing almost the full length of the ship, Sørensen turned left into an open hatchway and led them down a short series of steps into what was obviously the break room. About the size of a small bedroom, it was furnished with a table and two benches, all of which were bolted to the floor. Along the far wall lay a counter equipped with a microwave, a refrigerator and a small sink. "This is the dining area," their guide announced. "Some of the crew like to spend time here as well, although it is generally for civilian use. The crew's mess is in an adjacent room and is off limits to us. At times like this, when there are guests aboard, someone will deliver breakfast and dinner, buffet style, from the kitchen. We are on our own for lunch. I suggest you do as I do and save something from the dinner tray to tie you over for tomorrow's lunch."

"What sorts of food do they serve?" Marcie asked.

"Ah yes, that is a very good question, Marcie. I wouldn't classify the fare here as four star, but it is capable of keeping the human body alive and functional without causing major discomfort. For protein there is mostly fish, specifically herring, either smoked or marinated. For diversion there is usually offered sliced meat as well, generally pork or beef, and of course we have wonderful Danish cheeses. Steamed vegetables, potatoes and rice round out the menu. All of the food is either frozen or vacuum sealed; the cook merely heats it up. If there is a culinary bright spot on this ship it is the bakery. The cook bakes fresh bread and pastries each day. He starts with frozen dough, to be sure, but nothing is ever stale. The pastries are especially good," he remarked while smiling and patting his ample gut. "One should expect nothing less on a Danish vessel."

When no one asked any further questions, they proceeded back the way they had come and stopped a few doors down. Sørensen opened the metal door but didn't go in. The room was so small there wasn't space enough for more than two or three people to stand. Two fold-down bunks were closed against one wall. Opposite them was a narrow, enclosed space that could be sealed off from the rest of the compartment. Its opaque fiberglass door lay open and one could see that it was a small bathroom. A sink and showerhead were mounted on the wall nearest the passageway, and a small "head" or ship's toilet sat at the other end. The bathroom was about twice the size of a phone booth.

"Marcie and Jocelyn, these are your quarters. They are probably smaller than what you are accustomed to, but they are the finest available; you should consider this a 'penthouse suite.'" The rucksacks belonging to the two girls were lying in one corner. The highly efficient crew had already distributed their belongings.

"The room across the hallway is identical and it is reserved for Morgan and Debbie. Aside from the captain's quarters, these are the only spaces with private facilities." He turned to Spencer and Jack, "You boys will sleep in the civilian bunkhouse with me and one other individual. There are eight berths there and only four are occupied, so it will not be so crowded. There is a communal water closet next door." Sørensen paused to allow for questions. Once again there were none.

The four occupants of the 'penthouse suites' had gone into their rooms to unpack and the other three had left for the bunk room when the burly Dane stopped, turned around and assembled everyone together once again. "I have just remembered something important," he said. "When the ship last stopped for provisions we could not take on fresh water. Now we are running dangerously low. Please use as little water as possible. Washing one's face and teeth, drinking, and using the toilet are, of course, acceptable, but until the ship docks again in southern Greenland, and that won't happen for several days after we leave, everyone must comply with strict water rationing."

"This is so cool!" Marcie exclaimed. Sørensen had just left with Jack and Spencer in tow and she was taking measure of their accommodations. "Look, the whole bathroom, what there is of it, becomes the shower area. You can sit on the commode while you take a shower. And the bunks fold up against the wall to make room for us to sit and chat...what an efficient use of space." She was grinning from ear to ear. "So, which bunk do you want? Upper or lower? I'd prefer the top one, but you can have it if you want. I really don't care that much."

"Fine, I'll take this one," Jocelyn said, sounding bored and pointing to the lower one.

"Great, thanks, Jossy." Marcie immediately unfolded the bunk, hoisted up her rucksack and then ascended wall-mounted rungs to get into her sleeping nook. "Man, they gave us clean sheets and a heavy blanket, and look," she said excitedly, "there's a neat built-in reading lamp up here. This is so cool!" she repeated. "Dr. Sørensen said this was the penthouse suite. He got that right!"

Jocelyn was no stranger to the Spartan arrangements aboard ship. To her, the accommodations were indeed sparse and uninspiring. In a way she envied Marcie's excitement, her thrill of discovery, but immediately discounted it for what it was: the ignorance and enthusiasm of youth.

Marcie bounced down from her perch and announced, "I'm gonna go to the break room. I bet some of the others'll be there. You wanna come?"

"Nope"

"Okay, I'll see you later, at dinner maybe." Brimming with exuberance and a healthy sense of adventure, the young girl disappeared into the corridor leaving Jocelyn to her thoughts. The room went eerily silent save for the steady thrum of the ship's engines.

Jocelyn hadn't slept well in Reykjavik. She also hadn't bothered to shower at the hotel. Putting up with her period—it had conveniently started on the plane flight from New York—and the hassles of an extended trip, had put her in a foul mood. The summer was becoming a nightmare. She ran her fingers through her long, blonde hair. It felt dirty and greasy. "God, I need a shower," she muttered, "but I can't because I can't use any freakin' water." The irony of her situation made her angry. Why have a 'penthouse suite' with a shower if you weren't allowed to use it?

"Oh, screw it!" Jocelyn delved into her rucksack and extracted a bottle of scented shampoo. "I'm taking a quick shower, and if anyone objects, the heck with 'em."

The break room was indeed the social gathering place for the archeological passengers. Both Holloways, Jack Malinowski and Marcie Van Wormer milled around, snacking on a tray of cold cuts, cheese and fresh bread. The food was an impromptu 'welcome aboard' gift brought from the galley. Conspicuously absent was Spencer Bowen. Jack had informed the others that his roommate wanted to rest for a while before gracing them with his presence. A fresh pot of coffee rested in a gimbal to keep any sudden motions of the ship from spilling its contents. Debbie and Marcie opted to choose from a wide selection of teas stocked in a drawer beside the microwave.

Morgan sipped his beverage contentedly. He decided this would be a good opportunity to educate his young assistants about life on Eviskar Island and the nature of the encampment where they would be living in the near future. "As we sail onward towards what I believe will be the experience of a lifetime for all of you, I think it is appropriate to contemplate the trials of those who preceded us a thousand years ago. What an amazing journey it must have been for those intrepid Norsemen who braved these same waters, piloting their longboats through heavy seas for hundreds of miles searching for habitable land." He looked at his watch. "By my reckoning, we've just crossed the Arctic Circle and we still have to go more than 700 miles further north. That reminds me; one of the main adaptations you'll have to make is getting used to the lack of darkness. Some folks suffer from severe insomnia up there. I can pretty much guarantee, however, that all of you will be fine. Believe me, after a long day of very rewarding but backbreaking field work, a little sunlight won't keep you from getting your requisite shuteye."

Morgan continued on about the work they'd be doing and the excitement it would provide. Most of what he was saying they had already heard during gatherings in New York and Reykjavik and on the bus ride to Olafsvik. He was obviously really into his profession, and although the students were looking forward to their summer jobs, it was difficult for them to work up a high level of enthusiasm by just listening to him talk. They actually had to be there.

Jack and Marcie were leaning against the counter. Morgan's back was to them, and while their leader droned on about excavation protocol, Jack explained to his young admirer the astronomical reason for the long northern summer days. Marcie was, to say the least, in heaven. Not only was her cabin on the ship the neatest accommodation she'd ever experienced, but Jack Malinowski was giving her his undivided attention.

In a page of Marcie's notebook, Jack drew a circle to represent the Earth in cross-section and then ran two mutually perpendicular lines through its center. "Okay, say this is the Earth, this is its axis of rotation and this is the Equator," he began, "You can see that if one's latitude is high enough and if the Sun's declination is high enough—that is, if their sum is greater than ninety degrees—then even when the Sun is on the other side of the Earth, at local midnight, it will still be above the northern horizon.

"The Sun's maximum height above the Equator, its maximum declination, is about 23 ½ degrees. That means only at latitudes above 90 − 23 ½ or 66 ½ degrees can the phenomenon of twenty-four hours of daylight be observed. That latitude is called the Arctic Circle. Eviskar's latitude is about 76 ½ degrees and that means the Sun's center won't set until August 17th. Also, due to the effect of atmospheric refraction and the fact that the Sun isn't a point source, some part of the Sun will lie above the horizon for several days beyond that. Only in the last ten days or so of our stay there will we experience darkness."

"Wow, that is so cool!" Marcie exclaimed with her characteristic enthusiasm. The outburst, to her chagrin, was loud enough to interrupt Morgan. He turned around to face them.

"What's so interesting?"

Thinking quickly, she responded, "Sorry, I just, um...what you were saying about the island...it sounds fascinating."

Morgan beamed, "It is, isn't it. Don't worry, Marcie, in a matter of days we'll be up to our ears in archeological work, and I promise, this summer will be one you'll never forget."

Jocelyn entered the break room just as Morgan's speech was winding down and the others were preparing to leave. She wore a clean shirt and jeans, light deck shoes, and her hair was wet, smelling of apricots. "Hi, everyone," she said pleasantly, "did I miss anything?"

"Not really," Morgan said, "we were merely brushing up on what we'll be doing once we get to Eviskar—things you'll be aware of soon enough."

She spotted the tab of a tea bag draped over the side of Marcie's cup. "Oh, man, I could so use a cup of hot tea. What kinds do they have?" She sidled over to the beverage drawer and began sorting through the contents.

Marcie leaned over and said in a half whisper, "Jossy, you didn't take a shower did you? Don't you remember what Dr. Sørensen said about the water shortage?"

"Relax, I didn't use much. You're such a worrywart. Nobody'll even notice. All right!" She pulled a packet from the drawer, "orange-flavored green tea. Perfect, just what the doctor ordered."

Light conversation and laughter filled the room as Jocelyn nuked a cup of water for her tea. Marcie gravitated away from her roommate to ask Jack more questions about daily light/dark cycles at high latitudes.   She wanted to engage him in stimulating conversation before Jocelyn finished preparing her drink and inevitably tried to usurp his attention. Before she could speak to him, however, there was commotion in the hatchway.

Sørensen walked in followed closely by a slender, petite woman in uniform. Behind her was one of the crew, also in uniform. Sørensen bore a worried look and began to speak, but the woman stepped forward and cut him off.

Captain Katrine Magnussen came from a distinguished maritime family and wore the uniform of the Royal Danish Navy with extreme pride. Her blonde hair was tucked neatly under her cap, her black deck shoes shined like mirrors, and the uniform that she sported was immaculately pressed. Piercing blue eyes lined with fine crow's feet attested to decades at the helm, enduring the effects of sun, wind and salt air. Although diminutive in size and delicately featured, the way she carried herself indicated that Magnussen was a solid, wizened mariner. A highly respected officer, she had a reputation not only for fairness and impartiality, but also of someone who harbored no tolerance for anyone who broke the rules. As commander of the *Stjerne*, she had absolute authority over all that took place on board, and she was about to demonstrate that authority in the civilian break room. Her laser-like gaze scanned the room and settled upon Jocelyn and her wet hair.

The captain addressed those in the room in Danish, pausing periodically for Sørensen to translate. "In the past half-hour there has been a noticeable drop in my ship's potable water supply. This is unacceptable."

Jocelyn knew the lecture was meant for her and she didn't appreciate it one bit. Standing a good four inches taller than Magnussen, she wasn't intimidated in the least. Taking a shower was no crime. The woman's imperious attitude was insulting. "Just who do you think..."

Sørensen stepped in front of Jocelyn and interrupted. "I am very sorry, Captain Magnussen. Perhaps I, uh...perhaps I didn't emphasize enough the gravity of the water situation in my introductory remarks to our passengers. I accept full responsibility. There will be no further problems; I assure you."

Magnussen wasn't listening. She stepped around Sørensen and stood two feet from Jocelyn. It was at that instant Jocelyn realized her mistake. The captain's eyes were cold, almost encouraging the girl to escalate the encounter. The famous Clint Eastwood line "...go ahead, make my day," radiated telepathically through the captain's gaze. Jocelyn fell silent.

"Any further rule violations will result in immediate incarceration. Our brig, for your information, is located opposite the main crew quarters and has a chain-link door—no privacy. It also does not have a water supply. All bodily wastes must be deposited in a steel canister, in full view of any passersby. Have I made myself clear?"

Jocelyn's obduracy faded and she looked away, nodding meekly. Magnussen abruptly turned and headed for the bridge, her subordinate in tow. She had a ship to run and couldn't waste any more time chastising passengers.

Sørensen breathed a heavy sigh of relief. He clasped his hands together in a beseeching gesture and said to everyone in the room, "I assure you; Captain Magnussen does not make idle threats." He turned to Jocelyn, "Please do not antagonize that woman, Ms. Delaney. She is also the chief martial arts instructor on board, and I'm told that she and her husband are the fleet's Tae Kwon Do sparring champions. We have little more than a day left in our voyage. Let us not cause any more trouble."

Jocelyn remained in the break area after the others had left. Her mood was one of anger and self-pity. She was definitely jinxed. Trouble seemed to follow her wherever she went. Even the simple act of bathing was enough to get her in trouble. "What's next?" she thought bitterly. "Will that bitch captain decide to execute me for breathing some of the ship's precious air?" She suddenly had an overwhelming desire to go back home to Corpus Christi. The aggravations she'd experienced in just the first three days of this trip made her regret her decision to apply for this stupid program.

Spencer entered the room. He appeared to be in discomfort; his hair was tousled and he looked pale. "They got any Pepto-Bismol in heah?" he asked as he took a seat at the table and buried his face in his hands.

Recognizing the unmistakable signs of seasickness, Jocelyn smiled, "Hi, Spence, you look a bit under the weather."

"Yeah, it's real funny; that's why I'm laughin'."

"You want me to ask Morgan for some Dramamine?" Spencer just shook his head. "C'mon, I'm just trying to help."

"You've been enough *help* already. Jack told me all about it. If the captain had her way, we'd be swimmin' to Eviskah Island. She's pissed at all of us, not just you, even though you're the one who broke the rules."

"Hey, I took a shower, okay? It's not like I killed someone or robbed a bank."

He looked away. "Whateveh"

Jocelyn wouldn't let it go. "You know, for someone who's supposed to be really smart, some kind of kid genius, I'd expect you to be more objective, Spencer."

"Just leave me alone, would 'ya. I'm not feelin' a hundred percent right now."

Her temper flared. "Well then, maybe you need something to eat, to get your mind off the miserable motion of the ship. I've been seasick before and I know what you're going through, Spence: the headache, the shakes and especially the nausea. About all you can do is to hang in there and try not to think about it. I remember one time I was out in the Gulf on a friend's boat when a squall rolled in. We must have been four or five miles out and the storm was between us and land. There was nowhere to go. We just hung on through twenty foot seas. Huge swells took us on a roller coaster ride. We'd get lifted up high and then we'd slam down into a trough, sending up a mountain of spray. One of the girls with us was a heavy smoker. Being in the confined cabin of that boat, sitting there, nauseous and breathing that foul, secondhand smoke—it makes me queasy thinking about it."

She paused to monitor his countenance. He was pale and swallowing repeatedly. His downcast expression indicated he was almost there. "I'm getting hungry," she continued, "let's see what's in the fridge." She bent down and opened the door of the small refrigerator that was under the counter. Stuffed within were numerous containers of food. Hardly a square inch of empty space remained—the unit hadn't been cleaned in quite a while. She rummaged through an assortment of paper bags, Tupperware-type plastic tubs, beverage bottles and cans, most of which bore labels in indelible marker identifying their owners. Finally she found what she wanted. Stashed way in the back was a transparent re-sealable container, the contents of which had been long forgotten. She opened it and curled her nose. "Yech! Some people are so disgusting. I would never leave something like this in a public refrigerator. Look..." she shoved it under Spencer's nose.

Weeks earlier the container had held some sort of casserole, a slice of pie or maybe some stew. It was now identifiable only as a decomposing organic mass covered with several types of mold. Greenish slime coated what had once been the entrée, while around the periphery and on the underside of the lid grew delicate, feathery whiskers of something both beautiful and pungently aromatic.

What may have been a microbiologist's delight proved too much for the ailing Spencer. "Noooo..." the poor boy groaned. He pushed away from the table and dashed for the trash can by the door.

He almost made it.

Marcie came back just in time to witness Spencer regurgitate the last of his lunch. "Spencer, are you okay?" she asked with concern.

Jocelyn stepped over a puddle of half-digested chum and slipped past Marcie, making her way to the door. "He's just got a touch of 'mal de mer.'" She looked back at Spencer with undisguised contempt. "Don't worry about him; he'll live."

VI

The Stjerne anchored a hundred yards off the Eviskar coast. The Holloways, the four students and Johan Sørensen stood packed and ready while sailors readied the two rigid-hulled inflatable boats, RHIBs, that would transport them to shore. Tough and maneuverable even in the heaviest of seas, the twenty-three-foot-long craft had strong, solid hulls and sported inflatable tubes that surrounded the gunwales for added buoyancy and stability. Most modern navies employed some version of this design as tenders for their warships.

Strong hands reached up to guide them into the RHIB after each traveler had negotiated the short metal loading ladder that had been placed against the Stjerne's hull. The command to cast off came as soon as Morgan, the last passenger to board, had taken his seat.

Marcie thought for sure they would crash as the boat skimmed the water and rapidly approached shore. At the last instant, the pilot reversed the engine and the stout hull slid smoothly up onto the gravel beach using the craft's residual momentum. No sooner had the Eviskar group exited the boat, the two sailors who'd accompanied them jumped out and gave a hearty yell as they pushed the craft back into the surf and began their return trip.

They had arrived. The four students stood where they'd landed and surveyed the place they'd gone through so much trouble to get to. It wasn't exactly an idyllic tropical getaway replete with palm trees, hibiscus flowers and pretty girls in grass skirts. This place was rugged and desolate, but it was impressive nonetheless, exuding the majestic charm of a pristine locale essentially uninfluenced by mankind. They now realized how important this settlement was to historians. How anyone could have made such a long voyage in small open boats now became a topic of wonder. Much of what Morgan had been telling them was beginning to sink in.

The beach itself was open and broad and consisted of basalt gravel and sand, weathered by thousands, if not millions, of years of wave action. A few dozen yards from where they landed, three large rubber craft, zodiacs, rested on the gravel above the high tide mark. Farther inland, the terrain rose gradually and plateaued at a height of about eighty feet above sea level. It was there that numerous structures could be seen. Several large canvas tents, each at least twenty to thirty feet long and of similar width, had been set up uphill from the zodiacs. Farther down the beach, to the south, they could make out crumbling stone walls surrounded by ropes, flagging and yellow tape—the remnants of the Old Norse settlement. That was where they would be spending most of their working hours.

Two people were making their way over from the work site. Clad in mud-caked work boots, coveralls and wide-brimmed hats they waved and shouted greetings as they got close. "Welcome, welcome back," the man in front said. He shook hands with Morgan and Johan and then gave Debbie a hearty hug. "It is so good to see you. How was your trip?" The words came out in heavily accented English. He removed his hat to wipe his brow. With his head uncovered he lost a good six inches to his apparent height and revealed a shock of fine black hair, flecked with grey, atop a round face. Stocky and fit, his weathered appearance gave the impression he'd be just as comfortable mushing a sled in a minus-forty degree blizzard as he was working at an archeological dig.

"We had...uh...a very eventful trip," Sørensen replied. "Ittuk, I have the distinct honor of introducing you to these fine young students who will be joining us for the summer." He beamed with pride, as though speaking about his own children. "During our voyage on the Stjerne, I have gotten to know each of them, and I expect they will be of enormous help on this project."

"That is wonderful. It is always good to have youth and enthusiasm around. It will help to keep us old people on our toes."

Sørensen addressed the students, "This, my friends, is Professor Ittuk Inunnguaq of the University of Greenland. He is the one who discovered this remarkable site and he is our much appreciated expedition leader."

"As usual, Johan, you are too kind. I must say that local Inuit people, seal hunters, have known of these ruins for many years. They simply decided to honor us with that knowledge. We should give credit where it is due." He turned to his companion and said something in a foreign tongue. Reverting back to his halting English he said, "Dr. and Mrs. Holloway, if you would be kind enough to introduce our young employees to their rustic accommodations, the rest of us will retrieve the supplies."

Professor Inunnguaq's colleague, also a man of Greenlandic heritage, had gone to get one of the zodiacs. He was now bringing it around to where a pile of crates and boxes sat on the sand—additional supplies offloaded by the sailors of the Stjerne. The ever-inquisitive Spencer asked, "What's all that stuff?"

"Mainly food and fuel," said Sørensen. "In particular, you will be glad that we have a good supply of kerosene for the heaters in our tents. Even in June the nighttime temperature here sometimes falls below freezing. We would burn wood, but there is none that grows this far north. That is another reason why it is so unusual to find evidence of such an old settlement at this latitude. A major goal of our research is to determine why people traveled all the way up here. It was for seasonal use, of that we are reasonably certain, but it still doesn't answer the question: why?"

The women's bunkhouse was one of the three large tents they'd seen from the beach. Adjacent to that was the men's dormitory, and the third one in line was the kitchen. A fourth tent, located closer to the actual dig site and out of view of the beach, was a combination supply room and infirmary.

"Wow, this is what I call camping in style." Marcie was impressed with the living arrangements. She pushed her rucksack under the cot to which she'd been assigned and then lay down to test its effectiveness as a bed. "Just awesome," she added, jumping back to her feet.

Jocelyn was horrified. "This is it?"

"What did you expect?" Debbie replied. "The literature we sent with the acceptance letter contained specifics about the accommodations."

"It said we'd be in a bunkhouse. This is a *tent*. And where the heck is the bathroom? How am I supposed to wash and...stuff?" She caught herself, realizing that to mention 'taking a shower' might be a tad inflammatory after what had happened on the Stjerne.

"Actually, Jocelyn, these canvas tents are amazing. It can be windy and minus twenty degrees outside, but with the flaps closed and the kerosene heater going we'll stay warm as toast—in shirtsleeves no less. Now, if you'll follow me outside, I'll show you our, uh, 'facilities.'" Debbie smiled at Marcie, "I think you'll find the way they've set up camp to be quite clever."

The three women exited their living quarters through the back door and hung a left. Located about twenty yards away were two tall canvas enclosures. The flaps were pulled back, and even from a distance it was obvious what purpose they served. Inside each was a sturdy frame about three feet high which supported a toilet seat. Small step stools were positioned in front of the frames to accommodate shorter individuals. Underneath each seat was a ten-gallon bucket.

"These are what we call our 'throne rooms.'" Debbie flashed a sly grin at Jocelyn, "Any questions?"

"Yes, as a matter of fact. Which one is the ladies room?"

"Both actually. They're unisex—first come, first served."

"I don't see any doors," the girl continued, "how the heck can anyone be guaranteed any privacy?"

"It's obvious; just tie the flaps shut. No one will bother you; we're all adults here. Oh, before I forget, both of you be sure to check the white board in the kitchen every morning. It lists each day's work assignments. The first time either of you is assigned to 'bucket brigade,' I'll come with you to show you where to dump these guys. Mikkel Dalgaard, one of the other researchers, is a master gardener. He's set up a most remarkable compost pit. All of our biodegradable kitchen waste gets tossed into a trash can and it, along with these 'honey pots,' gets emptied daily into the pit. It's absolutely amazing how effective the system is. By next year, the waste we discard this summer will have turned into soil. There won't be any residual odor; it will have been completely broken down by microbial action, even in this cold environment. All of our combustible waste is disposed of by burning. We use an old oil drum as a burning barrel. I'll show you that process as well when the time comes."

"No way"

"What's that?"

"I said, 'no way,'" Jocelyn repeated. "Debbie, I didn't sign up to come half way around the world to empty shit buckets."

Debbie was fed up with Jocelyn's attitude. Working hard to control her anger, she said in a calm voice, "Neither did anyone else, Jocelyn. You're not being asked to do anything more than the rest of us. We all have to take our turns at the less desirable chores." Jocelyn started to protest, but Debbie interrupted, "If you have any further complaints, please take them up with Ittuk. He's the fellow who came to greet us when we landed, and he's the official leader of this project. I must warn you though, he doesn't respond favorably to those who don't pull their weight. In fact," her tone hardened and she looked Jocelyn squarely in the eye, "I feel obliged to note that he will not be as warm, personable and benevolent as your friend Captain Magnussen. And, Jocelyn—neither Morgan nor I will intervene on your behalf if we feel you are in the wrong."

Debbie, Jocelyn and Marcie stood at the edge of the pit looking on with interest as Magnus Strøm carefully brushed dirt off of their latest find. Magnus and his wife Liva were veterans of the Eviskar project, both of them providing invaluable expertise with regard to what they were now doing. Last summer the team had unearthed the skeleton of a middle-aged woman. A week ago, while digging in the same area, about twenty yards from the main, stone 'house,' they'd found another.

"I believe you are absolutely correct, Liva. We have the remains here of a young female, of perhaps twenty years old."

Magnus and Liva were both physicians by training. He was a retired cardiologist, and she was a pathologist and world-renowned forensic anthropologist. Together they were the team's undisputed authorities when it came to dealing with any human remains that were found. They were also the project's medical team, bearing responsibility for all physical ailments or injuries that befell any of the archeological workers.

"How can you tell all that?" asked Marcie. She was leaning over them, fascinated by the assemblage of bones and nearly completely decomposed clothing that lay before her.

"The gender is readily apparent," Liva said. She lowered herself next to the remains and pointed with her pen at the pelvis. "See how wide the pelvis is? How far apart the ilia are? A male pelvis would be much narrower. Also, this person was probably Scandinavian." She ran her fingers along the backs of the upper front teeth and nodded, as if to confirm her hypothesis. "Yes, definitely European. The arch of the maxilla and the spatulate incisor surfaces strongly suggest these are Norse remains. That is important because indigenous Inuit people also might have settled here at some time.

"Her age is difficult to determine exactly, but we can come close." She brushed more dirt from the skull and ran her pen along its divisions. "You can tell the sagittal and coronal sutures are not completely fused. That means we are dealing with someone younger than, say, thirty. In addition, all of the permanent teeth are present except for the third molars, what the English call 'wisdom teeth.' Those have not fully erupted."

"Wow, so just from the skull and the teeth you can deduce her age?"

"Those are perhaps the best indicators, yes. There are others, however. Another reliable age marker is the major joints. The end of the femur, right below the knee joint, appears not to have ossified completely. However, I will need an x-ray to confirm this."

"That means she was still growing, right?"

"Why, yes, that is correct." Liva was impressed. "You seem to know something of human physiology, Marcie."

"Not much," the girl replied modestly.

"Well, for the benefit of the others, I should probably explain my last observation. You see, an individual's long bones have cartilage at their ends which grows until he reaches his teens. The cartilage cells adjacent to the bone itself, as opposed to those nearest the joint, gradually convert to bone. As Marcie said, that is how we grow. When our growth rate slows, most of the cartilage will have turned into bone, a process termed ossification, and the cartilaginous zone, called the epiphyseal plate, at the bone's terminus, becomes very thin. I conclude that when she died, this young woman was not much older than you, Marcie." Liva looked at Jocelyn. "She was about your age, Jossy."

"Look at this, Liva." Magnus pointed to a spot below the base of the skull. "It is like the other woman."

Liva examined the spot and shared a somber, knowing look with her husband. She then said to everyone present: "Last summer we found a neck fracture which we felt might have resulted when the other corpse was buried. This one has the exact same injury. That sort of coincidence seems unlikely." After a moment's hesitation, she continued, "There is a good chance that these two women, who endured so much hardship in this remote place, did not die of natural causes."

Debbie and the two female students had been assigned to help exhume the skeletal remains for further study. Jack and Spencer worked fifty yards to the east, assisting Morgan, Ittuk and several others excavate the area around what appeared to be one of the primary buildings of the ancient village.

What remained of the walls displayed expert craftsmanship. The blocks of local stone from which they'd been constructed had been dryfit together so precisely as to leave no gaps for wind and rain to get through. The mere fact that parts of the structure were still standing, after a millennium of abuse by Mother Nature, was further testament to the masonry skill of the builders.

Jack had set up the surveying gear and was turning angles and shooting distances to various points of interest. Most were control points, set to define and outline the research area. Others were locations where artifacts and other objects of interest were unearthed.

Spencer had made it his job to work with the CAD software Morgan had brought with him. The young technology wizard would download data that Jack acquired and store them in such a way that they could be viewed as a 3-D image from any perspective. He had even included links to .jpg camera images, allowing anyone running the software to visually examine the locale where an artifact lay while simultaneously noting its exact position within the dig site. In the evenings, Spencer would amaze many of the older, less computer savvy, archeologists with the powerful data display tools he and Jack had implemented.

Debbie left the grave site and sauntered over to where Jack and Spencer were hard at work. She was extremely proud of how her students were performing. It was now three weeks into the summer's work, and all four, even Jocelyn, had become accepted, even indispensable, members of the crew. But in the last few days she'd noticed subtle changes in their attitudes. It was as if they were on auto-pilot, performing their duties in admirable fashion, but without the same level of enthusiasm they had exhibited earlier. In other words, her students were becoming bored. The work had become slow and monotonous for them—they needed a break. After watching the boys work for a spell, she said, "Guys, it's almost lunchtime. Let's meet in the kitchen in about fifteen minutes. I've got a proposition for you."

It was Ittuk's turn to make lunch. Instead of the usual fare of tasteless, re-heated canned mush, he'd decided to treat his compatriots to a real Greenlandic meal. Delving into their small freezer, he'd extracted a slab of seal meat which he was now frying alongside potatoes and onions in a large skillet.

The students sat at one of the tables, waiting patiently for Ittuk to finish and speculating about what Debbie had in the offing. The pungent smells wafting over from the stove piqued Spencer's curiosity. "What 'cha cookin', Ittuk?"

"It is a special treat for my new American friends—fresh seal meat. I killed it this spring, a female...very tasty."

"Smells like fish."

"It has the taste of the sea, Spencer, and it is full of nutrients: iron, protein, calcium...you will like it, of that I am certain."

Moments later, the students and the rest of the lunch crowd filled their plates, buffet style, and sat back down. While the hungry Scandinavian researchers dove into their food, looks of apprehension passed among the newcomers. Each was waiting for one of the others to take the first bite.

It was Jack who summoned his courage and gave in. "Here goes," he said. Cutting off a good-sized piece of seal, he chewed it slowly, savoring both the taste and the attention bestowed upon him by his captive audience.

"Well?" Jocelyn asked impatiently.

Jack held up his hand in a gesture for her to wait. When they saw him swallow, all three leaned forward, anticipating a verdict. Jack merely smiled and cut himself another piece. It was obvious he was toying with them. Marcie took the hint and followed Jack's lead. She took a bite and ate it in silence. Another agonizing minute passed.

"Aw, you guys," Spencer admonished. There was nothing to do but to try it himself. Soon, the three of them were eating their meals, waiting for Jocelyn to join in.

Their wait continued. The young woman from Corpus Christi picked at her vegetables and pushed the slice of seal meat around her plate. She was still gathering her nerve when Ittuk stopped by.

"It is good, is it not?" he beamed. "In winter, the seals are what keep us alive here in the North. The fat keeps you warm, and," he added, making a fist, "the meat makes you strong." The expression on Ittuk's face was one of hope. Part of his culture was on display, subject to criticism by his new colleagues. Sensing this, Marcie, Jack and Spencer offered enthusiastic replies.

"It's really good," said Spencer, "kinda like liveh 'an onions."

"Yeah," Marcie agreed, "like you said, it tastes like the ocean, sort of. I would say it's similar to beef, but with a hint of fish. I like it."

While Jack rendered his opinion, Jocelyn finally took a small bite. Ever since Debbie had warned her about Ittuk's volatile temperament, she'd been afraid of him. It certainly wouldn't pay to antagonize this man, out here in the middle of nowhere, with two months left in what she now considered a sort of prison sentence. When his expectant gaze fell upon her, she put on a fake, warm smile and said, with her mouth full, "Delicious!" Once he was gone, however, she spat it out, frowned and shook her head. "Yuk."

"Okay, maybe it's not filet mignon, but it's not that bad," Marcie said. She and the others cleaned their plates.

Jocelyn waited until Ittuk's back was turned and then quickly got up and scraped hers into the trash. When she returned to her seat, she sounded bored and frustrated. "So much for lunch," she growled. "I wonder what Debbie had in mind when she called for this meeting?"

A response wasn't long in coming. Debbie had just entered the tent and was headed their way. "Hi, guys, thanks for waiting up."

"You better hurry up and serve yourself some seal before it's gone," Jocelyn said sarcastically.

"I will in a bit. Ittuk is very kind to have prepared that for us. Did you like it?"

"I thought it was great," said Marcie. "So, why are we here? Jack said you have an important proposition for us."

"Morgan and I just got through talking. Work is pretty slow right now, so I was thinking: how would you guys like to go on a short expedition?"

"All right!" Marcie perked up. "What kind of trip? To where?"

"I was looking at satellite images of the island and noticed a small beach about twelve miles south of here. The weather seems to be holding up, so what do you say we camp there for a few days and do some exploring, maybe some rock climbing?"

"Awesome," Marcie said.

Debbie turned to Jocelyn. "You're on bucket brigade tomorrow, Jossy. If you go on this trip, you'll have to miss it."

Jocelyn let out a fake sigh of regret. "Let's see...go on a trip, or haul drums full of human feces...that's a tough call. Ah well, I guess if everyone else wants to go, I'm in."

Both boys nodded their assent.

"Great," said Debbie. "I'll pack one of the boats with our tents and supplies. Each of you should bring your heavy sleeping bag and a rucksack full of warm clothing. We won't be bringing kerosene heaters with us and it'll be cold there. We'll meet at 0600 tomorrow morning down by the zodiacs."

VII

Waves splashed against the launch, the larger ones spraying those seated in the bow. Jack wanted to stay close to shore but Jocelyn yelled at him over the roar of the outboard, "Take us farther out. Move past where the swells start to break." He dutifully pushed the handle away from himself and gave it some gas. The zodiac arced gracefully towards the horizon and the ride became noticeably smoother. Jocelyn sat in front, exhilarated to be at sea, breathing in the salt air. This was her element; she always felt happy, rejuvenated, out on the water.

They rounded yet another bend of the undulating coastline only to discover that the beach they sought had to be quite some distance ahead. Nowhere along the seaboard could one even consider landing a boat. Dangerous rocks jutted from the water and breakers crashed against them to create a cauldron of mist and foam.

"According to the satellite images our destination is about twelve miles from the dig site," Debbie reminded everyone. She glanced at her watch. "I estimate we're making about eight knots, so it will take us another half hour or so to get there."

Further out to sea there were patches of blue sky, but the island and the waters immediately surrounding it were covered by a thick layer of heavy, grey cloud. Patches of fog obscured the summits of the higher basalt cliffs that ran right to the water's edge. Spencer held onto his Yankees cap as the boat turned into the steady headwind blowing up from the south. Although the day was calm by Eviskar standards, the breeze nonetheless impeded their progress and roughened the seas. "At least I'm not seasick," he thought. He realized it was the fear and anxiety of the trip that was holding his nausea at bay. Pangs of regret at having agreed to come on this little excursion came over him whenever the small craft plunged through the larger swells. He longed to set foot on land, and the sooner the better.

Finally, out of the mist there appeared a break in the mighty seawall. Beyond an enormous rock that had tumbled into the surf eons ago, a sloping patch of ground, perhaps 100 yards wide, lay within a small cove. As they approached they could see breakers gently washing up onto a rocky, pebble-strewn beach.

"Make sure you're well clear of that rock outcrop," Jocelyn commanded," then swing around and come in straight."

Jack did as he was told and within minutes they were headed for shore, helped along by waves and the incoming tide. Spencer breathed a sigh of relief as the ride became much calmer and terra firma rapidly approached.

Picking the spot where he wanted to land was easy. It was in an area nearly devoid of large boulders, and from a distance it appeared to offer the smoothest and least objectionable surface for the rubber hull to scrape against. Waves were hitting the beach at a slight angle from the south, so Jack swung past his target and let the surf and wind help to propel him inland.

Just when he was about to throttle down, the zodiac slammed to a halt and listed sharply to one side. Jocelyn was nearly thrown from the boat and Marcie lurched forward into Debbie's lap. A loud crack accompanied the event followed by an awful scraping noise coming from the engine.

"Rock!" Jack yelled. He was grabbing for the control stick which had been ripped from his hand by the impact. Regaining it, he tried to steer the boat but discovered he had lost all control. The grating sound intensified and smoke began to spew from the engine. He immediately pushed a button on the handle that cut fuel to the motor. Within seconds the outboard sputtered and died leaving behind an eerie silence. An ugly oil slick began spreading out from the back of the boat.

For a while no one spoke. The only sounds were of water gently lapping the rubber gunwale and the whoosh and growl of waves as they washed onto the beach and then receded. "Is everyone all right?" Debbie finally asked. Looks were exchanged among the group, each person checking his companions for any sign of injury. "OK then. Let's find the oars and get this thing to shore."

Spencer and Marcie, who were sitting along the sides of the craft, each grabbed an oar and began to paddle. Assisted by the surf it didn't take long to beach the boat. Jocelyn leaped out and pulled on the bow line, heaving the rubber vessel firmly onto land.

The rest of the party disembarked and each found a rock upon which to sit while they contemplated their predicament. There was little doubt that the boat's motor was probably done for, but Debbie told Jack to check it out just in case.

"We'd better run it further up onto the beach," Jocelyn cautioned, "tide's coming in.   Motor or no motor, the thing is still seaworthy." She smiled, "Marcie and Spencer may have to paddle us all the way back to the dig."

"Yeah right," Marcie said sarcastically, "but you're right about the tide. If we're stuck here for any length of time, we may have to use the boat as a shelter." Spencer rose to help Jack move the zodiac and check out the condition of the motor.

"Let's not jump to conclusions," Debbie said. "I brought one of the satellite communicators with me. We'll get Morgan or one of the other guys to come and pick us up in another launch." She looked at her watch. It was only 9:00 AM even though it felt like it was close to midday. None of them had yet fully adapted to the long summer days at such high latitude. "Well, I for one intend to make the most of our little side trip," Debbie continued brightly. "We still have a good six weeks of excavation work to do back at the site. This may be our best, if not only, chance to have some fun on this island paradise." She turned and studied the surrounding terrain.

The island was essentially a steep-sided extinct, or dormant, volcano. The wall of the caldera rose high up into the clouds to Debbie's right and left. Directly in front of her, however, a long scree slope extended to a saddle between the spires on either side. Long ago what was once a cliff had crumbled, perhaps as a result of some seismic event, and broken bits of rock had cascaded down to form the beach where they now sat. The upper reaches of the slide formed a ridge, barely visible below the mist that hid the surrounding summits, perhaps a thousand feet above them. "Anybody have any doubts about his or her ability to climb that?" Debbie asked, pointing upward. "I don't know how many people have ever seen the interior of Eviskar Island. Between what I've seen at the dig site and from satellite images, this place right here may be the only way to access the volcanic interior without having to use technical gear. This is really unexplored terrain. What do you say?"

Debbie's enthusiasm was so infectious that no one declined. Marcie was particularly eager to visit the unknown. Her spirit of adventure was in high gear. She immediately began to hike up slope. "Wait a minute, Marcie," Debbie called, "there's no great rush."

"Oh, I know. I'm just going to scout around while you guys get ready. Plus, I gotta pee," she added sheepishly.

"Moi aussi," said Jocelyn. The two girls headed for a group of rocks. No sooner had they left than Jack and Spencer returned from the boat. Jack was frowning.

"So, what's the verdict?" asked Debbie.

"You want the good news or the bad news?"

She laughed. "Give me the bad news first. Is it dead?"

"In a word, 'yes.' The cylinder head is cracked. It's bad enough that the thing won't run again. It's a total loss. Not only that, the propeller shaft is bent and this is what's left of the prop." He held up a small, conical shaped piece of metal.

"That doesn't look much like any propellers I've seen. Where are the blades?"

He pointed towards the ocean and shrugged. "Somewhere out there. To put it bluntly: 'a niech to licho.'"

"What does that mean?"

"It's Polish. Loosely translated it means, uh, 'we're screwed.'"

"And the good news?"

"Oh, I'm not through with the bad news yet. The really bad news is that there is no good news." He gestured to the raft. "Like Jocelyn said, it's seaworthy, but I was fighting some pretty stiff currents on the way out here. There's no way we can propel a sluggish thing like this all the way home with those two tiny paddles."

Debbie appraised Jack and Spencer of the day's plans. Both were amenable to a pleasant hike to the rim of the caldera, although neither expected much of a view from the top. Patches of mist were rising rapidly up from within the island and dissipating once they met the offshore wind.

"There may be some places along the way where we might rope up and do some rock climbing," Debbie said to Jack. I brought enough gear so that we can practice and maybe teach the other students a thing or two. In the biographical info you supplied to me you mentioned climbing as one of your hobbies. Are you any good?"

Jack smiled. "I don't know how good I am, but there's a climbing wall at the local YMCA. I've helped to set a couple of 5.13 routes. One of them has an awesome overhang."

Debbie looked astonished. "5.13 puts you into the expert category."

"Hey, I said I set some routes of that difficulty. I didn't say I can climb 'em. But, yeah, on a good day...who knows?"

"Let me see your hands."

Jack tentatively held out his hands for Debbie's inspection. She regarded them carefully, turning them over, noting the slightly enlarged knuckles, the worn and damaged nails. He certainly had the physique of a climber as well; his arms were wiry and strong and his shoulders were well muscled. "You're a climber all right. This should be fun." She turned to the others. "You guys grab your backpacks and water bottles, and let's take our lunches with us. C'mon, Jack, you can help me carry the climbing gear." She hesitated and looked around. "Where's Marcie? Jocelyn, what happened to your partner in crime?"

"I see her," Spencer announced, "way ovah there, see?"

Sure enough, Marcie was carefully negotiating her way down slope. She had obviously been exploring. In her right hand she grasped something small and gray, and waved it in the air as she approached. "Hey, Debbie, look what I found." Proud of her discovery, she presented a knitted cap for all to see. "Looks like we're not the first people to visit this place. Someone was here recently; I don't think the old Norsemen could have woven something like this. Besides, wouldn't something made of wool decompose over several hundred years?"

Debbie regarded the object and adopted a worried look. "Where did you find this, Marcie?"

"Right over there. See that big rock? That's where I went to go to the bathroom. It was just lying there."

"Was there anything else that looked man-made?"

"Nope, I looked around some, but there was just this cap. Why?"

"I don't quite know, to tell the truth. I just, well, I'm trying to figure out if I've seen this before." After a moment's contemplation she changed the subject. Jack was approaching with the climbing gear. "OK ladies and gentlemen," she said, setting the cap down, "let's have a closer look at Eviskar Island."

The hike to the top of the ridge took approximately two hours. Despite the damp air that greeted them as they ascended the slope, the offshore breeze would occasionally push the haze away and allow sunlight to filter through. These rare periods of sunshine had dramatic effect on the party, warming them up by offsetting the cold brought on by the evaporation of perspiration during the arduous climb. All in all, by Eviskar standards, it was a gorgeous summer day.

Enthusiasm infused everyone present as they reached the ridge, not only because of the euphoria of reaching their destination, an effect mountain climbers dub "summit fever," but because the view that greeted them towards the island's interior was quite unexpected. It was like looking out of an airplane. The mist surrounding them would break periodically to reveal a continuous field of white cloud tops below. It gave them the impression of being much higher than they really were.

Through rare gaps in the clouds lay obscure dark areas. The urge to investigate was palpable.

Debbie took stock of their immediate surroundings. Where they sat, high up on the ridge, the ground was level and windswept. Not surprisingly, no grass or other vegetation was present. The traces of snow that still graced the nearby cliffs suggested that their present location had itself been clear of the white stuff for only a few weeks. Picking her way across the plateau she came to a group of large boulders near a precipitous drop-off. She moved cautiously to the edge of the cliff. There was a sheer drop of perhaps 60 feet ending at a wide, flat shelf. Beyond the flat area the ground sloped downward, gradually disappearing into mist. Was this a viable route to access the interior of Eviskar Island? If so, then a rare opportunity was afforded them. They had the gear to safely climb or rappel down the cliff and the weather was extremely favorable. She carefully examined the cliff face. The rock was solid basalt. One large crack ran diagonally from just above its base to about halfway up. Above that, numerous small holes permeated the rock where gas and volatile matter had escaped as it had cooled. "Perfect!" She thought. The climb would be short, easy and safe, an excellent place to introduce novices to the sport of rock climbing. In addition, they might be able to explore a short distance further into the island before returning to the beach. Mindful of the need to arrange a pickup from Morgan, she glanced at the sky. Their luck was holding. If anything, the weather was improving.

The students were finishing lunch when she returned. Jack was flaunting a coke he had carried all the way from the dig. Besides his backpack he had carried more than 40 pounds of climbing gear in the hike up to the ridge. Because of this, he considered the sugary drink to be a just reward. Brandishing the can for all to see he popped the top and settled back to savor his prize.

Jocelyn smiled seductively and sat beside him. "Say, Jack," she said sweetly," you wouldn't by any chance have another one of those, would you?"

He took a large swig and belched, "Nope."

Marcie, who was carefully watching the interaction of the other two, snickered at Jack's reply.

Jocelyn gave her a deprecating look and turned back to Jack. She batted her eyes shamelessly, "Can I have a sip?"

"Shucks, you're too late." He waggled the empty can between his fingers. "I tell you what, though, next time I'll give you the honor of bringing the refreshments."

Both Marcie and Spencer laughed. "Yeah, 'an put me down for a root beah, "Spencer said. "Coke ain't my drink."

"Actually I'd prefer something else as well," Jocelyn's temper flared, "a good wine perhaps. Something more civilized than a soft drink."

"You're too young to drink alcohol," noted Marcie.

"Oh, lighten up, Marcie. I'm not a child like the rest of you. My folks always have wine with dinner, and I imbibe with them. It's no big deal. It might surprise you to know that I'm not a drunk, and I never drink and drive. That's more than can be said for a lot of adults."

"It's still illegal," Marcie said soberly. "Your folks are breaking the law."

Jocelyn rolled her eyes. "Sipping a good Napa chardonnay isn't the same as guzzling moonshine. I mean c'mon, there are frivolous rules and there's common sense. I believe in the latter."

Marcy shook her head and finished her sandwich. Jack smiled, "Napa? You mean in Texas they sell wine in auto parts stores?"

"Very funny," Jocelyn grumbled. "It doesn't surprise me that someone from Cleveland would say something like that. You know, it's no wonder that I was twelve before I learned that 'damn Yankee' is two words."

"Ouch!" Jack laughed. "That's pretty good, a little insulting perhaps, but good."

"Yeah, but be careful, Jocelyn," quipped Spencer. He pointed to his ball cap, "You're outnumbud heah."

"OK, guys, lunch is over." Debbie said, brimming with enthusiasm. "Jack, grab the climbing gear. All of you follow me."

"So, what do you think? Safe enough?" Debbie wanted Jack's opinion of the anchoring setup she'd constructed for their cliff descent.

Her climbing partner nodded in approval as he walked around the two large boulders Debbie had selected. Straps of webbing were wrapped around each, and they led to loops through which carabiners could be used to attach a rope or harness. The rope itself was 10 mm in diameter, professional grade and had to be at least 70 meters long. "Nice rope," was all Jack could think to say. "Must have set you back a bit, three hundred bucks at least."

"Almost," she replied. "As a certified instructor I get a substantial discount, but, yeah, it's a good one."

Jack began to step into one of the harnesses. Spencer and Jocelyn stood by, watching silently. Marcie was fascinated. She regarded his harness with a mixture of curiosity and awe. Dangling from loops situated around the waist band were dozens of pieces of hardware that clanked and jingled while he fiddled with the adjustment straps. "I recognize the carabiners," she observed, "but what are those?" She pointed to pairs of carabiners linked by short lengths of webbing.

"Those are called 'quick draws.' They're used as guides. One beener attaches to an anchor point, a piton or a cam for example, and you feed the climbing rope through the other. If you're free-climbing you should set as many anchors as you can. If you fall you're going to drop twice the distance to the last one you've set before the rope goes taut. Trust me, it can really get your attention if you free fall more than about thirty feet, especially if you're using an old rope that's lost its elasticity."

"Cool! And what are those funny looking things with springs and jaws?"

Jack looked approvingly at the items in question. "It looks like Debbie's invested in some pretty nice protection devices. Most of my climbing experience has involved top roping." He shrugged. "She must do a lot of sport climbing."

"What do you mean by protection devices? You mean like condoms?" The descriptions of the equipment had attracted the attention of Jocelyn and Spencer. It was Jocelyn who posed the risqué question.

"Now, Joselyn, do those look like condoms to you?" Debbie laughed. "They're for fall protection, gizmos that wedge into cracks in the rock to serve as anchors. I'm going to set a few for our climb back out later today.

"Okay, so here's the general plan for our trip down and up this cliff." Debbie made sure she had everyone's undivided attention before she continued. "For the climb down the cliff, Jack will belay us. There will be some slack in the rope, but in case of a fall it will go taut immediately. Jack will feed it out as needed. In climbing parlance it's called 'top roping with belay from above.' Once we've gone down safely, Jack will rappel down. I'm going to practice free climbing on my way out, hence the need for me to set protection. Once I'm back on top, I'll anchor myself there and belay the rest of you when you climb up." She sat on a rock and stepped through the leg loops of her harness. As she cinched it around her waist and legs she explained in detail what she was doing. "Spencer, there's one important point that I want to emphasize because you're male. The leg bands should be cinched tight against the inside of each thigh, not so tight that they impede circulation, but tight without much slack. In the event of a fall you don't want the family jewels getting caught underneath them. That might be a tad painful."

Jack added more advice. "And, Spence, make sure your pants are loose between the loops. Otherwise, if you fall, the leg loops will pull the fabric tight. I had that happen once; I walked bowlegged for a week."

Debbie untied a small pair of shoes from her harness and, with considerable effort, pulled them on. She then stood and walked in tight circles, wiggling her toes until the shoes conformed to the shape of her feet like a pair of custom made gloves. "Why the ballet slippehs?" asked Spencer.

"These are climbing shoes," said Debbie. "I don't really need them for what we're about to do, but they can really make a difference. On a difficult climb they help your toes and feet actually grip the rock. It's almost like having an extra set of hands." She then inspected Jack's harness, noting that he had anchored it well and had set up his ATC belay device properly. She then tied the end of the rope to her own harness, describing each step in great detail. "Once I climb down safely I'll step out of the harness and Jack will pull both the rope and harness back up to where he's standing. He will assist each of you as you put the harness on. Jack, make certain you check the tension of both the figure-eight knot and the safety knot before each person begins to climb. Any questions?" She surveyed her group with a critical eye. No one looked bewildered or lost. All seemed eager to get started. She turned to Jack and said, "On belay."

He responded, "Belay on."

Debbie sat at the edge of the cliff, swung both legs into the void and began her descent.

Within minutes she was on the ground and had untethered herself from the rope. Jack dutifully hauled it up and began to help Marcie put on the harness.

Marcie had insisted upon being the next to climb. This was the type of activity she craved, and to have Jack standing so close, giving her his complete attention, was a wonderful bonus. When she was prepped, she took a deep breath, grabbed a solid rock outcrop with both hands and lowered her left foot onto a well-positioned basalt nub.

She continued to descend while concentrating on the climbing tips Debbie had given to them earlier: "Always try to support yourself at three points—using two hands and a foot for example. Only then should you reach forward with the fourth appendage. Use your legs as much as possible for support; if you must transfer your weight to your arms, do it with elbows straight—hang from your shoulders—otherwise your biceps will tire and cramp. Finally, keep your center of gravity as close to the cliff as possible, don't stick your butt out away from the rock." Marcie contemplated the advice as she reached out with her left hand and hooked her fingers into a small crack. Pressing her belly against the rock she slid her right foot over to the diagonal fissure that ran down through the wall. The large crack afforded a myriad of good climbing holds and within a minute she was standing on level ground, beaming from ear to ear.

Debbie gave her a high five. "Nice climb, Marcie. You looked great up there. For someone who's never done this before you exhibited phenomenal technique. You're a natural, my dear; if you enjoy this, and if you practice, you can become really good."

Marcie didn't need much in the way of encouragement. She was hooked. Visions of her and Jack climbing together as a couple, with the occasional romantic interlude taking place between climbs, occupied her mind as Jocelyn prepared to descend.

The older girl looked awkward as she picked her way down. Several times while she was still in the higher, more difficult part of the route, she leaned back to rest letting Jack support her with the rope. Marcie had never allowed that to happen; she had negotiated the climb by herself; the rope had been slack the entire time. When Jocelyn was standing beside her, Debbie gave her the obligatory thumbs up and complemented her on a job well done. In effect, she'd done very well for a neophyte. Debbie was pleased but made the mistake of referring to the extraordinary skill level demonstrated by Marcie. "When we climb out, watch what Marcie and I do. I want you to take note of how we control our bodies, press our hips against the rock and use our legs to climb. It makes all the difference in the world."

Jocelyn bristled at what she considered to be criticism rather than helpful advice. "Yeah? Well don't forget, Debbie, some of us have more developed hips than others. That makes it harder for us to get the hang of things."

Debbie knew the comment was meant as an insult to Marcie, an uncalled for reference to her youth and lack of physical maturity. Hurtful as it was, there wasn't much she could say in reply without making matters worse. In addition, Jocelyn's statement did have an element of truth to it. "Let's get you out of that harness," she said sharply, "it's Spencer's turn."

Spencer was nervous as he began his trip down the cliff side. Initially he watched Jack and listened to his more experienced comrade as he meted out advice about where to place his feet, where the next hand hold was, etc. Once Jack was out of sight, however, Spencer's apprehension level spiked, and he soon made an unfortunate mistake: *he looked down*. Panic set in. He grasped the rope tightly with both hands, and instead of searching for foot holds, he began kicking at the rock trying to find purchase with his boots as though he were trying to run back up.

"Leggo' of the rope, Spence," Jack instructed him, "it's just there for safety. Don't worry, I've got you; you're not going to fall. Put your hands and feet on the rock and climb down."

Spencer wasn't listening. His eyes were tightly shut and his brain was on autopilot, focused on the terror of the moment, unable to function analytically. Debbie had seen this sort of behavior many times during the years she'd been a climbing instructor. She knew that, in some people, the fear of heights is so strong they panic the first time they experience exposure and the concomitant sense of falling. The majority of them come around with experience; their apprehension fades with each climb as they gain trust in the equipment and protocol that go with the sport. A few individuals, however, never get used to it. Climbing just isn't for them. In such cases, their fear is absolutely insurmountable.

Debbie had also, on rare occasions, come across people who are at the opposite end of the fear spectrum. These individuals are so addicted to adrenaline that they can't climb *with* a safety rope. Without the thrill associated with the danger of falling, they don't climb well at all; it takes away their buzz. Sadly, the vast majority of these 'thrill climbers' rarely live past their late twenties or early thirties. Each climb compels them to attempt something even more difficult until, ultimately, the probability of survival drops to zero.

Even if Spencer suffers from mild acrophobia, he should be able to manage this simple climb, Debbie thought. She knew of his heritage, that his grandfather was one of the famous Mohawk high-rise iron workers who played such a pivotal role in creating the New York skyline. The kid certainly had a good genetic lineage for climbing.

"Spencer," she yelled, "Jack is going to lower you about fifteen feet. When he's done you'll be able to stand in a cleft in the rock. Once there, you'll find plenty of hand and foot holds around you. It should be easy to climb down the rest of the way—sort of like climbing down a ladder. There will be nothing to it." She nodded to Jack and he carefully played rope through his belay device until he was ordered to stop.   He could see Debbie, who at the moment was standing out away from the escarpment, but Spencer was beneath him, lost from view. He was also beginning to tire. His harness was firmly anchored through webbing to the rocks behind him, and the climbing rope was well fitted through the ATC and carabiner attached to the harness—Spencer was quite safe; he wouldn't fall. The problem was that Jack was standing, and his legs were supporting much of Spencer's weight. His quads were fatigued because the young man was just hanging in midair, petrified, making no effort to climb.

"Debbie," Jack shouted, "can you get Spence to at least stand somewhere for a minute or two? He's getting heavy."

"Hold on a moment, Jack. I'm coming to help."

Spencer's feet were fewer than twenty feet above where she stood. She knew it was too high for her to safely boulder to where he was. "Bouldering" is rock climbing parlance for practicing one's skills on a cliff or a wall while staying close enough to the ground such that a safety rope isn't needed. But in this instance, with a deep fissure to provide support and fall protection, and with her climbing shoes on, Debbie figured her chances of falling were almost non-existent.

Marcie and Jocelyn watched with a mixture of awe and apprehension as Debbie quickly and effortlessly scrambled to a point immediately below Spencer's feet. "Okay, Spence, let's climb down together." She took his left foot in one hand. "Relax and let me guide your foot to a stable hold." Spencer complied, and soon he supported most of his weight on the rock. "Excellent," Debbie remarked, "Now, let's do the same thing with your other leg." She grasped his other foot and pulled it down towards a nice wide shelf within the large fissure. That action, however, caused Spencer to turn his body and lose his balance. He reacted by kicking down with the foot, crushing Debbie's fingers against the rock. Instinctively she pulled her hand free, but in doing so her weight shifted away from the cliff.

Debbie Holloway let out a brief cry as she fell nearly twenty feet to the ledge below.

"Oh my God! Oh my God!" Jocelyn shrieked as Debbie, hands flailing wildly, plummeted towards the ground. She hit with a thud accompanied by a loud crack, and lay where she fell, crumpled and motionless.

For a split second no one moved. Jack's vantage point didn't permit him a view of events, but Jocelyn's screams left no doubt that something horrific had transpired. "What happened? What's wrong?"

"Debbie's hurt," Marcie yelled in reply.

Jack was overcome by the urge to help, but he had the presence of mind to remain calm and tend to Spencer who, once again, had become little more than dead weight. "Spencer," he said with authority, "get the hell off the rope. Climb down...NOW."

At the sight of Debbie lying motionless below, Spencer's fear disappeared. Adrenaline took control and he nimbly maneuvered down to the ledge. After struggling out of his harness, he moved well off to one side, far away from where Debbie lay, and began to cry. An overwhelming feeling of culpability welled up within him; he was frightened, embarrassed and ashamed because of the predicament he felt he had caused.

When Jack arrived he beheld a sobering scene. Debbie lay where she'd fallen, barely conscious and moaning softly. Marcie knelt beside her, intent in the study of the older woman's injuries. Jocelyn had disappeared, but at the sight of Jack, she stumbled over to where he stood. Her face was ashen. She looked to be in shock, and at the moment was wiping flecks of vomit from around her mouth—part of the lunch she'd lost after having caught sight of Debbie's injuries. Jack patted her shoulder in a gesture of reassurance before walking over to check on Debbie. Marcie saw him coming and stood, motioning him to a place where they could talk and not be overheard by Debbie.

"Is she hurt badly?"

"Yes and no," Marcie replied. The young girl was shaking and scared, but she was fighting to maintain control of her emotions and succeeding admirably well. "When I asked her to move her fingers and toes she did so easily. Her pupils are responsive and both are dilated to the same degree, that's the good news—it appears she isn't suffering from acute brain or spinal injury."

"But?"

"But I can't be sure. She's in an awful lot of pain, Jack. Normally, in a case like this we'd just call the paramedics and be done with it. They would sedate her and splint her for transport to a hospital."

Marcie bit her lip in concentration. As far as she was concerned, Jocelyn and Spencer were out of it. They'd be of little help. She and Jack had to assume the responsibility for Debbie's care. "Her lower right leg is badly broken just above the ankle. The fracture isn't compound, but the ends of the bones are severely displaced." She motioned for him to follow and the two of them returned to Debbie's side.

"Debbie?" Marcie asked. The injured woman looked up at her. The initial trauma of the fall was wearing off; she was in agony, but was lucid, comprehending. "Debbie, we have to get you out of here. Can you move at all?"

"It hurts too much. There's no way I can climb. My leg…" She raised her head slightly and regarded her injured appendage. It was swollen; her foot was canted inward at an unnatural angle, and the end of the tibia pushed outward above the break producing a prominent bulge. She settled back down and murmured, "Oh, God; I'm so stupid. Why did I do that? It was too high…Just get Morgan here. Please. The emergency communicator—it's in my pack. All you have to do is turn it on, push the red button and hit 'send.' Morgan will receive a prerecorded text stating that we have an emergency situation and it will display our exact GPS coordinates."

Jack nodded, "I'm on it." He began to make his way towards the rope.

"Wait," said Marcie. "Before you go can you help us move Debbie to that level place over there?" Enlisting the others to help, they prepared a "bed" near the base of the cliff where she'd be out of the wind. They cleared a spot by brushing away small rocks and pebbles. They then extracted wind-blown sand out of rock crevasses, spreading it around to act as cushioning for their patient. When all was ready they placed jackets under Debbie's torso and legs to act as litters. Then, with two people on either side grasping the coats firmly, they awkwardly, but successfully, transferred Debbie, teeth gritted against the pain, to her new bed. As they set her down, Jocelyn's knee accidentally bumped Debbie's right shoulder. The woman uttered a sharp cry of pain.

Jocelyn recoiled defensively, "What did I do? I didn't mean to hurt you. I swear!"

Debbie's reaction puzzled Marcie. Earlier she'd done a thorough accounting of Debbie's injuries. The woman had a laceration of the scalp which had bled profusely but didn't appear to be too serious. As far as she could tell it wasn't associated with a severe concussion. She also had either sprained or broken her left wrist and had several bruised ribs. But by far the main concern was her lower right leg. The latter was potentially life threatening if she didn't get proper care soon.

Now, however, there appeared to be something she'd missed, an injury to the *right* arm. Marcie carefully poked and prodded Debbie's arm starting at the wrist and moving upward. All was fine until she reached the shoulder. At that point Debbie winced in agony. Carefully pulling Debbie's shirt sleeve aside, Marcie saw the end of the clavicle jutting out.

"The fall dislocated your shoulder," Marcie observed. She studied the arm closely, feeling all around the joint. "It's not that bad. In fact, it's something I can fix. Do you feel up to it?"

The older woman nodded and looked at Marcie pleadingly. "Will it hurt much?" She had resigned herself completely to the care of this fifteen-year-old girl, a child really, whom she'd known only for a few weeks. There was something about her, an air of confidence, that was reassuring not just to Debbie but to the others as well. Marcie Van Wormer was incredibly well versed in first aid, a godsend given their perilous situation.

"It won't be painful if you force the arm to relax. That's the key." Without waiting for a reply, Marcie began to massage Debbie's neck and shoulder muscles helping to relieve tension. "Just relax," she repeated softly as she held the upper arm firmly against the woman's side. Then, with the elbow bent at ninety degrees, she carefully rotated the lower arm away from Debbie's torso while pulling gently downward. The ball of the humorous slid neatly back into place. The other students gawked in amazement.

Debbie smiled for the first time since the fall. "That was awesome, Marcie. The pain's almost completely gone. Where the heck did you learn to do that?"

The girl blushed. She was elated at what she'd just done, even more so than her patient and the others around her. "I was playing in a soccer game last year and one of the girls on the other team fell and dislocated her shoulder. My dad was watching in the stands." She shrugged as though it were no big deal. "I watched him pop it back in."

"So, your dad's what? A paramedic? A physician?"

"He's an orthopod, you know, an orthopedic surgeon—a bone doctor."

Debbie sighed, "We could sure use him right now." She then tried to smile, "but having his daughter here is almost as good."

VIII

I t has to be done, Jack." Marcie and Jack stood just out of earshot of the others. He'd just returned with the day packs they'd left at the top of the cliff.

Jack was frowning. "Can't it wait until her husband gets here? They have real medical facilities at the dig site, you know, an x-ray unit, prescription drugs for the pain...someone with a medical degree." The last comment stung Marcie somewhat but she knew what he meant. The kinds of decisions she was making could get her into messy legal trouble. Only trained health professionals are permitted to practice serious medicine, and even they are professionally and legally bound to follow rules for standard care. But she also knew that "good samaritan" exceptions existed for emergency situations, and their present predicament certainly qualified as such. Besides, she was right, dammit! Debbie's leg was in bad shape. Further damage would assuredly result if they didn't do something.

Tears welled in her eyes, "I don't want to do it any more than you do, but she's going to lose her lower leg if we don't at least try." The conviction in her tone was enough to persuade her colleague. They assembled the other students at Debbie's bedside.

"Debbie," Marcie began in a soft voice, "we're going to have to set your leg."

Surprisingly, her patient nodded grimly. She knew enough first aid to know that Marcie's diagnosis was probably right.

"It's gonna hurt like a sunofabitch, but afterwards, I mean, if things go well, then you'll feel better." She attempted to sound upbeat and confident, but underneath that façade, Marcie was scared to death. She had watched her father set bones in the emergency room at Albany Medical Center. Because of his stature as a senior physician, he'd secured special permission for her to attend. All of those patients were trauma cases, like Debbie, but those people had been stable and sedated, and x-ray facilities in the same wing of the hospital were available to verify that the broken ends of bone had been set into proper alignment. What they were about to attempt, here in this extremely remote place, was risky and could potentially do more harm than good. That knowledge weighed heavily on Marcie. She also knew that the procedure would probably require more physical strength than she possessed. Jack had reluctantly agreed to help.

Like most parents, Steven Van Wormer doted on his daughter. Years earlier, when at the tender age of only ten or eleven she had exhibited interest in what he did for a living, he had begun to provide opportunities for her to learn, first hand, the intricacies of the discipline of orthopedics. He'd provided her with a lab coat, replete with an embroidered nametag, to wear whenever she assisted him in his office. Her tasks ranged from the mundane, such as handing clipboards laden with forms to patients for gathering medical histories, to more advanced jobs like mixing up resin or plaster preparations for making casts. Steven's rationale for doing this transcended his desire just to spend quality time with her. It wouldn't be long before she attended college and began contemplating career paths. If in fact she still wanted to pursue work in either this or any other medical specialty, he wanted her to go forth with eyes wide open, knowing full well what lay ahead of her. He felt he owed her that much, but he had never considered that the simple training and experience he'd given her so far might mean the difference between life and death for either Marcie or someone else.

The setting of Debbie's shoulder had inspired an extraordinary change in attitude in both Spencer and Jocelyn. Both were now offering to provide assistance wherever they might be needed. The initial shock of viewing Debbie's injuries had worn off, to be replaced by a determined resolve to get through their current predicament. In short, all four students were rising to the occasion; they were imbued with a professional resolve to conquer circumstance and to help one another to survive.

Jack had taken his pocket knife and cut out the metal stays of the large internal frame pack that contained their climbing gear. Due to the absence of timber in their present locale, these were the only structural materials that could serve as splints for Debbie's leg. Marcie placed an extra T-shirt and a length of parachute cord from her own pack beside the metal braces, and nodded to the others when all was ready.

Spencer had hold of Debbie's left leg and Jocelyn supported her under her left shoulder. Debbie bit down on an extra pair of socks as Marcie took charge.

"On my count: Ready? One...Two..."

On 'three' Jack began to pull steadily on Debbie's foot. Debbie unleashed an unholy scream that was, thankfully, muffled by the sock. "That's it, Jack, steady pressure," Marcie said. She had one hand on Debbie's foot and the other around her lower leg, monitoring the positions of the bones as they moved. Once Jack had pulled the ankle free, Marcie turned the foot to bring the bones into alignment. "Okay, I think that's got it," she said with excitement, "hold it right there, Jack." She quickly wrapped the shirt around the leg as padding, then applied the splints, winding paracord around everything to hold it all in place. After what seemed like an eternity, but was actually less than three minutes, Marcie relaxed and sat back to review her handiwork. The leg looked straight and reasonably normal. There was the inevitable swelling, of course, but, most importantly, the bulging end of the tibia was no longer visible. Based upon appearance and the way the limb felt, Marcie had successfully set her first displaced fracture.

It was then that she shed her first tears of relief.

Marcie couldn't stop crying. Collapsing into a heap, the poor girl just let it all out, her slight figure trembling uncontrollably. The release of tension was so overwhelming that she had just lost it. The boys sat still, dumbfounded at the sight of this remarkable young individual who had only moments earlier been so composed and stoic. But Jocelyn understood. She held Marcie and spoke quietly to her, calming her down until her cries became little more than whimpers. Soon the shaking ceased entirely. "That had to be the bravest, most courageous act I've ever seen, Marcie. You were great, really great!"

"The unit seems to be working well; it displays our GPS coordinates but it keeps giving me the message 'satellite unavailable.' I guess we just have to keep trying," Jack said. He'd again turned on the satellite communicator to try to send for help. He shrugged, "Debbie said this thing uses the GPS constellation to derive our location, but it uses the Iridium satellites to send the message. Apparently the Iridium guys are finicky. They fly in low orbits and coverage can sometimes be sporadic." He replaced the device into Debbie's pack and sat with the others.

"I overheard Debbie telling Morgan we'd be gone for several days," Jocelyn offered. "Today's Tuesday, right? Unless they get a call for help, they won't come looking for us until Friday at the earliest." She turned to Marcie, "If it comes to that, waiting for three more days, well...what will happen to Debbie?"

The question had been on everyone's mind since Jack had announced his inability to get a message through. It was certain they'd have to spend at least one night where they were, possibly more. None of the students harbored much concern for their own comfort; Debbie's health was foremost in everyone's mind. They were currently conferring far enough away from her to allow them to speak bluntly about her condition.

"It all depends upon the extent of any internal injuries she may have," Marcie said. "Of course she's in a lot of pain as well, but we can control that to some extent. I brought a full range of analgesics in my first aid kit. I got her started on ibuprofen a few minutes ago and she's resting as well as can be expected. To answer your question, Jocelyn, I think her chances of survival are good, but she's going to be awfully uncomfortable, and I'm still really concerned about that leg."

The air was noticeably cooler now that late afternoon had arrived. The Sun would soon set behind the ridge that marked the caldera rim. Jack stood and held out his fist at arm's length. Pointing it in the direction of the Sun, he moved his arm slowly downward and then looked at his watch. Satisfied with what he'd done he began to put on one of the climbing harnesses.

Jocelyn gave him a questioning look. "I give up. What are you doing?"

"Someone has to retrieve our camping supplies from the boat."

"Let me go with you." It was Spencer, of all people, who had stepped forward. "You're gonna need help carrying all that gear."

"With all due respect, Spence, I have to go alone. Climbing without a belay is tricky—it takes practice. We can't afford to have any more casualties. I'm only going to bring back what we need to spend the night. It should take me about three hours if I leave right now; there won't be enough light after that."

Nods of agreement passed among the group. All knew that Jack was right.

"That scene where you stuck your fist in the air," Jocelyn repeated, "what was that all about? Some sort of Sun worshipping ritual?"

Jack smiled, "That's how I know how much time we have before the Sun passes behind that mountain." He pointed to the large spire off to the northwest. "One's fist, extended at arm's length, subtends an angle of about ten degrees, give or take. I was just measuring the angular distance along the Sun's path between it and that mountain." When he received questioning looks, he elaborated. "It's easy really, crude but effective. Because of the Earth's rotation, the Sun appears to move fifteen degrees every hour—that's easy to get, you simply divide 360 degrees by twenty-four hours to get fifteen. Fifteen degrees corresponds to one-and-a-half fist widths per hour. The distance from the Sun to the hill is four-and-a-half fist widths—three hours." He shrugged. "I gotta go."

"Prove to me you'll be safe," Jocelyn said. "How can we be sure you won't fall like Debbie did?"

Jack displayed a strange device that was attached to his harness. "I'll be roped up through this. It's a self-arresting cam; it acts like a one way valve. As I climb, I'll pull the rope through this way, but if I fall..." He yanked the rope the other way and the jaw on the device clamped down.

Within seconds, Jack seemed to be attached to the rock face. He ascended with almost no effort. Marcie and Jocelyn were particularly impressed with what they saw, in more ways than one. Strong hands locked into the smallest of cracks in the rock as powerful muscles in his legs and back propelled him upwards. He reminded them of Spiderman, except this wasn't a movie, it was 100% real. The young man's strength to body-weight ratio was enormous and his climbing technique flawless. No wonder Debbie had wanted to go climbing with this guy, Marcie thought. And, she reminded herself, allowing a slight smile to cross her lips, this was definitely a sport she would be really good at someday.

Jack returned as darkness fell. He was bone tired. The second hike from the beach up to the ridge, heavily laden with supplies, had totally gassed him. He'd left the tents behind, they were just too heavy, but he'd brought a rain fly so that they could at least construct a waterproof canopy. Three bulky sleeping bags and a heavy pack full of food rounded out his haul. Into the stuff sack of each bag he'd thought to include various items of warm clothing scavenged from the individual packs they'd left in the boat.

Jocelyn and Spencer engineered a clever shelter by tying one edge of the rain fly to protuberances on the cliff face and then weighing down the opposite side with rocks from the ledge. They packed one sleeping bag around Debbie and lay the others out onto the ground for the rest of the party to lie on. After a dinner of cold, canned beans they donned all the clothing they had and then huddled together for the night.

No one got much sleep. Cold, humid air with temperatures in the low forties settled in when the Sun went down, sucking heat from their bodies. A campfire would have taken away much of the chill. Marcie had brought waterproof matches, but there was no fuel nearby: no timber, no straw, not even dried moss, nothing but rock—everywhere. In the early hours of the morning it rained, a slow but steady drizzle that gave new meaning to the word "clammy." Long before Mr. Sun made his reappearance over the peaks to the northeast, all of the students were up, shivering, waiting and hoping for warmth and daylight.

"Lord, what I wouldn't give for a cup of hot coffee," sighed Jocelyn.

"More like hot chocolate," Spencer retorted, "'an some scrambled eggs wit' bacon, buttered toast 'n jam."

"Don't forget the grits."

"What's a grit?" Spencer asked with a grin.

Jocelyn mockingly rolled her eyes, "You mean your cousin Vinnie didn't tell you? Goodness me, you have a lot to learn about good oldfashioned southern cookin', young feller."

A moan from Debbie brought all levity to a halt. Concern for her predicament roared back into the minds of the others. Jack arose and pulled the satellite communicator from Debbie's pack. He went outside the shelter to attempt another rescue request. The rain had abated and a soft yellow glow to his left heralded the arrival of morning and an end to their miserable night. He returned moments later shaking his head. "Same message...'satellite unavailable.' I've been thinking..."

"Uh oh," Jocelyn laughed.

"Even if Morgan brings a rescue crew, it won't be easy lifting Debbie up that cliff. They won't have the equipment needed for an alpine-type extraction. As soon as it's light enough, I'm going to reconnoiter to the southeast." He pointed towards fog-shrouded hills nearly concealed from view. "When I brought the boat around to head in to the beach, I looked further down the coast. The hills there didn't seem to be as high. If there's another sheltered cove or beach down that way, maybe we can find a route to get there, one where we can carry Debbie without resorting to ropes and tackle."

"You're right." Marcie had been attending to Debbie, but had overheard Jack's plan. "Her leg still hurts pretty badly but it's doing well. She's able to wiggle her toes and it doesn't look any worse than it did yesterday. She's hanging in there, but with those really short splints we had to use, lifting her up that cliff is out of the question—too much chance it will dislocate again. As if that weren't enough, her ribs are what's bothering her now, they make breathing painful. We're going to need a real stretcher when it comes time to move her."

"I'm going with you, Jack," Jocelyn interjected. "I won't be of much use if I stay here. Plus, someone has to keep you out of trouble."

"That makes tree of us. You're not gonna leave me heah. I'm comin' wit' you too." Spencer was already shouldering his day pack. He was wracked with guilt. No matter how much the others tried to console him, he was firmly convinced that their present circumstances were entirely due to his fear of heights.

Jack was anxious to leave, so the three of them quickly prepared packs for a day trip through the island. Jocelyn packed what few things she had and turned a sympathetic eye to Marcie. Sensing the inner turmoil that was bothering the young girl, she took her aside, brushed away a tear and gave her a big hug.

"I know what you're going through, 'doc." Ever since she'd set Debbie's leg and shoulder, the other students affectionately referred to Marcie as 'doc.' "You've been the glue that has held us together through this ordeal and you're the only one who has the knowledge and skill to look after Debbie. I just...well, I want you to know how proud I am of you, and I swear, once we get out of this, we'll all come back and explore this rock together. Okay?" Marcie smiled in gratitude. "Oh, one more thing: I promise I'll look after Jack—make sure he comes back to you in one piece."

Marcie blushed crimson. She tried to sound indifferent, as though that last comment meant nothing. "Before you go I've got some things you should take with you." She retrieved her pack and began extracting items from the side pockets. "Here are some matches. They're waterproof and won't be of any use to Debbie and me. Also, take these water purification tablets. The snow melt up here is really clean. I filled my water bottle last night and drank the whole thing with no ill effects. You guys should take these, though, just in case. And here," she handed Jocelyn six energy bars, "if you have to hike any great distance you'll need fuel. Deb and I can subsist on the cans of beans that are left. The energy bars are light, easy to carry."

Jocelyn thanked her and rushed to catch up with Spencer and Jack, who had nearly disappeared into the morning mist.

A steep but manageable downslope greeted the three students as they departed their cliff-side encampment. The terrain to the east, the direction in which they had intended to go, was strewn with large boulders, forcing them to go, for the time being, along a route to the southwest. Visibility was poor. Light mist at higher elevations gradually gave way to dense fog as they moved downhill. Water from numerous seeps and rivulets flowed from the high peaks that formed the rim of the volcano, sourced by extensive snow melt. As they dropped in elevation, these trickles merged into a single stream that they followed, enjoying the sound it made as it gurgled and wound its way down through the rocks. Within half a mile from where they'd spent the night, barely 400 feet lower in elevation, many of the rocks bore a covering of lichen and moss, and further on, below an impressive waterfall, the banks of the stream were choked with small ferns.

"These aren't the kinds of plants one expects to find in the arctic," Jocelyn remarked. She bent down to examine the first flora they'd seen since Olafsvik. "I just spent half a semester in biology identifying plants," she added absentmindedly as she carefully counted the delicate leafy branches on a stem. "My teacher is a botanist and has a real hard-on for keying stuff like this." She stood and shook her head. "There appear to be at least three distinct varieties here, but none of them match anything we studied in class." Taking her cell phone from her pack, she snapped a quick photo.

Spencer shed his pack and took off the light jacket he'd worn since he'd first set foot on the island. He tied it around his waist and proceeded to fill his canteen from the clear stream that fed the deep pool at his feet. "I think these plants have been here for a while. They dint' just start growin' two months ago when winter ended. It's incredible. I'm sweatin' from the heat 'an we're only a little ways from snow 'an ice up on the mountains."

"Spencer's right," said Jocelyn. "It's got to be seventy degrees here, and muggy," she sloughed out of her coat as well, "and it's still early in the morning. I know of places like this where the climate changes rapidly with altitude. My family took a vacation to Colorado two years ago. We were in Colorado Springs sometime in June and it was hotter than blazes, almost ninety. Anyway, my dad wanted to climb Pike's Peak, so he and I left my mother and brother at the hotel and drove to one of the trailheads. We never made it to the top. A couple thousand feet from the summit it started raining and within minutes it had turned to snow. I was in a T-shirt and almost froze.

"But the elevation change on that trip was maybe four or five *thousand* feet. This is weird; Marcie and Debbie can't be more than a thousand feet above us—probably less. And it was really cold on the beach, and that's lower than we are now. Something more is going on here."

Jack's attention was split between what the others were saying and what was happening above them. He had his arm extended once again, fist in the air, alternately pointing it towards the Sun and glancing at his watch.

Spencer was intrigued, "Yo, Jack, what are you doin' now?"

"Trying to determine where we're going.   I don't want to alarm you guys," he smiled, "but can you tell where we are?"

Spencer looked around and realized what Jack was saying. They were surrounded by fog. The mountains had completely disappeared from view; none of the landmarks they'd familiarized themselves with were accessible now. Mild panic came over Spencer as the fact dawned on him that he had lost his sense of direction; he was completely befuddled. If necessity compelled him to return to the beach where they'd landed he wouldn't have the slightest idea how to get there. Jocelyn momentarily stopped thinking about climate and listened to Jack.

"Last night I used the angle between the Sun and the point where it would set to determine time—the number of hours until 'sunset.' Now I'm using the same technique in reverse; I'm determining azimuth, you know, direction, from the time of day. We don't have a compass with us and because of the fog we can't use terrestrial landmarks to great effect. Like blue water sailors in the days before LORAN and GPS, all we have to navigate by are celestial objects, basically the Sun, Moon, and stars."

The only object available at the moment was, of course, the Sun. Because of the dense cloud layer overhead, Jack could look directly at it without hurting his eyes. It was a nearly perfectly round, glowing orb, hanging over them like a divine beacon, offering to guide them through the unknown.

"Knowing what time it is is really the key. Our local time is almost exactly one hour earlier than Greenwich Time and I've set my watch accordingly. I know that at local noon the Sun will be due south, and I know from my watch how many hours we have until noon. That number of hours, times fifteen, is the number of degrees, along the Sun's path of travel, that the Sun needs to move until it is due south of us. I'm using my extended fist, my handy built-in angle measuring device, to find the south point. Once we know that, we can face in any direction, estimate the number of horizontal degrees from south, and that's our compass bearing."

His companions were impressed. "So, fearless leader, which way do we go?" asked Jocelyn.

He pointed slightly to the left of the Sun. "That's where we want to go, but the landscape is too rugged." He shrugged, "I say we follow this stream until we find a way to circle back to the east. If we don't catch a break soon, we'll have no choice but to turn back. It will also mean we'll have to hoist Debbie up that cliff to get back to the dig," he added ominously.

The party trudged on. Small streams continuously joined the one they were following until it justifiably could be called a river. They soon came to a deep gorge where the water became a torrent of foam and spray, crashing against sheer cliffs on either side. Forced to backtrack, they searched for a crossing to the other side. Near a large boulder, where the stream abruptly altered course, they came to a suitable spot; a log jam, of sorts, had formed a bridge. Bunches of something resembling scaly bamboo had been uprooted and swept downstream to form a dam.

Once they were on the far side, they stopped to drink and to refill their water bottles. The combination of heat and humidity was taking its toll. All three were perspiring freely; hydration had become a central issue.

Jocelyn again took a few moments to survey the strange plants they'd encountered. "These small trees, or whatever they are, don't look like anything I've ever seen, not even in books. Look at this," she pulled a log from the jumble of sticks at the water's edge and held it up for inspection. "It's got a bark layer that overlays dense wood, but the interior is pithy, almost hollow. And see these segments as you move along the trunk? At every node there are these skinny leaves, and this bushy part on top has some sort of seed cone. It's just...bizzaro."

"Didn't you say it's some type of bamboo?" Jack asked.

"Parts of it kinda look like bamboo, but that's deceiving; I don't think they're related at all. If I had to guess, I'd say—now don't laugh—it may be some sort of strange conifer. Who knows?"

Spencer dipped his bandana in the stream and wrapped it, soaking wet, around his head before replacing his Yankee's cap. The others took the hint and took similar measures to stay cool. Jack jokingly challenged his colleagues to a wet T-shirt contest and immediately declared Jocelyn the winner. She gave him a deprecating look and shoved him none-to-gently down the trail.

Gradually the slope of the ground lessened and the rushing, churning stream turned into a lazy, flowing river. Ferns lined the banks, lush and verdant, a seriously out-of-place landscape at seventy-six degrees north latitude. As one moved away from the mud adjacent to the river, strange looking trees appeared, some of them soaring to heights of nearly 100 feet. The going was easiest in a narrow zone between the wet, fern beds along the river and the sandy soil where larger plants took over. They made excellent progress, but all of them knew that they weren't on a mission to explore the island. Somehow they had to cross the river again and wind their way to the east, to find a route to the coast where they could safely transport Debbie for pickup. It was now almost noon. In another hour or so they would probably have to turn back, their brief excursion having failed.

Straight ahead they could see an upcoming break in the tree canopy. It suggested a widening in the river. "Let's see what's around the next bend," Jack said. "If we don't find any way to get across the water, I vote we turn back. We can load up with that 'bamboo' stuff Jocelyn was so jazzed about and use it to make a bosun's chair to lift Debbie up the cliff. It might also make good firewood. I personally don't want to spend another night like the last one."

The others concurred. Jack took the lead, followed by Spencer. Jocelyn, more interested in plant life than exploration, brought up the rear. As they entered a small grove of what looked like palm trees, a strange buzzing sound could be heard. It grew in intensity as they wound their way through the trees, eventually becoming loud enough to drown out the sound of the river.

"What the heck is that?" Spencer asked. "It sounds like an engine, like someone's runnin' a lawn mowah or a chain saw."

They stopped and looked around, bewildered and somewhat apprehensive. What could possibly make that kind of noise? Without warning, something slammed into Jocelyn's shoulder. She stumbled and fell, unhurt, but startled. "Oh my God, something hit me," she cried. Clambering back to her feet, she brushed dirt off of her hands and the knees of her jeans. "It felt like...I don't know, a model airplane, like one of those drones."

"It was a bird, I think," said Jack, "It looked big too, like an eagle or a heron."

"You're both wrong," noted Spencer. As if on cue another one flew by, passing inches over their heads. "It was a dragonfly, a great big dragonfly, with a wingspan of about two feet."

IX

Marcie sat staring at Debbie. The older woman had suffered through a bad night. Every time she moved, the pain in her leg and ribs woke her up, and every time that happened Marcie wound up at her side administering pain medication when appropriate and just holding her hand or making her more comfortable when little else could be done. Finally, just before the Sun poked over the ridge to the northeast, Debbie had slept.

After Debbie finally quieted down, Marcie had dozed off. It was dew dripping from the edge of their shelter that had woken her. She regarded her patient with concern. Debbie's care was her primary responsibility, but she found her thoughts constantly shifting to her friends who had yet to return. They'd been gone for several hours. It shouldn't take very long to explore along the coast for a mile or two. She began to fear that something may have happened to them.

"Have I been asleep long?"

Marcie smiled at the remark. Color had returned to Debbie's face. She looked much improved after having gotten some rest. "About four hours," Marcie replied.

"I feel so much better," said Debbie. "The ibuprofen you gave me helped enormously." She glanced around the shelter, "Any word from the others?"

"Naw, they haven't been gone very long." Marcie tried to sound upbeat, "I don't expect them to return until late today, maybe not even until tomorrow."

The same worrisome thought was on both their minds: Jocelyn, Jack and Spencer might have to spend the night 'out there' somewhere with no shelter and no sleeping bags. They had to be cold and miserable right now. They hadn't taken much warm clothing. Debbie's brow knitted in concern, "God, I hope they don't freeze out there." Her voice suddenly broke and she sobbed, "I am so sorry for what I've put you all through. This side trip was a terrible idea. If anything happens to any of you I'll never forgive myself."

Marcie didn't want Debbie to get upset. Her patient's level of pain and discomfort seemed to be highly dependent on her emotional state. "Nonsense, Debbie," she said firmly. "The four of us are fine, and before you know it, you'll be sitting by a fire with Morgan by your side and we'll be talking about the most exciting experience of our lives. Everything is going to be just fine."

"I suppose. I shouldn't underestimate their ingenuity. Perhaps I shouldn't tell you this, but I spoke with many of your teachers during the selection process. I wanted to know how creative, self-reliant and hard-working all of you were. Aside from a few uncertainties, none of which had to do with you, we knew we had chosen a talented group. Your colleagues are a resourceful bunch. If they get too cold, they'll probably just find some grotto and huddle together to keep warm."

"I know if I were with them, Jack wouldn't get cold," Marcie said wistfully. "My problem is: I bet he wouldn't even notice."

"I don't blame you for having a crush on him. I would too if I were in your shoes."

"He's so different from the guys in my school. I mean he's kind, considerate, funny, and it's all I can do to keep from running my fingers through that gorgeous curly hair of his. And let's not forget those pecks, deltoids and glutes...he has the cutest glutes! I just wish I had boobs. He might take me seriously then." She sat back and pouted. "I suffer from the curse of 'retarded development.'"

"You're a beautiful young woman, Marcie, fit and well proportioned. Having big boobs isn't important. Heck, look at me, I'm not exactly well endowed. Morgan loves me for who I am, he doesn't give a damn about my bra size."

"Well yours are a lot bigger than mine, and that's not all. I've been getting my monthly scourge for less than a year. I'm the last one in my class to 'graduate into womanhood' as the saying goes. Guys like Jack aren't going to take me seriously if I look like a little kid."

Debbie winced as she turned to face her charge. "Listen; don't be in such a hurry to grow up. You'll get there in due time. I know it's difficult, but in a few years this won't matter."

"That's what Gail, my stepmom, says. She's sweet and tries to help, but it's really hard for me to talk to her about stuff like this. I don't know why exactly; maybe it's because she and my dad are, you know..." Marcie made a circle with her left thumb and forefinger and slid her right middle finger in and out.

Debbie laughed. "Marcie, you don't have to be so graphic. Just say it: they have sex. In case you aren't aware, most couples do that. Why should it matter?"

"When you're intimate like that with somebody, you tend to talk about private stuff. At least I think you do. That's what Sharon Pendergast says. She's done it already, or at least she says she has. I don't want my issues with puberty to be THE topic of conversation in my parents' bedroom."

"I think it's time to change the subject," Debbie said. "What do you think of Spencer?"

The question took Marcie by surprise. "He's okay I suppose, kinda hard to talk to..." She reflected on their conversation in the bus while en route to Olafsvik. "...and he can be a real jerk at times."

Debbie smiled, "I can imagine." Her tone softened, "Do you think you could ever have romantic feelings for him?"

"I don't know. He's cute, but...why? What do you know?"

"I can tell he really likes you. He's constantly looking your way when your back is turned. He likes you, but he's too shy to let you know."

"Get outta town! Really?!"

"Yes, really."

Marcie looked stunned.

"Is something wrong, Marcie?"

No, no. Nothing's wrong. It's just, holy cow, I've never had a guy take an interest in me before. What do I do?"

"The best advice I can give is to be yourself. He'll come around eventually if his feelings are genuine. Once the ice is broken it'll be easy to get to know one another." Debbie felt like a school girl gossiping with one of her old friends. Perhaps it wasn't right, talking about Spencer behind his back, but Marcie was a good kid. She would handle the information in an appropriate way, and right now her young caregiver needed the emotional lift.

Whap! The wing of another giant bug hit Spencer in the face.

"Ow! You bastehd." The blow knocked both his glasses and his cap from his head.

Jocelyn had squatted down and was covering her head with both hands, playing defense. Jack, stunned at the flock of huge insects coming from all directions, took an offensive approach; he was trying to swat them. One lucky blow landed squarely to the head of a fly, causing it to change its flight path but otherwise having little effect.

"I'm gettin' outta heah." Spencer had had enough. He ducked low and blindly rushed through the trees while flailing his arms to keep the insects away. First Jocelyn, then Jack, adopted Spencer's technique, and soon all three were out of the palm forest and free of the swarm of monster flies.

"Boy, there's something about those trees they really like," Jack said. The relief in his tone was profound. "On our way back, what say we avoid this place?"

Jocelyn wasn't listening. Apparently she had already dismissed the episode with the dragonflies and was bent over a small tree of the type that populated the grove they'd just left.

"See this cone type thingy?" She pointed to a reddish-brown mass in the crown of the plant. "There's a sticky, smelly sap around its base. That's what's got those dragonflies so hot-to-trot." She sniffed and wrinkled her nose, then backed away to study the leaves and trunk. "And this is no palm tree," she said with excitement, "it's some sort of cycad."

"You must be part dragonfly," Jack quipped, "that plant's got you pretty excited too."

"Oh, stick a sock in it, Jack; this is important. Cycads are rare. Even though quite a few species are known, they aren't found in large numbers. They're prominent in the geologic record, but encountering one today constitutes a significant find."

"How come you know so much about these things?"

"I told you; I just learned about them last semester in my biology class."

She thought about Mr. Powell and the horrible cheating episode in which she'd played a leading role. Social problems aside, Jocelyn had to admit that Powell was a wonderful teacher. At times he'd captivated her with his lectures. His enthusiasm for such mundane subjects as lichens, mosses and, yes, even cycads, was infectious, and she felt very fortunate to have learned so much about such a large segment of life on the planet. Her hand ran to the top of the crown and fingered a sharp spike that projected from its center. "I've never heard of an example like this," she mused, speaking more to herself than to the others, "anyone unlucky enough to fall on this guy would have a really bad day."

The three of them continued ahead. Although the thick, humid air was oppressive, visibility had greatly improved. Gone were the mist and fog. All the clouds were above them now that they'd reached the valley floor. Low, heavily forested hills lay far off in the distance, well beyond the clearing to which they were headed. Spencer took the lead. An adventurous spirit had taken hold of him. Wary of the airborne dragonfly threat, he kept a sharp eye out for cycads and hiked through a sandy area populated by another type of tree, one with distinctive, flat, tongue-shaped leaves. Climbing a small knoll, they finally saw the reason for the break in the trees. The vista gave them pause.

It was a huge lake, a widening in the river at least half a mile wide and perhaps twice as long. The water here was a deep greenish-blue. Its surface was like glass, undisturbed by even a hint of a breeze. Thick vegetation lined most of the shoreline. They recognized large patches of the 'bamboo' that they'd seen at higher elevations, as well as several more stands of cycads, presumably laced with swarms of dragonflies. Dark green patches of taller trees located further from the water appeared to be coniferous, something they had yet to see up close. Earlier they had detoured around the area where the river ran into the lake, and now, looking back, they saw that it was a delta, the flat valley floor causing the river to branch out into several smaller streams. Jack decided that if they hoped to cross to the other side, the delta would be the place to try. None of the streams seemed to be very deep or fast-moving, and islands of rock and sand with little vegetation lay between them.

Jocelyn, Jack and Spencer plodded through the estuary-like terrain at the head of the lake. The ground alternated between mucky patches laden with ferns, to dry, sandy areas with larger plants, mainly 'bamboo.' Beyond that grew some of the tall conifers they'd seen from the knoll. Spencer led them in a wide arc around a cycad grove before cutting through a stand of tall conifers en route to the river. These were definitely pines. The similarities to trees of North America were apparent, but there were also marked differences. These had short, regularly-spaced branches that ended with large seed cones. Nonetheless, they had familiar-looking needles and they smelled right, having a pungent, pine 'pitch' odor that evoked memories of home in the midst of this strange, alien land.

At the edge of the stream Jack knelt to splash water on his face. They had stopped beside a small pool. "I suggest we cross back where those rocks..." The water in front of him began to boil. Movement just below the surface brought apprehensive looks to each of the students. Their imaginations instantly conjured all sorts of weird thoughts as to its source, but there was little time for speculation. A large, green head suddenly burst into view. Sheets of water cascaded down its leathery cheeks as a thick neck and powerful shoulders slowly rose above the waterline. A massive animal as big as an ox was emerging from the pool, and it was headed straight towards them.

The students ran. Visceral fear suffused them with one objective: to get away and seek shelter from this imminent threat. The nearest cover afforded to them was a large rock pile perhaps thirty yards upstream. Fueled by a rush of adrenaline, Jocelyn headed straight for it, Jack right on her heels. Spencer was having trouble. He'd twisted his right foot, the one that was slightly deformed, and he was limping badly. Jack looked over his shoulder and, seeing the terror in the younger boy's eyes, raced back to help. A glance at their pursuer, however, set him at ease. The beast was lumbering slowly out of the water and not following them at all. Apparently bath time was over and the animal was simply moseying up to the riverbank.

Safely ensconced within the rock pile, the students stared in wonder. The creature wasn't really green. It was chomping contentedly on a huge, dripping mass of plant matter it had dredged from somewhere within the pool. Its mouth was beak shaped with two tiny tusks poking out from either side. Its eyes were mounted on the sides of its head, much like those of a horse, and its short, muscular limbs were widely set, giving it an appearance more like a tank than a gazelle.

The beast stopped to chew its meal. Slow, circular motions of its lower jaw ground the stringy, aquatic vegetation into pulp. It reminded Jack of moose he'd seen dining in the shallows of ponds and streams in Northern Ontario.

"Just how the heck did hippos get onto this island?" Jocelyn wondered.

"That's not a hippo," Spencer replied. He was staring intently at the odd looking creature as it waded back into knee-deep water, searching for more nourishment. "I'm pretty sure it's a dicynodont."

"A what?" Jack asked.

"They're prehistoric."

"It's a dinosaur?!"

"No, believe it or not, this guy predates dinosaurs."

The animal sloshed along the bank, oblivious to the gawking humans hidden nearby. Making its way to a patch of reeds in the shallows of the pool, it lowered its head and plowed its stubby tusks through the muck, raking up another batch of water plants. Spencer looked on in fascination. "I'm shuah that's what it is—a dicynodont!" he affirmed. "It's exactly like the reconstructions scientists have come up wit' from fossils." He chuckled, "Looks like a cross between a turtle and Homah Simpson."

The beast turned and plodded downstream. Its funny beak, short hind legs, and thick, stubby tail did indeed give it the appearance of a turtle without a shell, and Jocelyn and Jack had to admit that it bore strong resemblance to the well-known cartoon character.

They continued to stare at the odd-looking animal, all of them contemplating Spencer's statement that it was a living fossil. After a moment, Jocelyn frowned in disgust. "Eeeww, do you smell that? Dinosaur or not, our friend, Homer, stinks. Maybe he farted or something—smells like road kill."

The two boys now smelled it too. Jack wrinkled his nose and gagged, "Holy crap, you're right, he smells worse than my gym locker." Sniffing the air again, he paused contemplatively, "But, what little wind there is is blowing the other way. I don't see how..."

The sound of cracking branches and rustling leaves came from behind them. Instinctively, all three ducked and hid from what was approaching. Although they'd been in this strange valley for no more than a few hours, the students had now seen enough that nothing would surprise them. Whatever was coming was big, and all knew there was no guarantee the new arrival would be as benign as Homer.

The true source of the foul scent gradually emerged from the foliage. A long snout atop jaws filled with sharp, jagged teeth poked through the brush as the animal moved toward the open terrain of the beach. To the trembling humans cowering just a few feet away, the new creature's dietary needs were obvious. This one was a carnivore.

Its evil-looking, slanted eyes darted back and forth in search of prey. The students ducked down further, as low as they could, trying to blend into the sand, fervently praying that the small pile of rocks around them was enough to render them invisible. Spencer was closest to this new, ominous threat, and had a terrific, albeit dangerous, view of the animal as it approached. Taller than a man and much heavier, it had an elongated skull full of razor-sharp teeth. Its tongue flicked around, sampling the air for scent as it slunk from the stand of 'bamboo,' pausing every few seconds to process data. It was hunting. Spencer's heart was beating so hard, he was certain the creature would hear him.

"Spencer, what's it doing?" Jocelyn whispered urgently. "Is it still there?"

"Shhh..."

There would be no escape if the predator found them. The only clear way out of the rock pile was the open stretch of bank between them and the dicynodont. Beyond that lay open water and the prospect of more untold dangers...not that they'd make it that far if they were foolish enough to try and make a run for it.

The animal had now fully emerged from the foliage and Spencer had a ringside view from less than twenty feet away. Although its forelegs were only about half the length of its powerful hindquarters, it seemed to be comfortable walking on all four limbs. Spencer's first thought was that it was a strange hybrid crocodile. The head seemed crocodilian but the legs were much too long; this animal walked upright, like a dog or a cat.

It was now right beside him. If Spencer were bold, or foolish, enough, he could have reached out and touched it. He held his breath as the crouching beast stealthily crept along the other side of the rock behind which he was hiding. It was heading for the river bank. Large scale-like plates lay along its spine, from the crest of its oversized head to the tip of the tail. Perhaps twelve feet long, it conveyed the impression of power, grace and speed. This was a killing machine.

Once the animal had passed them and they realized they hadn't been seen, the students' heads bobbed up and down amongst the rocks, in the manner of prairie dogs. Despite the obvious danger, the desire to observe this awesome creature was impossible for them to resist.

The head was primarily what captivated them. The skull was narrow but massive. Jocelyn thought it looked strangely familiar—like the gators she'd seen in South Texas and Louisiana. Its cheeks, where the heavy jaw muscles attached, were thick, indicative of the crushing strength of its bite. The eyes were located under a boney ridge that ran along the top of the head, and, at the moment, they were fixated on the activity going on in the shallows of the pool.

Without warning the animal bolted. It lowered its head and charged forward with amazing speed. Kicking sand in Spencer's face on the way, it headed straight for the dicynodont.

Jocelyn's 'hippo' let out a cry of alarm and began a lumbering retreat towards the apparent safety of the water. But it was much too slow. The predator caught it right at the water's edge. Burying its teeth into the dicynodont's neck it raked its foreclaws across its victim's back while trying to wrest it back onto dry land. The heavier prey animal's momentum was carrying it deeper into the pool, but the aggressor hung on, its hind legs scratching for purchase in the soft river silt, trying to haul both of them away from deep water. A guttural wail resonated from the throat of the dicynodont. The pitiful sound was like the braying of a donkey except deeper and more pleading. Instinct and adrenalin drove it into frenzied thrashing in desperate attempt to free itself from its mortal predicament.

"Holy crap, Holy crap!" Jocelyn cried as the vicious attack continued. "I wish we could do something to help poor Homer."

Jack recognized opportunity in the epic struggle. They had to find a better place of refuge—and fast. The fearsome, malodorous predator would make short work of them if it were to suddenly disengage from its present struggle. "I'll tell you what we can do," he said, "Run!" He grabbed both Spencer and Jocelyn by their arms and pulled them away from the rocks, pointing them inland, away from the water. "I think we'll be safe if we can get to those pines over there."

Just as he spoke, the dicynodont threw its weight into its attacker, catapulting them both into deeper water. Both animals submerged, and for a moment the water settled until the carnivore exploded back to the surface and began thrashing its way towards shore. Swimming, apparently, wasn't its strong suit. It had been forced to release its dinner and was making exasperated hissing noises.

Spencer thought it sounded pissed. He'd been mesmerized by the life-and-death struggle taking place before him and had fallen behind. Jack and Jocelyn were almost through the tangle of 'bamboo' and well on their way to safety when Jack realized Spencer wasn't with them. His eyes grew as big as saucers when the frustrated predator drew a bead on his young companion and began to charge.

"Run!" Jack shouted, "Spencer, Run!"

Spencer didn't need to look behind him. The urgency in Jack's voice told him all he needed to know. He was in the bamboo thicket, picking his way through, when he heard Jack's plea. With an alacrity that rivaled an Olympic hurdler, he began to climb, duck and weave his way through the twisted forest. But it wasn't enough. The animal was gaining. Because of its size, the 'bamboo' thicket provided little resistance. Spencer wasn't making enough progress. Jack began waving and yelling in a futile attempt to divert the animal's attention, but it was like trying to distract a laser-guided missile that had locked onto its target. Spencer's movement was all the beast could see.

There was nothing else Jack could do. He turned to Jocelyn, who was safely climbing through the branches of a large pine, and began to run towards her, to save himself. "Don't look," he yelled at her. She turned and saw a look of pure agony in his countenance. "For God's sake, Jocelyn, don't watch him die." At the very least he felt he might be able to spare her the trauma, the horror, of watching their young friend being torn apart by a savage beast. He reached the tree and began climbing with a heavy heart, reciting at the same time a short Polish prayer he'd learned as a child, and hoping fervently that Spencer wouldn't suffer. If the boy screamed, Jack knew he would forever be haunted by the sound. This wasn't the way an archeological dig was supposed to be. For heaven's sake, a summer spent learning about ancient Norse settlements well above the arctic circle shouldn't involve seeing someone die in the jaws of a monster in the midst of a steaming jungle.

"Go, Spencer, that's it. You can make it. Run." Jocelyn's yells of encouragement made Jack turn and look. It was as though his prayer had been answered. As it was leaving the 'bamboo' grove, the attacker had tripped and fallen. It had been so intent on its kill, finding itself only yards from an easy meal, it had failed to notice a heavy fallen log in its path.

It seemed that Spencer now had a fighting chance. Sprinting through a field of ferns he began to pull away.

However, his good fortune lasted but a moment. His pursuer rallied. Quickly rolling upright, the crocodilian lunged forward with amazing speed, propelling itself on all fours at an alarming rate. When it was mere yards away from its victim, it rose up onto its hind legs and prepared to strike. Jocelyn let out a wail of despair and Jack averted his eyes. The young man from Brooklyn, New York was doomed. The beast was going to grab him long before Spencer would make it to the safety of the tree.

X

Marcie and Debbie watched the Sun through the small opening at the entrance to their shelter. A last brilliant arc seemed to hesitate before darting behind the towering mountain above them. The shadowless landscape of rock lay in the muted twilight of another approaching bitter, cold night. Both women felt a twinge of hopelessness at the thought of another day having passed in this inhospitable no-man's land. Almost a full day had gone by without word from the other students, and no surprise rescue party had come to end their plight.

Marcie was hungry. In the excitement of preparing for her climbing lesson, she'd decided to put off eating any of her energy bars until later. Having subsequently given those to Jocelyn, Jack and Spencer for use during their journey, she was now carefully rationing what was left of the supplies Jack had brought up from the beach: three cans of pork and beans and two tins of smoked herring. Occasionally she would take a bite for herself, but Debbie desperately needed the nourishment and the patient's needs superseded those of her caregiver. Debbie hadn't thought to ask about the status of the food supply, and Marcie was glad. Even though lying to her mentor might be justifiable given the circumstances, Marcie would nonetheless feel uncomfortable doing it.

The reddish glow of arctic twilight had fully arrived now. It would remain dark like this, growing ever colder and damper until the Sun circled around the peaks to the north and made its reappearance in a few hours. As the chill began to set in, Marcie made an announcement:

"I'm going outside to try the communicator. Maybe we can get satellite lock now that the Sun is behind the hills."

She slid aside the rock that was tethered to one corner of the tent fly.

High winds the day before had compelled her to secure the tarp more firmly to outcrops along the cliff face. She'd also scavenged several heavier, loose rocks from around their narrow shelf and piled them along the base of the tarp. Nearly all of her para cord had been committed to securing the shelter, but when she'd finished, Marcie was impressed with her handiwork. "A hurricane couldn't move this thing," she'd thought with pride.

Moving to a locale far from the escarpment, she fumbled with the buttons on the unit. Her fingers were numb with cold. It would have been nice to activate one of her last two chemical hand warmers, but she decided against it. She considered those to be sacred, only to be employed once the Sun had been down for at least an hour. Once that happened, though, she would place the tiny package between herself and Debbie, deep within the folds of their sleeping bag, and the two of them would nurse every calorie that emanated from it for the four hours or so that it lasted. By then the Sun's reappearance would keep them from freezing for another tortuous day.

The screen glowed green, its hourglass icon telling her to wait. "Searching for satellites" was displayed in bold letters at the top. "Come on, baby, come on," Marcie urged. She pulled the collar of her windbreaker against her neck with her free hand. The wind was beginning to gust now as it did every evening at this time—cold air spilling down from the high peaks as the Sun skirted the horizon on the other side.

Suddenly the screen began to dim. At first Marcie thought the problem lay with her eyes. The cold wind caused them to tear up when it came howling through like this. But Marcie's eyes were fine. She stared in disbelief as the display became dimmer and dimmer, finally fading to black.

"Uhgggh...son of a bitch!" she groaned through clenched teeth. Anger flooded through her at this new setback, a cruel betrayal by a stupid piece of equipment. "What a piece of shit." She nearly threw the thing against the rocks, smashing it to bits in a moment of exasperation. But she held back. The apparatus didn't belong to her. As her temper subsided, Marcie's ire was replaced with something worse—fear. The satellite communicator was the only link to the people at the dig site, and it was now useless.

Circumstances were suddenly far worse. Concern for their absence wouldn't manifest into a search effort for at least two more days. Jack, Spencer and Jocelyn had effectively disappeared; they could be lost or in terrible trouble for all Marcie knew. The wind picked up again sending a chill straight through her body and into her soul. Debbie's condition was worsening bit by bit, they were almost out of food, and the chemical heat packs that made the nights bearable were nearly gone. As far as Marcie Van Wormer knew, she might soon be the sole survivor of their ill-fated trip to explore the island. A tear streaked her cheek as she slowly walked back to the makeshift shelter, and its origin had nothing to do with the wind.

Spencer could feel hot, fetid breath on the back of his neck. This was it. His life was at an end. It was strange, he thought, that in the last few seconds of his existence he would experience a clarity of mind he'd never before encountered. Images of his mom and dad flashed by, and scenes from his neighborhood came to mind: Charlie standing beneath the umbrella of his hot dog stand, old Lady Perrault holding a chicken wing in her boney fingers.... But the last fleeting snapshot to enter his mind's eye was one of Marcie. It was lunchtime, right after they'd dined on fried seal meat prepared by Ittuk, and she was beaming at the thought of going on an expedition to explore the coast of the island.

Spencer suddenly realized he would never see his folks, his friends or Marcie again. That thought didn't sit well with him—not at all. A surge of resolve shot through him. He decided then and there that no ugly, two-bit, oversized swamp rat, with a severe case of halitosis and a brain the size of a walnut, was going to turn him into its next meal. That was NOT going to happen.

Knowing that he wouldn't make it to safety in time, he came up with a last-ditch plan. When he sensed that his nemesis was just about to pounce, Spencer juked to his left, then broke sharply right. It was a beautiful move, executed to perfection. If his basketball coach had been there as a witness, it would certainly have earned Spencer an immediate spot on the team.

Although fleet of foot, the large carnivore wasn't as agile as its prey. The animal fell for the fake and took a hard left. Propelled onward by its own momentum, precious seconds elapsed before it realized what had happened and tried to change direction. Spencer headed for the tree. He began to climb as the attacker skidded to a halt and reversed course, once again accelerating towards him. This time, however, it was too late. Jack's strong arms reached down to grab Spencer and pull him to safety as the fearsome jaws of the leaping crocodilian snapped shut mere inches from his foot.

Pale and trembling, Spencer collapsed against the trunk of the tree. He closed his eyes, and for several minutes stayed motionless as his breathing slowed and his heart rate returned to some semblance of normal. The predator began circling the tree, knowing that a meal was still just a short distance away. When Spencer had sufficiently recovered, he looked down and his eyes locked on to those of his aggressor. The looks they exchanged conveyed more than words. Cold, spiteful, malevolent thoughts seemed to radiate from the animal's primitive brain. Extending both middle fingers, Spencer unleashed a stream of expletives sufficient to make a sailor blush. He then slumped back against the tree and received a very spirited and relieved pat on the back from Jack.

"Nice going, Spence. I gotta tell you though, that guy down there doesn't drive a cab. This isn't New York."

Spencer was too tired to laugh. For several more minutes no one spoke. Together they watched the huge beast pace beneath them until it finally gave up and trudged away. Jocelyn was the one to break the silence. "There is no way I'm leaving this tree with that...that 'thing' down there." She relaxed and heaved a deep sigh. "What have we stumbled into here, guys? Admit it; this is like no other place on Earth. Are these things from outer space or did they just evolve in some freakishly isolated way?"

To her surprise, Spencer definitively answered both questions. "They're not from outa space, 'an they 'dint evolve in a freakish way. The fact is they stopped evolving...period."

"What do you mean?"

He shrugged, "I mean they 'dint evolve. That animal that chased me? It was an archosaur."

"A what?"

"An archosaur. Probably hasn't changed much, if at all, since the late Permian or early Triassic. That's what I mean when I say these animals 'dint evolve. This appears to be some sort of isolated, stagnant ecosystem."

"I don't know if I buy that, Spencer," Jack said. "You mean to tell me that this is some sort of prehistoric place?"

Jocelyn thought for a moment and suddenly grew excited,

"Gymnosperms!"

"Huh?"

"All of the plants we've seen; they're all gymnosperms."

Jack was amused, "Sounds a bit racy to me. Are you saying these plants have macho sperm that work out in the gym?" He adopted a fake German accent and did a body builder flex, "Ya, dey get all pumped up—for dey're eggs."

"Men," Jocelyn chided, "why do guys always have to relate everything to sex?" Jack and Spencer laughed and shared a high-five. She groaned and continued, "Gymnosperm is Greek for 'naked seed.' There are plenty of gymnosperms in the modern world, pines for example, or cycads like those I identified earlier. But most modern plants are what are called 'flowering plants;' they produce seeds in ovaries."

"So, what's your point?" Jack asked.

She looked at each of them in turn, for emphasis. "Flowering plants didn't enter into the fossil record until about 140 million years ago."

"That fits wit' the animals we've seen," concurred Spencer. "Near as I can tell they evolved through the late Permian to early Triassic, 'an then something weird happened. This island somehow isolated this whole environment," he swept his hand to indicate everything around them, "'an it just stayed this way."

"So how long are we talking about?" asked Jack. He was becoming more accepting of Spencer's theory—at least it sounded good, and he couldn't come up with anything more plausible.

"If I hadda guess, I'd say all this sorta froze in time about 250 million years ago."

Long shadows and the orange glow of reflected light off clouds, heralded the arrival of nightfall. Their friend 'Malarkey,' a name created by Jocelyn by combining the words 'malevolent' and 'archosaur,' had been gone for hours, no doubt engaged in a continuing hunt for sustenance.

Before it got too dark, Jack decided to make their campsite a bit more comfortable. They had no choice but to spend the night in the tree, and he didn't want anyone falling out. Tentatively he descended to ground level and began gathering dead branches to pass up to the other two. At one point he risked a trip to the 'bamboo' grove to retrieve several stout logs to serve as flooring for the treehouse. Using lengths of paracord supplied to them by the resourceful Marcie, they constructed a platform just large enough for all three to lie on. Per Jack's instructions, each tied a four foot length of cord from his belt to a limb of the tree to guard against an inadvertent fall.

Jocelyn fidgeted in her seat. Jack's platform was uneven and one particularly stubborn twig was poking her in the butt. She rolled onto her side and propped up her head using her backpack as a makeshift pillow. "Spencer, how come you know all this stuff? What grade are you in anyway?"

"I'll be a sophomore in Septembeh."

"Well, I'm impressed. They must have pretty good schools in New Yoahk." She drew out the last word in an exaggerated imitation of his Brooklyn accent.

Spencer smiled and acknowledged her effort by flipping her the bird. "Actually I 'dint learn this in school; I read it on my own."

"Ah, you were one of those kids who was interested in dinosaurs," said Jack.

"Eh, yeah, I guess. But I ask ya, who wouldn't be? They're fascinatin' animals. But I was more interested in where the dinosaurs came from. They 'dint appear outta nowhere, right? They evolved. These 'tings here are their ancestahs. We owe a lot to 'em when you think about it. These guys survived the Permian-Triassic extinction. We wouldn't be here if they hadn't."

"I thought it was an asteroid that killed the dinosaurs."

Spencer rolled his eyes and explained. "That was the Cretaceous-Tertiary, or K-T, event of 65 million yeahs ago. I'm talkin' about what happened almost 250 million yeahs ago. Since life on Earth began, scientists have noted at least five major extinction events from their study of the fossil record. Everyone is familiar with the last one, the one that you just mentioned, but by far the biggest was the Permian-Triassic event. It almost wiped out all life. More than 90% of species went extinct, and that included about 95% of marine life and 30% of insects. It's really impressive that insect life was so significantly affected; no other extinction put that kinda hurt on bugs."

"It must have been some asteroid to do that much damage," Jocelyn said. She'd forgotten about the nuisance twig and was fascinated by the lecture, becoming ever more impressed with what this kid knew. He was a walking encyclopedia. "Do they know how big?"

"Nobody knows for shuah. It might notta been an asteroid, or it might 'a been a series of asteroids that hit over a period of a coupl'a million years. Another popular explanation is that volcanic activity stepped up 'an put so much ash 'an CO_2 in the air that it radically changed the climate."

"Like global warming?"

He shrugged, "Yeah, maybe. What I find interestin' is the big effect on ocean life. You'd 'a thought that bein' in the water would 'a protected most of the fish 'an stuff, but that 'dint happen."

There was no moon that night. Even though the Sun never dipped below the horizon this far north in the summer, it did drop below the level of the mountains to the northwest of where they were. That and the heavy cloud layer plunged their world into near total darkness. That's when the noise began.

"I can't sleep," complained Spencer. He rolled to his left, onto Jocelyn, who pushed him back.

"C'mon Spencer, for heaven's sake try to get some rest; have some sympathy for the rest of us."

"He's got a point, Jossy, the darn bugs are making an awful racket," groaned Jack, "not to mention the creepy crawlies that seem to have come from nowhere." He brushed one away from his face. "We should be thankful they don't bite." No sooner had he spoken than he slapped his arm, "Ow!" His assailant was a nondescript insect that absconded unscathed. "Correction: *most* of them don't bite."

Jocelyn attempted to run her fingers like a comb through the tangled mess that was once silky-smooth hair. She could feel little visitors moving around on her scalp, occasionally scurrying across her face or getting into her ears and nose. But until Jack had brought up the subject she'd been too exhausted to care.

"They're roaches," Spencer noted.

"Eeeew," Jocelyn sat up straight and began flailing at the little critters. "Roaches...that's disgusting. I hate those things."

"Get used to it," Spencer grinned, "about 90% of all insects in the early Triassic were roach relatives."

"That's just great," Jocelyn's tone was laden with sarcasm, "90% of the bugs around here are revolting roach kinfolk and the rest are noisemakers. Almost makes me want to throw myself at Mr. Malarkey's feet, ask him to put me out of my misery."

"For youah edification, the noisemakehs are probably some type of cricket, which makes 'em roach 'kinfolk.' Most people don't know that roaches 'an crickets are distantly related."

"For heaven's sake, Spencer, I've got to stop talking to you. All your fascinating tidbits are things I'd rather not know about." She curled up into a ball and did her best to wrap her head and neck in her windbreaker, leaving a hole barely big enough to breathe through. "Good night," she said with finality.

Morning dawned on the three exhausted travelers. None had gotten more than four hours sleep in the last two nights. They were listless and bleary-eyed, and selfconscious of bad cases of morning breath. Without a word, each consumed his last energy bar. Red, itchy welts had appeared on wrists and ankles, souvenirs from tiny nocturnal blood-sucking guests, all of which required scratching until the skin was raw.

"These are flea bites," Spencer stated matter-of-factly, "they hadda lotta fleas back in the Triassic—along wit' the roaches."

"I'm warning you, Spencer," Jocelyn growled, "Until I've had my morning coffee, I've been known to gut and dismember purveyors of unwelcome insect trivia." She massaged her neck which was stiff and sore from lying in her cramped spot in the tree nest. "Shit," she moaned, "I've got to pee so bad my eyeballs are floatin', but I don't want to leave this tree."

"My bladder's about to burst too," Jack confided. "If you'll turn the other way, I can relieve myself right from here." Jocelyn gave him a hard stare, which, of course, was just what he wanted. "That reminds me," he continued, "and I think you'll have to agree, there's one thing that men can do far better than women."

"What's that?"

"Pee on a campfire."

She rolled her eyes. His logic was unassailable. "Okay, that may be the *one* thing men can do better, but I can't list the things at which women excel, it would take too long—and I really do have to pee."

Jack smiled but again turned serious, "We can't stay up here much longer; that's for sure. Let's cross the river and hike up the east side. For Debbie's sake we've got to find a way out. If we stay close to the water, at least until we get out of the valley, we should be relatively safe from Malarkey and his buddies. Keep your noses on high alert though, just in case."

With Jack's words of advice lingering in their minds, they cautiously descended from their perch. All was quiet save for a few residual insect troubadours plaintively trolling for mates. Fog had rolled in during the early morning, but was beginning to lift as the Sun's influence intensified. The first few steps toward the river were psychologically difficult. Each remembered the speed which the archosaur had mustered in its attack upon Spencer, and every meter of distance from the safety of the tall trees represented a potential life-or-death defining interval.

At the water's edge, just above the lake, they stopped. They were at the head of the delta where the first of three significant streams flowed past. The first was the largest of the three and presented the greatest obstacle. Upstream from where they stood, the stream was rocky and the current dangerously strong. Right where the lake began, however, it fanned out to about forty feet in width, and the water was slow-moving and deep. Jocelyn looked at the other two. "If we're going to cross, this is the spot," she said definitively. There was no doubt in the minds of everyone that she was the expert when it came to such matters. Having grown up on the coast, Jocelyn had spent the better part of her life either in or on the water. Whether it was swimming with friends in a river or sailing in Corpus Christi Bay, she had developed an uncanny ability to analyze surface flow patterns, wave chop, ripples, underwater obstacles—anything that might pose a hazard to the activity involved. "See where the water gets deep about ten feet out?" She pointed to where the water was calm, "we'll probably have to swim for about twenty feet until it's shallow enough to stand. Those reeds near the other side are the same as those on shore, off to the left. When we get to them the water can't be more than a few feet deep—piece of cake."

"I don't know, Jossy." It was Jack who spoke. "Heck, you're the expert here, don't get me wrong, but wouldn't it be best to pick a spot to just wade across?"

"Like where?"

He nodded to a point upstream.

"Jack, the current is way too strong there; don't underestimate its power. If you try to cross up there, you'll be knocked off your feet and swimming in this hole before you can count to three."

"Well, what about that hippo we saw yesterday? Something like that may be lurking here. You never know."

"That dicynodont is a herbivore," said Spencer. "He made no aggressive move toward us. Remembeh? My vote's wit' Jocelyn. Let's swim across heah."

Jocelyn knew something was wrong. The apprehension in Jack's demeanor was obvious. "What's the matter, Jack? Is it that you can't swim?"

"I didn't say that, did I?" He sounded exasperated. "It just pays to examine all the possibilities, that's all." He stared at the others for a few moments. Finally his shoulders slumped in defeat. "But, yeah, I can't swim." He looked away, embarrassed. "I had a bad experience at a lake when I was a kid; I almost drowned. Ever since then, well..." his voice trailed off.

"But what about our trip out here in the zodiac?" Jocelyn asked in wonder. "You didn't seem scared then."

"I wasn't scared, okay. Maybe I was a bit nervous, but I had a life jacket on and another one at my feet. I figured the risk was minimal."

After a brief silence, she said, "Give me your pack." She took off her own and held both over her head as she waded into the lake and then swam, uneventfully, to the other side. She deposited their gear on the bank and made her way back easily. The entire trip took her less than two minutes. "I only had to swim about fifteen feet," she reported. "I was a lifeguard for several summers. If you relax and trust me, I can swim across with you, Jack. No problem."

Jack was frightened. He felt helpless, trapped by his inadequacy to perform such a simple task, and worried that his friends would lose respect for him, believe him to be a coward. Jocelyn had made it look so easy. Maybe he could do what she did; the distance was minimal. "Sounds like a plan." He smiled disarmingly, doing his best to adopt a brave, carefree façade.

She gave him a confident look in the eye. Inwardly she knew that this might be difficult, but there was little choice. "Remember," she said soberly, "you have to trust me. Let's wade out a bit." She led him out to where the water was chest deep. "Now, turn around and face me. You're going to float backwards with your head tilted back, your arms extended, and with your hands on my shoulders. It's called the 'tired swimmer's carry.' You float, I swim, and we reach the other side in no time. Okay?"

Jack nodded bravely, and Jocelyn pushed off the bottom, propelling them both forward with a powerful breaststroke. At first Jack floated comfortably, but within seconds his feet began to drop, rotating his body until his chin fell below the surface. Instantly panic overcame him. A gut-wrenching fear displaced all reason as the deeply buried memory of the awful experience of his youth consumed him. He began thrashing violently, grabbing Jocelyn in a desperate attempt to keep his head above water.

"Jack! Jack, stay calm!" she shouted to no avail. He was much stronger and heavier than she, and was carrying her down with him. Jocelyn fought to stay focused. Her lifeguard training kicked in. She grabbed a quick breath and did what all panicked drowning victims fear most—she submerged. Jack immediately let go of her and began churning the water with his arms, trying to stay afloat. Jocelyn deftly swam around and approached him from behind. Throwing one arm across his chest, she put him in a 'fireman's carry' and resumed her swim to shore.

At first he tried to grab her again by reaching behind his back, but failed in his efforts. He quickly realized, though, that they were moving and that he was out of danger. Forcing himself to relax, he made it easy for Jocelyn to complete the rescue, and within seconds they were standing on soft gravel, wading the last few meters to shore. Jocelyn was exhausted. Dealing with Jack's weight, superior strength and panic had almost been too much to handle. As she slogged toward where she'd left the packs, she slipped and did a 'face plant' in the soft mud. Jack rushed to her aid. Lifting her to her feet, he tenderly worked at removing clods of gunk from around her eyes.

"I'm so sorry," he repeated over and over. There was hurt and sympathy in every word. "I don't understand what happened. I thought I was in control..." He quieted as Spencer came up beside them.

The younger boy looked like a drowned rat. His clothes were plastered against his thin frame, and his backpack, which he'd failed to remove prior to his swim, had filled with dirty water which was now dripping as though from a fire hose. A wisecrack pertaining to Jack's crossing formed on his lips, but never made it out when he noticed the embarrassment in his companion's countenance. The episode was best forgotten.

Two more stream crossings lay before them, neither of which required the need to swim. Jack again took the lead. The first segment presented little difficulty. Although the slippery rocks were difficult for Spencer to negotiate because of his foot, they were soon assembled on a small fern-covered island. The last stream was wide, rocky and very shallow. Looking across they could see the terrain rise, transitioning quickly from a broad beach into a 'bamboo' grove and finally to an expanse of larger trees where the slope increased toward the hills. What lay beyond the trees was of particular interest because that was where they had wanted to go all along. If there were an accessible eastern route to the sea, above and beyond the mist and cloud that enclosed the valley, it might prove to be Debbie's salvation. Alas, only after hours of hiking over difficult and potentially dangerous countryside would they learn whether or not their trek was successful.

Jack began to pick his way across the final stream while the others held back. If an archosaur or some other danger were lurking nearby, the shallow water would pose no impediment to it. There was no use endangering the entire party by crossing simultaneously.

Halfway across, Jack stopped. In front and slightly to his left there was a commotion in the 'bamboo.' Something, some animal of significant size, was making its way towards the beach. Jack slowly started to back up, preparing to run at the first hint of danger.

The beast that emerged from the foliage was a quadruped. It was stocky, but leaner than the dicynodont they'd seen the previous day, and it was quite a bit smaller. The way it moved suggested that it spent considerable time on land vs. water. Roughly the size of a large dog or goat, it was built low to the ground, its reptilian lineage in evidence. It weighed perhaps forty or fifty pounds, sported a short tail, and its snout was round and whiskered. Its most striking feature was its coloration. The larger animals they'd seen the day before were both a dull greyish-brown, with a skin or covering that was tough and scaly. This creature had smooth, leathery, brown hide covered with irregular dark patches—reminiscent of the camouflage clothing worn by hunters.

It paused at the edge of the clearing, appearing to sniff the air prior to leaving the safety of the forest and heading to the river. One could immediately tell that it was hurt. It limped badly from a wound to its left shoulder; blood stained the rocks as it slowly moved to the water's edge. There it stopped and lowered its head to drink. Jack crouched to lower his profile and remained motionless. He blended well with many of the rocks that dotted the stream. All three students watched in rapt fascination this wounded animal from a past epoch.

More rustling and crashing sounds soon came from the nearby vegetation. Spencer and Jocelyn sought refuge among tall ferns and Jack scooted over to a large rock. Jack's cover was too small to conceal him completely, but there was nothing else available. He felt particularly vulnerable considering that whatever was coming through the brush was larger and seemingly more aggressive than the animal drinking at the river bank. The same unmistakable thought ran through everyone's mind: the creature that had wounded this animal was probably moving in for the kill.

A shrill cry accompanied the appearance of the hunter. It leaped onto the beach and ran on its hind legs towards its prey. In marked contrast to the other quadrupeds they'd seen, this one was purely bipedal and had a head surrounded by fur. In one forelimb it brandished what appeared to be a weapon. Sure enough, close inspection showed the object to be a spear. Swift on the attack, it plunged its lance into the chest of the other, killing it instantly.

The figure looked around apprehensively, wary of the arrival of yet another creature. The three students now realized that the spear-wielding killer was human. He had long, brown, disheveled hair, an unkempt beard and wore crudely constructed leather shoes and a breechclout. As they processed this astounding new information, that a human was living and hunting in this primordial world, they too heard what had captured the attention of the man standing before them. Another animal was indeed approaching. A series of high-pitched grunts accompanied the occasional snapping twig as this new arrival slowly maneuvered towards the beach.

The breechclout-clad man adopted a defensive stance and pointed his spear at the 'bamboo' grove as the new arrival broke into the open. In body style it was similar to the animal the man had just killed. It had a short, stocky, lizard-like body with leathery skin and a short tail—overall length: just over four feet. The head, however, was that of a carnivore. Surprisingly dog-like, in both appearance and mannerism, it had its nose to the ground, following the recently deposited blood trail. When it looked up and saw the man standing there, its upper lip curled into a snarl, revealing sharp canines and incisors. Like the archosaur they'd encountered the day before, this creature had a head disproportionally large for its body, at least by modern standards, and its jaws were filled with sharp nasty-looking teeth.

The carnivore began circling the human, who staunchly positioned himself between his kill and the unwelcome interloper. Spear point and teeth flashed as the standoff progressed. Every lunge by the animal was countered by a well-placed thrust of the human's pike. The man was eventually able to jab his point into the animal's neck, not deeply enough to cause significant damage, but sufficient to end the altercation. The carnivorous beast squealed and grunted as it slunk back the way it had come, pausing once to look back in envy at the meal it had been denied.

The human watched intently the animal's departure. When he was certain it wouldn't return, he turned his attention back to his prey and wasted no time binding its legs together with twine and looping them over his shoulder as a means of carrying it away to another locale for butchering.

Jack stood up from behind his rock. The man with the spear was concentrating on his preparations to leave and had no idea he was under observation.

"Hello," Jack yelled. He made no move towards the man, not wanting to appear aggressive. The man whipped his head around at the sound and stared at Jack. Jack held up his hands as though surrendering—the universal sign that he held no weapon and meant no harm. "Can you understand me? Do you speak English?"

It was difficult to gauge the fellow's immediate reaction because of his fully bearded countenance. When recognition set in he adopted a relaxed stance and waved, the crinkles around his eyes belying the presence of a smile. "I bloody well do speak English," the man boomed, "and just who the hell might you be, friend?"

Jack stepped forward and held out his hand. The man clasped it heartily. "I'm Jack Malinowski. My colleagues and I were working on an archeological site and had an accident while exploring the coast of the island." He waved for

Jocelyn and Spencer to join him, but needn't have bothered. They were already almost entirely across the stream, both sporting broad grins.

"Loren Endicott," their new acquaintance said, "I also worked at the Eviskar excavation—until last year." His voice trailed off as he remembered the circumstances that had brought him here.

"You're one of the three researchers who disappeared last June," Jocelyn recalled. She and Spencer had arrived in time to hear Endicott introduce himself. "What happened? Where are the others?"

Endicott shook his head. A look of sadness replaced his previously eager demeanor. "We have a lot to discuss," he said soberly. Taking an apprehensive look around, he continued, "It would be prudent to talk back at my camp. The blood from this pig will attract more lizard wolves. We'd best not be here when that happens." Abruptly he began walking away from the river and beckoned the others to follow.

XI

As they hiked single file along a jungle trail, the students excitedly related to Endicott the story of their experiences of the past several days: about Debbie's fall, the failure of the satellite communicator to send an SOS message to Morgan and the others at the dig site, and of their perilous journey through the valley. For his part, Endicott listened solemnly. He asked a few questions about the satellite unit, but, in general, his attitude became ever more sullen. What might have been a rescue party, his salvation, had turned out to be nothing more than a group of kids who shared his predicament.

It was a long way to camp. Dr. Endicott explained to the group that the best hunting was in the valley, but it was too dangerous to live down there. In this exotic land, lush and humid meant food and sustenance, while arid and cool, where they were headed now, meant fewer predators and bugs. Slogging along, they meandered through vegetation that became more and more sparse as the trail wound up into low hills. The older students expressed interest in routes to the eastern coast and whether or not Endicott knew of a convenient path to get there while bearing a stretcher. The response they got was disheartening.

"I've been in this God forsaken place for over a year," their host began. "Sure, there are places where one can overlook the sea, but you need to be a mountain goat to get there. I'm afraid the most likely way to get your injured friend to safety is by going back the way you came in."

"I don't get it," Jocelyn commented. "If that's the only way out, why do you live way over here?"

"How much food and vegetation did you see there?" came the rather curt reply. "It snows up on that ridge regularly, right through the month of June. It's a day's hike from anything edible as well as anything that can be used for constructing a shelter or fueling a fire. I stayed there for nearly a week after our accident and damn near died. The wind up in those high peaks routinely gusts to over 100 miles-per-hour. There is one thing of which you can be entirely certain: your two colleagues buggered down on that shelf are having a miserable go of it."

"I'm sorry to have offended you Dr. Endicott. I know you've been through hell here, but we're desperate to help Debbie." Jocelyn's strong-minded nature was unaccepting of Endicott's defeatist attitude. "We're getting out of here no matter what it takes. Even though we've been unable to call for help, a rescue party should arrive in a couple of days. Snow or no snow, wind or no wind, I will personally be on that beach to welcome them. For Debbie's sake I simply wanted to know if we could get her out of here sooner."

Endicott pondered her statement. "That's very noble of you," he said, "very admirable indeed, but tell me, just how do you intend to get to the beach? Can you fly?"

"We have all the climbing gear we need to scale the cliff," Jack interjected. "That's not the problem. The key issue is how to get Debbie up over that ridge and down to the beach without killing her."

Endicott stared at Jack and Jocelyn. He'd fixated on one thing that Jack had mentioned, and as he contemplated it he became excited. He grasped Jack by the shoulders and exclaimed, "Ropes? Climbing gear? Why didn't you tell me that in the first place? My God, I should have realized—that's the reason you're all uninjured. You had to have proper climbing equipment or you wouldn't have made it here. Let's hurry now and get back to camp. At dawn tomorrow we'll gather supplies and head over to that blasted cliff. How long did you say it will be until they begin searching for you?"

"They'll probably set out on Friday if they don't hear from us," Jocelyn said.

Endicott laughed. "My dear girl, how presumptuous of you to think that I have the slightest idea of what day of the week this is. Please, just tell me, again, how many days until they come for you."

"Two," Jocelyn replied, "possibly three."

"Ah, excellent, I'll pack food sufficient for six people for three days. We can certainly manage to camp on the beach for that long. Come, my young liberators, we've no time to waste."

"What do you propose we do about Debbie?" Jocelyn asked. There remained the important question of how to extricate the badly injured woman from the mountainside.

Loren Endicott's eyes again hardened. "She'll live," he snapped. "Her husband can stay and care for her for a few hours once the cavalry arrive." Fighting to control his exasperation, he said almost apologetically, "Think, my dear girl. When your...our... colleagues arrive they'll be able to send a Sat phone call to Daneborg. Within twenty-four hours, probably less, a rescue chopper will arrive to pluck that poor woman from peril and transport her to a proper medical facility."

He paused to rest. Dropping his 'pig' to the ground, Endicott sat on a rock and rubbed his eyes with filthy, weathered hands. Jocelyn made note of his long, broken fingernails, cracked lips and numerous cuts and sores. She began to fathom what he'd been through in the past year and the psychological toll it had taken. His volatile temperament was understandable.

"Don't for a minute think that I've no sympathy for your friend Debbie," the Doctor continued, "I and my colleagues shared a similar experience. A fall, it was, but in our case I'd guess you'd say it was more of a landslide. On a rare, clear day we hiked from the beach just as you did, anxious to catch a glimpse of what all of us thought was the bowel of an unexplored, smoldering volcano. One minute we were gazing into the interior of the island and the next...it was an eerie sensation of freefalling amongst a shower of boulders. Fate favored me, I suppose. My injuries were astoundingly minor: a few broken ribs, a badly sprained wrist and a number of bumps and bruises." His eyes were hollow. He was staring at nothing in particular as his mind resurrected the details of that fateful day. "It happened quickly, but the terror of the episode seemed to drag it on forever. I'll never forget the enormous pressure exerted by one of the rocks that rolled over me once I was prostrate down slope. Like a truck it was; it must have weighed several tons. I believe that's when my ribs fractured.

He looked down and shook his head. "Aage, that would be Dr. Aage Randrup, he was killed outright, crushed and mangled by tons of rock. A finer man I've never known, a native Greenlander who had such passion for his work. That archeological dig meant so much to him. You see, he was part Inuit and part Nordic, and he considered the Eviskar settlers as distant relatives. Learning about them was a link to his own past.

"And Karlsen, the Dane, he was very badly hurt in that fall, mortally so. Of course I could do nothing for him given my own circumstances. The memory of his moaning, beseeching me for help I couldn't render, still haunts me every day. Finally, when he knew the end was near, he pleaded with me to make certain to tell his wife and children how much he loved them. That was his dying wish: that I relay those sentiments to his family. Strangely, those words were largely what have kept me going. I promised that man that if it's the last thing I do, I'll fulfil his dying request."

Endicott stood and shouldered his quarry. As he did, the sadness left his voice to be replaced by bitterness, "Karlsen might have lived had they come for us. He lived in misery for several days, but no proper rescue attempt was made."

"But they did search for you," Jocelyn said. "Morgan told us they patrolled the coast for weeks and saw no sign of you or your vessel."

"Well, it wasn't enough, was it?" He fairly spat the words. "My exile here proves to me that we just didn't matter."

Endicott's words hung in the air as they resumed their trek.

The mood lightened considerably while they walked. Telling the students about his misfortunes was ultimately cathartic for Endicott. Now someone from the outside finally knew what had happened to him and his friends, his colleagues. Their conversation turned to the nature of the world around them. Spencer, in particular, began asking questions of his new hero, the man who'd managed to survive here alone and unaided for so long.

"We've nevah seen one of those yet," he observed, pointing to the 'pig,' "It looks like some kind of cynodont."

Endicott gave him an interested look. "You're very perceptive, young man." They hiked for a few minutes until they reached the top of a bluff. Endicott then turned to address Spencer again, "I'm intrigued. Just how is it that you can identify a prehistoric creature such as this? Are there others back at the dig site, paleontologists perhaps, who've taken an interest in this island?" His last question was directed at all three of them. The request seemed important to him. He had stopped walking, expecting an answer.

"Nope," Spencer said with pride, "I just know this stuff from readin' 'an doin' my own research."

"Impressive, impressive indeed."

The trail abruptly branched to the east and wound through several switchbacks up a steep, rocky slope. Endicott grunted with the effort of carrying his heavy quarry uphill. At the top, he spoke. "Spencer, my lad, you're observation is spot on. This is one of several species of cynodont that inhabit this part of the island. Most are herbivorous, like this fellow here, and at least one type is carnivorous. You saw a specimen try to take this kill from me."

"It did look pretty fearsome," Jack offered.

"They most definitely are. I refer to them as 'lizard wolves', or simply 'LWs,' as they seem to serve the same purpose here as do modern wild canines such as coyotes and wolves. Their amphibious/reptilian ancestry is obvious when one considers their morphology, but they also have characteristics indicative of their mammalian progeny. Did you happen to notice the whiskers on the snout of that LW?"

"I couldn't see past its teeth," Jack laughed.

"A point well taken; their dentition is indeed formidable. What are perhaps more interesting, however, from an evolutionary standpoint, are the unmistakable presence of small amounts of fur, and an uncanny sense of smell. Their olfactory capabilities are nothing short of amazing. A bleeding wound can draw them from a considerable distance, a quarter mile or so, maybe more if the wind is favorable. 'Land sharks' might be another appropriate nickname for them."

Spencer was absolutely enthralled with Endicott's accounts of the island's fauna. His own readings and research into the fossil record of the Triassic meshed perfectly with what he was hearing from this man. "Are they primarily hunters or scavengers?" he asked.

"A bit of both I'd say. Again, the moniker 'lizard wolf' fits them to a tee. I often see them feeding on carrion, but they're quite proficient at taking small prey. In fact I suspect they fill the important ecological niche of controlling the population of small herbivorous cynodonts—the early Mesozoic equivalent of the relationship between foxes and hares."

"Aren't you worried they might come afta' you?"

"I suppose somewhat, yes, especially if I have a major cut or a large open sore. Like I said, the scent of blood can draw them from far away. Ordinarily a single individual will shy from a full grown human, but all bets are off if he's bleeding. Blood lust imbues them with a fantastic instinctive courage. They can be extraordinarily dangerous in that sort of scenario, especially if there's more than one of them. Like their modern canine counterparts, they'll sometimes travel in groups of two or three, and they're smart enough to coordinate attacks. What has saved poor Loren Endicott's bacon on many occasions is the noise they make. You heard it—that high-pitched grunt sound. One always knows when they're nearby."

"You'd think they'd learn not to do that," Spencer reasoned, "I bet it scares off a lot of their prey."

"One would think so, yes," Endicott agreed, "but evidence suggests they don't hear well. From the small auditory openings in their heads—ears, if you will—and the internal arrangement of bones in their skulls, I believe that these cynodonts, both predators and prey, have poor hearing. Theirs is a predominantly silent world; virtually all their sensory input comes from sight and smell."

The trail veered to the north. As they contoured around a small hill, there appeared a cluster of boulders near the top that had been turned into a dwelling. Strong 'bamboo' logs were strategically placed between some of the rocks and also across the tops to enclose the structure. Large leaves, belonging to a vine-like plant brought up from the river bank, were interlaced with conifer boughs to create a thatch that lined the roof and sides. It was a well-designed and well-constructed abode, capable of keeping its occupant safe and dry against whatever challenges Mother Nature had to offer.

"Make yourselves at home." Endicott pointed to several rustic 'bamboo' chairs and a table as they entered. "Sit wherever you like. I've got to skin this pig, dispose of the guts and cook him before it gets dark. It won't take long."

None of the students were much interested in sitting around. They all accompanied Endicott to a clearing fifty yards from the dwelling where there was a flat rock set up as a butcher's block. Drawing a large folding knife from his belt, Endicott made a careful incision between the animal's hind quarters. "It's like carving up any large game," he noted as he worked. "The principal things to watch out for with these guys are the musk glands. Puncture those and you ruin the meat."

Endicott worked with an efficiency and precision borne of considerable practice. In minutes he'd disemboweled his kill and carefully flensed its hide, intact. Jocelyn was surprised that he wanted to save the animal's skin given their imminent rescue, but decided it was being done out of force of habit. The good Doctor was apparently still in survival mode. Tossing the head and the lower portions of the limbs in with the entrails, he harvested two tenderloin strips from along its back and stripped slabs of shoulder meat for what he called 'pot roasts.' He then wrapped the edible portions in the hide for transport back to the shelter and stood back to appraise his handiwork.

"Now it's time for a little show," he said with a grin. There was a twinkle in his eye as he gathered the detritus of his labors and beckoned the students to follow him to the edge of a deep cleft in the hillside, another fifty yards further away from his shelter. A trickle of water gurgled through the ravine, barely enough to supply the few ferns and stunted 'bamboo' that grew there. "Allow me to introduce you to Moe, Larry and Curley." With that, he flung the guts into the gorge, sat down, and waited.

The two boys eagerly anticipated what was to come. Jocelyn, however, shivered when she thought of the dangerous creatures about to pass so close by. Within minutes they heard the characteristic soprano grunts of approaching lizard wolves.

"That's Moe," Endicott remarked excitedly while pointing to the largest of three animals that sauntered up the stream. Heads moving back and forth, up and down, noses sampling both air and soil, the pack homed in on its evening meal.

With quick, savage lunges the three carnivores attacked the remains of the cynodont carcass. Powerful jaws ripped chunks of flesh from the pile, and the crunch of bone reverberated eerily off the walls of the gorge until absolutely nothing remained except red stains on the rocks. It was a feeding frenzy comparable in intensity only to the boiling of an Amazon pool inhabited by crazed piranhas.

"Awesome!" Spencer noted when it was over.

Endicott smiled. "I knew you'd be impressed." He again pointed to one of the creatures as it moved away. "That one's Curley. You'll note he's missing his right eye. And see the scars on his cheek? At some point he either got in the way of one of his hungry associates, or he attacked something that put up a terrific fight. The smaller one with lighter spots is Larry. I believe she's a female because of her size. It's really tough to determine gender among these brutes."

Joselyn had seen enough. Lizard wolves gave her the creeps. She couldn't understand the interest exhibited by her male colleagues; it seemed excessively primitive, and it made her uncomfortable. "Can we go now?"

"Girls!" Spencer chided.

"I just wanted to give you an indication of the fate one might expect if one isn't careful out here," Endicott said dismissively. "Normally lizard wolves won't venture up to this altitude—not enough food here I suppose—but those three hang around perpetually. They've been regular diners at 'chez Endicott' for several months now. Smart little buggers they are, 250 million-year-old moochers." He shouldered the cynodont hide stuffed with their upcoming dinner and led the way back to the hut.

The roof of the structure had a trap door which the professor opened. A ring of soot surrounded the hole, indicating its purpose. He then got down on his knees and carefully brushed aside the top layer of ash in the centrally located fire pit to expose coals left over from the previous fire. Grabbing a handful of dried moss he expertly nursed the new fire along. Soon there was a roaring blaze that cast warm shadows on the walls.

Twilight had brought with it a chill, and the fire lent much appreciated warmth to the evening. They weren't high enough to experience the low temperatures of the distant mountains, but it was significantly cooler here than in the river valley. The increased altitude didn't alter the humidity though, and the setting Sun left the still air clammy and uncomfortable. Jocelyn noted that Endicott didn't possess anything in the way of warm clothing, and asked him how he'd coped in winter.

Her host shrugged as he skewered slabs of cynodont tenderloin onto a stout stick and suspended them over a fireplace now glowing with hot coals. "I told you earlier that I have no idea what day it is, and the only way I have of knowing what month we're in is by the lengths of shadows of certain vertical posts I've been using as crude sundials. Part of what depresses me about this prehistoric prison is the lack of seasonal change. Aside from the fact that the Sun doesn't come up for months, one wouldn't know it was winter. The monotony of a climate like this wears on you. Day after day, month after month, nothing changes. The geothermal springs and vents, most of which lie far to the south and west, inject a constant supply of heat into this huge, bowl-shaped caldera, turning water to steam which, when it hits the cold air spilling down from the mountains, turns to cloud. Those constant clouds effectively insulate the valley, keeping conditions the same, day after bloody day."

"That's why the satellite images don't show anything but cloud?" Spencer observed.

"Precisely. Even in our modern technological society, the details of what this place is like, here under all these clouds, have remained a mystery. Actually, mystery isn't the proper term. I suspect nobody's ever really thought to explore this island. It's fairly small, as islands go, terribly remote, and it's far enough from the ice pack that no humans or polar bears can walk to it. Although it's readily accessible by sea, the caldera rim presents an imposing rampart, one sufficient to discourage all but hardy, properly equipped mountaineers from venturing forth. And what possible reason would compel a climber to visit this place—to gain access to a supposedly steaming volcanic cauldron high above the Arctic Circle, in the middle of nowhere?"

"We did it," said Spencer.

Endicott gave him an icy stare. "Yes, you certainly did. And look where it got you—me as well. We both found the most promising access point to the interior, that small beach and the weak, broken ridge that has eroded just enough to entice one to hike in and explore. This island is like the Greek isles inhabited by sirens, those sultry beings who beckon the unsuspecting and curious to explore their charms, only to lure them to their deaths."

Jocelyn shivered. Whether it was the chill or the nature of the conversation she couldn't tell. She found Endicott's mood swings unsettling. Most of the time he appeared to be perfectly normal—at least as normal as could be expected for someone who'd been through such a harsh period of exile. He was a strong man, not just physically, capable of dealing with, and overcoming, the hardships he'd faced. Stubbornness and a determined will had put him in this hut, where he lacked nothing essential to life: food, shelter, warmth...he had what he needed. But there was something else, perhaps the lack of human contact, that had instilled in him this disturbing erratic attitude. He definitely harbored an enormous sense of abandonment at having been marooned here. The thought of his exile made him despondent, but when he was reminded of the accident that cast him into this world, and the real or perceived lack of a successful rescue attempt, it had made him angry. The most innocent of questions seemed suddenly to trigger his ire, and she could tell he fought to control himself, to avoid a transition into rage.

Jocelyn had friends at school who used drugs. No high school in the country was immune to the problem. She'd borne witness to similar mood swings, especially among football players who took anabolic steroids. "'Roid rage" is what they called it. It often affected them badly enough that other students openly shunned them. Jocelyn regarded those players with a mixture of revulsion and pity. It both fascinated and appalled her to see what people would do to their bodies in desperate attempts to win glory and recognition for doing nothing more than playing a game.

Endicott, however, wasn't on drugs. He had lived for the past year about as far from a pharmacy as one could get. Jocelyn attributed his behavior to either the stress of his exile or to some sort of brain imbalance—schizophrenia perhaps.

Regardless of the cause, she felt he wasn't a stable man, and that made him a dangerous man. Jack and Spencer didn't see it. To them, Loren Endicott was someone to be admired for his cleverness, knowledge and perseverance. That was true, of course, but they couldn't also see the dark side, the inner turmoil lying beneath the tough exterior, the curse that made him a tragic figure.

It was easy to lose track of time in the everlasting twilight of summer at high latitudes. Jack's stomach growled as the scent of almost fully cooked cynodont steaks assaulted his nostrils. He had no idea of just how late it was nor did he care. He was famished. None of the students had had a proper meal in over three days. In an attempt to take his mind off of food, he looked around Endicott's dwelling and his eyes settled upon the spear the Doctor had used to kill tonight's dinner. He walked over to pick it up and returned to sit by the fire.

The weapon was robust and extremely well made. Its shaft was about six feet long, strong and lightweight, made of a stout piece of the ubiquitous 'bamboo' with which they were so familiar. The end of the piece had been split to accept the crown spike of a cycad tree; tightly wound animal sinew held the blade firmly in place.

Endicott noticed Jack's interest in the object. Setting the steaks onto a crudely constructed table to cool, he said, "That pike's kept me alive in more ways than one. Food and protection are what life is about in this land. Maintaining a supply of cynodont meat and keeping lizard wolves at bay would have been nearly impossible without it."

"You did a good job," Jack said admiringly. "This cycad tip is as hard as hickory, and sharp too."

"I carved an edge onto it and filed it sharp using an abrasive rock. I then hardened it carefully over a fire," he said with pride. "Believe it or not it's the only tip I've used. Several times I've lunged and accidentally driven it into the ground, but it never broke. That wood is a better quality material than many modern synthetics. Those cycad trees have been of great importance to me."

"They're real important to those dragonflies too," Spencer quipped.

"Ah, so you've noticed that have you? Well, here's something you haven't experienced." Endicott pulled several flat objects that looked like thick tortillas from a pouch made of cynodont hide and handed one to each student. He then grabbed one for himself, took a bite, and beckoned the others to do the same. Jocelyn nibbled hers and nodded approvingly. "So, tell me what you think," her host asked.

"It's really tasty," she replied, "sort of like bread with a flavor that reminds me of—it's hard to describe—kind of a carrot-potato blend, almost like a soup."

"'An it's sweet," Spencer added, "has a high sugah content."

"There's a pith layer in the crown of the cycad," Endicott explained, "right below where the point projects and under where the seeds grow. It's very much like the modern bread palms they have in Africa. Although I've never tried those, I daresay they can't taste much better than this. Mashed up with a bit of water, I knead the pulp and bake it to make these." He indicated what the students held in their hands. "Obviously it yields a delicious and very important source of carbohydrate to one's diet. And that's not the end of it," he added with a smile, "The cycad seeds provide me with something much more delectable—my most important discovery to date. I found that when you rinse off the objectionable goo that attracts those pesky dragonflies, the small, black seeds are most useful. When dried and roasted they may be steeped to yield a delightful beverage, one very similar to coffee."

Endicott's last statement caused Jocelyn to draw a breath. She was about to say something, but suddenly thought better of it and held her tongue. Instead, she commented on the weapon in Jack's hand. "What I find interesting is the wood you used to make the shaft. There's something familiar about it, but I can't recall what it is; it looks sort of like bamboo, but I'm virtually certain it's not."

"Well now," the question brought approbation from Endicott, "you're quite the botanist, Jocelyn. Most people would not have noticed the odd nature of this plant. You've undoubtedly noticed them growing almost everywhere. They're called horsetails, and the varieties on this island, I'm fairly certain, have been extinct elsewhere on Earth for 100 million years or more."

"Mmmm...this is superb." Jack hadn't been able to wait any longer. The steaks had cooled enough to handle, and he was savoring his first taste of cynodont. Spencer took the hint and dove into another piece of meat.

Despite her hunger, Jocelyn held back. Convincing herself that the boys made good guinea pigs, she thought she'd wait to be sure the food was safe. If it didn't cause them any gastric distress, she would eat some herself. No use taking chances. But harbored deep within her psyche lay the real reason she was reluctant to taste the cynodont: she'd seen the animal when it was alive. Knowing that's what she would be eating was affecting her appetite. It had looked so terrified and helpless back there on the river bank moments before Endicott had dispatched it, and now a portion of it was sitting in front of her, grilled to perfection, smelling wonderful, sort of like the pork chops her mother prepared. *Oh, knock it off,* she chided herself. The animal was dead now. Cows, pigs and chickens probably look the same before they go to slaughter—except perhaps the chickens, she reasoned, after all, they were just birds—but all consumers ever see are dismembered cuts sitting on display in the meat section of the supermarket. And what about the fish she caught in the Gulf? She was never squeamish about eating the snapper or the reds she and her friends caught.

"You better dig in, Jossy," Jack said when he noticed her staring at her dinner. "But if you aren't hungry, just pass your steak down to me. I could eat a horse."

"Unlike the rest of you heathens, some of us say grace before we eat," came her specious excuse as she picked up her portion and began to nibble. It was surprisingly good. Whatever her jumbled thoughts had led her to expect, this was different. Cynodont, she decided on the spot, would be tops on her list of favorites if they were available back home. Its taste was a delicate blend of chicken and pork, not gamey at all, and very tender. She slowly forgot about the source of the food and concentrated on her own hunger. Within minutes she was done, her earlier trepidation replaced with the opinion that she'd just had the most remarkable meal of her life.

"So tell me again what this thing is and where it came from. By that I mean what time it came from, you know, how long ago." Jack was working on seconds, talking with his mouth full. He'd made a sandwich by putting cynodont meat between two small pieces of cycad "bread" and topping it with what Endicott had called, for lack of a better term, 'cress,' a nondescript but tasty water plant.

"Go easy on the cress," Endicott warned, "or you'll be up all night. It has a mild laxative effect."

The warning caused Jack to pause in mid-bite.

""Yeah, you better not eat too mucha that grass," Spencer laughed, "we don't want you runnin' into the bushes every five minutes on our hike tomorrow."

Jack made a face and reluctantly pulled the cress from his sandwich. It would have made for a tastier meal, but he figured it best not to take chances.

"Our repast this evening, Jack, comes from a beast that hasn't changed much, if at all, for perhaps 250 million years," said Endicott.

"No offense, but I have trouble putting that into context," Jack replied. "I'm afraid my knowledge of geologic time is rather limited. Jocelyn knows when this world originated because of the plants that exist. Spencer happens to be an expert because he's so darn smart: I think he reads encyclopedias or something. And you—you're one of those professional guys who studies dinosaurs, what do you call 'em, proctologists?"

"Paleontologist," Endicott offered. "I'm an archeologist, actually, PhD from McGill in 2002. My thesis research dealt with primitive cultures of the northeast Canadian seaboard, and the flora and fauna of the time. That explains why I became involved with the Eviskar dig. Prior to that, however, I had strong interests in geology and paleontology. I took numerous courses in both of those subjects during my undergraduate years in Halifax."

He crossed his arms and sighed, "I wish I were more knowledgeable in so many areas. Sometimes I feel that I became trapped here through divine providence, that instead of feeling cursed I should embrace the extraordinary scientific good fortune of being able to live amongst these ancient beasts and plants, and to study them in the most intimate manner. Many of my colleagues would give almost anything for such an opportunity, but, frankly, after having spent so much time here, I just want out. Throughout most of the past year I've contemplated how in Heaven's name this place came to be, but all I think about now is how much I crave a cold glass of beer and a good hockey game." Endicott turned to Spencer. "Before we retire for the evening, Spencer, would you care to enlighten me and our friends with your thoughts about this bizarre place? I personally would like to hear the objective opinions of another knowledgeable human being who has experienced this world."

Spencer couldn't believe what Endicott had just suggested. Here was a distinguished scientist asking for *his* opinion, the views of fifteen-year-old Spencer Bowen, a high school student from Brooklyn. After taking a moment to collect his thoughts, he began his discourse by addressing Jack:

"Like I said befoah, 250 million yeahs ago there was a major extinction event, the most extensive die-off of life the planet has evah known. Among the higher land-based life forms to have survived the cataclysm were tetrapods, animals that paleontologists have divided into two distinct sub-groups: sauropsids and therapsids. That archosaur we met yesterday was a saurapsid. They eventually evolved along two lines: dinosaurs and birds on one branch, 'an crocodiles on the other."

"Wait," interrupted Endicott, "did you say you encountered an archosaur the other day?"

"Yeah, he chased me up a tree, almost ate me, why?"

"You're one lucky fellow, Spencer. Those big archosaurs rule the western part of the island. Fast and lethal, there is no question they occupy the very top of the food chain. The climate down there is much more to their liking, the abundance of geothermal vents keep it warm and moist, decidedly more tropical than these parts. I've long felt that the cynodonts that live up here may be warm-blooded, at least to some extent. The archosaurs and dicynodonts that thrive in the swamps to the south and west are much more reptilian. They need the constant eighty degree environment down there to maintain reasonable body temperature. When I say you were lucky, I mean it in two ways. You were fortunate to survive, that's obvious, but you were also blessed to have seen one. If they could exist in these cooler regions for any significant length of time, they would decimate the populations of all reasonably-sized prey. Even within the narrow confines of this island universe, there are well-defined separate ecosystems. It would be fascinating to study so much of this world if I didn't bloody well have to live here."

"So, getting back to what Spencer said," Jack interrupted, "archosaurs are related to dinosaurs?"

"Yeah, according to analysis of their fossils, dinosaurs evolved from sauropsids...archosaurs...within fifty million years or so. The therapsids, the otha' main group to have survived the great extinction, existed in three main types: dicynodonts, cynodonts and therocephalians. Therocephalians went extinct pretty fast 'an the dicynodonts, like the one the archosaur went after in the river, they went extinct in the Triassic. It's the cynodonts that were the important line. While dinosaurs, birds 'an crocodiles evolved from archosaurs, cynodonts were the progenitors of mammals."

All four individuals were silent for a moment, contemplating what Spencer said.

"I think I get it now," Jack admitted. "This world is perhaps 250 million years old, predating the time when dinosaurs ruled. And it was a dinosaur ancestor who almost turned you into lunch yesterday. The critter we ate tonight, and the guys who ate his guts in the ravine, are our distant ancestors." He paused before adding, "That makes a lot of sense to me now. Those cynodont lizard wolves bear a striking resemblance to my Uncle Fred."

Outside it began to rain, a gentle drizzle bringing a chorus of soft plops from the leafy thatch covering of the hut. Endicott carefully covered the coals with ash from the periphery of the fire pit and closed the smoke hole in the roof.

"Tomorrow will be a monumental day," he announced soberly. "You'd best make ready and catch some sleep. We've got quite a distance to cover."

Jack yawned by way of assent. Crawling to a corner of the one-room shelter, he draped a cynodont hide over his tired frame and used another as a pillow. "Boy, when this is over, when Debbie is tended to and we all get back to the archeological dig, the first thing I'm going to do is disappear into my nice warm, comfy sleeping bag and sleep for twenty-four hours. Then, I'm going to write down everything that's happened to us on this island..." Suddenly he was asleep. No sooner than he'd lain down, Spencer too was sawing wood. Neither boy had slept much in the past two nights, and their overwhelming fatigue, coupled with a full and satisfying meal, had abruptly caught up with them.

Jocelyn was just as tired as her companions, but sleep eluded her. Something she couldn't logically comprehend bothered her. It had to do with Endicott. Just before Jack had dozed off, she noticed Endicott staring at him. The look on his face was hard to define because of his thick matte of facial hair, but his eyes for a brief moment were cold and disapproving, almost hateful. The man was an enigma. As someone who was good at reading the moods of others, Jocelyn found the Doctor's personality to be impenetrable. At times he was jovial, willing to engage in stimulating conversation and eager to discuss his life in exile. Often, however, he'd turn cold and spiteful, a man lost in gloomy thoughts and bad memories. Right now, in this remote shelter and in the presence of this unpredictable man, Jocelyn knew she wouldn't go to sleep. There was danger here, she could feel it, sense it. For the sake of herself and her two friends, instinct compelled her to stand guard.

Endicott slept on a straw-lined bed against the wall opposite from where the students lay. The interior of the hut was only as dark as a night illuminated by a full moon. The glow from the Sun that lay just beneath the mountain peaks filtered through gaps around the door and windows, enabling the occupants to observe one another in silhouette. For a while, Jocelyn sat on a woven mat made of coarse reeds and leaned against the rock wall. Rhythmic snoring resonated from where Spencer and Jack lay, their minds peacefully ensconced in dreamland, secure in the knowledge of an imminent return to the civilized world.

After sitting for perhaps half an hour Jocelyn stood and made her way to the door. As she passed Endicott she whispered that she was stepping outside to pee. Regular, heavy breathing emanated from the prostrate form. The good Doctor was asleep. Leaving the door wide open, she turned the corner and squatted out of view of Endicott, but she maintained a direct line of sight to where the boys lay. Upon her return she left the door partially open. Her eyes were now sufficiently dark adapted to allow for a closer look around the residence.

There wasn't much to see. A leather poncho and the now famous spear were located just to her left. Otherwise the only item of note was a pile of what looked to be homemade clothing or hides resting on a chair near the back of the hut. She tiptoed over to inspect. Cautiously she lifted the top skin. Underneath were a small backpack made of nylon and a steel pot of moderate size. She was about to lay the cynodont hide back into place when she noticed something else. Something reflected the weak twilight streaming in through the open door. It was tucked into the main pocket of the pack. A glance in Endicott's direction reassured her that he was indeed sound asleep, so she reached inside and pulled out a book. The corner of the dust cover was what had reflected the light. Holding it up for view she read the title: 'The Vikings—Canada's first European Immigrants.' It was a large, profusely illustrated history of Viking settlements in North America. Jocelyn frowned. Certainly this was a volume likely to be in the possession of an archeologist like Endicott.

A rustling noise off to her right made her start. Turning quickly she was relieved to see that it was just the professor rolling over in bed. She returned the book to the pack and replaced the hide that concealed it. In doing so she happened to notice yet another item that lay beside the pack. Small and dry, she couldn't identify it at first, so she walked to the door to examine it in better light. It was a desiccated apple core. Jocelyn's brow knitted in concentration. This wasn't the sort of item one expected to see in a primitive, prehistoric world. Again she replaced her find exactly where she'd found it and quietly went to shut the door.

Intrigued by what she'd discovered, Jocelyn Delaney felt her way towards the back of the hut and to the thin bed where she would wait out the night. Without realizing where she was, she stubbed her toe on one of the rocks lining the fire pit. Dropping to one knee, Jocelyn grabbed her foot and grimaced in agony. *'Sonofabitch that hurt!'* She mouthed the words. She wanted to cry out and tell the world, in very explicit terms, how that stupid rock, in this stupid place, had, without provocation, attacked her poor little toe. But she couldn't. Slumping to the floor, she stayed where she was, massaging her foot until the pain subsided to a tolerable level. "At least I don't have to worry about falling asleep now," she told herself in a tone dripping with irony. She finally let go of her throbbing appendage and leaned forward to inspect the damage.

If fate hadn't led her to trip over that rock, she never would have found it. In the dust beside her toe, half buried by the rock that had attacked her, another object glistened in the weak light coming through a crack in the door. She picked it up and knew immediately, from its reflectivity and its weight, what it was.

Most high school girls, especially those who pay attention to their looks and personal adornments, know real gold when they see it. This was a large bracelet. It appeared to be very old. The surface was slightly pitted, indicating the presence of impurities, and it was covered with small hammer marks. Due to the darkness she couldn't tell if it had a jeweler's mark, but there were certainly no large engravings or inlays of any kind. It was a very heavy, very simple piece of gold.

Jocelyn put the bracelet back under the rock and carefully walked back towards her sleeping mat. The items she'd seen were, to say the least, curious. What to make of them?

Baffled by her discoveries, Jocelyn was lost in thought as she turned to sit. Out of the far corner of one eye, something else caught her attention. Endicott's head seemed to be raised, silhouetted against the lighter background of the wall behind him. A quick glance was all it had been; she may have been mistaken. Had he really been propped on his elbow, watching her, studying her while she snooped through his stuff? She took a closer look back in his direction, and saw that his head was on his pillow. He appeared to be sound asleep. She stared for a while and then lay down, passing off the vision as a figment of a paranoid imagination. Her premonitions about Doctor E. were probably unfounded, she tried to convince herself. Despite the man's idiosyncrasies he had accepted them into his abode, hadn't he? He'd fed them a decent meal and in the morning he would lead them away from this horrible place. And the objects she'd found? There was undoubtedly a logical explanation for everything. Chiding herself for being so suspicious, she relaxed to let some of the pent-up anxiety of the past two days melt away. But not all of it. The one thing she needed most, a good night's sleep, was something she knew she wouldn't get.

The "coffee" made from roasted cycad seeds was surprisingly palatable, if not a tad more bitter than the real thing. Even with syrup made from rendered tree sap—a precious and difficult to produce commodity in which Endicott took tremendous pride—the students didn't consume much. They did, however, bestow numerous compliments regarding the exotic beverage. Doctor Endicott was in a chipper mood and his guests weren't about to say or do anything to change that. They ate a sumptuous breakfast of cold cynodont, coffee, cycad biscuits and a fleshy vegetable, a tuber of some sort, somewhat akin in taste to an overripe pineapple. Endicott took his time, relishing what he considered to be the last meal in his camp of the past year. The other three hungrily wolfed down their food, barely taking the time to savor and chew. They wanted to get started. Images of Marcie and a suffering Debbie clouded their thoughts and lent urgency to preparations for the trek to the inhospitable cliff where their comrades were enduring another cold, damp morning.

Jack was the first to stand and grab his backpack. "I've got plenty of room in my pack," he announced to no one in particular. "Load me up and let's move out."

Jocelyn stood and stretched. "Sounds good," she said brightly. She was exhausted but didn't dare show her fatigue. To satisfy her curiosity about her recent find, she "accidentally" kicked the rock under which the gold bracelet lay. Bending down to pick it up, she examined it thoughtfully, as if for the first time.

"Ah, I was wondering where that was." Endicott took the object from her and smiled. He nodded with satisfaction and added wistfully, "Randrup's good luck piece." Despondency crept into his tone as he ran his fingers over the pitted surface. "Aage Randrup. You may recall he was one of my two colleagues who died in our tragic fall of a year ago. He recovered this from the Eviskar dig site. From the moment he found it, he exhibited a profound attachment to it. Viking gold. He wore it on his wrist henceforth, wouldn't even take it off to bathe."

"That's stealing," Spencer noted. "It's an archeological artifact. He had no right to just take it like that."

"You are entirely correct, Spencer. His actions were decidedly improper. Of course everyone knew what he'd done, but..." Endicott heaved a sigh in remembrance of his former friend. "Most of us excused what he did. You had to have known him to understand why. Aage was a proud Greenlander, a complex man who treasured both his Inuit and Norse ancestries. This bracelet, it, well—it represented his Scandinavian heritage, his Viking roots. His attachment to it was obsessive. It was as though he drew some immense inner strength from its presence; it established a link to its former owner, a Norseman of obvious stature due to its size and weight."

"It was still wrong for him to take it," Spencer frowned.

"Yes, yes it was," lamented Endicott, "but Randrup dutifully logged it into our inventory of artifacts. He never hid what he'd done, and we all knew he would care for it better than any museum could. So we let him wear it." He looked in turn at each of the students. Tears welled in his eyes as he dropped his gaze and stared at the ground. In little more than a whisper he said, "I took it from his corpse, and I want to show it to his next of kin once we get out of this wretched place. I was going to give it to someone who loved him, but you're right, Spencer. It belongs to the public, and it should remain on display here in Greenland to be forever associated with the fine human being who discovered it."

Endicott stood and walked to the back of his shelter to take stock of the supplies that were piled there. He regarded the assortment of hides, food stores and wooden implements he'd needed to support his long stay on Eviskar Island. "I need time to assemble the gear necessary to construct a litter to haul your friend Debbie safely up that cliff face." He shook his head, "Yesterday I may have been a tad overly optimistic about her rescue. The more I think about it, the more I fear it may be too dangerous for a helicopter to lift her to safety given the high winds and the mist above that steep cliff. If the three of you would be willing to carry out the food, and a few provisions, I'll set out shortly with the other materials we'll need."

The two older students were itching to get started and needed no further encouragement. "Let's split the remaining cynodont meat between us," Jocelyn said to Jack, "and, Spencer, you carry the cycad biscuits, but be careful not to get them wet when we cross the river."

"I'm staying wit' the professor," her young colleague announced. "You guys take most of the food 'an leave enough for the two of us. Doc Endicott is gonna need help carryin' all this stuff."

Jocelyn didn't like the idea of leaving Spencer behind. She figured the best way to coerce him to accompany her and Jack was via a lighthearted approach. "C'mon, Spence, we're gonna need you for protection. What if Malarkey or some other what-do-you-call'em, gorillasaur attacks us? Who's going to distract him?"

Spencer rolled his eyes. "It's 'archosaur,' 'an like I said, Professor Endicott may need help. There's a lot 'o stuff to bring to help Debbie. I think he's gonna need me."

Jocelyn was flustered but didn't let it show. Maybe Endicott was all right. Maybe, in fact almost certainly, her premonitions about the guy's mental stability were totally unfounded. She half-heartedly made one last effort to change Spencer's mind. "I'm just worried that if we show up without you, Debbie will freak out. She'll be concerned for your safety."

Spencer chuckled, "It's youah safety I'm worried about. Dr. Endicott has lived here for a year. I'll be a lot safer wit' him than wit' you."

"If the lad wishes to accompany me, I welcome the fellowship," Endicott said jovially. "He and I have much to discuss. You and Jack be careful on your hike to the cliff. It would be best for you to go back the way you came—through the valley, across the river and then up the gentle slope to the northwest. Do you think you can manage that?"

"No sweat," Jack responded. "I know the approximate bearings and distances we travelled to get here. We'll just reverse them for the return trip."

Jocelyn patted Jack on the back and quipped, "I trained him well, Professor. His built-in angle measuring device is well calibrated. We'll be fine." Endicott appeared to be in excellent spirits. All concern for Spencer's safety went away as she and Jack cinched their packs and prepared to leave. "Please hurry, Professor Endicott," she said as they departed, "Debbie's life depends on us."

"Spencer and I will be along shortly, Jocelyn. We'll take a shortcut through the hills to the north. It's rugged, but lessens the distance somewhat. I suspect we won't arrive too much later than you will."

Jocelyn and Jack waved as they rounded the hill behind Endicott's hut and disappeared into the mist.

For the first half hour Jack and Jocelyn walked with singular purpose. Time was of the essence. Their leisurely breakfast and late start meant that they wouldn't make it to the cliff before darkness set in, but they wanted to cross the river and camp at higher elevation once the time came to stop. Already the thermometer had hit at least eighty degrees and the air had become much more thick and humid than it was at Endicott's camp.

"I feel like a sieve," Jocelyn complained, "like one of those cartoon characters that gets hit with a shotgun blast. When they take a drink it just pours out all the holes. I've never sweated like this before."

Jack regarded her with concern. Something was bothering Jocelyn. She wasn't just dehydrated; she looked haggard. She was exhausted and cranky, even more cranky than normal, but of course he'd never comment on that. He was certain she hadn't slept the night before, and he didn't think it was from worrying about Debbie. "A penny for your thoughts," he said when they stopped to refill their water bottles from a small stream. "And I mean your thoughts. Don't hold back. What's on your mind?"

She looked at him and saw the seriousness in his countenance. He wasn't the usual smiling, upbeat Jack. His eyes were boring into her with evident concern. "Dr. Endicott is weird," she muttered.

Jack waited for her to elaborate, but Jocelyn merely sat on a nearby rock, closed her eyes and massaged her neck. He wasn't about to drop the subject. "I agree," he replied, "but I don't see why that should upset you so much, keep you from sleeping."

"I spent hours last night thinking about Endicott's situation, and a bunch of things don't make sense."

"Such as?"

"First of all, he doesn't seem to be too concerned about Debbie. And he wasn't exactly in a hurry to get started this morning. You'd think he'd want to get to the beach as soon as possible, you know? After all, he's been marooned here for over a year."

"That might not be as abnormal as it seems," Jack noted. "The fact that he's been here for so long—that can have all kinds of psychological effects on people."

"And look how fit he is. The guy faced down a lizard wolf that wanted his kill. And after that we had trouble keeping up with him on the hike to his hut, despite the fact he was carrying a dead forty-pound silo-whatchamacallit thingy."

"A very tasty cynodont," Jack offered.

"I started thinking how easy it would have been for him to scale that cliff. There are plenty of vines around, and tough pieces of leather. He could have fashioned a strong rope and safely climbed up that steep top part. It's only about thirty feet and there are good hand holds. A desperate and determined man would have tried it. What would you have done in his situation?"

Jack nodded thoughtfully. "Yeah, I guess I'd have climbed out, but I'm an experienced climber and anyway, that rockslide he was in had to have been traumatic. That might explain any apprehension on his part."

Jocelyn shrugged. Jack had a point. He was using logic—sort of—but she was using something more powerful—feminine intuition. The more she thought about it, the more convinced she became that Endicott was hiding something. She shouldered her pack and motioned for Jack to get moving. Once they were on their way again, she asked, "Did you happen to notice some of the possessions he had in his shelter?" She didn't wait for a response. "Of course you didn't. He had a coffee-table-sized book about Vikings and a large cooking pot. Who the heck goes hiking along a rocky ridge carrying books and cooking pots? And I saw an apple core lying under his pack. What about that? It certainly wasn't something left over from a year ago, and there are no apple trees on this island, no flowering plants, remember? Even if there were, you can't just drop a seed into the ground and grow, say, a tree that produces Golden Delicious or Macintosh apples. You wouldn't know what to expect. All modern eating apples are grafted cultivars."

Jack abruptly stopped and turned around. "Just what are you implying, Jossy?"

"The only ways Endicott could get those things would be to either raid the supplies back at the archeological site or make trips to and from the island. I suspect the former explanation is by far the more likely of the two. In other words, he knows a way out, yet *chooses* to live here. Something strange is going on, Jack, and as for you, you poor guy, you can't see it because, like all men, you lack women's intuition, that sixth sense we have when it comes to understanding human behavior. All other indications aside, Dr. Endicott's behavior and mannerisms tell me he's lying. He's hiding something."

Jack pondered what she'd said. "So I'm clueless and lack intuition, but at least you admit that I'm a man."

She put her hands on her hips and glowered. "Really?! That's all you got from what I just said: the fact that I'm aware of your gender?" She pushed past him and continued walking down the trail.

They moved along smartly for some time before Jack said meekly, "I was just kidding."

Another moment passed before she spoke. Still walking briskly, and without turning around, she said, "For what it's worth, I've definitely noticed you're a guy, okay? A really nice guy. Furthermore, I find you very attractive."

"Professor Endicott, I got enough meat 'an biscuits packed for the bote of us. What other stuff do you want me to take?"

"Ah, good. There's a satchel in the hut containing several large animal hides. We may be able to use them to fashion a basket in which to carry your friend Debbie. Just how big is she? How tall?"

"She's about my height, but she weighs a little moah."

"Good enough. Come sit here while I select what we need."

Spencer sat just outside the entrance while the Doctor rummaged inside, searching. Moments later he heard Endicott's footsteps and turned around.

A fraction of a second before impact, Spencer raised his hands to protect his face. Endicott swung the handle of his spear like a baseball bat, aiming a vicious blow at the boy's head. The club knocked Spencer's hand against his face and the youngster fell to the ground. Endicott stood over his stunned victim with malice in his eyes.

"Wha...what'd 'ya do that foah?!" Spencer asked in disbelief.

"Good, you're bleeding. Stabbing you would have been painful—for both of us," was all the man said. He produced a leather thong and expertly bound Spencer's hands behind him.

Spencer had a bloody nose. The front of his shirt was gradually turning crimson, and the sweet taste of the blood running down the back of his throat made him gag. The Professor lifted him to his feet and propelled the stumbling and thoroughly confused young man to the ravine into which he had jettisoned the cynodont entrails the previous evening. Upon reaching the precipice, they half-walked, half-slid down the steep slope to the bottom. They then made their way along the stream to the rocks where the lizard wolves had dined only hours earlier. Shoving Spencer onto his stomach, Endicott bound the boy's legs together. "I'd taken quite a liking to you, Spencer. You're a smart young bloke. It's too bad you have to die."

"Why?" wailed Spencer. His face was streaked with tears and blood. His nose and cheek were swollen and painful. But the real hurt was psychological. Endicott was someone whom Spencer had looked up to. This survivor, this world expert, had treated him as a kindred spirit, almost as a professional equal. The incredible turn of events had broken Spencer's heart.

"Yes, I suppose I owe you an explanation. Young man," he bent down and patted Spencer on the shoulder, "I hate to do this, but I mustn't allow any of you to return to civilization to tell of this mysterious world. You see, a thousand years ago, give or take, there were other visitors to this island, and like you and me they discovered its secrets. That archeological site up the coast?" he waved dismissively, "it's really nothing, a few huts and an old fishing village. I do believe the reason for its existence was merely to lead the curious away from the beach and low ridge that you and your colleagues stumbled upon as a route to the island's interior."

Endicott thrust his left wrist up close to Spencer's face. It bore the bracelet Jocelyn had uncovered back at the hut. "This is Viking gold, my young friend, and it represents but one piece among the thousands that have been cached in several places within this prehistoric world.

"Well," Endicott stood and stretched, "I'm afraid I must be off. It's time to stage what promises to be a nasty ambush of your friends. I'm afraid there's no other way. I would have clubbed all of you to death last night but for the watchful eye of that bitch, Jocelyn—stayed up the entire night she did. I daresay she might have dozed off if she hadn't stumbled, literally, upon the bracelet. Ah well, in a few hours none of that will matter." He scrambled several feet up the slope of the ravine before turning to address his victim one final time. "As a budding paleontologist, there may be some consolation in knowing the scientific name for the beasts which will soon devour your remains. 'Cynognathus' is the technical term. It's a bit bland in comparison to 'lizard wolf,' don't you think? And for what it's worth, I don't believe you'll suffer much. On several occasions, having watched them make a kill, I was impressed with how calmly their prey succumbed. I do believe they're somewhat venomous; their saliva must contain some sort of powerful anesthetic." With those final words, Endicott disappeared over the edge of the ravine.

Spencer lay still against a moss-covered rock. The air was calm and humid; the only sounds he heard were the gurgling of the little stream and the desperate beating of his own heart. He pulled against the thongs that bound his hands, but Endicott had tied them so tightly he couldn't move his wrists at all. Similarly, the Doctor had lashed his legs together from just below the knees down to his ankles. In the back of Spencer's mind, beneath the numbing fear, he knew that in order to survive he had to extricate himself as quickly as possible from this macabre dining place of the lizard wolves. His efforts to move, however, were decidedly unsuccessful. So securely had he been trussed, he couldn't so much as roll over.

Spencer began yelling for help. He pleaded for someone to come and cut his bonds. He cried out to his parents in English, in French, in Mohawk. He conjured up desperate hopes that searchers or rescuers might be looking in this vicinity for him and his lost colleagues. He called out to Charlie, his friend with the hot dog stand, the man who knew him so well, who always rendered such sage advice whenever Spencer had a problem. What counsel would the old man have for him now? Finally, he called out to Jack and Jocelyn. If either of them were suspicious of Endicott's motives, maybe they had circled back to check on him.

But all of his entreaties went unanswered. Abruptly Spencer stopped yelling and began to whimper. Who was he kidding? No one was coming to help him. He began to cry softly.

It was between sobs that he first heard it: a chorus of short, high-pitched grunts. They were approaching quickly up the ravine. Spencer stopped crying as panic overwhelmed him. He launched into a superhuman effort to break the leather straps that immobilized his hands, but it was for naught. The thongs simply grew tighter, cutting into his skin. A horrified look crossed his face as the foliage below him rustled and the first animal broke into the ravine.

XII

Jack stopped abruptly. "What's the matter?" Jocelyn asked. She plopped down onto a fallen tree and took a large swig from her water bottle. She then soaked her bandana before replacing it around her neck. Grateful for the break, she relaxed and looked up at her companion. He was standing exactly where he'd stopped, a look of serious concern on his face.

"We took a wrong turn," he replied. Extending his fist at arm's length, he did his navigation thing and nodded to himself. "Yep, we're too far south. Darn it! I should have been paying closer attention. We should have veered to the west over an hour ago. If we want to cross the river at the head of the lake, we have to turn back."

She looked around and sighed. "I think you're right. This terrain is strange. We certainly didn't come through here yesterday." She looked at him and sensed bitter disappointment. "Hey, it's not your fault. I should have been more attentive as well."

Jack shrugged by way of assent. "We may as well head back. Who knows what we'll encounter if we cross this valley this far downstream. Doc Endicott said the archosaurs live down south, and we're on our way there. Let's just go back and swing west once we get to familiar territory."

They hoisted their packs and plodded back the way they had come. Both were hot and exhausted, and the enthusiasm of the morning had long since worn off. It was a long way back and the only way to get there was to keep moving regardless of the fatigue that had set in.

After an hour of slogging through fern fields, conifer forests and circumnavigating one large cycad grove, Jack spoke. "My navigational error really cost us, Jossy." He was bitter and angry. Jocelyn had never seen him upset like this. "What with that late start we got, we're not going to make it to the river by nightfall." He turned to face her. "And that," he added emphatically, "means we won't get to Debbie and Marcie until late tomorrow. And THAT means," he continued, "Debbie won't make it to the beach until the day after tomorrow." Tears of frustration moistened his eyes. "The poor woman, she's so badly hurt and I've singlehandedly prolonged her suffering."

The strain of being away from Debbie, of not having yet rendered any real help to her, was having a profound effect on Jack. Jocelyn felt it too, but not nearly to the same extent. In her mind they'd done all they could, but Jack's sense of responsibility evidently ran much deeper. He was really upset.

Acting on impulse, Jocelyn put her arms around him and held him close. The bold move surprised Jack. Anxiety abruptly replaced frustration, and he stood stock still, not knowing how to react. Jocelyn held on, pressing her head against his chest. Soon he responded. At first he gently patted her shoulders, then he relaxed and returned the embrace, hugging her tightly and stroking her hair. They stood that way for some time, neither wanting to let go, both considering the awkward moment when they would separate and be forced to admit to the attraction they had for one another.

They finally drew apart. She was smiling. Her gaze was soft and understanding. Jack blushed deeply but forced himself to look her in the eye. "Thanks, Jossy," he murmured, "I don't know why I got so worked up, but...thanks."

"She grinned, "We'd best be going."

"Yes," he admitted, "we still have a long way to go."

From a dense clump of ferns the first animal appeared. It moved quickly towards Spencer, coming up the incline of the gulch with its head down and urgency in its demeanor. And it wasn't a lizard wolf. It was a creature he'd never seen before, but there was, nonetheless, something familiar about it. As the distance closed, Spencer made out a human-like face hidden behind extensive facial hair. It moved with a hobbled gait, an extreme limp, but it moved quickly and was promptly by his side. Brandishing a knife, the "bearded ape" worked quickly to free his legs, whereupon it grunted, "Come," and helped to propel him out of the dangerous ditch. No sooner had they left when three fearsome lizard wolves, salivating in anticipation of an easy meal, sniffed their way to the spot where Spencer had lain.

At the top of the embankment, Spencer collapsed. A combination of shocks to his system had caused his brain to shut down; he blacked out from sensory overload. Everyone has limits to the extent of psychological trauma he can endure, and Spencer couldn't take any more. The intense fear he'd just experienced, coupled with the helpless feeling of being bound hand and foot, the betrayal of the man he'd come to admire so much, and the blow to his head, had simply been too much.

When he awoke, the "cave man" was staring down at him. Spencer's hands were free and he found himself lying in Endicott's hut, sprawled upon the Doctor's straw bed. His rescuer poked and prodded him, looking for signs of injury. Apparently satisfied with his examination, the man ushered him to the door and pointed to the north. "You go...uh...mountain. No here safe. Mountain...der."

Spencer began to ask questions, but the man cut him off. He was agitated and apprehensive, anxious to be on his way. He handed Spencer a crudely made knife and a spear, and again pointed to the northern hills. "You go now. Safe at mountain." Giving Spencer a reassuring pat on the shoulder, the bearded savior hobbled away to the south, towards the river valley, along the route taken by Jack and Jocelyn earlier that morning.

Spencer was alone but he was no longer frightened. He had experienced fear, real fear, only minutes earlier, and the incident had somehow hardened him. A feeling of intense resolve now consumed him. He knew he was lucky to be alive, and, dammit, he was going to stay that way. But remaining here at Endicott's place would lower his chances considerably. Mr. "cave man" had indicated that safety lay in the mountains, so he'd follow the man's advice and head that way.

His mind was functioning cogently now. Already he'd formulated a plan. A route along mountain slopes to the north and west would ultimately bring him back to Debbie and Marcie. If he encountered obstacles, he'd drop in elevation until he cleared them and then continue his trek upslope. That should keep him clear of most predators and out of the steamy, humid jungle below.

Taking off his blood-soaked shirt, Spencer tied it around his waist. He then tucked the knife into his belt, grabbed his spear and jogged in the direction indicated by the mysterious fellow who'd saved his life. Along the way, Spencer wondered about the man, who he was and why he'd appeared when he did. How long had he been in this Godforsaken place? Where had he learned the few English words he'd spoken? And where the heck was he off to and why did he leave in such a hurry? "The answers don't really matter right now," Spencer reasoned. He was quite certain the two of them would meet again, and he sincerely hoped that when they did, it would be under less stressful circumstances.

Long shadows stretched across the trail in front of the two tired students. The reddish tint to the Sun warned Jack just how low it was in the sky and how little time they had before it would slip behind the distant hills.

"We should be near the crossing point now," Jack said with confidence. "Like I predicted earlier, we don't have enough daylight left to ford the stream today. What do you say we look for a place to camp?"

Jocelyn didn't need any encouragement to stop. She was exhausted. They instinctively began meandering uphill, away from the river where wildlife would be expected to congregate at this late hour. There would be no comfortable shelter to stay in like Endicott's hut. A tall tree with strong, level branches upon which to construct a crude platform would be the best, most hospitable abode they could reasonably hope for. On a nearby hill, a solitary large tree stood apart from the rest. Majestic in stature, it seemed to beckon the two weary travelers. Jack headed straight for it.

"Okay, Ms. Botanist, here's a specimen for you. It looks like an oak. Even I know that's out of place in this world. I wonder how it got here? Whoa," he said as he neared the trunk, "it smells like someone lost his lunch. We can't sleep in this guy; he stinks."

Jocelyn wasn't listening. She stooped to pick up something from the ground, sniffed it, wrinkled her nose, and then became absorbed in the study of the tree's leaves. Knowing better than to interrupt her when she was in "plant examination" mode, Jack waited for her to speak.

"It's incredible," she remarked.

"Told ya," Jack said with pride. "The headlines will read: 'Malinowski finds oak tree in gymnosperm world.' I even remembered the term 'gymnosperm,'" he beamed. "You may now applaud if you wish."

Jocelyn smiled. Jack was back to his carefree self. She liked that. "Sorry to disappoint you my fine phytogenetically astute friend, but this is no oak."

"What?"

"It's a ginkgo tree."

"Hey, I've heard of that. Ginkgo balboa. It's a vitamin supplement or aphrodisiac or something. They advertise it on TV."

"Ginkgoes are an ancient variety of non-flowering plant. The only surviving member in the modern world is *Ginkgo Biloba*. This one's different though, similar, but different. Like those horsetails we've seen all over the island, this plant has been extinct for over a hundred million years."

"As fascinating as all that is, let's move to the pine grove over there. I'm tired."

"We can stay here. Look at the branches in this ginkgo. It's the perfect place to sleep."

"Maybe you can stand the smell, but I can't. The smell of puke makes me want to do the same."

"I agree, but the smell is down here, Jack." She picked up a handful of soil. "See there?" She held several small objects up to his nose. He wretched and turned away. "The rotting seeds, the ones on the ground, are what stink. Butyric acid is produced as they decompose. Once we're higher up we won't smell it."

Jocelyn was right. About fifteen feet off the ground, three large branches extending horizontally from the trunk served as joists upon which Jack constructed another crude sleeping platform. In the growing darkness, he began to search their surroundings for strong sticks and branches. Once he'd gathered an armload, he'd pass them up to Jocelyn and then scramble up to supervise their placement. She marveled at the ease with which he ascended the tree following each successful foray. He climbed as easily as if he were walking down the street. In almost no time they had a comfortable place to rest, a solid platform of wood covered with soft cynodont hide.

"I swear, you must be part monkey," Jocelyn said once they were settled. "You're so athletic. What sports do you do?"

"In addition to climbing you mean? None, really." Delving into his pack he produced two cynodont sandwiches. After offering one to a grateful Jocelyn, he continued, "Actually, I'm surprised that your feminine intuition didn't peg me as the captain of the swim team."

"Do you have to make a joke about everything? You're an enigma to me,

Jack. Don't take this the wrong way, but you're the most unusual guy I've ever met, and," she added in a low voice, "apparently you didn't hear me on the trail earlier today when I told you that you're not exactly, entirely without a modicum of acceptable assets in the area of physical appearance...as it were."

"Huh?"

"Gee, Jack, do I really have to spell it out for you? I think you're attractive, Okay?"

Jack was at a loss for words. He stopped chewing his dinner and stared.

She let out a deep breath. "Now that I've made a complete fool of myself, I'll leave you to your dinner. I'll eat mine as well." She took a big bite of her meal and turned her back to him.

"I'm really attracted to you too, Jocelyn."

"Oh, right." She once again faced him. There was pain in her expression and sorrow in her voice. As they'd plodded through the afternoon heat, the young woman from Corpus Christi had become reflective. She'd found herself thinking more and more about Jack, and about how different he was from her friends back home. "How could you possibly harbor any feelings for someone like me? I'm an argumentative, unsupportive, mean-spirited, self-centered bitch. And you know what? I'm the unhappiest person alive because I hate myself. I despise the way I've behaved towards people on this trip, I despise the way I've acted in school, and I'm a real lemon picker when it comes to choosing friends."

Jack smiled. "I wouldn't call you 'unsupportive.'"

She laughed. "What you lack in tact, Mr. Malinowski, you make up for in humor and honesty. I guess that's what I like about you."

"You know, if you don't like who you are, then change, Jossy. One of my dad's favorite expressions is: 'Today is the first day of the rest of your life.' He's always throwing out phrases like that—he thinks he's quite the philosopher. But if you think about it, that saying makes a lot of sense. People change. I've seen it many times. If you don't like who you've become, make this the first day of the rest of your existence."

She nodded tearfully and leaned against him. Jack put his arm around her. "You know, you have a lot of good qualities, Ms. Delaney. You've shown that you can be understanding, caring, helpful, and you haven't complained about anything throughout this whole ordeal with Debbie. I admire how you can be honest in recognition of your faults, but don't be too hard on yourself."

"Can I ask you something," Jocelyn said. "What did you think of me before Debbie's accident? Until then we hadn't interacted much."

He thought for a moment. "Well, when you showed up with most of your worldly goods at the airport and caused Debbie all that grief, I was..." He searched for the right word, "...I was perplexed. I thought, 'She must know she's got to fit her stuff into two bags. What's going on?' But, as long as we're being up front here, I was concentrating more on your looks than anything else. I fell prey to that fault most guys have of excusing a girl for the way she behaves simply because she's pretty.

"Then when you used up all that water on the boat to wash your hair...well, I guess that's when I saw a side of you I really didn't like."

"Neither did the captain," Jocelyn said. "She was pissed; I thought she was gonna throw me overboard."

"Ah, yes, I do believe she wanted to. But look at the bright side; you've had your vocabulary greatly enriched by a Danish sailor. Let's be honest here, old Doc Sørensen didn't translate *everything* the Captain said. Certainly you can use some of those colorful phrases to great effect at the dinner table back at the archeological site."

She poked him in the ribs, "Hey, I may have run the ship's supply of potable water dangerously low, but my hair was silky and smooth. The sharks would have been impressed with my flowing locks if we'd been introduced."

"Ha! Now who's making jokes?"

"You're right. I'm sorry. Now, tell me exactly what you thought of me after I pulled that boneheaded stunt, and don't hold back, Jack. If I'm going to reform, I have to really understand the errors of my ways."

Jack was uncomfortable with Jocelyn's request to be critical of her. He didn't see the point of this exercise. It was up to her to evaluate her own shortcomings and, if necessary, to alter her behavior. The change had to come from within. But when he saw the pleading look in her eyes, he gave in. After a moment's thought he said, "Back then I figured you to be a vain and manipulative person who played at two different games. On one hand, you're very smart and get good grades. Those are things that get you in good with your parents, teachers, etc. In fact, that's what got you accepted for this archeological study. I also thought, however, that you were good at playing the popularity card; you'd learned how to be mean and cliquish, and I would have bet money that you hung out with friends who value social standing more than anything substantive.

"At least that's what I thought back then," he added defensively. "In the last few days, I've seen a different Jocelyn Delaney." He hugged her and said, "I've, uh...I've really fallen for this one."

Jocelyn sat up and looked quizzically at him. "You figured all that out? It's like you really knew me. No offense, but I've always believed you to be a typical guy when it comes to reading people's character, you know—oblivious. You're really very perceptive."

"What I am is a high school student, like you. The kids at my school fall into the same categories as those in Corpus Christi. People are the same everywhere." He smiled, "Now it's your turn, Jossy. What did you think of me when we first met? I came clean to you, so hit me with the cold, hard truth."

Jocelyn perked up, grinning from ear to ear. "Okay, here goes. Are you sure you're ready for this?"

"Uh, yeah, I guess." Jack became mildly concerned, but he'd asked for it. "Go ahead, hit me."

"You're 'Mr. Perfect,' and I found that intimidating. When we first met, I thought, 'He's cute, friendly, probably a teacher's pet, a real goody-two-shoes.' That didn't surprise me, though. I expected the other kids on this trip to be over-achievers: you know, class Presidents, honor roll regulars, members of every club known to man. Did you read the essays written by the four of us that Debbie sent out once we were selected as winners? When I read Spencer's I thought, 'There is no way a fifteen-year-old wrote this, a Pulitzer Prize winner maybe, but not some high schooler from Brooklyn.'

"Anyway, I thought, mistakenly of course, that the only guy I could possibly be attracted to, and who would likewise be attracted to me, would be someone with attitude, a 'bad boy.' I never considered you to be my type. I was also unprepared, both mentally and emotionally, for this trip. The only reason I accepted the invite was to get far away from a difficult situation at home."

Jack considered her words. "It's funny how we tend to pre-judge people, how we form opinions about them before we get to know them. Jocelyn, I just realized something; you and I are a lot alike, you know that?"

"You've got to be joking again."

"No, I'm not." He shifted around on the platform so that he could see her face. "We both are hung up about pleasing others. You work hard in school to please your folks, and you go along with stuff that bothers you, and that you know is wrong, in order to be popular."

"You don't seem to be so insecure, Jack. You're perfect, remember?"

"Hell, I'm ten times worse than you, Jocelyn. I strive for good grades because I don't want to let my parents down. I'm an only child and they're immigrants who've worked hard to provide me with the American Dream. It sounds corny, but it's true. They dote on me. I hear my mom telling her friends all about me, about how I'm such a great student. My dad thinks I'm this super mechanic who'll take over his business and turn it into a big success. The pressure is incredible. I love them and don't ever want to give them reason to doubt me or be ashamed of me.

"And, do you know why *I'm* on this trip? For the same reason you are: to get away. I simply couldn't stand to work in my dad's garage this summer. I don't want to be a mechanic for the rest of my life, but I just don't have the guts to tell my dad. It'd break his heart." He sighed and said despondently, "You're lucky, Jossy. Your situation is passing. After high school your troubles will be behind you. I don't know if I'll ever be able to do what I want without disappointing my folks."

"So what do you want to be other than a mechanic?"

"It may seem silly to you, but I want to be an astronomer. It's funny, really; I've never studied astronomy in school. Spencer and I have that in common. He developed an interest in paleontology outside of his 'halls of learning,' and I love reading about the night sky."

Jocelyn listened attentively as Jack launched into a grand soliloquy about the nature of stars: their sizes, temperatures and chemical compositions. She admired the passion he had for the subject and envied him the joy of having an interest that so captivated him. There certainly was more to this kind, considerate man than she could possibly have imagined. She suddenly felt a closeness to him that came as a pleasant surprise. Admiration for how he balanced his passion for astronomy against his concern for his parents' feelings, with his folks taking precedence, spoke volumes about his character. He'd become an inspiration to her. Now, more than ever, Jocelyn knew she had to effect a change in her own outlook on life.

While Jack carried on about stellar distances, magnitudes and lifetimes, she found herself fiddling with the matted, tangled ends of her hair. It hadn't been washed in ten days, and for the past three it had become a snarled mass of knots, dirt and bugs. What had once been a symbol of status, beauty and vanity, had become, of late, a nuisance. Moreover, it represented the lifestyle she wanted to leave behind. "Jack," she interrupted, "I have a favor to ask."

He stopped in mid-sentence when he saw the pleading look on her face. He knew immediately that whatever it was, she was asking for something she considered very important.

"Cut my hair."

"What? You serious?"

"Please, Jack, take it off right here." Her fingers held a lock about an inch above her shoulders.

"All I have is my pocket knife, Jossy."

"That will do just fine, Jack. Just fine."

Spencer was making good time. He was trying to stay more or less at the same elevation as Endicott's camp, contouring around hills and up gorges, every so often moving higher or lower to circumvent obstacles. He knew that sooner or later he'd run into the field of huge boulders that had diverted him and his colleagues to the south two long days ago. Finding his way around that would be tough, but it was something he'd just have to face when the time came. There were miles to go in the meantime.

Ahead of him lay one of the kinds of obstacles he was anticipating. Far upslope, an impressive waterfall tumbled from high among the coastal peaks. Over eons, water had carved a deep gorge that meandered through the foothills over which he was hiking. Somewhere downstream, this stream would flow into the large river coming from the east, the one he, Jocelyn, and Jack had forded earlier. The gorge was too steep to navigate at his present location; he'd have to find an acceptable place to cross.

Spencer sat for a moment to collect his thoughts and ponder the situation. He looked to the east, to the source of the water, and realized he'd never be able to negotiate the cliffs that rose out of the mist beside the waterfall. That meant he had to move downstream. He didn't want to descend into the valley itself, with its high heat, humidity and the threat from predators. This stream would also merge with others along the way thereby increasing the size of what was already a formidable hazard. At last he made his decision. He would hike downstream and cross at the first available opportunity.

Spencer couldn't believe his luck. At a point where the stream cut between two low hills, a tree had fallen across. It was a large conifer whose roots had been exposed during periods of high runoff. Enough soil had eroded away that its base couldn't support it, and it had toppled over. Unfortunately the trunk didn't span the entire waterway, but it did form a nice bridge over the faster-flowing water beside the near bank. He decided this was it. This was the best place to cross.

At the water's edge, Spencer took a deep breath. The water was much deeper and faster moving than it had appeared from a distance. Nonetheless, he tightened the chest strap of his backpack, clenched his teeth and stepped onto the log. He tried to focus on the stationary trunk and the placement of his feet rather than the disorienting sight of the foamy water roiling below. Inch by inch he moved across, carefully picking where to place his hands and feet in order to maintain balance on the wet, slippery moss-covered wood.

Crack! At just over halfway his luck ran out. He fell into the creek still holding the branch that had given way. He'd put too much weight on it and the frail limb had pulled right out of the rotted trunk. His left arm slammed into a rock sending a wave of pain through his shoulder, and the shock of ice cold water numbed his senses as he was swept dazedly downstream, unable to stop moving. Desperately grabbing for any sort of hold, he tumbled onward, feeling helpless and out of control.

Struggling just to keep his head above the surface of the churning water, he caught a glimpse of a large, jagged rock about fifty feet in front of him. Located mid-stream, it was right in the way. He was going to hit it, and hit it hard. Two choices flew through his mind as he catapulted towards it. He could try to deflect off of it, push away with either his hands or his feet in order to stave off a collision, or he could take an awful risk: he could try to grab it. He might be swept directly into it with devastating consequences, but, if he could move to the side at the last second, maybe, just maybe...

Steeling his arms for impact, he grabbed for the rock as he simultaneously rolled his body to the side. The powerful current yanked at his legs trying to force him onward, but his grip held. It felt as though he were hanging from a chin-up bar with a fifty-pound weight strapped to his ankles.

The strain on his shoulders was incredible. He knew he couldn't hold on for long, so, summoning all the strength he could muster, he pulled with his arms and kicked with his legs, somehow managing to move his body into the eddy at the upstream end of the rock. The far shore was still more than ten feet away. A daunting stretch of turbulent water lay between him and safety, but the boulder to which he clung was a godsend—it had stopped him from moving downstream. Exhausted, he rested for a moment. He needed to look around, collect his thoughts. Water splashed against the side of his head and into his eyes, making it difficult to see clearly. Staring ahead, he gradually focused on something that protruded out over the water. It was a branch. What he couldn't make out, however, was whether or not it was attached to anything. If he grabbed it, would it prove to be his salvation, or would he continue his trip downstream with a new piece of rotted wood for company? "I don't really have a choice," he realized. He had to get out of the water before hypothermia made it impossible to move. He was going to drown if he didn't act soon. With a mighty shove, he propelled himself towards the river's edge and grasped for the branch with both hands.

It held. He hung there for a moment, clinging to the branch, resting. Finally, summoning what little strength he had left, Spencer clawed his way along the branch and pulled himself up onto the bank. The cold, shivering fifteen-year-old lay in a mass of ferns and muck, spent from his labors, but aware, also, that he'd overcome a major hurdle on his trip to get back to Debbie and Marcie. Gone were his spear and his coveted Yankees cap, precious and valuable possessions now given up to the awesome natural forces that ruled this strange land. But once again, Spencer Bowen had prevailed. As he continued to win at this battle for survival, his confidence increased and his resolve strengthened.

A noise in the foliage startled him and he quickly drew his knife from his belt. A snout soon appeared, followed by a small, squat body about the size of his neighbor, Mrs. Benavidez's, beagle. To Spencer's relief, its features were benign. It was a small, herbivorous cynodont. The two stared at one another, neither showing signs of either fear or aggression. The cynodont extended its whiskered face until they were nose to nose. It carefully sniffed and analyzed the scent of this odd interloper, this alien visitor to its realm. Spencer was likewise enthralled with the idea of interacting with a living fossil. Months earlier he had been reading about beasts such as this, imagining from pictures of their petrified remains what they might have been like. Slowly he reached forward and ran his hand across the animal's smooth, leathery head, and looked into its amphibian-like eye. The cynodont snuffled once before turning and waddling away.

Spencer watched the animal disappear into the shadows. Darkness was coming. The Sun, heavily muted by leaden cloud, was marching inexorably towards the high hills to the north, and would soon be hidden for the hours that masqueraded as 'night' in this odd land high above the Arctic Circle. Cold, tired and wet, he realized he needed to find a tree in which to wait until morning. To continue his journey in darkness would be dangerous and foolhardy. It hurt to stand, but he forced himself onward, trudging toward a small, nearby grove of conifers. Tomorrow he'd get an early start and push himself over the last uphill stretch that, hopefully, would lead him to the cliff below the ridge where this whole ordeal had begun. He'd soon be reunited with Marcie and Debbie—unless Endicott got there first.

Where the heck were they? Endicott recrossed the river at the place he'd expected Jocelyn and Jack to have forded. Again he carefully examined the muddy bank for footprints—none. He'd dispensed with Spencer quickly enough, and his pace along the trail had surely been sufficient to overtake the others prior to the river crossing. Confused, he stood still and pondered what must have happened. "They didn't ford here," he surmised. "That's obvious. They must have gotten lost and crossed elsewhere." For the life of him, Endicott couldn't imagine a better place. Upstream the current in the river was just too swift. And downstream? He didn't know this part of the valley well enough to answer that question. But along the lake and below, it was absolutely choked with vegetation and all but impassable. Unless they were to have stayed at higher elevation and wandered south, they couldn't cross the valley for some distance. He finally concluded that they were still on this side of the river.

The sky was darkening. Searching for the two students would be difficult in the fading light. Morning would come soon enough. He'd find them then, and when he did, their unexpected visit would come to an end. Consideration would then shift to the other two, the injured woman, Debbie, and the young girl, Marcie. If Marcie hadn't wandered too far from the cliff, might it be best to let them live? If she and Debbie knew nothing of the island's prehistoric character, they might not pose a threat to him. "No," he abruptly decided, they had to die too. Were they to make it back alive they would certainly report the disappearance of the other three students and a massive search would ensue. All evidence must be removed from the beach and cliff areas to keep rescuers from snooping around that ridge and stumbling into the island's interior.

Hefting his spear, Endicott jogged back up the trail to find a place to pass the night. In the morning he had business to attend to, nasty business, but, in the end, it had to be done. This world and the treasures it contained, his treasures, had to be protected. He soon found a nice tree and settled into its lower branches. Unbeknownst to him, less than half a mile away, Endicott's prey had just finished their evening meal.

XIII

The platform in the gingko tree was littered with patches of blonde hair. Jack Malinowski sat back and closed his folding knife.

"Oh, how I wish I had a mirror." Jocelyn was carefully feeling the ends of her hair, trying to generate a mental image of how she must look.

"You look great, Jossy," Jack assured her, "It's the best haircut I've ever given."

"Really? You're kidding."

"Nope," he smiled, "It's also the worst haircut I've ever given—it being the only one." She pouted, but he added brightly, "You look great with short hair, honest." In fact, Jack couldn't stop staring at her. At that moment he thought she was the most beautiful woman he'd ever seen. She caught him looking and it made him blush. "Of course, you have to give enormous credit to your barber for that crazy cut. I can see it now. When we get back to civilization, people will see you and marvel at what henceforth will be called the 'Malinowski Doo.' All the finest salons will offer it. Hairdressers will be sharpening their pocket knives to give customers that 'Tarzan-cuts-Jane's-hair-in-the-jungle' look. I'll make a ton of money to augment my meager salary as an astronomer."

"Very impressive," Jocelyn noted. "I didn't realize you had such savoir-faire when it comes to style. So, are you gay?"

The question stunned poor Jack. "Aw, shoot. All I did was what you asked me to do. I mean, it's not like I'm into, I don't know, flower arranging or anything. You wanted me to cut your hair. It isn't a big deal."

She took his hand in both of hers and couldn't resist a sly smile. She'd put him on the spot, insulted his masculinity, and it was making him squirm. "Sorry," she swooned, "I guess it wasn't fair to ask you that...but are you?"

"What?"

"Gay"

"Heck no!" He smiled when he saw the mischief in her eyes, eyes that were pale blue and tinted by the setting Sun, the most beautiful eyes he'd ever seen. "But, what if I were? Would it make a difference?"

"Oh no, most certainly not, at least not when it comes to friendship." Now it was her turn to feel uncomfortable. "You have to admit, however, that if there were to develop any sort of romance between us, then maybe it would be problematic..." She trailed off when she noticed Jack was no longer looking at her. Instead, he seemed fixated on something above them. She followed his gaze but didn't see anything. What could be more important than her subtle hints about starting a romantic relationship? Maybe he really was as clueless as she'd believed earlier. "A penny for your thoughts," she sighed.

He was doing his extended fist thing again, alternately measuring the sky and glancing at his watch. Pointing to a rare break in the clouds he said, "Yep, that's Deneb. It was tough to identify without being able to see the surrounding stars in Cygnus, but, yeah, it's him. It's my favorite star." Both of them watched as wisps of cloud gradually moved in to cover the faint sparkling image. Once again the sky became a dull, grey blanket. "I say it's my favorite because it's truly impressive." Jack sounded as though he were speaking about an old friend.

"Really?" said Jocelyn in a tired voice. She admired Jack's enthusiasm, but she herself didn't think stars were such a big deal. Sure, it was nice to look up and see them on clear nights, kind of romantic even, but when you got right down to it, they were just faint spots of light.

"Yeah, really. It's one of the largest, most luminous stars known. Even though it's about two thousand light years away, it's still one of the brightest stars in the sky, one of the three that make up the 'summer triangle' asterism. Think about it, Jossy, the light we just saw left Deneb around the time Christ was born! It puts out fifty to a hundred thousand times as much light as the Sun."

"So it's bigger than our Sun?"

"Bigger? I'd say! Try twenty solar masses. There's a limit to how big stars can get, and Deneb's right up there. When one gets to be that size it burns fuel at an enormous rate. Of course that means Deneb won't live long. It's maybe ten million years old, give or take, and it probably can't last more than a few million more before it dies in a supernova explosion. It may already have exploded. If that happened today, we wouldn't know about it for two millennia."

"Yes, it's very impressive," Jocelyn said with a yawn, "but I think all the technical talk detracts from the charm of camping out on the beach, or sitting in a smelly gingko tree and looking at tiny lights twinkling against a black void." The Sun was now lost behind the hills and the air was noticeably cooler. She snuggled up to him. "Sometimes I wish we lived in the past, Jack. Not the 250 million years ago past, but long enough ago to where the stars were a mystery to mankind. The majesty of the heavens has been lost to some degree, now that we know so much about them."

Jack put his arm around her shoulders and pulled her to him. "When I was young, maybe ten years old or so, my dad took me camping. We went to some park up in Canada, somewhere in northern Ontario. What I remember most about the trip is the view of the sky at night." He shifted so that he could see her face. "You have to understand that I was a kid from the city. From my house I'd seen the moon, Jupiter, Venus, Saturn and a few bright stars, but didn't think much about them. Up there in Canada, my dad pointed out a bunch of stars, the same ones that are above us right now hidden from view, and he told me about the Milky Way and the constellation Cygnus, 'The Swan.' And you're absolutely right, Jossy. As a kid I was awed by the majesty of what I saw and fascinated by what was then a mystery to me. Now that I've learned more about stars, they continue to fascinate me, but much of the mystique isn't there anymore.

"Now, in ancient Greece the sky was the realm of the Gods. Nothing could surpass the grandeur of what they saw in the heavens, and numerous explanations arose about how the constellations like Cygnus came to be. In fact, Cygnus is one whose lore I know something about because Deneb is one of its defining stars, representing the swan's tail.

"One account says that the Gods were so enamored with the poet Orpheus that, upon his death, he was turned into a swan and placed amongst the other constellations. Another claim is that Cygnus was the pet bird of the Nubian princess Cassiopeia. But the predominant Greek myth holds that Cygnus is the image of the form taken by Zeus when he fell in love with the mortal woman Leda, wife of Tyndareus, the King of Sparta."

"Zeus was more or less the number one God of the Greeks, wasn't he?" Jocelyn interjected. "What could possibly have made him fall in love with a mortal?"

"I would presume," Jack said after a moment of mock contemplation, "that Leda was a great botanist and swimmer. I can definitely see him falling for someone like that. Also, as a young swan Zeus could have needed swimming lessons. That would have given him the excuse he needed to approach her."

"Right, right, that must have been it," she said sarcastically.

"So, Zeus, who's now a swan, seduces her and she lays two eggs..."

"Yuk! You mean she had sex with a bird?"

Jack again thought for a moment. "Maybe they did things differently back then?"

"I doubt it."

"Yeah, me too, but anyway, as the legend goes, Leda bore four offspring, two sired by Zeus; Pollux and Helen of Troy, and two others, Castor and Clytemnestra, fathered by her husband. You probably know the story about Helen, about how beautiful she was. She married the King of Corpus Christi but was terribly unhappy and ran off with her true love, Paris, a stud from Cleveland. Of course things got really ugly at that point. Her husband assembled an army to get her back, and the resulting conflict became known as the Trojan War."

Jocelyn gave him a disapproving look. "I remember studying the Trojan War in my World History class and I believe you're mistaken about a few of the place names. Although I don't care much for that legend, it would be nice if you would point out the constellation Cygnus to me—once we get somewhere where we can see the darn thing. This eternally grey sky is depressing."

"I can't argue with you. This place isn't exactly an astronomer's paradise. As long as we're on the subject of Cygnus, would you care to hear the Chinese explanation of how it got there?"

"Does it involve a hunk from Cleveland?"

"Of course."

"Okay, let's hear it."

Jack lay back and covered both of them with his windbreaker. A gentle breeze had come up carrying with it cool air from the mountains and the strange nocturnal songs of thousands of prehistoric insects. "Long, long ago," he began, "there was this hot guy from Cleveland, or maybe he was a shepherd from China; I can't remember. His name was Niu Lang which I suppose supports the notion that he was Chinese. Of course he still could have been from Cleveland. Anyway, Niu fell in love with a beautiful fairy princess named Zhi Na. They were happy until the Goddess of Heaven found out about their relationship. It seems that Niu, although he was quite the hunk, was a mere mortal, and fairies are forbidden to consort with mortals. The Goddess got mad and banished them to heaven. Zhi is now the star Vega, in the constellation Lyra, and Niu, the mortal stud, became Altair, the brightest star in Aguila, 'The Eagle.' To keep them apart, she separated them by a river of stars that we now call the Milky Way."

"How mean," Jocelyn said. "It's amazing how we humans use prejudice to deny happiness to others. People can be so cruel."

"I totally agree, but the myth has a happy ending...sort of. You see, the constellation Cygnus lies in the Milky Way and the swan's wings span the 'river.' Once a year, on the seventh day of the seventh month—according to some old Chinese calendar—all the magpies of the world fly up into the sky and form a bridge, the Magpie Bridge, 'Que Qiao,' across the Celestial River, right where the swan lies. They do it so that the lovers might spend one night together. Legend has it that if it rains that night, it's because the magpies couldn't make the trip and the raindrops are the tears of Zhi and Niu who know it will be another year before they can possibly be together again."

Jocelyn lay quietly beside him, so quietly that Jack assumed she'd fallen asleep. He knew how tired she was, how she hadn't slept the night before, and how physically drained she must be after hiking all day in stifling heat. It wasn't long, though, before he felt her shaking. He sensed something was wrong and touched her shoulder. "Jossy, are you all right? You cold?"

She sat up and looked at him. Tears streaked her cheeks; she'd been sobbing. Jocelyn wasn't just tired, she was emotionally spent. The ordeal they were going through was taking a heavy toll. Reaching out to him she cupped his face in her hands and looked deeply into his eyes. "Jack, I just want to..." She choked-up, desperately searching her tired and foggy mind for words to express her feelings. She finally wiped away her tears and took a deep, cleansing breath. "I want to thank you for being such a good friend, and for cutting my hair, and for telling me that wonderful story. I liked it a lot better than the Greek one." She smiled, leaned forward and kissed him gently on the lips. Then she snuggled up against his chest and fell into a deep sleep.

"Wiggle your toes for me, Debbie," commanded Marcie. There was movement there, but not much. Debbie had had a horrible night. The previous two nights had been difficult, but this had been worse: much, much worse. Her leg was throbbing, and her moans prohibited both of them from getting any real rest. Finally, partly because of the cold, but mainly out of concern, 'doc' had decided to thoroughly examine her patient. Something was very wrong. When she donned her LED headlamp and unzipped Debbie's sleeping bag, the problem was apparent. The injured leg had become badly swollen; taut skin and fluid pressure were squeezing the fracture, causing intense pain.

Marcie bit her lip in the characteristic way she always did when she really concentrated on something. Of one thing she was certain: action on her part was required. There were several things she could do to help alleviate some of Debbie's suffering, but each carried consequences.

Throughout this ordeal, Marcie had carefully regimented the pain medications she had in her pack. What were supposed to have been enough pills to relieve the occasional headache or back pain afflicting one person over a three month period, had become needed therapy for a major injury. The supply was now nearly exhausted; only two ibuprofen tablets remained. Debbie wasn't due for another dose for at least two hours, but Marcie quickly decided to administer them immediately in a prompt attempt to arrest the swelling. She also decided to elevate the limb by several more inches, and then do something she had been trying to avoid.

Because of the intense cold, Marcie had refrained from icing the injury. Now she felt she had little choice. No snow or ice existed on the shelf where they were camped, so Marcie improvised by soaking one of her Tshirts with cold water. Easing Debbie's leg out of the sleeping bag, she wrapped the compress around it and then closed the bag around the rest of Debbie's body as best she could. The risk here was from hypothermia. Using cold to stop the terrible swelling would suck heat from Debbie's body at an alarming rate.

Both women already shivered constantly through the short but miserable nights when the Sun passed behind the mountains, and this therapy might push Debbie's body temperature to a dangerously low level. To combat this inevitable heat loss, Marcie activated her last remaining chemical heat pack and tucked it between the two of them.

"Hang in there, Debbie," she said in a soothing voice to her barely aware patient. "Tomorrow's going to be an eventful day. I promise."

In fact, the day would be eventful because Marcie, having taken stock of their rapidly degrading circumstances, had just made a momentous decision. If help didn't arrive in some form by early afternoon, she would try to rig some mechanism to haul Debbie up and over the cliff edge. The woman's condition was worsening. Enduring one more night with no more pain killers, no heat and no food, might prove too much for her. If Marcie couldn't get Debbie to the beach, and if a rescue party didn't arrive within a day or two, her newfound friend and mentor would die.

Jocelyn sat up and rubbed her eyes. It took a moment for her to collect her thoughts and get her bearings. She'd been so tired and her sleep so deep, it took a while for her to remember where she was. As her mind cleared, a sudden mild panic set in. Jack was gone. Looking quickly about, she was ready to shout his name when he catapulted up from below and handed her a stick. "A present for you, Miss Delaney, from your favorite story teller."

She examined it. It was a straight horsetail stalk. Embedded in the end, and tied tightly with a short length of Marcie's paracord, was a short but nasty-looking cycad spike. Jack himself sported a similar-looking spear that lacked the spike. It had instead been carefully sharpened using his pocket knife. "In case we encounter trouble near the river," he said by way of explanation.

He immediately attended the business of stuffing his pack full of the animal skins they were to carry back to the cliff. Without speaking, Jocelyn touched his shoulder. When he turned, she embraced him and gave him a lingering kiss. "Just to let you know that last night was...that I really meant it."

Jack didn't blush. Their relationship was now past that awkward stage. The Jocelyn Delaney who had emerged from her cocoon and spread her new wings over the past three days was the polar opposite of the girl he'd met in New York. This one was smart, insightful, caring, and he liked her—a lot. Needing no further encouragement, he held her close, rubbing her back, running his fingers through her recently cut hair, and gazing soulfully into her wonderful blue eyes. With a heavy sigh, however, he soon let go, picked up her pack and handed it to her. Without a word, Jocelyn nodded and they set off towards the heart of "Eviskar Valley," as they'd come to call it, heading for the river a scant mile away, a river that stood between them and the high cliff where a badly injured Debbie still lay. Endicott's engineering skill, in conjunction with their climbing gear, was now the only hope of removing the poor woman from her cold, rocky prison and saving her life.

Ten minutes after Jocelyn and Jack's departure, a half-naked man clad only in a breechclout and homemade leather shoes, knelt at the base of a large gingko tree. He smiled sadistically as he plucked strands of blonde hair from among the foul-smelling seeds that littered the ground. Looking up, he beheld a crudely constructed sleeping platform nestled in the branches, and examination of the soil around the trunk clearly revealed two sets of human footprints. None of this had been here when he'd passed by yesterday afternoon, of that he was certain. With a triumphant nod he grasped the handle of his spear and arose to scan the foliage in the direction of the river. How long had it been since they left? His smile broadened at the thought. Not long: perhaps twenty minutes, he guessed—given the amount of light they'd need to find and follow the trail. If he could double their pace he could likely orchestrate a surprise reunion in one of the glades lying just uphill from the river bank. Loren Endicott broke into a jog and padded swiftly and silently through his Triassic world. Among horsetail and fern, conifer and cycad, the hunter advanced toward his unsuspecting victims.

With the rising Sun at his back, Spencer trudged slowly uphill. He'd learned through careful observation how to gauge his elevation based upon air temperature. Staying above the clouds made it easier for him to navigate, but because he was still wet from his horrendous stream crossing, the cold air chilled him. He was therefore forced to spend much of his time down low where the air was thick and humid, and the bugs and vegetation a nuisance.

Now, however, he was angling uphill on a foray to look for landmarks. He had to be paralleling the coastline because he was moving among the foothills of the mountains. He also had the Sun more or less behind him which, at this time of day, put him on a northwesterly course, exactly where he wanted to be.

The mist was thinning up ahead, not much farther to go. He would rest there and eat something, but not linger too long. A dreadful thought had come to mind in the last hour or so, one that he blamed himself for not having considered much earlier. That Endicott was after Jack and Jocelyn was obvious. The bastard had smugly revealed his evil plans before leaving Spencer to become brunch for a pack of hungry lizard wolves. But what about after that? If Endicott killed Jack and Jocelyn, a thought Spencer refused to dwell upon, he would then make a beeline for Marcie and Debbie. Spencer had to get to them first. The two women would be sitting ducks the moment they turned their backs on the charming professor. That wasn't going to happen. Spencer picked up his pace, pushing the thought of fatigue from his mind as he powered uphill.

Soon the sky began to lighten. Instead of dark, slate-grey it was the color of toilet paper, at least the cheap bargain brand his mother bought. "When you consider what we be usin' it for, I don't be spendin' the good money," she would say jokingly. The thought of his mom brought a smile to his face and further strengthened his determined mood. Up higher, the clouds turned to wisps and blue sky beckoned.

When he finally stopped, Spencer took a long, well-deserved drink and looked around him. To the south lay the valley, socked in by cloud. The view was surreal, making him feel like he was in an aircraft, crossing miles above terra firma. Somewhere within that atmospheric soup, Jack, Jocelyn and the malevolent Dr. Endicott were destined to meet in a deadly denouement. Spencer forced himself to look away. He agonized over his inability to help his friends, to warn them of the peril posed by their traitorous "savior." There was always the possibility, he thought optimistically, that they had enough of a head start. But so what if they reached the cliff ahead of their foe? The professor would still have the element of surprise; Jocelyn and Jack still considered him a decent man. All four of his colleagues would be sitting ducks. Spencer had to get to the cliff first.

He awoke from his reverie, resigned to be on his way, when he spotted it. Between two towering mountain peaks, a low spot, like the crossbar of a football goal, lay in the distance. The longer he stared, the more excited he got. It had to be the ridge. No other breaks existed in the mountains flanking the eastern part of the island, at least they hadn't seen any from the boat or on Debbie's satellite image.

The intervening terrain was rugged. Steep-sided basalt in the highlands gave way to lush, dense vegetation down low. How far was the ridge? Spencer paused to estimate the distance. He looked back the way he'd come and tried to correlate what he'd just been through with what lay ahead. Three or four miles, he finally concluded, but that was as the crow flies. Depending upon what he encountered, it might be hours before he arrived. Hefting his pack and a sharp stick he'd picked up as a weapon, Spencer once again hit the road.

"I have to stop, Jack."

"We're almost at the river."

"I know, but I have to visit the little girl's room. Thinking about the river, well, it has a stimulating effect on my bladder."

Jack smiled and moved ahead to give her some privacy. They were at the edge of a glade, a hundred yards from a significant source of rushing water. It was probably the nearest of the three tributaries they'd crossed the day before. That meant the crossing point should be just to the south.

The soft rustling of foliage off to his right caught Jack's attention. It was probably Jocelyn returning from her break, but in this world full of dangers one never knew. "Jossy, is that you?" he enquired. When she didn't answer, Jack gripped the spear he'd made that morning and went on high alert.

Expecting the worst, Jack watched as the thicket parted, and then he uttered a huge sigh of relief. "Hey, Doc, I thought you and Spence were taking the other..." Something was wrong. Why would Doc Endicott want to throw a stick at him? Realization came in the nick of time. Jumping quickly to his left Jack watched in horror as the point of Endicott's spear passed within an inch of his neck. Not knowing how to react, he stood stupefied, like a deer caught in headlights, trying to fathom what was happening.

Sensing bewilderment in his victim, Endicott pressed the attack. He sprinted straight at the young man. Powerful legs propelled his stocky two-hundred pound frame, kicking up sand, closing the gap between them in a matter of seconds. Jack's eyes bulged when the professor pulled a long knife from a sheath, and his confusion turned to dread as Endicott screamed and dove for him.

Once again Jack's reflexes barely saved his life. He successfully dodged the thrust of the blade, but the big man's shoulder delivered a glancing blow as both fell sprawling into the sand.

Endicott immediately sprang to his feet. Leaping onto Jack's prone form he swung the knife downward. Jack hit his arm, deflecting the blow. He managed to grab the hand with the knife in both of his own and pull it to one side. The professor responded by savagely hitting Jack with his other hand and then grabbing him by the throat.

The pressure was unbearable. Jack's windpipe was in a vise; he couldn't breathe in or out. His eyeballs felt as though they would pop from his face and he drifted towards unconsciousness. Nonetheless, he gamely held on. To relent was to die. But he was losing strength fast.

"Don't struggle, Jack," the Doctor said. A contorted smile formed on his countenance as he squeezed his victim's neck even harder. "A clean cut will make you bleed out faster. It will make things considerably less painful."

Jack's ability to resist was failing. He thrashed his legs and tried to dig his fingernails into Endicott's hand, but he was just too weak. His attacker sensed the end was near and laughed sadistically. This athletic young man posed the only true threat to the secret of Eviskar Island. The three women who remained of this ill-fated group would be easily subdued. Within seconds he would slit Jack's throat and his principal adversary would be gone.

Whap! Endicott pitched to the ground when the haft of Jocelyn's spear smashed into his head just above the right ear. The young woman had heard the struggle and run from the bushes to aid her friend. She immediately moved to where Jack lay gasping for air and holding his neck.

Jack was now breathing, sucking small amounts of air, glorious air, into his starved lungs. But his head was spinning; he was disoriented. His brain had been deprived of oxygen long enough that he'd nearly blacked out. He was now in the foggy world of those who've fainted and fight to reenter reality.

"Jack, get up! Come on, Jack!" Jocelyn was trying to pull him to his feet.

It was taking too long. Jack simply wasn't coherent enough to stand. He needed time—time to recover.

Out of the corner of her eye Jocelyn noticed that Endicott, although dazed, was beginning to stir. That was unacceptable. Running to the Doctor, who had now risen to his knees and was trying to get to his feet, Jocelyn kicked savagely at him with her size nine Reebok CrossFit Nano 2.0 Lite TR crosstrainers. One smartly delivered blow caught him across his left cheek and spun him to the ground. Moving in for the coup-de-grace, Jocelyn aimed for his groin and delivered a mighty kick that would have settled the issue once and for all. Unfortunately, her aim was poor. Her right big toe, the same one she'd stubbed on the rock in Endicott's hut, rammed smack into the professor's knee. "Ow! Sonofabitch," she yelped, grabbing the pained appendage.

If the situation hadn't been so dire, a disinterested party viewing the scene from afar would have found humor in the strange, absurd sight: a young woman hopping around on one leg, burning the ears of surrounding prehistoric beasts with a string of obscenities, while two men writhed in the nearby sand.

Jack responded first. Shaking his head to clear the remaining cobwebs, he slowly stood and picked up the spears he and Jocelyn had dropped. Jocelyn hobbled over to him and they embraced. Their respite didn't last long, however. Jack was still attempting to breathe normally, but kept clearing his throat, coughing and massaging his neck. He was about to try to speak when Jocelyn stiffened and pointed. "Jack, look!"

Endicott was on his hands and knees and moving quickly to where his spear had landed.

"Run!" Jack's voice was little more than a hoarse whisper. Clinging to one another for support, she limped and he staggered as they struggled through a dense horsetail patch—one that stood in the general direction of the river. For several minutes they pushed onward, stumbling over logs and swatting away branches covered with dew that slapped them as they passed. Brambles scratched and clawed at their faces and clothing, seemingly trying to delay their escape. Soon, patches of fern gave way to dense forest and the sandy soil turned to thin, watery mud. They were heading into a swamp.

"I don't remember this," Jocelyn noted with dismay.

"Me neither." Jack paused to look around. "We're too far north. The wide area where we want to cross is thataway." He pointed toward the blackest, densest part of the swamp.

"You want to go through that?" she exclaimed.

"It can't be that far. The valley opens up down there. Trust me."

"But what about, you know...creepy crawlies? Who knows which is worse, Endicott or whatever lives here."

He took her hand. "Are you coming or not?" He took a step forward, and as if on cue a huge dragonfly whizzed above them and lit on a rotting stump a few yards away. Undaunted, they slogged through muck and shallow pools of foul-smelling stagnant water. Their feet made loud sucking noises with every step, the mud slowing progress to a slow walk. The air was so thick and humid it was hard to breathe.

Jocelyn was petrified. As the forest grew darker and darker because of the thick, claustrophobic overhanging canopy, she began to shiver with fear. After all she'd been through in this primitive world, it was this place, this dark, gloomy, fetid morass, that had finally extracted primal fear from deep within her psyche. She clung tenaciously to Jack's arm.

Jack wasn't exactly enjoying the landscape either, but he marshaled a calm, brave façade for Jocelyn's sake. He gave her a hug. "Jossy, I haven't thanked you yet for saving my life back there."

She smiled, "You know I got your back, Jack."

"That kick you delivered to Endicott's head—that really got his attention. It was awesome."

"Those tae kwon do lessons I took as a kid finally paid off."

"Yeah," he pointed at her sore toe, "that second kick didn't go so well though, huh?"

"Hey, I had a couple of lessons; I didn't say I was a black belt."

"Too bad."

"Yes," she sighed, "it really is too bad."

Another dragonfly buzzed past. It flicked left, crossing their path, ultimately settling on a low-lying moss-covered branch. Both students were awed by the huge insect. Seeing one up close like this was truly breathtaking. Enough muted sunlight fought its way through heavy cloud, forest canopy and water-laden swamp air to reveal the bug's dazzling colors. Its foot-long wings shimmered with all the colors of the rainbow as light diffracted off of their delicate membranes.

"It's so beautiful," admired Jocelyn. "I guess there's beauty even in a place like this. When you least expect..."

The pool beneath the dragon fly suddenly erupted, and an oddlooking animal launched itself out of the water. A long tongue shot out from an enormous head and plucked the giant insect off of its perch. The attacker fell back into the water with a resounding splash and then climbed out onto a large log to savor its meal.

"Ahhhh...!" Jocelyn freaked. She jumped into the arms of a surprised Jack, nearly making him fall into the mire.

"Jossy, let go. It's just some sort of dragonfly-eating...something or other." He peeled her arms from around his neck and helped set her back on her feet. They watched in fascination as this weird-looking life form, this creature from the black lagoon, devoured its prey.

Curiosity overcame her fear as Jocelyn scrutinized this newest of prehistoric beasts. "Well butter my butt and call me a biscuit," she muttered in amazement. "Man, that thing is ugly. If I had a dog looked like that, I'd shave his ass and teach him to walk backwards."

To the 21st century mind the creature was, as Jocelyn so eloquently stated, 'butt ugly.' The head was large and frog-like, but behind stocky forelegs its body tapered sharply. The hind quarters were small, and it sported a long tail. Overall it was a very, very peculiar-looking organism. It chewed slowly and with its mouth open. One could make out rows of short, but very sharp, teeth crushing the dragonfly's exoskeleton with an audible crunch every time it closed its jaws. Jack and Jocelyn stood transfixed until the creature was done with its meal. Cold, primitive eyes stared back. By and by, the animal tired of watching the two funny-looking strangers. It uttered a guttural croaking sound and bounded from its log back into the pool. Using its tail for propulsion, it swam, snake-like, until it was out of sight.

"I'm gettin' outta here," Jocelyn swore. She picked up the pace and marched forward with purpose. Brandishing her spear, slogging through the syrupy muck, she announced, "Any of you swamp critters try to mess with me, I'll gig you, batter you up and fry you Cajun-style. Got it?!"

Jack was impressed. He followed his partner, and her new-found courage, until they were out of the swamp and onto a flat, fern-laden stretch of river bank.

XIV

The water was deep, slow-moving. Jocelyn stopped marching. She turned and met Jack's gaze. Both knew what had to happen. Jack was going swimming.

Urgency compelled them to hurry. Jack took a deep breath and let it out. There was no use stalling for time; he was as ready as he'd ever be. Jocelyn took his hand and led him hip-deep into the river. The current was insistent but gentle. She explained that they would be carried a slight distance downstream, but not to let it bother him. She then quickly went over the rules, telling Jack what she needed him to do: relax, tilt your head back, keep your arms straight and let me do the work.

"Let's do it," he said without hesitation.

Jack beamed from ear to ear as he sloshed onto the far bank. Jossy had been right; he'd done exactly as he'd been told and they'd crossed without a hitch. She leaned forward to kiss him, but never got the chance. Jack grabbed her arm, pulled her from the beach, and headed for the safety of the forest. Looking back, she saw the reason for his behavior. Loren Endicott had just appeared on the far bank.

Stumbling through the sand, Jocelyn followed Jack into the underbrush, but before they were lost from sight she looked back and her eyes locked on to those of their pursuer.

The expression on Jocelyn's face troubled Endicott. Her stare was hard, almost challenging. It was contrary to what he'd expected. Apparently the students were no longer afraid of him. Respectful? Yes—or they would have held their ground and stayed to fight. If they felt they'd have the advantage in open combat, they'd have dug their heels in the sand and attempted to bring this situation to an end. Things were different now, though. The rules had changed. Endicott had his work cut out for him.

"Well then," he thought as he stepped into the muddy water, "Let the chase begin."

Cascading down the slope of a towering coastal mountain was the field of boulders that had forced the intrepid students to move south and into the valley three days earlier. Crossing it was a must, and the terrain was as rugged as Spencer had ever seen. But the reward was great. On the other side lay a long but gentle walk uphill to the cliff where Marcie and Debbie were trapped.

The view from this side was sobering and impressive. Rocks of unimaginable size were strewn about forming an impassable barrier. There was nothing to do but to strike out downhill and search for some path where he could slip through. Compounding Spencer's dilemma was a second significant obstacle. The sound of rushing water coming from under the boulder field promised more trouble for the young man. "This is great," he muttered, "anotha stream crossing. 'An this one sounds like it's gonna be a bitch 'an a half."

Yet a third major difficulty soon presented itself. Spencer had already dropped more than five hundred feet in altitude. Hot, wet, fog-enshrouded vegetation had suddenly appeared around him, and he would have to be ever more alert to sounds and movement. As he continued to move closer to the valley, a large stream emerged from within the rocks and it now thundered past just off to his right.

Here, near the valley floor, the ground became less sloped and the boulders thinned out—the river was now the principal obstacle. Spencer began looking intently for some sort of natural bridge to get across, but nothing presented itself. Although tall trees now lined both sides of the torrential stream, none had fallen across in any useful way.

He stopped briefly to rest and assess his situation. Squatting beside a calm eddy he filled his water bottle. It was beginning to look as though he would have to travel all the way to the heart of the valley, to where the water was calm at the spot where he and the others had swum across before. He was reluctant to do that. Such a large detour meant he wouldn't make it back to the cliff until tomorrow.

A small cynodont appeared from within a stand of horsetails downstream and ran past him. The smaller ones were numerous around here. They seemed to live amongst the boulders and scree that merged with thick foliage. Another ran past and then a third, reminding Spencer of rabbits running from a fox.

The thought made Spencer look up with a start. Something was chasing them. Suddenly he heard it: a high-pitched grunt; the sound of its presence had been masked by the roar of the stream. He turned as panic gripped him. Jumping to his feet, he had just enough time to grab his spear before the first of two lizard wolves rushed him.

Spencer stumbled into the creek. The nearest assailant lunged at him, narrowly missing his leg. Spencer awkwardly thrust at its face with the spear, driving it back. The second animal moved around the first, trying to attack his flank. For creatures as primitive as these, their hunting methods were amazingly well developed. There was little Spencer could do. He flailed away with his small spear, first slashing at one attacker and then the other, repulsing well-coordinated rushes that were becoming ever more aggressive. The lizard wolves knew they had him cornered. Instinct told them success was imminent.

Spencer wasn't about to admit defeat. Sure, he couldn't hold them at bay much longer, but he knew he could end the standoff at any time by simply diving into the turbulent water behind him. Given what he'd been through during his last stream crossing, however, he also knew his odds of surviving another such dunking were only slightly better than a fight to the death with two blood-thirsty lizard wolves. But that's exactly what he'd do if there were no other way out.

His attackers didn't appear to be particularly fond of water. As Spencer backed away from his foes and into the shallows, he was surprised, and much relieved, to find that they refused to do more than get their feet wet. Whether it was the water itself or the strong current that acted as deterrent wasn't apparent, but whichever it was, Spencer found that he had a narrow safe zone in which to stand: far enough away from the long, snapping jaws of his tormentors, but not so far into the stream that the current could sweep him from his feet.

In much the same way his grandfather had walked on slender I-beams high above the streets of Manhattan, Spencer carefully began to negotiate his way downstream, mindful that to slip on a moss-covered rock would end his life at the hands of either current or predator. He was heading for a bend in the stream where tall conifers lined both banks. Progress was slow but steady, and it gave the young man ample time to consider the details of a new escape plan. An idea had come to mind, one that would not only save him from being eaten by his two new friends, but, in addition, would solve the vexing problem of how to cross the stream.

"We can't out run him, Jack."

Her companion nodded grimly, but there wasn't anything they could do except push on. For the past hour they'd been engaged in a high-stakes game of cat and mouse. Moving uphill at what had been a relentless pace, the two students were unable to shake their pursuer.

Endicott was like a wolf, biding his time, patiently waiting for his prey to falter. Once they tired or became trapped by some insurmountable natural obstacle, he would seize the advantage and move in for the kill.

For the most part they'd been easy to track. The soil near the river was moist and soft; their footprints were so well defined he could read the imprint of the Reebok logo in those left by Jocelyn. At one point he'd almost lost their trail. When they'd moved up a rocky slope with no discernable game trail or path to follow, they'd almost gotten away. Disaster had been avoided, however, when the two had spooked a herd of small cynodonts from a grove of horsetails directly upslope from him.

But it didn't matter, really. They were headed for the cliff face where their two beleaguered colleagues were awaiting rescue. He'd briefly considered taking a shortcut, swiftly moving to the cliff, dispatching the two women who were there, and then lying in wait to ambush Jack and Jocelyn. But that alternative carried with it the risk, albeit very small, that the two older students might detour towards the coast and attempt to go for help. After all, there wasn't much they could do to save Debbie; they needed outside assistance.

Endicott rubbed his cheek. It was painful and swollen. He cautiously probed the teeth at the back of his upper jaw with his tongue. Ouch! One of the molars was chipped and the nerve was exposed. It throbbed in rhythm with his heartbeat. Jocelyn, that bitch, would pay for kicking him. Her death wouldn't be a pleasant one; he would see to that. The pain instilled in him anger and a need for vengeance. "It won't be long, my friends," he muttered through clenched teeth, "not long at all."

Jocelyn and Jack's worst fears were realized when they broke into a small clearing. Before them lay a sheer rock wall. To either side was heavy vegetation. They had no real choice but to backtrack and go around the obstacle, but that option was risky. Endicott was right on their heels.

"C'mon, Jossy, let's go this way." Jack motioned for her to follow him through a tangle of stiff ferns, but instead she planted her butt on a rock and looked at him.

"And exactly where will 'this way' take us?"

"Uphill, towards the cliff."

"Like I said, we can't out run him, at least I can't. I'm going to stay and fight, and this is as good a spot as any."

"Jossy, you can't..."

"You don't know me, Jack. I'm pissed, and when I get mad I'm tougher than a two-dollar steak. I aim to put some major hurt on that sonofabitch. Even if he guts me with that pig-sticker of his, I'll make him pay. He won't be of a mind to hurt you, Marcie or Debbie when I get through with him."

Jack stood and stared at her. He was overwhelmed by both her beauty and her bravery. She was right. All they accomplished by running was to delay the inevitable. It was best to confront Endicott before he got anywhere near their two companions, and as she'd just said, this was as good a place as any for a showdown. "Let's do it," he said grimly. She smiled and walked to where he stood. Overcome with emotion, Jack took her in his arms and held her tightly. God, how he wanted to take her away from here, to end the nightmare that threatened her. He couldn't imagine Endicott harming this wonderful girl whom he'd just gotten to know.

Abruptly she gave him a quick kiss and pulled away. "You stand there," she ordered, pointing to a spot about fifteen feet away. She brandished her spear. "If he attacks one of us, the other can flank him." Moments later, Dr. Loren Endicott broke into the clearing.

"Only a few more feet," Spencer told himself as he neared the pine forest. The water was a bit calmer here; he could stand knee deep without fear of being washed downstream. A third lizard wolf had joined the others, and all three were pacing back and forth on the bank, grunting excitedly while eyeing their prey that stood only a few feet away.

Spencer was getting cold. He was standing in snow melt. The water temperature was barely above freezing, and it relentlessly sucked heat from his skinny frame. His teeth chattered and his lips were blue. Although he'd formulated a good plan, one he was quite proud of, there remained one problem. He had to figure out a way of getting to shore and climbing the massive tree that seemed to beckon to him. Its branches hung only yards away, but, in front of it, stood snarling hellhounds, their presence representing a gauntlet between the river and sanctuary.

If his body temperature were to drop too far, Spencer feared his reflexes and strength might be compromised to such an extent that his plan might fail. He had to think of a way to get into the tree, and the sooner the better. He stared at the three snouts pointing in his general direction, saliva dripping from partially opened mouths, exposing evil-looking canine teeth. The lizard wolves were leaning forward, moving their heads slowly from side to side, sampling the air for Spencer's scent and growing more excited by the minute.

"That's it!" Spencer exclaimed. The solution to his problem flashed into his mind. "Oh, you guys are gonna be so pissed when one 'a your descendants fools your asses." Although he didn't relish this latest idea, he knew it was foolproof.

Spencer untied the shirt from his belt. After his last "swim," all of the blood it had acquired from his bloody nose was gone. He reached down into the stream, grabbed a baseball-sized rock and tied the shirt around it. Taking a deep breath, Spencer then gritted his teeth and drew the blade of his knife across the back of his left hand.

The cut wasn't deep. It wasn't designed to be. It took a moment for the wound to fill with blood, but soon Spencer was squeezing the incision and mopping up the blood with his shirt. The lizard wolves went wild. Their grunts increased to a fevered pitch. The prey they had cornered in the stream now smelled a thousand times better.

Spencer inched towards his admirers with extreme caution. Given their frenzied state he couldn't rule out the possibility that one of them might charge toward him despite its fear of water. Holding the shirt at arm's length, he slowly swung it back and forth. Like spectators at a tennis match, his adversaries followed the scent in rhythm. It had a hypnotic effect. So mesmerized were the lizard wolves that the grunting stopped; one hundred percent of their attention was fixed on the odor and position of Spencer's shirt.

When he felt the moment was right, Spencer gave the shirt one last backswing and then launched it onto the bank, twenty yards upstream from where he stood. The lizard wolves squealed in unison and took off after it. Stumbling over one another, they pounced on it and commenced to tear it apart in a frenzy.

With his adversaries now otherwise occupied, Spencer calmly waded from the stream and climbed into the tall pine. "Chumps," he chided once he was out of danger. A backward glance at the predators showed one of them licking the rock of all remaining blood trace while the others sniffed the air around them, apparently wondering where the rest of their meal had gone.

Spencer immediately refocused on the problem of crossing the stream. His plan was simple, really. He would fix a rope to the pine on the other side, tie the near end to this tree, and then, hanging by his hands and knees, inch his way across. If he could slant the rope, he might even turn it into a zip line—slide down like a contestant on some dumb reality show. Piece of cake. At least it had been a piece of cake in his mind while he stood in the stream dealing with lizard wolves. Now, reality sunk in. He looked down at the raging river below. Who was he kidding? This truly was a river, not a stream. There was no doubt he had to go over this river, not through it. But it was wide, almost twice the width of the one he'd crossed earlier that morning. He had a long way to go.

Beneath him, the three lizard wolves had returned and were now circling the base of his tree. From listening to Endicott he knew how persistent they were. As long as his scent was in the air, they'd hang around. This was it then. Climbing down wasn't an option. He was committed to his plan.

Imagining a rope bridge across the river was one thing, constructing it in such a way that it could bear his weight, and doing it from one side of the river while sitting halfway up a tree, was something else. How was he going to project the end of the rope into the other tree and anchor it there? He needed an arrow, one with a barbed point that would embed in the trunk. Fat chance. He hadn't exactly come equipped with Ninja tools.

Spencer tied one end of his length of paracord to the shaft of his crude, homemade spear. The paracord wasn't long enough to span the river, so he then attached a segment of braided leather rope to it. "We'll need the rope to help extract Debbie from that ledge," he remembered Endicott saying moments before the man had attacked him. The thought filled Spencer with bitterness and reminded him of the plight of his friends.

With an angry yell, he launched his spear across the river only to watch it fall into the raging waters. He reeled it back in and climbed higher into his own tree. Carefully coiling the rope into his non-throwing hand, he again hurled the spear on an upward trajectory towards the opposite bank. This time the ballistic projectile found its mark, penetrating the upper branches of the tree before cascading down through them. Spencer cautiously retrieved the rope until the spear caught crosswise between a stout branch and the tree's trunk. He hauled back mightily once the slack was gone, but the spear wouldn't budge. It had caught fast. Step one complete. Elation came over him when Spencer realized his plan was working—only to be dashed to bits when reality again set in. The rope was too short. Not enough remained at his end to properly anchor it to any part of the tree he was sitting in.

"Oh crap!" he moaned.   At the sound of his voice the lizard wolves started grunting in earnest. "Ah shut up!" was all he could think to say.

Spencer leaned against the tree and rubbed his eyes. He was exhausted. The thought of surviving both the attack by Endicott and his harrowing stream crossing, only to be undermined by a rope that was five feet too short, was almost too much to bear.

Life in this world was a game of inches and seconds. One's survival was really a matter of luck, he thought. It was luck that had enabled him to evade the jaws of the archosaur, and luck that had brought the timely appearance of the mysterious stranger in the ravine behind Endicott's camp. Now, however, misfortune had arrived in a big way. He needed a longer rope or he'd never leave this tree alive.

Suddenly he looked up. "That's it!" he exclaimed. The grunting from below again intensified, but he barely noticed. "The rope's too short. In fact, I hope it's real short." The solution to his dilemma was simple: he'd simply swing across...like Tarzan.

Now the issue became—is the rope too long? The last thing he wanted was to end up like one of those Darwin Award-winning bungee jumpers who used ropes longer than the heights of their platforms. Spencer contemplated the length of his rope versus the height at which his spear had become lodged in the other tree. It was close, but he'd make it. Even if the rope were to stretch, he figured it would barely be short enough. "I just hope my knots hold," he worried as he readied himself. He wrapped the rope tightly around one hand so that it wouldn't slip—he'd watched rodeo riders do that on TV—it seemed like a good idea. Then, he took several deep breaths, let out an ear-splitting yell, and launched himself from the tree.

Spencer rode an emotional roller coaster during his brief swing across the river. At first his heart nearly stopped as the surging water seemed to rush up to meet him. His fear quickly vanished when the rope went taut and he arced gracefully over the chasm, soaring over both salivating lizard wolves and treacherous watercourse. That euphoria was again replaced with dread when he realized just how fast he was approaching his destination.

He hurtled straight towards the lower branches of the pine and there was nothing he could do to slow down. In the last instant before impact he turned his back to the tree and buried his face in his armpit.

Cruunch! He slammed into the dense branches. Many of them broke, cushioning the impact and slowing him down, but the sharp, broken ends punctured and tore at his flesh, inflicting a multitude of cuts and bruises. Once he'd stopped, Spencer just hung for a moment, breathing hard.

He'd done it. A quick self-assessment suggested he'd made it across relatively unscathed. Pain radiated from every part of his naked torso where the skin had been slashed, but no bones were broken; of that he was certain.

Gathering his strength, Spencer then climbed the tree to retrieve his spear. He coiled the rope and stuffed it back into his pack. High-pitched grunts from the far bank could barely be heard above the roar of the river. Spencer glanced in their direction and couldn't help but smile. The lizard wolves' attention was directed up into the tree on the other side. They'd be there for hours, he knew, until the few remaining molecules of his scent finally evaporated into the warm, humid mist of the jungle.

A quiet calm came over the young man from Brooklyn. A deep sense of satisfaction and accomplishment settled in as he realized that the last major geographic obstacle that lay between him and the cliff was now behind him. Barring further mishap, he would be talking to Marcie in a matter of hours.

Endicott stopped and warily eyed his opponents. He hadn't expected them to make a stand, but here they were; this would be it. Both eyed him warily. Unfortunately he'd lost the element of surprise; that would make his job somewhat more difficult. Nonetheless, he would prevail. For the past year his life had consisted of one great difficulty after another, and he had, without exception, found solutions to all of his problems. Facing these two inexperienced foes wouldn't tax him greatly.

Jocelyn was standing slightly to his left, in front of a rock outcrop. Jack waited, weapon poised, off to his right. "A commendable strategy," he thought with a modicum of admiration. "They hope to attack from different directions, make me fight along two fronts. Well, I can remedy that." He slowly maneuvered to his right along the fringe of the clearing until Jack was positioned between him and Jocelyn. He smiled in satisfaction as his adversaries allowed him to "stack" them in this way. Only Jack now posed an immediate threat. Jocelyn would have to go around her partner to intervene.

His attention shifted to their weaponry. Both wielded short spears that were no match against his. Jack's, in particular, was nothing more than a flimsy sharpened stick, something he himself would be embarrassed to carry. He scoffed at what he saw; neither presented much of a threat. "You've selected a good place to die," he sneered.

"Perhaps," Jocelyn shot back, "but we're not gonna make it easy for you. We aren't sitting ducks like poor Spencer. Tell me, Endicott, how do you deal with the shame of killing an unsuspecting child, someone who admired and looked up to you? What a cowardly thing to do."

Endicott's eyes flashed in anger, but he maintained his composure. In a moment Jocelyn would pay for those ugly, hateful words. She was likely goading him into an ill-advised attack. He had to maintain discipline, strike out at Jack when the moment was right. Once his male adversary was out of the way, Jocelyn would pose no threat. "Spencer was an unfortunate casualty," he replied, "and for what it's worth, I didn't actually kill him. I merely incapacitated him and let Nature take it from there."

Jocelyn thought about what Spencer must have gone through. Had he been conscious and aware of what was going to happen to him? She couldn't imagine the horror he must have experienced in his final moments. Endicott was even more of a monster than she'd earlier believed. "You sadistic turd," she snarled.

Endicott feigned indifference to her comment and then rushed quickly at Jack, yelling at the top of his voice as he did so.

Once again the Doctor caught Jack off guard. The young man moved to one side, dodging the spear point but stumbling to the ground. Endicott moved to finish him, and would have gored his hapless victim if not for the screaming attack by Jocelyn.

He wheeled around to fend off Jocelyn's assault. Alas, despite the fervor with which she charged, the young woman was hopelessly outmatched. Endicott's size, experience and skill enabled him to knock her spear aside with as little effort as if he were swatting a fly. He grabbed her by the hair and viciously yanked her to the ground. A split second later she was completely immobilized with the point of Endicott's spear pressing against her throat.

Jack scrambled to his feet, but one look from Endicott made him stop dead in his tracks. A twist of the Doctor's wrist would end Jocelyn's life. The contest was over. Endicott had won.

"Hurt her and I swear you won't make it out of this place alive," Jack threatened.

Endicott laughed. "Chivalrous poppycock. It's now time you both met the same fate as your younger colleague."

Jocelyn's heart was beating so fast she felt it might explode. She was inches, moments from death. The adrenaline rush was almost overwhelming, the urge to flee nearly uncontrollable, but one false move and she knew her life would end. She fought to control her emotions and to think logically. "I've got to make him talk," she decided. "I have to make him settle down, buy us some time."

"I still can't fathom why you're doing this," she said, "but I bet it has something to do with that bracelet I found."

"It does indeed, my suspicious young insomniac. Although it didn't really matter that you found it last night. The decision to kill you all was made the moment we first met. You see, any information you might reveal about this Triassic jungle land would, of course, cause hoards to descend upon it." He sighed, "I simply cannot permit that."

"There are other artifacts around aren't there?" Jack offered.

"Heavens yes. The two of you are most perceptive." Jocelyn's plan was working. The man's grip on her hair had lessened, he was noticeably more relaxed.

She had to keep it going. She asked, "Just what have you found, Doctor. Why is it important enough to kill for?"

Endicott considered the question. "Well now, lest you think I'm not a civilized man, I suppose an explanation is in order. Killing is such distasteful business; to justify it requires an extreme reason. Allow me, therefore, to enlighten you as to why you must perish in this dreary world.

"From my research over the past year I've been able to paste together the fascinating history of this island. As you already know, its geologic legacy dates back hundreds of millions of years, to a time when cataclysmic events nearly extinguished all life on Earth. The remaining biological ashes included what you've experienced in your limited travails in this land, the progenitors of everything from dinosaurs to mammals to flowering plants, all fighting for ecological supremacy within the confines of this isolated, geothermally-heated singularity.

"Of course, revealing to the world the existence of this fascinating prehistoric land would have been a crowning achievement for any scientist. My reputation as an explorer and discoverer would have brought me fame and high academic standing."

"But it wouldn't have brought you wealth," Jocelyn interjected. "That bracelet isn't the only gold artifact you've found."

"Ah, you've hit the proverbial 'nail on the head.' You see, more than a thousand years ago there were others who visited this place, and they didn't come just to live in misery twenty miles or so up the coast where those ignorant archeologists are now blissfully pulling scraps of charcoal from the ground." He grunted and shook his head in disdain. "Men penetrated into the interior of the island and used it as a sort of bank vault, if you will. They left three large caches of Viking plunder here, two of which I have discovered.

Until I find the third, which according to record is the largest, I cannot allow anyone to know of its existence."

"Just how do you know all this?" Jocelyn asked. "How did you find out there are three stashes of Viking loot?"

Endicott's eyes brightened. He broke into a very self-satisfied smile. "There are records here, records that are quite literally engraved in stone: stones with runic inscriptions that describe in exquisite detail who those people were, what they brought with them, and how and where they hid it.

"Unfortunately I'll be forced to destroy most of the runestones in order to conceal the origin of what I'm going to sell on the antiquities market. If the Greenlandic government ever found out where those artifacts came from, collectors would have to give them up. I can't destroy the stones, however, until I've discovered the last of the treasure. I'm close; I know it. There are a few cryptic inscriptions that I need to decipher before I can pinpoint the location of the third cache. Then I'll be able to leave this bloody place and return to a life of opulence. God knows I deserve it after what I've been through. I might be there now if it weren't for interruptions from people like you and those two inquisitive busy-bodies from last year."

"Those two researchers didn't die in a rockslide did they?" said Jack. "That story you told us last night—that stuff about holding Karlsen's hand while he died, and about Randrup and his bracelet—it was all a load of crap wasn't it?"

The Doctor's expression hardened. "It was their fault. If they hadn't insisted upon exploring the interior, in much the same way you did, they would still be alive. I tried to stop them; I argued there was no point to climbing around in some bleak volcano, but once they learned of the lush ecosystem within," he shrugged, "they both died in tragic falls."

"Assisted by you, no doubt," Jocelyn said contemptuously, "and for what? So you can make a few bucks selling some old Viking stuff?"

The question angered Endicott. He increased the pressure on the spear. The point dug into Jocelyn's skin, drawing blood, and making it hard for her to breathe. "Just some old Viking stuff, eh?" He twisted the spear, making her grimace. "I suppose your ignorance can be excused; you've no idea of the magnitude of my discovery. It's perhaps appropriate that, before you die, I should enlighten you both as to the importance of what's at stake."

Endicott's face was right up against Jocelyn's cheek. It wasn't the sharp point of the spear or his pitiless grip of her hair that bothered her most: it was his smell. His body odor and his foul breath nauseated her. She felt as though she would suffocate. She couldn't take it anymore. She was about to make a violent and probably suicidal attempt to surge and break free when he suddenly turned his head and began to speak in an almost conversational tone—another abrupt mood swing from this insane man.

"Our story begins with a strapping, hulk of a man named Thorvald Asvaldsson Joederen, who in 960 AD along what is now the coast of Norway, committed murder. As punishment, Thorvald was banished from his homeland, and so he and his family, which included his ten-year-old son Erik, relocated to Iceland.

"Young Erik grew to be an imposing figure. He was a big fellow, and strong, just like his father, and he possessed the same volatile temper. At the age of thirty-two, trouble found him when he killed two men over a property dispute. In the same way his father was sent into exile, Eric was forced to leave Iceland for at least three years. That, my friends, is what led Erik Thorvaldsson, now known to history as Erik the Red, to the shores of southern Greenland to establish the first Norse settlement on that great island. You see, the Earth was warmer back then; it underwent a period of glacial melting much like what we are experiencing today. The balmy weather was essential to the success of Erik's settlement, and it was there, in Greenland, that one of Erik's sons rose to prominence.

"His name was Leif, Leif Eriksson, and he was the famous explorer who established the first European settlement in North America. I'm often troubled by the insistence of historians, particularly those in the U.S., who attribute the European 'discovery' of North America to Spanish and Portuguese explorers of the fifteenth century. Leif Eriksson, we now know, walked the shores of Newfoundland some five hundred years before then.

"All of this is known to the world, but it is here my tale takes an unexpected turn. You see, Leif was an explorer, not a brawler or a killer like his father and grandfather. He sired two sons, one of whom, Thorkell, succeeded him as chieftain of his Greenland colonies. Thorkell oversaw the home front while Leif was sailing to parts unknown. Historical documents simply list him as Leif's successor, but I now know that Thorkell did much,

much more than just lead a group of herdsmen in their hardscrabble existence in southern Greenland.

"Thorkell, it seems, took his job as magistrate very seriously. Sailing from village to village along the coast, he ruled with a firm but benevolent hand. He shuttled meat and grain from his settlements to Iceland and there exchanged them for the trade goods his people needed. The taxes he collected more often than not made their way into his own pockets, and this added to his already considerable fortune. Most of his riches, however, came to him by way of inheritance. When you think about it, it makes perfect sense. How do you think Erik and Leif, or even Erik's father, Thorvald, for that matter, financed their travels? Boats and boatmen cost money, as did the food and supplies they needed to survive on extended voyages, some of which took weeks if not months. All the endeavors of those great and powerful men were financed with Viking plunder.

"Thorkell made three trips to Eviskar Island. Each time he brought with him part of his family fortune, which he subsequently sequestered until such time as he might need it. The exploits of this vain man are documented on runestones, along with the cipher that links the three treasure troves to one another. I've not broken the entire code yet, but I have found two of the caches."

Endicott spoke gleefully about his discoveries. He harbored a driving need to boast of his prowess, and this would likely be his only opportunity. The secrets of Eviskar Island had to remain lost to humanity for his monetary scheme to work, but there was no risk in revealing the details to his two young captives. They'd be dead within minutes, and his secrets would accompany them to their graves.

"The riches of Thorkell are nearly unimaginable. They include numerous gold figurines, necklaces, buttons, arm bands and bracelets. One cache contained several magnificent bronze castings, the hilts of numerous heavy swords and hundreds, if not thousands, of silver coins. As far as I can tell, the items originate from all over Europe, from the Hebrides to the Mediterranean. The value of the metal alone is in the millions, but the objects themselves are worth far more to wealthy collectors in Norway, Sweden and Denmark."

During Endicott's rant, several thoughts raced through Jocelyn's mind.

Snippets of what he was saying provided answers to questions that had been bugging her. It was obvious to her now why the victims they'd unearthed at the dig site had had their necks broken. Greed is a powerful, sometimes overwhelming motivational force, one that if allowed to grow unchecked can lead to horrific consequences. Loren Endicott and Thorkell Eriksson had both succumbed to its spell. The women in those graves, almost certainly along with others, were killed, executed, because of what they knew of Thorkell's riches. A thousand years later, she and Jack would meet the same fate at the hands of Endicott—if neither of them could figure out a way to thwart the man's plans.

Ever since the students had dined with Endicott in his island shelter, another thought had been troubling Jocelyn. She had been wondering if it was the coffee substitute the professor used, the one prepared from dried, roasted cycad seeds, that might be responsible for his erratic behavior, especially his sudden and intense mood swings. Her biology teacher, Mr. Powell, had mentioned that the seeds of the bread palm were toxic. Might Endicott be under the influence of some powerful psychoactive substance produced in the seeds of this primitive cycad relative? Was he really just a normal person who's personality and actions, no matter how brutal and wrong, were simply the result of his unwitting ingestion of a powerful drug? No, she now concluded; that can't be the case. Endicott's revelation that he'd killed his colleagues at the start of his forced exile to the island's interior dispelled the idea that his behavior was pharmaceutically induced. Only later, as he adapted to life in this primitive world, had he discovered the area's culinary offerings. Nothing, therefore, could excuse what he'd done to Spencer and to his fellow researchers. The man was simply barbaric and evil, and that thought aroused a deeper and more primal hatred within her. She was now more determined than ever not to allow this vile man to inflict the same fate upon her and her friends as Thorkell Eriksson had done to those poor wretches back at the dig site.

XV

The vision before Marcie was surreal. Out of the mist a solitary figure approached, thin, dark, sporting a bandana around his neck, wearing a small pack and carrying a staff of some sort. As he got closer, she recognized Spencer and drew in a sharp breath. At least she thought it was him. He looked markedly different than he had three days earlier, much older than his fifteen years. His eyes had a hard, vacant look and the left side of his face was swollen and puffy. Dried, crusted blood extended from one nostril and cuts adorned his thin torso. He looked like he'd been in a fight, and the object in his hand wasn't a hiking staff, it was a small spear with a wicked-looking wooden blade.

"Spencer, my gosh, Spencer, what happened to you? Where've you been?" She regarded the spear, noted the materials from which it was made, and their eyes met.

"I don't know where to begin, Marcie. How's Debbie? We've got to get help or at least move her from here. We're in real danger."

They walked toward the shelter where Debbie lay. En route, Marcie peppered him with more questions. "You've been gone for three days, Spence. Please tell me where you went. And where are Jack and Jocelyn?"

The last question caused Spencer to stop. "I don't want to alarm Debbie, but I don't know exactly where Jocelyn and Jack are or what's happened to them." He paused to contemplate how to break the news of their friends' peril, or their own, for that matter. "They're being stalked, hunted, but they don't know it. That's why they're in such great danger; the attack will come as a surprise. If they can get away, they should be here by nightfall. If not...we may nevah see 'em again."

She was shocked by his last statement. He took note and put his hand on her shoulder. "There's nothing we can do to help 'em. But that's not all: if the man who's trying to kill 'em succeeds...we're next."

When they got to the shelter, Spencer was impressed. Marcie had beefed up its construction. She'd lashed the tarp more firmly to protrusions in the rock face. The structure was virtually indestructible, both rain-proof and wind-proof. Large rocks surrounded the perimeter of the lean-to, some of them seemingly too big for Marcie to have moved. She was obviously stronger than she looked. Inside it was much warmer than outside, and somewhat claustrophobic; Marcie had closed off all drafts and transformed the structure into a lifeboat against the elements. Her's and Debbie's body heat, together with the better insulation, had kept them alive.

"Debbie?" Marcie asked gently as she put her hand on the woman's shoulder. "I've got great news. Look who's back."

Debbie opened her eyes slowly, but she was too weak to turn her head. "Morgan? Is it you, Morgan?"

"No, Morgan hasn't come yet. It's Spencer. Spencer's come back to help us." Debbie closed her eyes again. Marcie whispered to Spencer, "She's been drifting in and out of consciousness most of today. I was hoping it's stress related: you know, pain, cold, lack of sleep, lack of food—but it may be more complicated. Her ribs are bothering her. She's having trouble breathing. I think she may have broken a rib and slightly punctured a lung. If she's bleeding internally..." Her voice trailed off when Debbie uttered a low moan.

Spencer motioned for them to exit the tent. "Have you been able to send a distress message?" he asked half-heartedly. His lack of optimism was apparent.

She shook her head. "I tried a couple of times, but the battery died." She poked her head into the shelter and retrieved the unit. "You can try if you like, but don't get your hopes up."

As a formality, Spencer pressed the power button. The screen glowed faintly then went black again. Sure enough, dead battery.

"The thing is supposed to work anywhere on earth," Marcie lamented, "I don't see why we haven't been able to get through. Maybe it's defective."

Spencer scrutinized the unit. "This thing uses the Iridium system," he said.

"Yeah, Jack mentioned that. He said something about the mountains interfering with reception because the satellites can be so low in the sky. I saw him walk way over there," she pointed off into the mist, away from the cliff, "but he still couldn't get through."

Spencer was only half listening. He was examining the side of the instrument. An idea came to mind. "I bet it might work on the beach," he said.

"But the battery's dead."

The young man grew excited. "I might be able to charge it. Look here, see that?" He pointed at the charging port. Removing his backpack he took out his cell phone. It had endured several stream dunkings in recent days, and it probably no longer worked, but it wasn't his intent to turn it on. Instead, he held it beside the satellite communicator. "They both have micro USB ports for recharging. The charging cable for my cell is down at the beach."

"So? In case you haven't noticed, we don't have too many outlets to plug it into. What good will it do?"

Spencer grinned. "It doesn't need a wall charger. Mine plugs into the USB port on my tablet. 'An my tablet is also in my overnight pack—the one down at the beach."

"So, you're saying we can hike to the beach, charge the communicator and send an SOS?" Marcie said excitedly.

Spencer put his hands on her shoulders. It was by far the most intimate gesture he'd ever proffered towards a member of the opposite sex, or, for that matter, to anyone other than his parents. "I'd better go alone," he said quietly. When she started to protest, he shook his head. "It's not just that Debbie needs care. I'm worried about the man who's trying to kill us. At least one of us has to survive. Someone has to make it back to the dig 'an tell the world what's happened. Believe me, Marcie, Doc Endicott, that's his name, is a real bastehd. After he comes here, he'll head straight for the beach and whoever is there will be trapped. Your only hope is to take this spear 'an hide. Don't stay in the shelter wit Debbie; hide over there in the rocks. You won't be able to defend Debbie if he shows up; he's too strong 'an he's well armed. I'll be back as soon as I can."

"You can't just leave us here."

The exasperation in her voice tugged at Spencer's conscience. Was that what he was doing, leaving them to their doom while he got away? No. Deep down, he knew he was right. Endicott knew about their boat; he knew about their supplies on the beach, and Spencer figured he had to get to them before Endicott did. Unless he could charge the communicator and send for help, he, Marcie and Debbie probably wouldn't make it off the island alive.

Spencer made his way to where the climbing gear lay at the base of the cliff. He began to don a harness while Marcie continued to plead her case. "We need more supplies here, Spence. Debbie and I have eaten two cans of beans in the last two days. Two cans. You're gonna need help bringing extra food and clothing back here."

Spencer buckled his harness, but before he roped in, he took off his pack. He'd forgotten about the food he was carrying. "Here," he handed Marcie a slab of meat. It was wet from having been dunked in the river. "You should rinse it off first, but it's good stuff."

"What the heck is it?"

"A cynodont steak. Don't worry, it's fresh; we cooked it last night. 'An here..." he pulled out a leather pouch that contained several cycad biscuits. These hadn't survived their immersion in water the way the meat had; they were now soft, roughly the consistency of wet bread dough, or stiff mashed potatoes. "These are a kind'a carbo. They're kinda mushy but I think they're still good." He shrugged, "I been eatin' 'em."

A perplexed Marcie took the food and stared in wonder. Spencer had a lot of explaining to do when he got back. Reluctantly she nodded. He knew far more than she did about what else was happening on this island. She looked up at him and he smiled. "I know what you're thinkin'. Just promise me one thing," he added soberly, "you see a guy looks like a cave man: run! 'An if you can't get away, no matter what he says, don't trust him."

Spencer clipped into the self-belay device and began his ascent of the cliff.

"Be careful, Spencer. Don't look down. Remember what happened before."

She heard him chuckle. "Don't worry. Last time I was on this cliff was a lifetime ago."

With those final words, Spencer maneuvered up through the fissure and began the technical part of the climb. With grace and confidence the young man of Mohawk descent nimbly moved from one handhold to the next, pulling slack through the belay device, using his legs to propel his lithe form upward. Neither fear nor hesitation slowed him down. His grandfather, the high altitude iron worker, would have been proud. In minutes he'd scaled the precipice and was over the ridge, making his way quickly down the long, boulder-strewn slope toward the beach. Time was of the essence.

Spencer's conscience nagged at him the entire way. While his journey to send for help was of critical importance, it left Marcie alone and vulnerable. Endicott was on the move and had gotten a good head start when he'd left Spencer to die. Dealing with Jack and Jocelyn would slow him down, perhaps even stop him, but odds were that hadn't happened. His friends were most likely dead; Endicott was coming soon.

Sending the distress call was of paramount importance. As soon as that was done, he had to quickly assemble what supplies he could carry and make the arduous trip back up the ridge. He was bone tired, exhausted by the trauma of that morning and the long hike that followed...and his foot was killing him. The slight deformity was generally little more than a nuisance, slowing him down, hampering his agility, but the long trek over difficult terrain made his shin, ankle and knee feel like they were on fire.

It was a combination of adrenaline and guilt that drove him onward. He had to accomplish the task at hand and then return to help defend Debbie and Marcie. To fail at that was unthinkable.

It took the better part of an hour to reach the overturned raft with its cache of supplies underneath. Thank goodness it was undisturbed. Endicott hadn't yet paid an unwelcome visit here.

The raft was heavy. It had challenged both him and Jack to invert it and set it into place. Unable to lift it by himself, he gradually raised one corner by propping rocks beneath it. When it was high enough, he scrambled underneath and began hauling items out onto the beach: individual rucksacks, two coolers full of food, paddles, rope, stakes and a tent.

Spencer carried his own rucksack to a large boulder and quickly rifled through the side pockets and main compartment, extracting his tablet computer and his cell phone charger. The moment of truth had arrived. His hands shook from both nerves and fatigue as he fumbled to insert the small connector of the charging cable into the satellite communicator. "C'mon, baby...work," he muttered. It fit. He breathed a huge sigh of relief. Now he had to hope that the power connector of the communicator was wired the same way as his cell. He crossed his fingers, plugged the USB end of the cable into his tablet and turned on the communicator.

Nothing.

Spencer groaned. All that effort—and for what? The letdown was emotionally excruciating. He instantly became acutely aware of the pain in his foot and his overwhelming fatigue. Worse, Marcie and Debbie were now at Endicott's mercy and he, Spencer, wasn't there to help.

Marcie. She was great. Her face came to mind with its winning smile and cute dimples. And he loved her marvelous, unbridled enthusiasm. Her eagerness to learn about everything they'd done on this trip, from the history of Iceland, to archeology, to rock climbing, had infected not just him but the other students with an added sense of awe and adventure. The summer had been much more enjoyable because of her. She'd been so outgoing and nice to him—and now look how he'd repaid her kindness and cheerful attitude. He'd deserted her when it mattered most.

Spencer hung his head. This recent failure was too much to bear. He rubbed his eyes and began to sob. Emotion poured forth as fatigue and the tumultuous events of the day began to take their toll. Feelings from deep within told him he wasn't done, that he had to get back to Marcie, to do all he could to help her and Debbie even though hope was dwindling. But he couldn't move. His sorrow had glued his butt to the rock on which he sat. A sense of futility overwhelmed him. "What's the point?" he muttered. "I'm a freakin' failure."

"Holy crap!"

There was a faint glow coming from the satellite communicator. It was lying in the sand where he'd dropped it in despair. He grabbed it and watched excitedly as the screen became brighter and brighter. A pulsing cursor appeared under the message "tracking satellites." Soon, that message dissolved and was replaced by another: "Iridium link acquired, type message below."

He realized the battery had been so low it had simply needed extra time to charge. Holding the unit in shaking hands, he fumbled with the buttons around the periphery of the screen. A small virtual keyboard popped into view and he discovered that he could move the cursor with a rocker key and enter letters one at a time into a tiny message box. Excitedly he composed what he wanted to say: "Send help, Debbie hurt." He scrolled down a list of contacts until he got to "Morgan." He hit ENTER and then pushed SEND. A blinking icon appeared for several seconds. A flood of relief washed through him when the words "message sent" filled the screen.

He'd done it! Help was on the way. Spencer jumped up and did a little dance. He allowed himself this brief celebratory moment before settling down and thinking once more about Marcie, Debbie and the peril they faced.

Sending the message changed everything. Taking supplies back up the ridge was no longer of primary importance; now the task was getting his friends to the beach and hoping a rescue squad came before Endicott showed up. Spencer appreciated that attempting to defend the women against Endicott carried with it much lower probability of success than the alternative of running away, of simply fleeing to the beach. It would be hard on Debbie, really hard; it might even exacerbate her condition to the point it would kill her. But it had to be done. And there was no time to lose.

He removed a long-sleeved shirt from his rucksack and put it on. Outside the caldera it was cold, with a biting windchill. His face hurt where Endicott had slugged him; his foot was killing him. The cuts he'd suffered during his Tarzan swing into the tree felt like they were burning in the salty air blowing in from the sea. Pushing all thoughts of discomfort aside, he dumped the contents of his own rucksack into the sand and began re-packing it with the limited supplies he'd take back up to the camp. The tablet computer and satellite communicator went in first followed by several items of warm clothing. Not wanting to carry too much weight, he only packed two cans of food—peaches and pears in heavy syrup—near the bottom where they wouldn't rub against his computer. If at all possible he didn't want to spend the night on the other side of the ridge, but one never knew. The women were starving—a days' worth of food was necessary.

Spencer hesitated before rifling through Marcie's rucksack. He felt guilty invading her privacy this way, but he also knew how well prepared she was for emergencies such as this. Among the outer pockets he found bandages, more aspirin, more paracord, a small mylar emergency blanket and a folding knife. Tossing all of it into his pack along with a few more items of warm clothing, he closed it up and hefted it. The weight was about right, twenty pounds maybe. It wouldn't slow him down too much.

He shouldered it and surveyed the rugged field of boulders and scree that lay along the slope up to the ridge. The trips he'd made up and down thus far had followed the south edge of the boulder field. He wondered if there were an easier route, and scanned the area to the north as he began the long walk uphill. It didn't look promising. The rocks in that direction were larger, the going there would be tough.

Before Spencer veered back to his left, to retrace his earlier path up the mountain, something caught his eye. At first, panic shot through him; whatever it was, it was moving. Was it Endicott, come to destroy their boat and supplies after murdering his friends? A second glance set him at ease. It was something small near the steep rock face, and it was flapping in the wind. He'd noticed it because it was yellow, a splash of color out of place in this muted, black-and-white landscape.

He needed to return. The compelling urge to be on his way conflicted with curiosity about the foreign object he'd spotted. In the end, curiosity won out, but only because the thing was so close. He would investigate and be on his way in less than a minute.

If his small party was the only group to have visited this desolate area in over a year, where had this apparently man-made object come from? Was it simply detritus that had washed up onto shore during a storm? If so, it must have been quite a storm; the yellow thing lay well above the high water mark.

When he reached the object, Spencer regarded it quizzically. It was an inflatable vest, the kind stewardesses on aircraft show you how to put on in case of a "water landing." Water "landing" my butt, he thought with a smile. The vest lay under a rock as if someone had put it there, anchoring it so it wouldn't blow away. That was strange. When he looked up, though, what else he saw astounded him. Wedged into a vertical fissure in the rock face was an inflatable raft. This was no zodiac like the one they'd taken from the dig site. It was an emergency type, the kind you inflate just prior to use. It was small, meant for two or three people.

He moved in for a closer look. Only when he was a few feet away did Spencer then notice that the fissure extended well into the mountainside. Powerful volcanic forces had ripped an ugly gash into the wall of the volcano.

Water trickled from the entrance. He bent down and tasted it. Fresh. In back of the dinghy there was more stuff. A small outboard motor was propped against a rock. Beside it sat a gas can. Further into the rift several watertight containers were neatly stacked together. Set atop the pile was an expensive, waterproof lantern. The reason for its presence became obvious as Spencer made his way further into the cleft. Very little sunlight penetrated into the narrow steep-sided passage, but it clearly ran much deeper into the rock.

The urge to explore clashed with Spencer's need for a speedy return. He looked back at their zodiac lying upside down in the sand by the surf, then ran his gaze across the rugged field of rocks that disappeared high up into slate-grey mist and cloud. His heart willed him to hurry as fast as possible to the ridge, but an unexplainable force held him back. Thoughts tumbled and whirred in his mind as Spencer agonized over what to do. As much as he hated to admit it, in a battle against Endicott he'd be of little use. Without superior weaponry of some sort, Spencer knew he couldn't hope to save Marcie and Debbie.

"Time for a change in plans," he said out loud, trying to sound convincing. He'd warned Marcie. She would simply have to hide from their enemy until help arrived. Besides, he had a hunch about this cut in the mountainside.

Grabbing the lantern, he flipped it on. A powerful beam shot out, illuminating the passage in surreal artificial light. The batteries were fresh. Someone had made recent use of this place, and Spencer had a good idea of who it was. What he saw on the ground purged all residual doubt from his mind about his course of action. Footprints in the wet sand down by his feet led back into the abyss. Without further hesitation, the young man marched forward into the narrow cut in the mountain.

XVI

While Endicott rambled on about the riches he had collected, Jocelyn had been communicating with Jack. In moments, their adversary would tire of talking and would again focus on slitting her throat. She had to break free, and soon, but to do it she and Jack had to launch a coordinated attack. Success would come only if she began to struggle at the same instant Jack were to rush him. They had to confuse Endicott, force him to hesitate before making a difficult choice: should he try to kill Jocelyn and leave his back vulnerable to attack by Jack, or should he repel Jack's advance and allow Jocelyn to run free? Their timing had to be perfect.

Jocelyn mouthed the words, "on three." Simultaneously she extended three fingers on her left hand, just like a catcher signaling to a pitcher what to throw. Jack looked her in the eye and nodded almost imperceptibly. Jocelyn mouthed the count:

"One, two..."

On three, Jocelyn grabbed Endicott's spear just behind the blade. Jack rushed in and struck at the man, forcing him to let go of Jocelyn. The plan worked; Jocelyn was now free, but Endicott was enraged. He'd been fooled by two inferior intellects, mere children, and he was as mad as a tormented bull at a bullfight.

The two men faced off and Endicott threw a vicious punch at Jack's head. The younger man ducked, then dove at his enemy, catching him in the solar plexus, driving him to the ground. Fists and kicks flew as the two grappled in the dirt, each trying desperately to land a disabling blow. Endicott raked his fingers across Jack's face in savage attempt to gouge his eyes. Jack countered by pushing the doctor away and landing a punch to his jaw. Endicott rolled to one side and howled in pain. Jack had gotten lucky. His punch had hit the same tooth Jocelyn had broken only hours earlier.

Jocelyn had retrieved Endicott's spear and had been hovering while the men fought, waiting anxiously for an opening. The one thing she absolutely could not afford to do was to accidentally injure Jack. Fleeting chances came and went. No clear shot at the bastard presented itself—until Jack struck the damaged tooth. When Endicott reeled back clutching his jaw, Jocelyn sensed her opportunity had arrived. She screamed for all she was worth and lunged, aiming her weapon straight at his heart.

Endicott reacted like a cat. With blinding speed he reached out and caught the spear by the blade. Jocelyn tried to pull it back, but Endicott held firm. Their eyes met, and for the first time that day, Jocelyn's courage faltered. True fear consumed her. Endicott's expression was that of a deranged man. Blood streamed from his hand but he seemed not to notice. Grinning sadistically, he yanked the pike from her hands and jumped to his feet. With a crazed laugh he then swung the weapon in a vicious arc. A sixth sense had somehow warned the doctor of Jack's rapid approach behind him, and the move caught the young man off guard.

Jack couldn't get out of the way. He had barely turned to the side when the blood-covered spear point ripped across his back and right shoulder, opening a long, deep cut. Endicott then savagely drove the haft of the spear into Jocelyn's abdomen, propelling her to the ground.

A sudden quiet engulfed the small clearing. Endicott stood triumphant, breathing heavily, smiling broadly as he looked upon his victims. Jack was on his feet, but stood stunned and in obvious distress. He gripped his injured shoulder with his good hand, blood oozing between his fingers, dripping to the ground at his feet. Hatred contorted his features, but reason held his emotion at bay as Endicott pointed the spear menacingly in his direction.

Jocelyn lay in a fetal position, gasping. The blow had knocked every bit of air from her lungs; she was fighting for breath.

"I must say that was an ill-advised plan," Endicott gloated. He looked at Jack. "You, young man, are as good as dead. That's quite a wound you've suffered. There's enough blood there to attract every lizard wolf in the valley." Turning to Jocelyn he sneered, "And you, you will suffer the same fate. I'm afraid I'll have to lacerate you in similar fashion, but first," his tone hardened and he spat the words, "I'm going to rearrange your dental work. Consider this retribution for what you did to me earlier."

He grabbed Jocelyn by the hair and yanked her to her feet. Balling his fist he prepared to deliver a cruel blow to her face. Jocelyn braced for the punch. But it never came. Endicott unexpectedly let go of her hair and stumbled to his right.

A small arrow had mysteriously appeared and was embedded in Endicott's right leg. The crudely fletched shaft protruded from his hamstring, just above the knee, and the stone point, which had passed clean through, now projected from his thigh. Endicott staggered and caught himself against a large rock at the far end of the clearing. Clutching his leg with both hands, he turned to face the others. The bushes behind Jack rustled and a strange, bearded figure emerged.

The man walked with a noticeable limp. Superficially he resembled Endicott. His face was nearly hidden by a mass of tangled hair and beard. He was clad in a sort of leather kilt and wore crudely-fashioned leather shoes that reminded Jocelyn of cowboy boots. In one hand he carried a small bow.

Jocelyn and Jack stared at the man uncomprehendingly, but Endicott's reaction was one of both recognition and disbelief. "You!" he bellowed. The two bearded adversaries eyed one another for several seconds before Endicott spoke again. When he did, his speech was indistinguishable to the students. Even Jocelyn, who prided herself on her skills as a linguist, had no idea what Endicott was saying or even what language he spoke.

But the 'cave man' did. The language was Kalaallisut, the native tongue of most western Greenlanders.

"I should have finished the job rather than leaving you to die," Endicott growled.

"Put down your weapon, Loren. You're wounded, bleeding. You know you're in great danger."

By way of response, an angry Loren Endicott flashed withering, hateful looks at all three of his enemies. He grasped his spear tightly and hobbled into the bush, heading in the general direction of the river. Their rescuer made no attempt to pursue his wounded victim; he simply watched for a moment and shook his head before turning to face the students.

"Who are you?" Jocelyn asked.

The man didn't speak. He went to Jack and carefully examined the wound. With an air of great urgency he tore Jack's shirt apart and used it as a bandage. When he'd finished dressing Jack's arm, he waved off further attempt by Jocelyn to communicate and beckoned them to follow him, his insistent gestures demanding that they hurry.

It was then that they heard it. Through the stagnant air from the valley came the distinctive grunts of numerous excited lizard wolves. "You run!" the man exclaimed. He pointed, needlessly, in the direction opposite to where the animal noises were coming from. The three of them scrambled up the trail, driven by primal fear of the growing assemblage of excited carnivorous cynodonts.

It was amazing how quickly the lizard wolves came. Grunts and squeals filled the air. So many predators, perhaps as many as a dozen, had miraculously converged towards the scent of blood.

They ran hard. Adrenaline and fear drove them onward; the effects of injury and fatigue forgotten. Only the need to put distance between themselves and those crazed beasts mattered. Suddenly, above the din of the predators, they heard a loud, pitiful human scream. Seconds later the grunting ceased. Jack, Jocelyn and their new-found friend stopped and exchanged grim looks. The lizard wolves weren't chasing them anymore. They'd stopped grunting because they'd made their kill. Now...they were feeding.

An hour later the small party stopped to rest. After taking a long, well--deserved swig from her water bottle, Jocelyn turned to the bearded stranger. He was inspecting Jack's injured arm, but he stopped and smiled when she spoke.

"What's your name," she asked.

"I name Aage Randrup. You name?"

"Jocelyn Delaney." She held out her hand. "Thank you. You saved our lives." She could tell he understood the gist of what she said, but he didn't speak much English.

"I English...little bit," he replied sheepishly, holding his thumb and forefinger a half inch apart. "You, Danish?"

"Nope."

"Czy pan mówi polsku?" Jack asked.

"What?" said Jocelyn.

"He doesn't speak Polish," Jack replied, "...and apparently neither do you."

She rolled her eyes and laughed. Addressing Randrup, she asked, "Se habla Español? Parlez vous Français?"

"Mais, oui!" came the enthusiastic reply. Est-ce que vous le parlez?"

The discovery of a common language threw the two of them into intense conversation. Jack listened patiently, comprehending just enough to follow the flow of what they were saying but not much of the detail. At one point, Jocelyn enquired about Spencer. Randrup's response caused her to let out a loud wail and bury her face in her hands. She began to sob uncontrollably.

Jack's shoulders slumped. Apparently, Spencer hadn't made it. Jocelyn had been right about Endicott all along. He chastised himself for not trusting her intuition; if he'd supported her arguments to persuade Spencer to go with them, the kid might be alive now. In large measure Jack felt responsible for Spencer's death.

It was Randrup who sensed Jack's confusion. Patting Jack's good shoulder, he smiled and said, "Spencer, le jeune homme avec un pied mal, il vit."

"Spencer's alive," Jocelyn choked out the translation. "Sorry, Jack, I guess I kind of freaked when I found out. It's such great news."

The pronouncement that Spencer was alive had an enormous uplifting effect on Jack as well. He too came close to tears once he understood what had happened. His immediate reaction was to find the young man, make certain he was out of danger. "So, where is he? Jack insisted, "If he's still back in the valley we have to help him."

"Maintenant, Spencer marche a l'endroit de votre professeur," Randrup volunteered. He explained what had happened back at Endicott's camp and what he'd told Spencer to do.

Jocelyn pondered what he said and then turned to Jack. "Dr. Randrup says Spencer is making his way back to Marcie and Debbie by way of the coastal mountains. He's suggested we should head that way as well. Spencer should get there before we do, but if he isn't there when we arrive, he'll go look for him."

"Randrup and I will go after him right now! I'm not leaving Spencer out there alone," Jack said with conviction. "Now that we know he's alive we've got to help him."

"And what about Debbie? For that matter, what about you? You need medical help too, Jack. I vote we just stay calm and see what the situation is back at the ridge."

Jack looked at her and nodded soberly. "All right," he admitted. Awkwardly shouldering his pack with his good arm, he added, "But we aren't doing anyone any good by sitting here. Let's move out."

Untold years of erosion had covered the floor of the crevice with a layer of sand and gravel. A small trickle of water ran through it, every so often crossing the path so that Spencer had to hop from one side to the other. But progress was good. He was climbing. The trail was gradually taking him up through the wall of basalt that formed the rim of the volcano. Water seeped from outcrops all along the way, lending a sheen to the rock when hit by the flashlight beam. At the base of the fissure, down where he was walking, the air was thick and stagnant, but up where the crack opened into the clouds, he could hear the moan of wind sweeping past.

Half an hour after leaving the beach, he came to a waterfall. A jumble of large boulders, thrown down by a massive rock slide, had at some point blocked the trail, but a resourceful person or persons had expended significant effort to create a staircase of stone that ran along the north wall of the chasm. Small rocks had been expertly fitted together to make the structure, and Spencer stopped briefly to admire the handiwork. This was a job that had been carefully planned and executed. Here, in the middle of nowhere, halfway up the side of a slab of basalt, someone had gone to a lot of trouble to clear a path. As he climbed the rock staircase, Spencer pondered its significance. There were two things of which he was now certain: this trail definitely led to somewhere important, and it wasn't Endicott who had made it.

The cave-in that created the waterfall had also dammed the rivulet that flowed through it. A crystal-clear pool of water lay beside a beach of fine black sand—silt carried down by past floods. Depressions in the sand, human footprints, caught Spencer's eye. Someone had passed this way recently. He bent down to study them. Whoever it was hadn't worn modern shoes, but the lack of individual toe impressions suggested some form of foot covering. That fit with the notion that it was Endicott who'd made them. Still, Spencer had to keep an open mind. Whoever it was had been heading towards the back of the crevasse, not in the direction of the beach. There were no return footprints. That made Spencer nervous. If this were a one way trip, if this trail had no other exit, he would undoubtedly run into his predecessor. How long ago had the person been here? It was almost impossible to tell. Hours? Days? A month perhaps? Deep imprints such as these wouldn't survive the freeze--thaw cycles likely to have occurred during late spring. Snow melt and spring floods would likewise have washed them away. Spencer concluded that they had to be less than about two weeks old. Beyond that he couldn't tell.

Just past the pond the fissure ended. Before him lay an irregular, gaping hole in the side of the mountain. At this point the cleft in the rock yielded to a volcanic blow hole of impressive size. While there had been a modicum of natural light that filtered down between the walls of the crevasse, inside the cavern that yawned in front of him there was none. Absolute darkness reigned. Without the lantern he would have had to stop. The footprints he'd been tracking for almost an hour disappeared into the void. Spencer followed.

Here the footing was poor. Instead of sand and gravel washed in by the action of water, the cave was lined with rocky projections. Sharp, scoriated edges stuck out from the walls, threatening to cut and lacerate those daring enough to pass through. Basketball-sized shards littered the floor of the tunnel—detritus that volcanic gases had deposited as they'd charged through with explosive, unimaginable violence, splattering plastic blobs of molten rock along the way. Some of the rocks were smooth, but most were jagged, infused with small holes left by escaping gas which turned them into giant Brillo pads. Spencer picked his way through carefully, thankful that his shoes had good, thick soles to protect his feet. He guarded against a slip that would hurl him against the nasty silicate knife edges that seemed to jump out from nowhere.

For the most part the tunnel was straight. Occasionally a huge boulder appeared, acting as a baffle to limit visibility down the shaft. Spencer stopped beside one such obstruction. This particular rock was glassy, a large block of obsidian that had caught in the throat of the ancient belching inferno. Indentations covered its surface, but these weren't the product of escaping gas. These were man-made. He swept the beam of the flashlight across its face. The carvings constituted some sort of text. No hieroglyphics or pictographs accompanied them. These were definitely letters, and they conveyed some sort of message. It was an alphabet that Spencer had never seen. Fantastic images of men from outer space came to mind. He envisioned them beaming down to Earth thousands, no, millions of years ago, long before humans were around to record their visits. He let his imagination take over. These strange writings could conceivably have been etched using some sort of laser or plasma tool, perhaps even a weapon like the light sabers in Star Wars. "Maybe the idea of a light saber isn't so far-fetched," he thought.

Continuing along the subterranean passageway, Spencer suddenly realized he wasn't climbing any more. In fact, ever since he'd left the fissure on the ocean side of the mountain and entered this cavern, he'd been moving slightly downhill. By his estimate he hadn't yet gained enough elevation to have reached the level of the ridge. He didn't think he'd even reached the height of the shelf on which Debbie lay. Nonetheless, he could tell he was headed in the right direction. If this tunnel continued much farther, he reasoned, it would eventually pass completely through the mountain. That thought spurred him onward. His spirits lifted into the stratosphere when the damp, cold, stagnant air of the cave seemed to move. He licked his finger and held it up. There was a very slight breeze, and it came from up ahead. "I'm gettin' close," he muttered.

A spot of light soon appeared—the light at the end of the tunnel. Relief surged through him and he picked up the pace. His thoughts turned to Debbie and Marcie. Where exactly was the outlet to this passage relative to the shelf where they were stranded? More importantly, were they still alive? If Endicott had gotten to them and killed them, this journey would be for naught. Also, if Endicott had indeed murdered his friends, the first place he would head for would be this cave. He would want to destroy all evidence of their landing on the beach.

His pace slowed at the prospect of an ambush by his nemesis. "I've got to dim the light before I reach the opening," he reasoned. Using his bandana, he covered the front of the lantern, allowing only a fraction of its output to illuminate his route.

Just before Spencer reached the cave entrance, the passageway opened up into a large chamber. Recognizing this as a superb spot for an ambush, he turned off the light, picked up a baseball sized rock and crept forward slowly, scanning the area, poised to react quickly should he have to defend himself. But no attack came. Once he assured himself he was in no immediate danger, Spencer took a look around.

Several more large rocks bearing strange inscriptions stood along one wall. Each weighed several tons, and it would have taken multiple men, or some futuristic anti-gravity device, to set them into place. Stashed among the stones were several plywood crates filled with an assortment of metal objects. Cautiously, a nervous Spencer turned his back to the cave entrance and bent to study their contents. He lifted the topmost item. It appeared to be the handle of a sword, heavy and made of a copper alloy covered by a thick layer of green tarnish. Underneath it lay a pile of metallic buttons and jewelry. Those made of gold gleamed brightly in the light of the flash. Most, however, were made of silver, thoroughly blackened by the sulfurous atmosphere of the cave. Next to one box sat satchels made of cynodont hide, secured by crude leather drawstrings. Spencer grabbed one but could barely lift it. When he opened it, he saw that it was filled with crudely-struck silver coins.

"Holy crap," he whispered in awe, "This looks like old Viking stuff—like that thing Jocelyn found at Endicott's place." He would have loved to stay and examine the treasure, but there just wasn't time. Stowing the lantern behind one of the crates, Spencer cautiously moved out into the muted sunlight of the island's interior.

It was getting late. Marcie Van Wormer fidgeted with lengths of paracord and the leather thongs that Spencer had brought back. Apprehension and curiosity caused her mind to wander from her current task. She was trying to fashion a basket in which to carry Debbie when the time came to haul her up the cliff, but her thoughts were slowing her down. Questions came and went, none of which seemed to have answers she could fathom. Next to her lay the spear Spencer had brought. Where had he obtained it? It was made of wood. She'd done some exploring in the immediate vicinity of the tent and hadn't seen anything but rock...nothing but rock, cold, mist and snow, as far as the eye could see. No trees, not even a blade of grass could survive here, and yet he'd shown up clad only in trousers and shoes, no shirt. How had he kept from freezing to death?

Marcie bunched up one corner of her sleeping bag and tied a length of cord around it. She cinched it tightly and then added another half-hitch. Just after Spencer left, she had come up with her design. She would run five lengths of cord from one side of the bag to the other. They would lay Debbie in the bag and slip the spear handle through all of the loops so that it could be lifted as a unit, keeping the patient secure and horizontal. They would still have to fasten the climbing rope to the ends of the handle for the harrowing lift up the cliff, but, hey, it was a start.

Again her mind wandered from her project. That meat Spencer had given her—she'd already eaten more than half of it and it was darn good. Of course it might just have seemed extra tasty because she was on the verge of starvation. It was certainly different from anything she'd ever had before, though, a blend of chicken and pork, with maybe a hint of fish—strange stuff that he'd identified by an even stranger name.

The odd food, although interesting, wasn't of immediate importance. What really bothered Marcie were the ominous words Spencer had uttered as he'd begun his ascent of the cliff. She eyed the spear as she recalled what he'd said: "If you see a cave man, don't trust him." So, Spence had encountered other people in the past few days. Correction: he'd encountered at least one other individual. And the guy was a cave man? Whom she was to fight off with this weapon?

She looked at Debbie and her heart sank. The woman's breathing was feeble and rapid. Pain racked her body during what had become all too brief periods of limited consciousness. Her brain was starting to shut down. Not much of what Marcie said to her seemed to register. Debbie had been only marginally coherent for more than a day now. Watching someone suffer like this was hard on poor Marcie. To assume such awful responsibility, to treat a gravely ill patient with the most meager of resources, had extracted a heavy psychological toll. The young woman's chronically upbeat attitude was in danger of slipping into despair. Spencer's arrival and the hope it engendered, had come just in time.

Forcing herself to focus on her job, Marcie fought to keep from losing faith. Unfortunately she'd begun to obsess over the sobering reality of what lay ahead for poor Debbie. If Spencer couldn't get out an SOS, Debbie was probably going to die of her injuries. Even if help were to come, in say, a day or so, if they could somehow signal a search party from the beach, getting Debbie out in time to save her life would require a heroic effort.

But that was all the more reason why this carrier had to work. It would save precious minutes in the effort to extract Debbie if it were ready when needed. Marcie willed herself into a resurgence of purpose and began to cut another length of rope. As she began to attach it to the sleeping bag, she heard the unmistakable sound of footfalls outside the shelter. Excitedly she pushed aside the door of the shelter to see who it was. Probably Spencer—the amount of time that had elapsed since his departure was about right. She fervently hoped he was bearing good news.

The approaching figure wasn't Spence. Marcie's heart caught in her throat. She turned deathly pale. It was a "cave man." So, Spencer's prophetic words were true. There was indeed another inhabitant in this awful place. She was trapped inside a tent alongside a dying woman, and a dangerous man had just found them.

Marcie fought the urge to panic. She had to suppress her sudden fear and think cogently. Maintaining her composure was the key to maximizing her odds for survival. But what to do? Clearly she had only two choices: to run like the dickens and hope to escape, or to stay and fight. One glance at Debbie and her mind was made up. There was no way she'd leave her friend and mentor to the whims of some barbarian. Grabbing Spencer's spear, she flung back the tent flap and adopted a menacing pose.

"One more step and you're history, butt-hole," she snarled. She took a step forward and thrust the spear towards the man's groin, causing him to jump back. "Yeah, you'd best crawl back under the rock you came from if you have half a brain. Make a move and you'll be singin' soprano in a heartbeat." Marcie trembled with fear, but her aggressive façade had the desired effect. The attacker clearly believed she was a threat.

"I friend," the fellow pleaded. He held out his hands in a gesture of supplication.

But Marcie didn't buy it. "Not according to my bud, Spencer, you're not. He warned me about you, 'cave man.' You're not to be trusted. Now...get lost."

"It's all right, Marcie. Wrong 'cave man.'"

It was a woman's voice. Marcie almost fainted when she recognized Jocelyn and Jack walking up the trail behind the bearded visitor. "Marcie, this is Dr. Aage Randrup. He's a friend who saved our lives as well as Spencer's." She addressed Randrup, "Monsieur, je vous present Marcie Van Wormer."

"Hello, I am nice to meet you," the fellow smiled, holding forth his hand.

Marcie paused and looked at Jocelyn. The other girl smiled and nodded her approval. Marcie slowly relaxed and lowered the spear. "Nice to meet you, too," she sighed.

XVII

A flurry of conversation ensued. The returning students insisted upon knowing of Debbie's condition, and Marcie was loaded with questions about what her friends had gone through in the past seventy-two hours. Randrup stood quietly in the background, listening intently, picking up bits of information about the plight of the members of this small party who'd stumbled into his world.

Marcie was explaining her plans for moving Debbie when Jack asked, "Have you seen Spencer?" Marcie stopped talking and the others looked at her expectantly.

"Yes," she replied, "he was here a few hours ago. He took the satellite communicator down to the beach. He had an idea about how to charge the battery, and..."

"Heah I am."

Everyone turned at the sound of Spencer's voice. Upon seeing her young friend, alive and well, an emotionally charged Jocelyn ran to him and threw her arms around him. "Oh, Spencer, you have no idea how glad I am to see you. Dr. Randrup told us what happened. I am SO sorry we left you with Endicott. We suspected...I mean, I suspected, he wasn't right..."

"Aw, fugetaboutit, Jocelyn. It was my fault I stayed wit' him, besides, I'm okay now, and what's more, I..."

"Bonjour, Spencer," Randrup spoke up, "Je m'appelle Aage Randrup. C'est un plaisir de vous rencontrer."

Spencer smiled and greeted the man who'd saved his life. "I can't thank you enough, sir, for what you did," he responded in French. His speech was tinged with a Creole lilt that Randrup found amusing. The two conversed briefly before Spencer asked, in English, of no one in particular, "Where's

Endicott?"

There were a hundred other questions he wanted to ask. He wanted to learn the details of how Jocelyn, Jake and Randrup had met, and how they had been forced to contend with Endicott. But those things would have to wait. The pressing issue of Endicott's whereabouts was more important.

Jack and Jocelyn glanced at one another. It was Jocelyn who responded. "After he left you for dead, Endicott followed our trail and attacked us. If it hadn't been for Dr. Randrup, we'd almost certainly be dead." Still shaken by recent events, she didn't want to go into detail. "We don't have to worry about him now, though. He's no longer a threat."

"Yeah," Jack couldn't resist adding, "when we left him, the three stooges were having lunch with him." The comment elicited a puzzled look from Marcie, a disparaging scowl from Jocelyn, and a broad smile from Spencer.

It was then that Marcie did something strange and unexpected. She went to Spencer and hugged him. Tension flooded from her trembling body as she held her friend. Even she, herself, was astonished by her feelings and the extent of her emotional outreach.

None was more surprised than the target of her affections. Spencer stood stock still, his arms pinned to his sides by the wonderful girl who was trying mightily to hold back tears of relief and joy now that he'd returned. Their collective discomfort was enhanced by the knowing look and smile they received from Jocelyn. Both blushed awkwardly.

Marcie sheepishly released her hostage and tucked away her emotions. "Happy reunions aside," she said primly, "we still have a huge problem with what to do about Debbie."

"What we hafta do..." Spencer began, but he was interrupted by Jocelyn.

"Dr. Randrup has figured out a way to stabilize her injuries."

"But when I was on the beach, I..." Again, Spencer was cut off, this time by Marcie.

"I've already taken care of that," she said proudly. "Using the spear Spencer brought with him, I've made a litter I think will hold her. C'mon, I'll show you."

"Wait a minute," Jack said. He had a bemused look on his face. Turning to Spencer he asked, "If you just came from the beach, how come we didn't see you come down the cliff?"

"That's what I been trying to tell ya'," came the exasperated reply. "There's anotha way to get to the beach. We don't need any ropes. All we hafta do now is make a stretcher to carry Debbie 'an get goin'." He then paused for effect. "The rescue party'll be here in a coupl'a hours."

"You mean you got through? You were able to send a distress call?!" Marcie asked excitedly.

"That's right," he proudly replied, "'an you'll NEVAH guess what else I found."

"You're going to need quite a few stitches in your arm, maybe one or two in your back." Marcie poked around the cuts Jack had suffered at the hands of Loren Endicott. "The doc at the dig site can do that. For now we should leave them somewhat open so they can drain. I put antibiotic cream on 'em and wrapped 'em in sterile gauze. As long as you don't develop an abscess you should be fine in a week or so. Plus, you'll have a really macho scar to show the ladies."

"Thanks, doc."

They were sitting in a temporary shelter against the wind, made by leaning their zodiac against a huge rock halfway up the beach. In front of them lay the North Atlantic, stretching out to the curve of the Earth. They were alone save for an unconscious Debbie, and both of them were anxiously watching for a rescue craft to round the point that lay to the north.

Marcie put her hand on Debbie's forehead. "No fever; that's good."

They were silent for a while. Both were tired from the long walk they'd just endured. Everyone had taken turns, even a one-armed Jack, carrying Debbie's stretcher. They were taking a well-earned break. Presently, Jack said, "That was quite a hug you gave Spencer back at the cliff."

The comment caught Marcie off guard. She let out a deep breath. "Yeah." She paused. "You know, I had a bit of a crush on you, Jack...for a while anyway."

"Really?" he asked, feigning surprise. "And now?"

"Um, don't take this the wrong way okay? You're a really great guy and all, but...let's be realistic, you're too old for me. And Cleveland is so far from Albany. And besides that, Debbie says Spencer likes me. I know what you must be thinking, 'What's up with that?' Right? Well, she seemed pretty sure about it and, I guess, well, I sorta like him too. You gotta admit he's kinda cute, and he really saved our bacon by getting that message through. And you should have seen him when he climbed up that cliff. I mean, it was the bravest thing I've ever seen, overcoming his fear, risking serious injury to send for help..." She stopped when she realized she was rambling.

Jack just smiled. "So, are we good then?"

She blushed and nodded.

"For what it's worth, I think Spencer is one lucky guy. Give yourself some credit too, Marcie."

Marcie stood to stretch and gazed back towards the fissure entrance. Jocelyn, Spencer and the 'cave man,' Randrup, had been engaged in serious conversation since they'd arrived at the beach. All the talk was in French, so Marcie and Jack had moved off to stay with Debbie. Marcie knew what they were talking about, though. It had to do with all the stuff they'd seen in the cave, all those old coins, jewelry, statues...

Dr. Randrup had been overwhelmed. He'd stammered words like 'encroyable!' and 'magnifique!' along with many others in language or languages that were totally foreign to her. But the meanings were clear enough. What had impressed him the most were the big stones with writing on them. "Runestones" he'd called them. Marcy had taken photos of everything they'd seen. As owner of the only remaining charged and functioning cell phone in their group, she'd been enlisted as chief photographer of what Randrup claimed was the largest, most impressive and by far the most valuable store of Viking treasure ever discovered.

She bit her lip in concentration. If Randrup were simply describing the significance of what they'd seen, shouldn't he be doing most of the talking? It looked to her as though Jocelyn and Spence were adding their share—and the discussion seemed to be a very serious one indeed.

"Hey, Jack," she said, returning to the rock on which she'd been sitting, "What do you know about the Vikings?"

"Not much I'm afraid. I know they're in the NFC North, along with the Packers, Bears and Lions. Why?"

His humor was lost on Marcie. She was deep in thought. "I don't know. It seems those guys have a lot to talk about, and that's the topic of conversation. The prehistoric world you were telling me about appears to play second fiddle to the relics we passed in the cave. What do you think about that?"

"Well, Randrup is an archeologist." He shrugged, "Finding those artifacts had a big effect on him. He was happier than a pig in slop when he saw what Endicott had collected. That, by the way, is a direct quote from Jocelyn."

"Hey, guys." Jocelyn ducked into the shelter. Randrup and Spencer were on their way as well. The meeting was over. Jocelyn pointed to Debbie and motioned for the other two to follow her outside where the older woman wouldn't hear them. Even though Debbie had been largely incoherent since their return, for some reason Jocelyn wanted to avoid involving her in the conversation.

A stiff breeze was now coming from offshore. The low-hanging Sun passed behind a cloud, causing an uncomfortable chill to descend upon the inhabitants of the beach. Jocelyn hugged herself and rubbed her arms to keep warm. "Dr. Randrup has asked a favor of us," she began, "Spencer and I agreed, but we told him it had to be a unanimous decision. You two have to approve it as well."

"What does he want?" Marcie asked.

"Dr. Randrup has asked that we not tell anyone about the early Triassic ecosystem in the island's interior, or about the Viking relics that we saw today."

"What? Why?"

"Yeah, these are important discoveries," said Jack, "especially the biological part. Scientists have to know about this; there's so much they can learn about evolution and adaptation, not to mention the possibility of finding new drugs, cures for cancer, produced by some of the plants. It's unethical to keep this from the rest of the world."

"Oh, the world will be informed, and soon; Randrup agrees with that. But think about what will happen if the island is opened up to study right away. The place will become a zoo. In addition to scientists flocking in from all parts of the globe, hordes of tourists and souvenir hunters will descend upon it."

"Okay, I get it, but once people find out about it, that's going to happen anyway."

"Maybe not. Spencer and I presented the same argument to Dr. Randrup. He's convinced that if strict controls are enacted by the Greenlandic government, the ecology of the island can be protected. He likens it to the Galapagos. Ecuador has regulated access to those islands very successfully for many decades. Randrup thinks Greenland can do the same thing with Eviskar. All he wants is time, time to set up Greenlandic and Danish naval patrol of the waters surrounding the island, and to establish protocol for access."

Jack and Marcie looked at one another. When Jocelyn had compared Eviskar to the Galapagos Islands, it made a lot of sense. "I agree," Marcie sighed. "I mean, let's face it, I don't know of any place on Earth where modern society openly lives in harmony with nature. Randrup has a point."

"Me too," Jack agreed.

"And, I think there's more to Randrup's request than he'll admit," Jocelyn offered. "He's a dedicated scientist, but he's also a proud Greenlander. I think he wants his country to play the lead role in the study of this fascinating place and its history. And, personally, I think we owe him a great deal. He saved our lives and he's lived here under the harshest of conditions for more than a year. He's earned the right to ask this of us."

"I think I detect a bit of feminine intuition at work."

"Yes, you do, most definitely."

"There's one problem I see with his plan," Marcie said. The others regarded her questioningly. "There's no way he's going to convince anyone that he's survived on this beach for a year. I mean, look at the way he's dressed—half naked in a land where the high temperature in the summer is a balmy sixty degrees. Those people at the dig site are scientists; he won't fool a single one of them."

"When the rescue crew gets here, he won't be around," Jocelyn said. "That's why he wrote this." Jocelyn produced a sheet of paper that contained a brief note. "It's written in his native language, Kalaallisut. I'm supposed to give it to Ittuk; he and Randrup are close friends and he's one of only two people at the dig who can read and understand it. Randrup is apparently going to take Endicott's raft a couple of nights from now, and land south of the excavation. Ittuk will hide him and find a way to smuggle him off the island."

"How?"

"Beats me. I suspect..." Jocelyn was interrupted by a shout from Spencer.

Rounding the point to the north, motoring through the mist, were two zodiacs. Standing in the bow of the lead vessel was a dapper man wearing a safari vest and bush hat. Clenched between his teeth was an unlit pipe. Morgan Holloway and the cavalry had arrived.

Debbie rested peacefully on one of the two beds in the medical tent at the Eviskar archeological site. Tethered to one arm was an IV, through which flowed electrolytes, antibiotics and morphine. She was weak but responsive. Her husband sat contentedly by her side.

"Morgan," she turned to him and smiled, "I'm sorry for inconveniencing you like this. It was my own stupid fault I got hurt. I know how important your research is, and I'm afraid I've ruined your summer. Thanks, though, for coming so quickly to rescue us. You really are my knight in shining armor."

He gave her hand a squeeze. "Nonsense, everyone here, the entire excavation team, wanted to help when they found out you were in trouble. They're a superb bunch. Doc Strøm says that you really owe a debt of gratitude to your students. In particular he praised the efforts of the young girl, Marcie—said she did everything right. He even intimated you might not have survived if not for her."

He loaded his pipe bowl and drew a deep breath—marvelous. A colleague had gifted him two hundred grams of a wonderful Danish tobacco blend called "Asgard Gold." He was dying to light it, but Strøm would crucify him for smoking in the presence of his patient. Content to savor the pleasant aroma without setting it afire, Morgan let out a satisfied sigh.

"So tell me what's been going on here since we've been gone," Debbie asked. "You seem pretty happy. I take it progress has been good?"

"Good?" he chuckled, "Good is an understatement. I don't mean to sound boastful, but we've been darned lucky on this trip, yes siree. Right after you left, one of the fellows ran a routine metal detection scan through sector nine." Morgan leaned forward, his eyes bright, animated. "You'll never guess what we dug up." He paused for dramatic effect. "A foot below the surface we found an axe head and what appears to be a ladle. Deb, you can't imagine the excitement that generated. Think of it, the first metal objects we've unearthed so far at this site. And what a find! The form of the axe is period for the 11th century. Gosh, it's exciting. I wish the students we brought along could have shared in that, but I think they'll be suitably impressed once I show them. Heh, heh...a lecture is probably in order as well, one that addresses the success rate of finds like this. I don't want them to get the idea that such extraordinary discoveries are the norm."

"Sorry I've made such a mess of things, sweetie. I don't want to take you away from here when things are going so well."

"Actually, you won't. The Danish vessel that brought us here is due to pass through the day after tomorrow. They've kindly agreed to take you to Reykjavik. I was going to go along, but two of the Greenlanders, Ittuk and Nunni, will accompany you instead. It seems they've just been informed of some urgent business they have to address. I feel bad for them—just when things are getting exciting around here they have to leave."

Debbie had closed her eyes. Morgan could tell she was exhausted. He stared at her, trying to imagine the hell she'd experienced on that cold desolate ridge. Four cracked ribs, a broken wrist and a shattered lower leg, serious injuries that were life threatening. A shudder went through him as he realized how close he'd come to being a widower. She was safe now, though. The serene expression on her face and the regular, unlabored breathing of sleep, told him all was well.

Morgan's gaze shifted to the piece of leather lying on the ground by her bed. The litter the students had made for her had been a clever one, constructed out of twine and one of their sleeping bags. This leather piece had been placed under the bag to serve as reinforcement for the arduous trip from the accident site—a harrowing climb up over a cliff, followed by a long hike to the beach.

It was flexible and tough, and it bore a strange pattern of spots. Several containers they had unearthed the previous summer, satchels that had contained grain a thousand years ago, were made of the same spotted leather. The coincidence pointed to a local source for the material. But what? Had the students killed and skinned a large animal during their three day exodus? Most definitely not, Morgan concluded. A more plausible explanation is that they found a dead animal near the shore and harvested the hide—some sort of pinniped, most likely. Morgan guessed it was either harp seal or walrus. Both species had been spotted along the island's coast. His thoughts wandered to the diet of the ancient Norsemen who'd lived on this shore and a thin smile formed around the ubiquitous pipe stem lodged between his teeth. The idea for yet another scientific publication was forming in his mind.

Two tender vessels from the *Stjerne* were beached on the sand near the Eviskar medical tent. A hundred yards offshore the parent ship lay at anchor, bobbing in heavy chop. The wind was incessant and the seas were rough. A storm was moving in.

Dr. Strøm, accompanied by Morgan and the four students, watched Debbie's transfer into the nearest boat. Her two Greenlandic chaperones climbed into the other craft, assisted by a third man who was heavily bundled against the weather. The man walked with a pronounced limp, and a high collar and long-brimmed hat hid most of his bearded face from view. To those on the beach he looked like a sailor from the Stjerne, assigned to help transfer the patient and the two researchers. To the men on the ship he appeared to be a fourth passenger. Only four of the people who stood on the beach in the bracing wind knew the man's true identity, and they were not about to divulge that knowledge. He and the two Greenlanders would see Debbie safely to the hospital in Reykjavik, and then all three would book passage on the next flight to Nuuk, the capital of Greenland. A sensitive meeting among top government officials and selected University faculty was scheduled for the instant they arrived.

XVIII

Icelandic Airways flight 3219 from Reykjavik touched down at New York's JFK international airport in the morning of September 2nd. The four weary high school students on board, those returning from three months of dirty, backbreaking excavation work on Eviskar Island, waited for the other passengers to exit before hoisting their bags and heading for the gate.

The flight had been a pleasant one for Marcie Van Wormer. It hadn't been completely full and Marcie had been lucky enough to find herself next to an empty seat. The fellow seated next to Spencer had been eager to swap seats with her, grateful for the extra privacy and elbow room.

As a cost saving measure, Morgan figured his charges could sleep on the plane, and had therefore booked their flight home for the morning after their water transport docked at Olafsvik. After four hours of bus ride across Iceland, they'd gone straight to the airport to wait for five more hours prior to leaving for the United States. All were travel weary, but the excitement of their return home denied them sleep on the plane.

Anticipation of the imminent reunion with her folks, had charged Marcie with a mix of excitement and apprehension. Three months was a long time for any young person to be separated from her family, but it was especially so for someone as young as fifteen. So much had happened in that time, it seemed as though an eternity had passed, and in a strange, nonchronological way, it had. Marcie knew she had changed, all of them had. The stresses and hardships they'd endured on the island had been life altering. A bond now existed among the four of them that was as strong, if not stronger, than that of siblings. Their close ties had been forged in the furnace of ordeal, developed over the stressful, life-threatening three days they'd been trapped in the island's forbidding interior. Marcie, in particular, considered her fellow students to be her best friends, and it was going to be difficult for her to say goodbye. Throughout the long ride to Reykjavik and on the return flight home, she'd been aware that the end to this eventful summer was fast approaching. That end was now only moments away.

There was a long line at customs. Another full aircraft had arrived shortly before theirs—an early morning plane out of Paris. The tired students from Eviskar stood waiting to be processed in lines in front of each customs agent that snaked through several switchbacks in the huge, crowded room. At the moment, Jack's line ran along one wall. He was seated on his rucksack, leaning against the wall trying to doze.

Jocelyn was in heaven. She'd maneuvered into a line containing a French tour group and was listening intently to snippets of conversation. It was a wonderful opportunity not to be squandered. As a student of their native tongue, she listened for subtleties in pronunciation, diction and colloquialisms. She also enjoyed hearing the thoughts and perceptions of these tourists as they prepared to set foot in the United States.

The two younger students had become inseparable. Both wanted to spend as much time together as possible which, for Marcie, afforded her the opportunity to broach a sensitive subject, one she'd postponed raising until they were off the plane. In letters to her father she'd mentioned it, and now it was time to discuss it with Spencer.

"Hey, Spence, mind if I ask you something? It's personal, so if you don't want to talk about it, that's cool." He gave her a questioning look. "It's about your foot."

"What about it?"

"Well, my dad's an orthopedic specialist, and..." She took his hand in hers. "He's treated a lot of kids with talipes, you know, 'club foot.' From what I gather it's real common. I was wondering if you, uh, might want him to look at it."

"First of all, I don't mind you askin' me that, Marcie. It's really nice of you. But from what I've read on the web, I think I'm too old for treatment. My bones have grown 'an I think it's too late. Like I said, though, thanks for the thought."

"What if you're wrong? What if he could really help?"

"Yeah, sure, I guess, but I gotta be honest wicha; my parents probably can't afford it. 'An besides, I can live wit' a slight limp. It's no big deal."

"Don't worry about money. My dad wouldn't charge you, and if you're too proud to accept charity, we could work out some sort of deal maybe." She looked away, somewhat embarrassed. "You could tutor me. I suck at math, Spence. My grades in it have been okay, but I overheard my dad and stepmom discussing the possibility of getting me some help."

"What makes you think he'll go along wit' that?"

"Oh, he will," she said with a sly smile, "I'm his daughter. He has no choice."

Standing just outside the door from customs, Marcie's father and stepmom waited expectantly for their daughter's triumphant appearance. Steven was trying valiantly to catch a glimpse of his daughter every time the exit door opened, but the crowds and chaos thwarted his attempts. Gail could tell he was excited. Although her husband prided himself on his self-control, always keeping tight rein on his emotions, the cold cup of coffee in his right hand revealed where his thoughts and feelings had been for the past twenty minutes. She'd never before seen Steven allow a good cup of java to cool down.

The moment Marcie exited customs, she spotted her folks. As promised, they had brought with them two large suitcases, the bags Jocelyn had been prohibited from taking to Eviskar. She ran first to her father and then to Gail, dishing out bear hugs along with the biggest smile either had ever seen. She'd really missed them. It was also apparent that she'd had a glorious, eventful summer abroad, but was overjoyed to be back.

One by one, her colleagues emerged into the airport waiting area. They too were dutifully welcomed by Steven and Gail. Jocelyn offered heartfelt thanks to the Van Wormers for safeguarding her belongings. After Jack and Jocelyn finished exchanging pleasantries with Marcie's folks, they loaded up with their mountain of luggage, preparing to depart for the main terminal to check in for their flights home. Before they could get away, however, Marcie embraced each of them. She choked back a sob while trying to smile, and admonished, "You guys better write to me or I'll be pissed, and I expect both of you to come visit me if at all possible, capiche?"

Jocelyn, in particular, reciprocated those sentiments. She held Marcie's hands in the manner of a loving older sister, and told her in heartfelt words how much she appreciated the time they'd spent together. "You be sure to write to me too," she said as she finally let go and hefted her rucksack, "that's what best friends do."

Gail watched the interplay among the four students with considerable interest. The pre-departure dynamic she'd noted back in June appeared to have changed significantly. Of course, she'd read Marcie's letters, and they had spoken briefly by satellite phone about every two weeks or so. Their daughter had kept her and Steven well informed of what had gone on at the archeological site. But Gail was the type of person who could learn far more about how Marcie's and the other students' lives had changed by watching the way they interacted, by reading between the lines. She knew that, in general, her stepdaughter had enjoyed her time in that remote place. However, she also knew how living in close proximity to a small subset of others, in a confined environment, always resulted in interesting friendships, interactions, and, oftentimes, conflicts. This group, it seemed, had grown very close.

One prominent physical change she'd noted right away dealt with Jocelyn's appearance. Her hair was much shorter than it had been when she left. A perceptive person like Gail knew it was a big deal for a woman to trim her locks like that. Primitive bathing facilities could account for it, but there was something else about the girl that accompanied her new look; she seemed friendlier, more gracious, and it was obvious that she and Jack had grown particularly close.

Gail also pondered the warm hugs Marcie had given the older students as a sendoff. There was no remaining evidence of her crush on Jack. And what circumstances had transpired to bring the four of them into such close friendship? Gail Van Wormer knew something profound had happened on that island, and it was something Marcie had yet to reveal. But Gail wouldn't pressure her stepdaughter to mention anything she didn't want to. "It may be best that what happened at Eviskar, must stay at Eviskar," she thought.

There were also real indications of just how much more mature her stepdaughter had grown. She wasn't the naïve little girl who'd once fretted at length about which headlamp to buy or what songs she would download for the trip. Now, she exuded real confidence and was considerably more outgoing.

Maybe it had to do with Marcie's exploits in helping that poor woman, Debbie Holloway, who'd fallen and been hurt so badly. Steven had been so worried when he'd found out about the accident, he'd begun to make arrangements to go to Eviskar himself. However, once he knew Marcie was all right, he'd settled down and cancelled his trip, and when the details came describing his daughter's first aid heroics, that she'd saved the woman's life, he'd swelled with pride. That had been a watershed moment for both parents. They realized that not only had Marcie survived the ordeal, she was the one who had stepped up and dealt with adversity in level-headed and life-saving fashion.

They had received a lengthy letter from Debbie several weeks after the accident, describing firsthand what had happened and how grateful she was for the remarkable care Marcie had given her. Gail swore that the moment Steven read that letter was the greatest thrill he'd ever experienced, even surpassing the joy she'd seen in his eyes the day they were married. Poor Marcie had no idea what her dad had in store for her on the train ride home. The interrogation would be intense, relentless.

"Ladies and gentlemen, in a few moments we'll begin boarding American Airlines flight 471 nonstop to Cleveland through gate twelve." The flight attendant summoned those travelling with small children, and those requiring assistance, to the checkin podium. Jack and Jocelyn stood and stretched.

"I'm going to miss you, Jack." There were tears rolling freely down Jocelyn's cheeks as she helped him put on his backpack.

"Hey, we'll see each other soon. I've been told Corpus Christi is a lot warmer than Cleveland during the holidays. Would you mind having a 'Damn Yankee' visitor around then?"

"I'd like that," she beamed. "I'll have to convince my friends that you're okay, though. Some of them have this idea that Yankee visitors are like hemorrhoids:" She put her arms around his neck, "they're a pain in the ass when they come down and it's a real relief when they go back up."

"If you'd prefer I didn't come, then..."

"No, no, please, I want you to visit. I'll make sure we have plenty of 'Preparation H' on hand. Everything will be fine."

Jack smiled, "I hate to change the subject, but what are your plans for when you get back? You can't discuss any of the important stuff that happened back at Eviskar, not yet anyway."

Jocelyn took a deep breath. "The first thing I have to do is to make things right with some folks. I owe apologies to a number of people. Then, I'll have my hands full, what with school work and applying to colleges."

"Where have you decided to go? I know your grades are first rate, Jossy. I bet you'll have your pick of schools."

"Actually, I'm leaning strongly towards a small school up in Minnesota. I'm pretty close with the wife of a professor of archeology there. They have a strong biology department and some great study abroad programs for students who are interested in languages." She took Jack's hand, "No pressure, but would you ever consider attending a school like that? Debbie says they're well known in physics and astronomy."

Jack hadn't expected the question. He looked away, embarrassed, and caught the eye of an elderly woman, wearing a Cleveland Indians ball cap, standing behind him. The woman smiled at him and nodded.

It's impossible to carry on a private conversation in a crowded airport, he fretted. A sense of déjà vu swept through him as well. Although he wasn't particularly superstitious, he hoped the woman in the ball cap wouldn't be seated near him. Collecting his thoughts, he replied to Jocelyn's question. "That's a great idea," he said, "assuming I can qualify for enough financial aid."

"And don't forget about our date."

"What date?"

Jocelyn rolled her eyes in mock aggravation, "Don't you remember? August 12, 2026, in Olafsvik, Iceland."

"Oh yeah, I'd nearly forgotten about that. Of course I'd like to go, but twelve years is a long time, Jossy. Who knows what..."

She put a finger to his lips. "Yes or no, Jacek Malinowski. Nothing on this earth will stop me from going if I know you'll be there."

"Ladies and gentlemen, at this time we will begin general boarding of flight 471 starting with rows 25 through 36. Will all passengers seated in those rows please present your boarding passes now."

"That's me," Jack noted. He and Jocelyn maneuvered towards the back of the quickly growing line. He gave her a hug. "I'll be there. You can count on it."

Inside the plane, Jack took his seat and stuffed his backpack under the seat in front. In a couple hours, he'd be home. Now that was a surreal thought. Since leaving the shores of Eviskar, he'd travelled for two days through rough seas, landed in several major airports, bid farewell to three others who'd become his closest friends and was now minutes from sitting at the kitchen table in his parents' house. Soon he'd be talking about his experiences abroad—most of them anyway. He'd also be back at school in only two days. Strangely enough, that last thought appealed to him. He needed to return to a routine; he needed some time to decompress.

Jocelyn's question about his educational future was stuck in Jack's mind. It was a subject he hadn't contemplated for several months now, but he would have to address it soon enough. He closed his eyes and relaxed. First and foremost, he decided, before dozing off, he would plan a trip to Corpus Christi, Texas. After that he'd turn his attention to college.

Something bumped Jack's shoulder. He turned and froze. It was the woman in the ball cap. "Pardon me," she smiled, as she took the seat across the aisle, "I can be such a klutz." She paused for a moment. "Was that your girlfriend back at the gate?"

"Why, yes as a matter of fact," came his guarded response. He was shocked by his own admission. It was true; she was indeed his girlfriend. He'd never had a steady girlfriend before.

"Well, I don't mean to pry, but I hope you don't have to wait twelve years before you see her again."

He smiled, "I'll try not to let that happen."

"She's very pretty, and I can tell she really likes you...a lot."

The plane had finished taxiing to the head of the runway. Their conversation came to a halt as the pilot revved the engines and they accelerated down the tarmac, headed for Cleveland.

Outside, it was a beautiful fall day in the city. Rain the day before had yielded to cool air and few clouds. Although days had been long at Eviskar, the Sun was usually never more than a weak, fuzzy ball attenuated by steamy-grey cloud. Here, it shone in all its glory, warming the skin and fighting off the morning chill.

Despite the uplifting effect of the weather, the two bone-tired younger members of the Eviskar team were in somber spirits. This was it, they realized. Jocelyn and Jack were in the air, winging their way home, and in less than an hour the next Empire Express would transport Marcie and her folks to Albany. The four travelers sat on a bench outside Madison Square Garden. Spencer's mother would meet them soon, down below in Penn Central Station, but until then they had an hour to kill. Steven bought coffee, and, according to prior arrangement with his daughter, broached the subject of Spencer's foot.

"Let me be blunt, Spencer. Marcie warned me that it might be difficult for you to talk about it, but I'd like to take you on as a patient, assuming you're willing."

The boy looked down, but eventually met Steven's gaze. "If you think you can help, then, yeah, I guess, but I don't know if I can afford it."

"I wouldn't think of asking for payment. If anything, Gail and I are in your debt. Marcie told us all about how you braved that hazardous climb up the cliff and found a way to summon help for Debbie and the other students. She also told me how good a friend you've been to her. Please allow me the satisfaction of treating your clubfoot. I must warn you, though; it will require a tremendous amount of effort on your part."

"How so?"

"First of all, I try to avoid surgery if at all possible. We'll use casts and a brace to gradually force the foot into proper alignment. It will involve some discomfort and it will take time, but if you're willing to try, let's do it."

"Do ya' think it'll help?"

Steven hesitated before responding. "I've never treated someone your age before. We'll just have to see what happens. But I am sure of one thing, and that is: it can't hurt to try." He smiled, "your condition isn't that uncommon, Spencer. A number of famous athletes have successfully overcome talipes and gone on to have very distinguished careers."

"No offense, Dr. Van Woamah, but I'm a basketball playah. That takes a lot 'a runnin'."

"Troy Aikman had talipes."

"Really?! The quarterback?"

"Yes, and Charles Woodson."

"Don't forget about Mia Hamm," Marcie added.

Spencer was incredulous. "Those are supastars. I mean, they aren't just good...they're the best!"

"I agree, and what undoubtedly has contributed to their success is their ability to overcome injury and adversity. The character those individuals displayed in dealing with this birth defect foreshadowed the tenacity they would later exhibit to become the best in their professions. Look, Spencer, you can't necessarily expect to become an NFL star or a World Cup champion as a result of this treatment, but I believe there is a good chance that your quality of life will improve. I'll be back in the city for a conference the week before Columbus Day. Why don't you come back with me to Albany the following weekend and we'll assess your condition."

Under the Garden, inside the bowels of Penn Central Station, a large woman dressed in a colorful robe exited her train and walked majestically from the platform. Smiling a million-dollar smile, she greeted those around her, strangers all, and received appreciative nods and smiles in return. Some people have the ability to make friends at a glance, to immediately put at ease those around them. Yolanda Bowen had this gift in abundance. As she turned heads, and as her radiance permeated the throngs of commuters in the station, she kept a watchful eye out for her son.

She soon spotted him standing by a bench in the middle of the concourse, conversing with three other people. "Spencer, my boy, welcome home!" She floated across the room with arms spread, and engulfed the young man in an enormous bear hug. "And, Marcie, welcome to you as well. Spencer tell me all about your adventures. Goodness me, I need hear all about it. But first, I must have a picture. Come, all of you, Mr. and Mrs. Van Wormer—all together now, and give me a big smile." She took several photos and then paused while she recalled and examined each one in the camera's LCD display.

Spencer whispered to Marcie, "Before we left, I set up a Facebook account for my mom. When I went online in the airport in Reykjavik, she already had more than a hundred friends 'an she must 'a posted twice that many pictures. She's hooked bad."

"So, I guess this is it," Marcie said solemnly, "our train leaves pretty soon;

we have to get to the track."

"Yeah, I think we betta go too." In a bold show of affection, Spencer took hold of her hand. Blushing deeply, he changed the subject, "I can't believe that in less than a week I'll be writin' one 'a those essays—you know, 'what I did last summah'."

His words barely registered. Marcie's heart was pounding. She tried to act casual, but she was now focused on the one thing that mattered—the touch of Spencer's hand on hers.

Throughout the last weeks of their archeological project, she and Spencer had been sharing smiles and glances and trying surreptitiously to spend time together without drawing attention to their budding relationship. Of course, Jocelyn knew what was going on. Her feminine intuition had picked up the strong vibes of attraction radiating from the two soon-to-be high school sophomores. Jack knew of their close friendship as well, but his main focus at Eviskar had been on his archeological duties...and on Jocelyn—not necessarily in that order.

Marcie gave his hand a squeeze. "So, um, what are you going to say?"

"That's a good question. I guess I can't mention the 'Malarkey' that almost got me killed." They both laughed. Marcie gripped his hand more tightly. "An' as far as the dig goes..." he shrugged, "I bet my teachers'll be real interested in that axe head they found."

This was it, she thought. It was now or never. On impulse, Marcie leaned forward and gave Spencer a quick kiss on the lips.

A camera flashed nearby. Yolanda Bowen sported a huge grin. "What a handsome couple," she cooed as she scrutinized the image.

Spencer rolled his eyes. "C'mon ma, give us some privacy heah." Turning to Marcie he said, "That'll be on Facebook by the time you get home. Sorry. Unless I hack her account, there's nothin' I can do. But, speaking of Albany, I guess I'll be up there soon."

Tears filled Marcie's eyes; she fought to maintain her composure. "You mean 'Small-bany,' that hick town up north?"

"That's the one. I hear it's a really nice place, though. Maybe I'll start spendin' more time up there."

"And I should spend more time in the city—find out how you city folks live. G'bye, Spence." She gave him a long hug that lasted through three camera flashes. She then shouldered both of her packs, took her dad's hand in one of hers and Gail's in the other. "C'mon, parental units; stop pretending you didn't see that kiss and let's go home."

FINIS

Made in the USA
San Bernardino, CA
01 July 2016